Reviews of Rohan Quine's novellas

See www.rohanquine.com/press-media/the-novellas-reviews-media for all links to the following.

"It would be remiss of me not to take this opportunity to bring people's attention to a truly remarkable book. Rohan Quine writes right at the boundary between literary fiction and experimentalism, and his new collection of four novellas, *The Platinum Raven and other novellas*, is a genuine masterpiece. This guy is as good as [Sergio] De La Pava, and deserves to be the next self-published literary author to cross over into mainstream consciousness."

"Rohan Quine is one of the most brilliant and original writers around. His *The Imagination Thief* blended written and spoken word and visuals to create one of the most haunting and complex explorations of the dark corners of the soul you will ever read. Never one to do something simple when something more complex can build up the layers more beautifully […] suffice to say he is the consummate master of sentencecraft. His prose is a warming sea on which to float and luxuriate. But that is only half of the picture. He has a remarkable insight into the human psyche, and he demonstrates it by lacquering layer on layer of subtle observation and nuance. Allow yourself to slip from the slick surface of the water and you will soon find yourself tangled in a very deep and disturbing world, but the dangers that lurk beneath the surface are so enticing, so intoxicating it is impossible to resist their call."

"Rohan is one of the most original voices in the literary world today—and one of the most brilliant."

"four stunning new novellas by one of the most exciting literary writers in the UK."
—**Dan Holloway**, novelist, poet and *Guardian* blogger

"Rohan Quine is a master of words, his world is also accessible, and it's a place you definitely need to visit. With echoes of Jennifer Egan's *Goon Squad*, Quine captures all that is beautiful, but he doesn't shy

away from all that is ugly. What links the four novellas together is that his characters are all searching for that something beyond the everyday, beyond the ordinary, and Quine is a god, having them dole out kindness and justice. In his world, everything that is commonplace would be annihilated. This is the kind of read you have to give yourself up to. […] When you emerge on the other side with a greater understanding of what it means to be 'that animal called human', then that will be the time to stop and ask, 'What just happened?'"
—**Jane Davis**, novelist

"Novelist Rohan Quine not only has several books out. He also has a career in alternative modeling and film to look back on. Naturally, he has gone on to make a series of silent short films to go with an audio track of the author reading from his work. It's flooded with city lights, drugs and darkness. One foot in the New York Nineties, and one foot in today's London, it's both hypnotic and gut-churning."
—**Polly Trope**, novelist and literary editor of *indieBerlin*

"A cautionary tale [*The Host in the Attic*] of the potential corrupting power both of vanity and of the internet plays out in modern London's high-tech dockland offices and luxury apartments, with brief forays to lavish West End hotels and country houses. […] As the story becomes ever darker, gentle touches of humour provide a little light relief. I particularly enjoyed the characterisation of the women, especially the wonderfully petulant Angel Deon […]. While at first this parable's main purpose may seem to rage against the principles of a high tech, monopolistic, capitalist world that enable individuals to lead unspeakably privileged lives above the law, it is at the same time a cautionary tale against narcissism and the abandonment of love and compassion for others. This broader theme gives the story its true heart and depth. Quine is renowned for his rich, inventive and original prose, and he is skilled at blending contemporary and ancient icons and themes. […] an interesting approach to dialogue, blending idiom and phraseology from different eras, from Victorian times through 20th century popular film culture to the modern day. […] There are some classic moments of horror that are very filmic, including one on a par with the *Psycho* shower scene. Without

giving too much away, I can imagine this book might put readers off accessing their own attics for a while."
—**Debbie Young**, novelist and Amazon UK 1,000 Reviewer, writing in *Vine Leaves Literary Journal*

"This is an extraordinary writer. I am going to gorge myself on these novellas as soon as I possibly can."
—**JJ Marsh**, novelist

"cerebral works full of brilliant imagery and invention. This series of novellas are all well crafted and designed to draw the reader in to the shifting realities of their settings. The title novella *The Platinum Raven* in fact has two young women in two narratives […] very vividly described. There are elements of magical realism and alternate reality throughout. At times the two Ravens appear to communicate but the levels of reality are enigmatic and intriguing. *The Host in the Attic* is a beautifully reinterpreted version of *The Picture of Dorian Gray* set in a high-tech dystopian world and a sinister computer global company—Mainframe Corporation, which appears to permeate every level of society. The hologram corporate image logo is in essence Dorian. All the main characters from Wilde's novel are here in more modern form. It has a tremendous and horrific climax. The horror novella *Apricot Eyes* is a fast-paced horror tale in a nightmarish New York. *Hallucination in Hong Kong* is a mysterious tale of past and present, dreams and waking with horror and love themes. The whole collection is a roller-coaster of at times nightmarish perceptions and strange surreal happenings brilliantly imagined. The tales leave a lasting impression and I recommend highly."
—**Alexander Gordon-Wood**

"a riveting read. The novella *The Host in the Attic* in particular is splendidly Wildean: in it, [Quine's] novel *The Imagination Thief* itself drives forward the plot of *The Host in the Attic*. He is a veritable Imagination Thief!"
—**David McLaughlin**

The following are reviews of Rohan Quine's *Hallucinations* (New York: Demon Angel Books), published in print in the USA only, which included earlier versions of: *Apricot Eyes*; *Hallucination in Hong Kong*; and a few chapters of *The Platinum Raven*.

"I have now been reading *Hallucinations* with great pleasure […] you are indeed a star."
—**Iris Murdoch**, novelist

"He has no equal, today or tomorrow."
—**James Purdy**, novelist

"Sometimes Quine succeeds with things you wouldn't think language could do, like describing a piece of music with an extended metaphor that reads something like watching the last half-hour of *2001*."
—**Ben Cohen**, *New York Press*

"*Hallucinations* at the end of this millennium is what Lautréamont's, Huysmans's and Wilde's work represented at the end of the 19th century […] a sadistically svelte structure on top of explosive, primal content that refuses to behave in a linear fashion. It can only be described as literature that strains between ecstasy and bondage […] one of the chic-est, most provocative things we have read in years […] one of those seminal works that goes on to be accorded the status of a classic."
—**Wayne Sterling**, *New York Web*

"The imagery is *Apocalypse Now*-era Coppola meets Wes Craven, or *Edward Scissorhands* meets *Barbarella* […] or Anne Rice (as screenwriter) on an acid trip […] the lilt and cadence of prose poetry laid end-to-end, resulting in a narrative that is frequently stunning […] sublime verbal renderings of the emotions and sensations of human love."
—**Hayward Connor**, *Union Jack*

"Most taut and clever in [*Apricot Eyes*]; it grips the reader and gives a provocative ride [… *Hallucinations*] develops 'alternative' characters with style and dimension, as well as challenging traditional forms of storytelling with admirable results."
—**Tom Musbach**, *Lambda Book Report*

"This is quite an extraordinary work, distinguished both by its originality and by the strength of [its] voice."
—**Anne Hawkins**, literary agent (John Hawkins & Assocs.)

"There's a reality in each sentence of *Hallucination in Hong Kong* that neither depends on nor is blurred by all its virtuoso fuckings of the English language."
—**Dr Michael Halls**, Intercom Trust

If you'd like to be notified of future print and ebook publications, you're most welcome to sign up for Rohan Quine's not-too-frequent newsletter at www.rohanquine.com/sign-up. Rest assured, such emails will be at supremely tasteful intervals and your details will be shared with no one else.

THE PLATINUM RAVEN

AND OTHER NOVELLAS
BY ROHAN QUINE

The Platinum Raven
The Host in the Attic
Apricot Eyes
Hallucination in Hong Kong

EC1 DIGITAL

The Platinum Raven and other novellas by Rohan Quine
ISBN: 978-0-9927549-1-4

The Platinum Raven
The Host in the Attic
Apricot Eyes
Hallucination in Hong Kong

Published by EC1 Digital, London, UK

Copyright 2014 Rohan Quine

www.rohanquine.com/the-platinum-raven
www.rohanquine.com/the-host-in-the-attic
www.rohanquine.com/apricot-eyes
www.rohanquine.com/hallucination-in-hong-kong

Cover design by Jane Dixon-Smith, www.jdsmith-design.co.uk
The Burj Khalifa, Dubai: photo by Anna Omelchenko / www.shutterstock.com
The Shard, London: photo by olavs / www.shutterstock.com
The Platinum Raven: photo by Subbotina Anna / www.shutterstock.com
Author: photo by James Keates

The four novellas in this volume are also available as four separate ebooks and
audiobooks published by EC1 Digital.

Earlier versions of a few chapters of *The Platinum Raven* constituted parts of
the novellas *Hallucination Downtown* and *Hallucination in New York*, within the
paperback collection *Hallucinations* (New York: Demon Angel Books), published
in the USA only. That collection also contained earlier versions of *Apricot Eyes* and
Hallucination in Hong Kong, with the same titles.

The Host in the Attic's digitisation of the plot of Oscar Wilde's *The Picture of
Dorian Gray* was based on an idea by Ray Mia for a feature film, which became
a screenplay co-written by Rohan Quine and Ray Mia. With Ray's written
permission, that screenplay has been converted into this novella by Rohan.
Towards the end of this novella's chapter IV, a few short paragraphs have been
incorporated from Wilde's novel (with minimal tweaks reflecting their new
context), in homage to the great O.W.

CONTENTS

THE PLATINUM RAVEN

TABLE OF CONTENTS

THE CHOCOLATE RAVEN

RAVEN

RAVEN

1 A SUDDEN WHITE RABBIT

Easing out of sleep into half-sleep, Raven remembers what she is waking into, while carefully prolonging her comfortable haze of mind a little longer. She's lying in bed at home, with her sleeping boyfriend's naked warmth against hers. It is early one Monday morning, not long before her alarm-clock will be going off, and bright sun is coming through the gaps around the window-blinds. Keeping her movements gentle so as not to wake him, she squirms around to face him and brushes her black hair out of her eyes. The white sheet fully covers both their heads as well as the rest of them, and the sunlight is passing through the thinness of the sheet, so she has a clear view of this familiar face and body that she loves, that she has loved deeply for a long time now, lying not quite on his back nor quite on his side—her best friend in the world, right beside her in shared comfort and silence here, just where he should be. As far as the angles of his position allow, she arranges herself so as to lie on her side and to feel his skin on her own in as many places as possible, up and down their bodies, but neither so as to wake him nor to result in any discomfort for herself. The result is something between a half-embrace and a simple proximity, touching in three or four places in several permutations of limbs or shoulders but remaining apart elsewhere, here under this warm sunny tent of sheet. The biggest area of space between them is somewhere midway down their length, where they happen to lie curved apart in an approximate mirror image of each other. Raven shuts her eyes and lets herself drift back down into her own haze. Then she half-opens her eyes once more, and in doing this she becomes aware of a third presence, as there flickers up the image of a being she has not seen before—a small white rabbit curled up peacefully upon itself, right here in the rabbit-sized space between her boyfriend's body and her own, in a state of semi-sleep like their own, its eyes half-opening and its perfectly white furry head and ears making slight movements from time to time, before its eyes close and its head and ears become still. Smiling, Raven whispers to herself in words she soon forgets, then sinks back into sleep, smiling still.

An hour later she kisses her boyfriend goodbye, pulls her front door shut behind her and heads down a nondescript residential corridor past a series of anonymous doors, each bearing nothing but the number of the flat behind it. In the lobby at the end she summons a lift, and while it starts its ascent from the ground floor she wanders to the lobby window. Far underneath are the lower buildings comprising this development, which is the Lansbury Estate in Poplar, East London; and over there in the distance is the spectacular building she is heading for this morning. In the lift mirror she double-checks the appearance of her office suit, her make-up and her long straight raven-coloured hair, which are all immaculate. Outside she walks to the station nearby, where a southbound DLR train happens to be waiting ready for her. Hardly noticing the journey, so habitual is it, she travels four stops to Canary Wharf station, then takes the Jubilee line three stops west to London Bridge station. A few minutes later she steps into another lift, manages to close the lift-doors upon herself alone before anyone else can get in, and gazes at the building information beside the lift-doors while she ascends past offices on floors 4-28, past restaurants on floors 31-33 and past hotel floors 34-50, during the last of which the lift decelerates. Through coming here a lot, and through her lifelong curiosity about how enormous buildings are structured (a curiosity she registers as mildly quirky, which has no connection with anything else in her life), she is well aware of what is above her, though she has never been there: a spa on floor 52, apartments on floors 53-65, viewing galleries on floors 68-72, and the spire on floors 75-87. But now the lift has stopped and, as always, she alights on the highest of the hotel floors. For Raven works on the 50th floor of the Shard, high above London Bridge station.

Despite this glamorous location, her job as a receptionist ties her to a phone that rings all day long, so in fact she encounters very little of this iconic building where so much of her life is spent. There are no windows she can see, from the seat where she is captive, and so generic is her immediate workspace that she may as well be working on the ground floor of a low-rise building in the suburbs.

Throughout these work hours, although in physical comfort, she is much put-upon. Numerous people talk down to her, both on the phone and off it, and there isn't much that can be done about this; it would seem to come with the position. The pay is not much and her horizons feel restricted. Still, there's an economic downturn, the job is stable and it's all she can access for the moment, so there's no point in moaning about it. Nor does she forget that she wakes up every morning with a beautiful friend—the boy whom the sunlight lit so clearly through their clean white sheet this morning. Nor, this morning in particular, can she forget the enchantment of that white rabbit that appeared between the two of them.

No; when she contemplates the bigger picture or looks at the news, Raven knows her own luck is well above the average. She sees the desperate hopeless anger of many around her; she lives in the real world. Despite the functionality of her life, she hasn't forgotten that if such functionality isn't proactively maintained, then the world quickly reverts to its habit of pressing forcibly into people with its favourite latent quality—the relentless, hard-edged, physical violence of reality.

That's the bigger picture. But there's no denying, either, that the real world leaves a lot to be desired.

THE CHOCOLATE RAVEN

2 THE MOST BEAUTIFUL BUILDING IN THE WORLD

In the late morning, in the course of routing hundreds of phone calls at the reception desk, Raven is hit by a phone call of such vile, vicious, sadistic rudeness that as soon as she has put the phone down afterwards, her eyes start welling up. This happens to be followed by a rare spell of several minutes uninterrupted by any calls. During this, she first succeeds in just about conquering her incipient tears, and then just sits there in the cubicle, immobile, her eyes still closed, aware of the simple sensation of sitting in an upright chair and those constant, bland office sounds filtering indistinctly down the corridor to her…

This closure of her eyes reminds her of the unexpected white rabbit's slowly-closing eyes this morning in that enclosed space between the mirroring curves of the two bodies underneath the sunny tent of clean white sheet. She lets the peaceful magic of this picture settle over her, while distantly aware that it cannot be long before the phone will ring again, whereupon the rabbit will of course be put from her mind and the telephone will rule her once more.

In fact she is interrupted not by the phone but by the scheduled arrival of a colleague to take over the desk for the duration of Raven's lunch break; time has rolled on without her noticing. She heads straight across the tower to a small empty conference room, where she often goes for her breaks, because its lack of windows is more than made up for by its being almost always blissfully empty of people. She opens her packed lunch and starts eating, seated there in silence with her eyes closed again; and she decides that right here during this lunch break she will first brainstorm and then plan exactly how to make certain, for the rest of her entire life as a receptionist, that the white rabbit will conquer, dominate, overshadow and even somehow possibly supersede the phone in the cubicle.

Sitting there chewing her sandwich, she finds herself instead picturing how she might look to a camera that was somehow able to see her from outside this angular Shard of glass and light, hidden deep within its angles, in this small antiseptic conference room, gazing through unknown partition walls and steel and glass towards the lens she's imagining. This camera zooms in to a close-up of her unfocused, thousand-metre stare, and then zooms back out again to embrace a wider shot including her as just one little detail among a myriad other bodies and objects stuffed into this glass tower. But she frowns, for the tower now looks different from how it did before the zoom-in a moment ago … in fact, it looks like a different tower, and an altogether more monstrous one.

Yes: from the middle of Dubai the tallest building in the world shoots up through the harsh dry heat, to the sky. It is the vaunting, inhuman-scaled Burj Khalifa. Visible from scores of kilometres away beyond the dunes or across the Arabian Gulf, it's an elegantly complex, telescoping spike, of a stunning, otherworldly fabulosity—its beauty cool, mineral and icy in the undulating shimmer of the desert.

And there she is inside it, just behind the glass, staring west from a window in her 63rd-Level apartment. Or rather, there is a woman whose face is just like Raven's face, but whose long straight hair is a beautiful chocolate colour instead of raven-black; and without consciously choosing the name, Raven straightaway thinks of this woman as the Chocolate Raven.

This woman is murmuring words to herself half-aloud, so Raven narrows her eyes and strains her ears to hear what they are, since they will probably reveal something about this person of whom she knows hardly anything so far. "Why, oh why," she is murmuring, as she runs her eyes across the cityscape. "Why, oh why…" and Raven strains her ears harder, so as not to miss it when it arrives, as it does at last: "Oh why are such a vast majority of people so very clunky and stupid?" the Chocolate Raven asks.

"Well *you're* a shallow creature, aren't you?" Raven snorts, back in her conference room in the Shard. "I was hoping for something a little deeper than that…" and she stops, in case her own words are being picked up somehow, over there in Dubai.

She peers into the Chocolate Raven's eyes, as best as she can: from this vantage-point in the outside air, the glassy surface of the 63rd-storey window is golden-brown in the late afternoon light, so it's hard to make out the details of her, though she's facing Raven full on. But no, she hasn't heard Raven's words, for now she's merely gazing almost downwards to the Burj Khalifa's base, where the world's largest shopping mall, the Dubai Mall, sits beside Interchange 1 of the city's main highway. Looking left, and being an avid shopper, the Chocolate Raven rests her gaze on the Mall of the Emirates, seven miles away—another gigantic mall that's really quite similar to the Dubai Mall but sits instead beside Interchange 4 of the highway. Likewise seven miles further, beside Interchange 6, sits the Ibn Battuta Mall—yet another glitzy shopping complex, comparably huge. On the coast are the flashy high-rise towers of the Marina, and beyond them the industrial expanse of the power station complex. A little to the right is the Burj Al-Arab hotel, planted on its miniature peninsula like the billowing sail of a ship. And beyond it, the Palm Jumeirah, that enormous artificial peninsula shaped like a palm tree, best admired from space. Far in the distance to the left, she can just make out another huge palm-tree-shaped peninsula, the Palm Jebel Ali. And finally, those scrappy islets out ahead would be the aborted World archipelago.

A footfall overhead brings her attention streaking back across the waters to where she is standing, and she glances up. She has long been aware that her immediate neighbours on the 64th Level possess one of the building's much-coveted terraces. She hasn't yet found a way of meeting these neighbours, however; for despite their physical juxtaposition, such meetings are not so easy to arrange in an environment such as this, whose cushioned opulence overlays a structure of such unmeltable compartmentalisation that nobody is really meant to meet anybody. If only her windows could be opened, then perhaps she could lean out far enough to twist her body and head around to face the shiny sky and bellow something upwards in a casual and relaxed fashion, through the dizzying height of wind and sunlight, and maybe thereby catch their attention and elicit an invitation to saunter upstairs for spontaneous cocktails on the terrace; but alas, her windows cannot be opened.

Her envy derives not just from traditional, feel-good, neighbourly hatred. It derives also from a lifelong curiosity about how enormous buildings are structured—a curiosity she registers as mildly quirky, which has no connection with anything else in her life. In this case the building comprises twenty-seven cylinders of different heights, with each cylinder's flat roof doubling up as a terrace for an apartment that's one storey higher in an adjacent cylinder (except for the highest of the twenty-seven cylinders, of course, whose top has no such subservient function). This special curiosity of hers was what led the Chocolate Raven to request viewings, while she was still apartment-hunting, of as many terrace-graced apartments as possible. And since she was among the building's earliest viewers, she did succeed in seeing as many as three of these, before the real estate sales agency insisted on establishing the extent of her finances to a point where they knew what she could afford, thereby frustrating her fixation without giving her the chance to amass anything like the complete collection of possible terrace visits. As a result of this, the only residential terraces she was able to visit were the ones on the 19th, 26th and 53rd Levels. That still left those on the 34th, 64th, 87th and 99th Levels—there being no higher terraces within the residential section, which ended at the 108th Level. Just to think, there were still *four* residential terraces, each aching to be visited...

For yes, experiencing all of the Burj Khalifa's terraces happens to be one of the Chocolate Raven's goals, albeit one that she knows better than to admit to—

"Well *there's* a lofty ambition, I'm sure," sniffs Raven in her Shard conference room. "Most inspiring, I don't think."

But it's no good Raven's pretending such disdain, for she can sense that this unexpected Chocolate Raven woman is, despite her seeming shallows, a VIP guest within the residence of Raven's own mind, and must be treated as such. What's more, Raven is, frankly, rather hooked on her already. Hooked on her flashy surroundings, on her chocolaty hair, on her all-around chocolatiness—on the exoticness of her version of Ravenity, in contrast with Raven's own. She knows little about this woman yet. But she's hooked nonetheless, because this lustrously edible-coloured version of herself is standing high up in the most beautiful building in the world, not getting abused down the phone behind a reception desk, but instead surveying the geometry of an entire city as if it belonged to her, and pronouncing blithe, bitchy judgements on most of its inhabitants...

Really, what is there not to like in that scenario, from this windowless vantage point on a Monday morning?

This beautiful Chocolate Raven woman clearly has an altogether different life from Raven's own. A life of comparative ease and pleasure. She has the manner of an authoritative, well-paid, popular, sybaritic party-animal, who lives in the fabulous Burj Khalifa in the desert kingdom of Dubai.

"And d'you know what?" says Raven aloud to herself, giving her mug of decaff instant coffee a stir. "That's just what she is. And really, she is *so* like me."

3 FRONDS A TO P

For the rest of the day, on her break and between phonecalls and even during phonecalls, Raven's gaze devours the Chocolate Raven, discerning more and more of her life, absorbing details through a mysterious kind of omniscience regarding her. To summarise: it seems that the Chocolate Raven works in one of the large hotel complexes at the Marina, somewhere on the corporate hospitality side of things. Many of the business travellers she helps look after are demanding (and a few are appalling), but the great majority are civilised and impersonal. Being at a middle-management level in this field, she does indeed have a generous salary—much more than Raven's own. She is briskly competent at her job. She is humorous, well-liked, and even enjoys a tolerable level of job satisfaction.

Through her numerous tourism and hospitality industry contacts, she is socially active across the whole Marina-based scene of moneyed hedonism and factitious frolic in grand hotels—as well as across the mostly residential Palm Jumeirah. And at the home end of her commute, she is also familiar with the Downtown Burj Dubai complex, where the Burj Khalifa itself stands, and with the neighbouring stretch of Sheikh Zayed Road, whose own concentration of grand hotels makes it, frankly, the relevant stretch.

In these two extensive neighbourhoods the Chocolate Raven thus enjoys an endless round of well-watered and well-fed fun, which tends to occur in bars, nightclubs and restaurants, in hotel suites and palatial lobbies, at house parties in shiny marble-walled lounges, beside back-garden swimming-pools, and on private beaches on the Palm at dusk, behind a few of those thousands of not-quite-identical luxury mansions built along each side of an array of not-quite-identical Fronds running the whole exotic gamut from Frond A to Frond P.

Behind the glitter of this social whirl, however, she sometimes becomes half-aware of an elusive sense of emptiness, absence or vapidity; and this sense leaves her discombobulated for a moment, before she lets herself be distracted back into the normality of her days. She's well-practised, after all, at using her all-purpose intelligence and fun-loving aliveness to interact with people in ways that achieve a reliable level of social success and worldly comfort, while embracing those around her in a simple, generous glow of glamour. And this reliable ease of achievement has quietly conspired (as why would it not?) with a small and unobtrusive streak of laziness in her, to drag her back just a little from filling out her own imaginative potential quite as far as its edges.

The Chocolate Raven's own half-awareness of this confirms the truth of it, for Raven.

And as Raven reflects upon this truth, she realises that she herself is slightly disappointed to have discovered it in the Chocolate Raven. For the latter's function was surely to be entirely enviable, like a film-star or a pop-star—or rather, like the image constructed and maintained around a film-star or a pop-star. Yet here she was, displaying to Raven an element of flatness in her inner life.

4 CHOCOLATE HAIR ON WHITE SILK

Standing at the far left end of a swanky hotel bar after lunch, looking at the tableau of people on view in the impeccable mirror on the wall behind the bottles, the Chocolate Raven contrives to snatch another discreet look at the figure at the far end of the bar. Dressed in a black suit, white shirt and charcoal-grey tie, he is slim, pretty, watchful, with dark brown hair and big brown eyes, set within a pale face. There's nothing overtly strange in his appearance, yet he strikes her as being somehow larger than life.

Within a few moments he becomes aware of her. Or was he already aware of her before she noticed him, and is he now returning his gaze to her? Usually she would have a sense of the answer to such a question, but this time she doesn't. Either way, the same thing is true: within the instant when their gazes meet, his eyes see too much into her.

She imagines this man's viewpoint on this same wide mirror tableau: standing again at the left side of the tableau (but in only half-profile this time) will be a glamorous young woman facing right, her long chocolate hair falling dead-straight and splashing softly off her shoulder, burning dark against the smooth white silk of her top. This is the Chocolate Raven herself, of course, though he won't know her name yet. She half-turns her head in his direction, through real space along the bar; and for him, her hair in the tableau in the mirror must therefore be splashing a little differently now upon the white silk of her shoulder, though of course she herself can no longer verify this directly in the mirror.

"He probably wants me to fuck him," she murmurs to herself. "I wonder if that's going to happen? Well, we'll see." The barman places her drink in front of her and she sets off across the room, where a business client of hers greets her, asks to join her and sits down with her at a table. She adjusts the position of her chair, to ensure an uninterrupted line of sight between her and the far-right end of the bar, but is then distracted from this sightline by her client's demanding chatter.

Presenting the vaguest and politest awareness of the Chocolate Raven, through the mildest of occasional quarter-smiles across the room in her direction, the figure at the bar bends his senses into focus and sets about gauging the line of least resistance he's likely to uncover in her.

He senses that almost as long ago as she can remember, she started to find that if she was just natural and direct in expressing herself, then people often reacted as if she was somehow being *too much* of something. That's interesting, he reflects. There was often a construal of her as too vivid, for example, or too bright, or too intense, or too who-knew-what kind of quality, by her companions back in childhood days. She came to realise, he observes, that this familiar reaction by people was unhelpful, because it distracted from what she was saying to them and subtly devalued her words and tended to alienate her in ways that were less than interesting. So ever since then, for nearly as long as she can now remember, whenever there has been stuff for her to convey to other people, she has muted herself and muted the expression of her thoughts and feelings downwards a tad, into tastefulness and reassurance, just far enough not to frighten those people. And being socially skilled and a good learner, and having done this for a while, she may now be relied upon to mute herself to a well-judged level—except on a few occasions when she forgets to do so, or underestimates the amount of necessary muting through being inebriated or distracted or both. These occasions are infrequent enough not to matter, though, so they don't worry her.

And she expects that on the whole she will carry on muting herself reliably, until she dies. She will do so because it benefits her, and because she likes people enough not to want to frighten them, and because she quite understands that this underlying fear in people is simply how those people are set up—whatever the reason and regardless of the fact that things would obviously be a good bit more interesting if they weren't that way.

But underneath, in secret, she's very tired of muting.

For she knows that this muting, never spoken of, will simply keep on draining away a small but significant portion of her energy, all the way forward through the years, until she dies.

And this is seen within her, too, from the end of the bar.

She's good at interacting with people, but sometimes, when responding to some bit of Palm Jumeirah small talk, she is overwhelmed for a moment by boredom and fatigue at the necessity for it. "So what are you doing this weekend, then?" might be asked of her, by some Jumeirah Jane with much money and much blankness in her eyes; and the eagerness of triviality in the question is so exhausting that the Chocolate Raven wants this face to be far, far away from her. She doesn't want to slap it, no. She just wants this Jane face gone, so heroically little do its concerns connect with the flux of images and echoes in the Chocolate Raven's own head.

Not that all this gets her down, as such. After all, such travails hardly constitute actual suffering. Actual suffering gets very quickly much worse than this, she's aware, and it's all too ubiquitous; everyone knows that. —Not that we can let the existence of actual suffering get us down either, come to that, because what's the use of doing so? If we don't like the presence of suffering in the world, then we'd better get over this because it will carry on in any case. People suffer, and she dislikes this, but she knows it won't be stopping in deference to her dislike. Complaining about it is dull, she has always felt: it just adds a thin layer of dullness to the world, on top of the world's much thicker layer of design blunders. If life has seriously hurt a person, as it often does, then she's sorry for them because she has compassion; and she will help them, up to a point. That point is reached fairly soon, however, because she has only finite resources of time, money and energy. This finiteness is also the case for the vast majority of other people, alas; so hardly any of them are going to be able to help the hurt individual either, beyond a point that's soon arrived at. She cannot help this fact, so she's not going to feel guilty that she herself is obliged to contribute to its trueness, nor judgemental that everyone else is obliged to contribute to it too. In this respect the situation sucks, certainly—but she didn't cause this. Truly immense suffering comes to a minority of people, arriving at any time between birth and death, with not much that anyone else can ever do to help, except to be kind now and then along the way.

At the same time there are a lot of people in total, and the happiness of many of them for much of the time is just as real as the suffering, despite the highest highs' travelling much less far upwards than the lowest lows travel downwards. A modicum of safety in numbers thus obtains. And a few of the lucky ones are able to do quite a lot of varied and interesting stuff along the way.

That too is real, she knows … and he sees.

The end result is that she expects and acknowledges the dreary deluge of pain and stupidity around her, yet she reacts not with judgement but by finding and adding to the beauty, humour, enchantment and compassion that exist amid the deluge, within her available resources. She expects little help or love from anyone, though she's unsurprised when these things appear and she's quick to recognise and return them when they do. Her lifelong rediscovery of her own powerlessness to correct the colourful array of screw-ups on view in the world has led her to a world-view in which three measures of sincere engagement are mixed with one measure of mirthful distance.

As a result, the figure observes, people tend to find her warm, humorous and compassionate; as indeed she is.

There are other elements he can see below her surface, however—with which he now forms an intention to engage.

He sees, for instance, that from back in her "too" days she still does retain a considerable sense of alienation from much of what preoccupies people from day to day. He sees that beneath her tolerance she also retains a wide, slow-burning anger at the stupidity and laziness in so many of them—at their lack of passion or compassion, and most of all at their hatred of thinking. He sees a wider, still-slower-burning contempt for the forces that landed them in this predicament where they find themselves. And finally he sees a smattering of the raw ingredients of honest-to-goodness megalomania, just waiting to be assembled and cooked.

He smiles to himself with the mildest of smiles, and gets up from the bar.

The Chocolate Raven, until this point, hasn't been thinking about him, since her brief initial sight of him. As soon as he gets up, however, she feels his presence again. She doesn't look in his direction but is aware of him setting off towards her, approaching her at a measured pace, his face in the corner of her gaze growing brighter like a thousand-watt light-bulb.

Now they're within speaking distance of each other, she can sense him pulsing like a cat through the stretch of space between them. She stands up, to ready herself, and looks up to face him.

"Hi, my name's Jaymi Peek," he says. "I have a card-key to return to you, from one of the corporate suites. It was handed to me, because the guy who booked it was called away on urgent business and had to leave Dubai this morning. Apparently the booking originated with you."

"Oh. Thanks," she says, pocketing the key.

"I have to head out now, but maybe I'll bump into you here again."

"OK, yes, good—see you soon," she says, somewhat on autopilot and nagged by a subtle disappointment.

And with a decorous smile he is gone.

5 THE BELLOW ON THE ROCK-SLOPES

Back home later that afternoon, the Chocolate Raven flops down into her leather sofa in the sitting-room. On the coffee table she sees the card-key she's just been given. She frowns in puzzlement. It's not uncommon for keys to be returned to her, from hotel rooms or corporate hospitality suites whose bookings she has had something to do with, including (all too often) keys with inadequate explanations or documentation, owing to some hotel employee's inefficiency. This one, however, is unusual in two respects. First, when she checked her corporate client lists earlier, she could find no record of anyone who had hired the suite in question. And secondly, instead of being located somewhere around the Marina, this is a suite that's located right here in the Burj Khalifa, somewhere above this very apartment—a less usual location for her to have been involved with, such that she would have expected to remember it now.

She picks the card-key up and inspects it. On its shiny plastic surface is printed nothing but this tower's familiar logo, the figure 152 and a mysterious red square.

There's only one thing to do next.

"Oh, all right, here goes," she says, heaves herself to her feet and glances at the clock. Five-forty-five. She checks that she has both this key and her own, leaves the apartment, takes the lift down to the main lobby and crosses to the lift serving the upper corporate suites. Displaying the new key to an underwhelmed lift attendant, she enters the lift-car and watches the doors close.

At 152 she steps out into a small, quiet lobby where several unnumbered but differently-coloured doors present themselves—one of them red. She tries the strange card-key in this door, hears the lock click open and pushes the door inwards.

Inside is an internal hallway with the neutral luxury she has seen in a thousand upscale corporate suites. The door snicks shut again behind her. She sees a window in the wall ahead and steps across to it. Unlike her own residential suite below, this high suite evidently has a terrace, for she can see a small corner of its floor planking through the lowest part of the window over there—

And she falls quiet, stops dead-still and stares across the room at that little corner of planking, which sits there as if it were just a natural, easy fact.

Er, hello: *there's a terrace...*

Well, doesn't that sound nice—and an *en suite* bathroom, no doubt. But to put the fact of a terrace into fitting context, it should be recalled that throughout this gigantically beautiful tower with its many hundreds of residential and corporate suites, there are no more than twenty-seven terraces in total. That's all. They form the tops of the twenty-seven cylinders that constitute the three wings of the tower's footprint—a footprint inspired by the shape of the hymenocallis flower, an important local flower about town. She shakes her head and smiles, recalling those visits she finagled to the 19th, 26th and 53rd Levels while she was still viewing empty apartments here; but despite those three triumphs, which loom legendary in the living-room of her memory, there has always been the sobering knowledge that she was never able to effect a visit to any of the much higher terraces gracing the corporate Levels. These were not open for her to visit, as she wasn't a corporate customer. (She has never regarded her visits to the publicly-accessible "Sky Lobbies", on the 43rd, 76th and 123rd Levels, as constituting terrace achievements of any note, of course.) Nevertheless, the inaccessibility and aloof perfection of these elite corporate terraces have left her no less aware of their location: she'd always known they were to be accessed through doorways, or possibly full-length windows, on only the 112th, 139th, 144th, and 148th Levels and—*yes!*—right here on the 152nd Level. In looking at that printed "152" on the card-key earlier, she was bizarrely failing to make any connection between those abstract numerals and her actual terrace knowledge. A knowledge rivalled only, perhaps, by that of the tower's architect Adrian Smith, who surely deserves a rent-free occupation in perpetuity of the tiny access platform at the very tippy-top of the Pinnacle itself, tucked in there in royal state, beside the metre-high beacons that scrape the sky...

So here she suddenly is, with sole and undisturbed access to the highest corporate terrace of all! In fact, she reflects, in a sense this is the ultimate "human" terrace: for it forms the flat roof of Tier 14, and it sends Tier 15 off upwards in fine style, rising a mere four Levels to the 155th Level, which is the highest corporate suite on the planet but lacks a terrace of its own. Above that, she muses, things get a bit too narrow to be "suites" as such: the private 156th to 159th Levels are taken up with communications and broadcast equipment, including an achingly inaccessible terrace on the 156th. Then, beginning with the terraced 160th Level (the highest thing to be called a Level), there's just mechanical equipment for the building, filling up those non-human, inorganic, mineral, *alien* Tiers 17 to 30… To be sure, this mechanical section, which in itself is the size of a small skyscraper in the sky, does contain eleven more head-spinning, eye-watering and doubtless diminutive terraces that form the flat roofs of Tiers 16 to 26—but alas, these terraces must remain forever aspirational.

Beyond that, in effect, is the silence and vacuum of deep space: just Tiers 27 to 30 consituting the skinny Spire, its interior a dark, tapering, mostly empty metal tube, rising to the Pinnacle. Not a place many people can access; but of all the places in the world, surely one of the strangest to reach.

The Chocolate Raven compresses her lips and sets off on her first approach towards this new-found terrace that has so unexpectedly become hers. The glass door is unlocked. She opens it and steps out across those planks, with trepidation—not so much from vertigo, as from an intimation of something momentous. Irresponsible. Irreversible.

Ahead, the terrace's edge is bounded in clear glass up to stomach height, with a railing near the top. At her approach to this, an enormity of space yawns up around and into her, pulling her too far forward towards jelly-kneed weakness and the end of all her chances in a hopeless, powerless, microscopic plunge into calamity—

She stops. Acclimatising herself by degrees, she extends her left hand above the railing, then dabs a finger down to touch it. Here at the centre of the railing's length, where the terrace's area comes to a shallow point, the view ahead is more or less to the west, just like the view from her 63rd-Level apartment window but eighty-nine storeys higher. After drinking this in, she heads to the terrace's far right-hand end, where its width narrows to nothing. She peers around the building, as far to the right as she can see, northwards to the skyscrapers of Bur Dubai and Deira, and offshore the aborted beginnings of what would have been the third and hugest artificial palm-tree-shaped peninsula, the Palm Deira.

Glowing with a dedicated terrace-hunter's excitement, she trots back along the terrace to its far left-hand end, where its width once again narrows to nothing. Through coming to these narrow ends, it contrives to surround almost three-quarters of the building, in effect; so here, when she peers as far left as she can, she's looking almost east. Holding the railing, she leans absent-mindedly out above the dizzying space beyond it, craning her neck around the side of the tower to peer along the lanes of horizontal lines that recede around its curve—then realises what she is doing and quickly steps back, her head swimming. Ahead of her the city stretches inland, into increasingly sparse suburbs. Over in Muhaisnah 2, she makes out the dismal grid of dormitories at Sonapur—now mostly empty, but for years an expanse of exhaustion and squalor, for a skyscraping labour-camp that spread across the cityscape. Then to the left of these, the airport in Sharjah, where a plane is taking off just now, tiny as a toy. Then the great expanse of desert, as far as the distant Hajar Mountains.

Perched high and tiny up here among the folds of this monster-building's curves, the Chocolate Raven's mouth gapes in an *O*, and a too-empowered force of noise blares out from this *O*, without exertion…

Was that herself? she thinks—and yes, she knows it was. She herself just produced that extraordinary, magnified bellow, which must only now be arriving over there, straight ahead where the mountains float in majesty beyond the desert sands.

Straightaway this knowledge is vertiginously scary, for she doesn't yet know if this immense unnatural bellow is controllable or not, but she knows already that its power is so great that it could do disastrous damage. And if it's not controllable, and if it then insists on emerging at the wrong time (but what would be the right time?), then her life may be finished, in effect, because… A nightmare erects itself, in sketchy form: the Chocolate Raven being quickly identified as somebody, or something, to apprehend and capture and restrain and enclose and imprison, then to sound-proof, then to bury in a tube far beneath the muffling sand, subsequently lowering her deeper, tier by tier, down an ever more unreachable, claustrophobic flue—an inverse Burj Khalifa underground, designed for her alone, a spike-shaped coffin sunk to isolate her further, as far and deep as possible, away from the fragile-eared species she'd belonged to, to bellow at herself in the darkness forever…

This alien voice that just took possession of her is associated, she feels, with a facial expression in which the mouth forms an elongated vertical slit with small rounded ends, and she realises in fascination and horror that her own mouth, while making the sound, did indeed become just this shape, after starting out as the *O*.

Her will ejects a jet of steel that hardens to a needle and she thereby hauls herself up from her wash of fear and into a decision: if she's powerless before the force that just came through her, and if it won't be explained, then she will run with it. She'll hunt for the access-points tucked away in plain view within familiar space, she will ferret out the overgrown gates and the spyholes winking in the wallpaper's pattern, and the keyholes and hyperlinks; and through them she'll invite, from that realm furled behind the skin of day, whatever eye-like fingers accept her invitation and poke back through at her, slanting up the bedroom air towards her in the dead of night, when mystery and horror bubble out from the mirror-glass.

Streaming off this terrace, her attention slices through the miles of air across Dubai to the mountains, and her glance touches down where her bellow strikes the rock-slopes. And there, a mad-faced tower shimmers up, rising through the haze, perched among the mountain-folds and staring back at her…

THE PLATINUM RAVEN

6 PLATINUM HAIR ON BLACK SILK

…And the appearance of that tower is a step too far, she knows. Its silent unfurling and rise, there in the mountains, is less overtly dramatic than her bellow was, but it feels more unnatural, alien, altogether ominous.

She tears her gaze away, returns to the wide centre-point of the terrace and forces her attention downwards, to ground herself in the familiar sight of the street grid running west beneath her. She's lost track of time; late afternoon has slipped into dusk. The city is almost completely covered in clean white clouds, here seen from above, so only the pinnacles or upper levels of a few skyscrapers poke up through them. They grow slowly pinker while the sun sets somewhere beyond them out of sight over the Arabian Gulf, and then they start to clear away in time with the falling of dusk, so that those protruding pinnacles grow longer and begin their ascent from progressively nearer the ground. Within twenty minutes all the clouds have boiled silently away, revealing the full beauty of the city in this pinky-brown-grey light of early evening. Thousands of lights appear, and soon the entire sky is dark except for a soft band along the Gulf's horizon.

Presently she will be brave, return to the left-hand end, and look back to where that tower seemed to appear, and perhaps it will no longer be there. To assist its absence, perhaps she can now break the spell by stepping back inside for a moment. So she turns and heads through the doors into the corporate suite. In its well-stocked kitchen she lights a cigarette, opens a bottle of red wine and pours a glass. Then she carries bottle and glass back outside, turns left, heads to the very end and places the bottle down in front of the railing.

Sipping the wine, she leans on the rail and looks downwards a third of a mile, to where the lights around the Mall twitch and flicker in the sticky air. A car-horn peeps thin and yellow for a second, like a pin sticking out from the city's endless thick electric pincushion night-roar.

Since the recent setting of the sun, it has come to seem to her that almost all of life is night. Alone in this eyry, she feels she is dealing now in night alone—the bright black night in front of her, cut with tracks of energy and pricked with coloured points of light. That's fine; she likes the night.

Across the city, towers shine—some huge and beautiful, but none as huge or beautiful as this one that she's in. Some bristle close to her; other ones rear up far away, colossal and alone, hard-wired to the same grid of lights. No one could know the whole city well, she reflects: many months might be spent, trekking all through its blocks, to the sad far marches on the edges of the desert.

She refills her glass, taps her cigarette ash off, draws in, exhales, and sees the smoke coil and hang and drift away to where the flood-lights catch it from below.

She thinks back perhaps twenty minutes, maybe half an hour, to the extraordinary voltage and transcendence she achieved, through forces of creation she'd not known she possessed, when her mouth went so terrifyingly into first an *O* shape and then a vertical slot-shape with rounded ends, and she birthed that mad-faced tower on the mountains. And there rises in her now a feeling rather like a rich blast of organ chords across the sky in harmonies that hold aloft a woman's song whose power and serenity and longing span the world. She knows that a second deployment of these new-found powers of hers will be occurring here, in just a moment or three—and she knows that this time the experience will be much calmer and gentler for her than that first time was.

So, she just starts doing it—and yes, it is indeed calmer and gentler, but nonetheless she feels it as electrically powerful, unnerving and excessive. Her hands grip the railing, as the voltage unfurls from her face and streams sideways, out across the desert to the mountain range. She shouldn't have this much power. It's too dangerous, in terms of what she might do with it down there in everyday life, instead of up here now—or whom she might turn it upon.

It's time to look again, where she's carefully not been looking.

Her attention shoots ahead, across the burn of the city and the blackness of the desert, to the canyon with the tiny glow of yellow-orange light…

And perched on the rock-slopes, just on a level with her, there is the mad-faced building she erected—still there, obediently waiting for her now. The folly made of iron, with the face of a mad tower: two round windows just beneath the turret, staring back at her…

So now what? she wonders. And while she does so, they hatch, right there in real time, tiny in the distant tower: fuzzy for a moment, till the auto-focus kicks in, but growing into sharpness as they swell to human size.

It's a bar scene, she sees. Standing at the far left end of the bar is a glamorous young woman, facing right and thus in profile from this point of view. Her face is half-obscured by the long platinum-blonde hair falling dead-straight and splashing softly off her shoulder where it burns dead white against smooth black silk, like a burnt-out exposure in a photographic print, or a photographic negative of raven-coloured hair. She half-turns her head in this direction, and the Chocolate Raven blinks to see the face is like her own face. So similar is the woman's build to her own, moreover, and so cleanly dramatic and unique is the opposition of her hair colour to the Chocolate Raven's own dark brunette version of the same style, that she thinks of the woman straightaway as the Platinum Raven.

The barman hands her a wad of banknotes, which she stows about herself with speed and discretion. Then she stands contemplating the tableau of people on view in the mirror mounted along the entire length of the bar's back wall above the bottles on the top shelf, looking in particular at the man at the far right-hand end of the bar. He is blond and attractive, his face alive with self-contained perceptiveness. The wide-set fluidity of humour in his eyes makes her think of Rutger Hauer in the desert: well-equipped, through ready charm, to hitch a lift.

She imagines this man's viewpoint on this same wide mirror tableau: standing again at the left side of the tableau (but in only half-profile this time) will be a glamorous young woman facing right, her long platinum-blonde hair falling dead-straight and splashing softly off her shoulder, burning white against the smooth black silk of her top. This is the Platinum Raven herself, of course, though the blond man won't know her name yet. She half-turns her head in the blond man's direction, through real space along the bar; and for him, her hair in the tableau in the mirror must therefore be splashing a little differently now upon the black silk of her shoulder, though of course she herself can no longer verify this directly in the mirror.

On her right will be a young Armenian man of maybe twenty-one, of a dark and delicate beauty in keeping with the silver scorpion pendant hanging at his neck, and whose glass she clinks with her own.

Without warning the Platinum Raven then turns her head further round, in slow-motion, to face this direction, as if she can see though the fourth wall of the bar-room and across the desert, to where the city of Dubai spreads out impaled by the Burj Khalifa's spike.

The Platinum Raven's eyes spend a few moments easing with infinitesimal precision up and down this building's 30 Tiers—then they pinpoint the Chocolate Raven's little *i*-shaped dot where it leans at the rail of Level 152, holding up a glass of red that's lit from within by the dusk-light passing through it here on the roof of Tier 14.

The platinum-lashed eyes stop their hunt. They focus more; and now they stare straight across, cutting clear and cool through the miles of desert in between, directly to their chocolate-lashed double's own eyes.

On the wet smooth curves of the Platinum Raven's eyes sits an identical pair of images of the Chocolate Raven herself, ever so tiny and ever so perfect: crouching in the glare of a parked car's head-lights, just beyond the power-station complex on the desert coast, over-exposed in a light that burns her face to white, moaning in pleasure there impaled on a man in shadow, crouching with her lus-cious straight chocolate-coloured hair across her face, until she raises her head and the hair slides away... And now her own devastating, desert-eyed perfection meets the Chocolate Raven's gaze full on, electrifying—animal, expressionless, an icon of ecstasy and chocolate and sweat in wailing silence in the headlights, as dust floats around her through the siren-song behind the air.

The Chocolate Raven's glance zooms back out again, to re-embrace the bar scene in the tower once more, where beside the Platinum Raven is the other one: the Armenian boy dressed in black, a Scorpio pendant at his neck. No smile there at all, too much tension and exquisiteness and fierce vulnerability.

For him it wasn't easy, no one-two-three. But here he is—just as if in some club, deep in a city. A sudden smile leaks through, a flush of light across his face, for an instant. Then once again, no smile. Fem in black, for this is realness. So waltz darling, deep in vogue.

—There he is, right now.

Perfection, for all time…

The Chocolate Raven thinks of him as Scorpio, murmuring the name as she watches him, unblinking so as not to miss a split-second's portion of this advent of an unpredicted figure whom she nonetheless feels that she's known all her life.

He snorts a line of cocaine from the bar's immaculate shiny top, then he turns his dainty head to one side and slightly up, to hear the Platinum Raven murmur something in his ear. And only now does the Platinum Raven release the Chocolate Raven's gaze and turn away, back towards the mirrored bar tableau and her own world, there in the mad-faced tower on the rock-slopes.

7 PURPLE AND RED AND YELLOW AND …
ON FIRE

The Chocolate Raven pours another glass of red, lights another ciga-rette and lets a mouthful of smoke streak away into the desert night. Thinking on what she's just seen up there in the Hajar Mountains, she recognises that the Platinum Raven and those others would seem to be in some kind of decadent nightclub. In labelling it so, she's not forgetting that many Dubai residents and visitors party hard in many venues; but this club's decadence would seem to be of a kind that's almost impossible to find in Dubai itself, namely the druggy variety. In the context of Dubai's draconian anti-drug laws, the Platinum Raven or whoever else runs this establishment must have some quite extraordinarily powerful financial or criminal associations, in order to have opened and be running it without immediate arrest, imprisonment and probable execution.

So, from her eyry here, the Chocolate Raven watches events unfolding tiny in that shaft upon the mountain-slopes. The Platinum Raven's gregariousness with the tower's other denizens never undermines her striking poise, and the charismatic smile in her interactions seems powered by a universal awareness of her authority. Little of all this lively verbiage can be made out, however, from across the desert. From here on the Burj Khalifa terrace, only snatches of chat make it through the desert dust-storms and the shiny-squinting wind-whipped sunlight, to the Chocolate Raven's ears; but even these snatches remain incomprehensible. As for lip-reading, she can make no sense of what those three sets of mouths are saying to one another. It doesn't seem to be English. Are they speaking in Arabic? Possibly; but strange, if so. Scorpio could pass as a native, but not the other two—and how many resident non-natives bother learning more than a couple of words of the language of their Emirati hosts, here in Dubai? Despite her best efforts, those tantalising vocal snippets therefore remain indistinct, like the archaeological scratches of human voices in a faint and intermittent radio signal.

This is mostly a limitation on understanding the Platinum Raven in particular. For Amber doesn't speak much: he seems rather to embody some inevitable darkness in the building, that prefers to show than to tell. And Scorpio's presence has a kind of divinely eloquent dance within it, which feels to be more the soul than the sound of the tower.

The eccentric beauty of the structure gives no clue to its function; but as she surmised, it is in fact the darkest, brightest and strangest of nightclubs, despite its bizarre location. Indeed it is no less than the Ultimate, Mythical Nightclub, because for a couple of recent years it housed a weekly party whose legendary scene cast a longer and richer-coloured shadow through the worldwide conception of *the city* than any other ever has: in particular, the city as nocturnal playground, stage and killing-floor for those who have the inclination and ability to inhabit the apex of fabulosity; the party monsters who reject the general herd in favour of those avid, self-selected few who strive without rest but always want more. The echoes of its nights have travelled down through the intervening months and years and seeped across the continents—in snapshots and video snippets, in the memories of the chosen who were present and who lived that crazy chic, and in the consciousness of all who have seen or heard or read of this scene before relaying it in Chinese whispers all around the globe. Higher than the underground pinnacle of that elusive night at That Venue, at an hour when the whole crowd was calling down the spirits: higher than the penthouse of that undated night at That Other Venue, in one of *those* months in *that* particular year when perhaps … well, if you weren't there or you couldn't get in or you didn't even know of it, then I'm sorry, baby, but you missed the ship. You missed a ship the like of which there won't be again. Sure, there will be other scenes in other times, with other little lifeboats to hop into. But in comparison with those little vessels, *this* was a crystal ship—an opalescent quinquereme gliding up the coast at night, dispelled by a morning light that still picks out the ship's glassy wake across the ocean...

The interlocking circles of people at this mighty venue have collaborated on a recipe that's been within the control of no single one of them, but whose flavour has been refined over the months to attain a unique authenticity. This recipe's raw ingredients were glamour, style, amorality and squalor; and when these four first came together here a couple of years ago, they did so with a lurch or two, a fresh-off-the-boat quality, even a clunky innocence. Then before many weeks had elapsed, the four had become prospective conspirators, coiling around one another at increasing speed, emitting smoke and flickers of coloured light. Within a few more months, though, they had mutated into a single conspiracy and had become the mad-faced tower itself. What followed came in three stages.

First, the tower spent a few months just providing a home to all those little misfits who'd felt the restrictions of the world outside as not so much a helpful thing, but rather a waste and mutilation dictated to them with the irrelevant fear of frightened masses throughout history. (The tower had once had to fight off an attempt to tame its own architectural nature, owing to petty politics in the architect's office, so it sympathised.)

Secondly, in an access of flamboyant love, the tower gave these bright sweet misfits such an addictively hedonistic playland, spread across a labyrinthine floorplan so filled with such enticing spaces and jam-packed with addictive substances, that the misfits were unaware of being turned into beings who would be unsatisfiable at any other venue on earth.

And thirdly came the flowering of the tower, where the lack of any surrounding competition helped it become the clearest channel for all that was suppressed throughout the region. There on its isolated hillside outside any city limits, this place became the epitome of such urban sophistication and sybaritic urbanity as to feel quite vertiginous, certainly for anyone stepping into it for the first time, but even to many of the assorted international party monsters who already made regular pilgrimages from New York, London, Los Angeles, Shanghai and European capitals, in search of the most fantastical and transcendent confluence of subcultural energy anywhere in the world. For here was where white rabbits not only conquered telephone cubicles, but made those cubicles scream and bleed, for the damage they'd inflicted on a million Ravens globally.

Sometimes the whirl of flesh and lights and hazy sound seemed to slow for a moment to a still frame, and eyes of experience would then be caught on camera, in a face amid the swirl—a face you'd half-recognise from before, when you'd seen it on a big screen perhaps, or in a memory seen through champagne upon a terrace under heat-lamps, while the music span forever on that summer night before—wide eyes, prominent and grey, camera-frozen in a face soaked in way too much experience.

At this point the fabulousness of the denizens grew so indefatigable as to become ferocious. The dance-floor was a cat-walk, under little fluffy clouds where the skies went on forever and the clouds would catch the colours—*purple and red and yellow and ... on fire.* And every night the anorexic models floated through, beautifully drugged-out and weak and untouchable, forever down the runways of their airport lanes, each expressionless in damage through the night-lit clouds, with their make-up flashing soft in the lights, like perfection, clad in shreds of lightest silk that concealed the needle-marks.

The clientele's long-standing ambiguity of male and female began to become more concentrated, as the rest began to diminish by slow degrees, leaving an increasingly hardcore population of fabulous monsters whose very gazes seemed intent on drawing blood. Soon the club came to be running almost 24/7, still profitably open to passing trade from around the world during regular nightclub hours, but in reality the permanent realm of a loose cadre of what can only be called transsexual death-ghouls—the global elite of that disparate band for whom this natural direction coincided with the means never to have to think of such dirty considerations as money, work or food. The mad-faced tower had become, in effect, a drug-den in nightclub drag.

And onwards it barrelled through the months, with its own unique momentum, pulling world-class DJs in and world-class spending in their wake. With all volume limits removed, the pumping of this building's music and the flicker of its sky-sweeping images came to populate the whole grand space: over the desert, in between the aeroplanes in Sharjah, over the labour camp at Sonapur, up through the night-time city sky, and up and out above the Gulf.

Within the air came the echo of a tower-spike to match the Burj Khalifa, made of giant plinks of light and shafts of sound branching upward, hard and colour-smooth and perfect—like the dream of a thousand-storey Dubai skyscraper, pitched like a rocket-launch upon a draftsman's screen with a mega-project soundtrack, to haul in investors. See the tower-spike sprout like an inverse water-spout, up among the mountains; and helter-skelter round its shaft at break-neck speed through the whistling air of night, via software magic, all set to the soundtrack's stunning flash and burst of perfection and echoes... Two voices glance through this world-circling flash and cool of music: first, a yearning woman's murmur rises through a howling wind, *"Noémi ... Noémi ... Noémi..."*; then that dead, passive, flat super-model voice again, weak and beautiful and affectless and Arizona-damaged, with her fluffy clouds and skies that went on forever, and the clouds would catch the colours—*purple and red and yellow and ... on fire.* You don't see that—you might still see them in the desert.

8 THE MAD-FACED TOWER IN THE MOUNTAINS

By now the Chocolate Raven has lost all track of time, here on her 152nd-Level terrace. She is starting to suspect, and nervously to hope, that she herself is perhaps in control of the tower; and decides that if this is found to be the case, then she will people it as she likes.

The Platinum Raven would then drive and anchor this tower, thinks the Chocolate Raven: she would embody what I love, so that in making her I can be making love with her. Intelligent aliveness, the clearest lens. Exuberance, with style and poise, confidence and strength. Charisma, attracting attention and loving it, a self-celebration, her heat and cool coiling like a serpent through the sea—yes! The richly-layered force, celebration and vengeance of electronic dance music. Fluid interaction, from flexible and fast perceptions. She would need the company of other people, but the length of time she'd want to spend with them wouldn't be very much and the number of them wouldn't be that great, for at heart she'd be a lone wolf, whose richest pleasures came when she was alone... She's what I want to leave behind me, thinks the Chocolate Raven: a creature of harnessed passion, recompense and mode for desires I had to sublimate...

She pours herself another glass of red from her bottle and lights another cigarette. It's less than a couple of hours since she first discovered the mad-faced tower, but already she is starting to wonder how she did without it until today. And how recent that was! Can there really have been such a stretch of time before that? And why on earth, during that stretch, did she never realise what was lacking? How could she have failed to realise this? Why did she never protest that it lacked? Why had she never put her foot down, in some way?

"OK," she thinks, "it's clearly time we drove there."

It isn't hard to arrange, after all: there's a car, there's a driver, there is certainly petrol, and there must surely be some kind of route to the tower, for all those party monsters to have chattered and preened their skeletal fabulousness all the way across the desert to its door.

...And hence it is that the Chocolate Raven's forehead is pressed against the rear left window of a car shooting down a road, dead-straight for hours, through the dunes and across the plain.

Presently the sand on either side of the road gets rougher, giving way to dirt and scrub. Stones push through the dirt, and then the dirt becomes stone. The knuckles of endless rock stretching away in all directions remind her of the tale of a castle she once read and now cannot remember.

By the time she reaches the first toes of the foothills, the weather is turning. The colour of the sky above the road ahead is dirty rust: its surface bellies out with a flicker underneath, then a giant gash of ochre lightning rips through its height. This dazzling crackle stands out a split-second, vanishes—reappears a long half-second—then is gone.

Now the car is climbing the foothills. The humming of the engine in the glass on her face is hypnotic. Electric pylons march beside the road, then swing away down a sudden valley with a giant span of metal struts and wires into dark. She catches a sudden glimpse of the tower, far up ahead on the rock-face, before it swings out of view behind an intervening hill. Her scalp gives a tingle.

Vertiginous, she leans forward with her elbows on her knees, feeling she is shrinking in the width of the back seat. Ahead through the windscreen she sees, with a dread-prickle, manicured toy-sized trees shaped as fluffy grey teardrops, flanking the road where it climbs straight ahead. These toy-land trees start swelling as she watches them: top leaves writhing and twigs tight-clenched, all bathed in an odd and windless milky-yellow light. She feels as if she's shrunk to a speck upon the seat, while the trees quiver ever upwards, as if they want to breathe: the fluffy tears of foliage have risen, so the car now climbs along a corridor of bare trunks as straight as metal bars. A rabbit springs across the road—ears in the headlights—and vanishes.

And now at the crest of the tree-chute, the mad-faced tower once again appears, this time very much closer and for real, with its two brown windows staring down upon her. Around the tower's base upon the rock-slopes (wreathing the space where the pug hangs sluggish in its pale blue strait-jacket in amongst the struts, spitting sand), a fog churns and eddies. Feelers seem to stir in it, and now the Chocolate Raven's scalp tightens even more, as a shape like a ram's head starts from the fog, statuesque as a bust, flings its snout up and bleats while its eyes cut straight down the road into hers with a look of such sadness and loss and desolation that she feels she is seeing something nobody deserves to see: the Great Lie.

Streaks of pain and horror shoot around her through the air, and among this buffeting she half-hears snatches of beauty winging past her in gusts, like a distant music blown around a mountain by the wind. She sinks her head between her legs, here on the back seat, blocks her ears tightly with the sides of her knees, screws her eyes shut and screams out "DRIVE BACK NOW PLEASE…"

9 THE SQUIRLY BROWN WINDOWS IN THE TURRET

Next day, the Chocolate Raven is back where she should be: in Dubai, on Level 152. She leans at the far left-hand end of the railing once again and grows attentive.

High upon the turret of the mad-faced tower there are two round windows, tinted with swirls of brown inside the glass itself. In one of these the Platinum Raven stands, looking down from the hills and out across the desert plains. She shuts her eyes a moment, and a smile pulls the corners of her mouth apart and upwards. She's excited, for tonight in the tower is a special night indeed: a brand-new, much-vaunted drug called mirror mist will infiltrate the air, gently filling up the club through the air-conditioning system. News of it has filtered underground around the world, bringing stories of a new and most sophisticated high—a high, so it's said, with the power and the beauty of a trip, but where the tripper runs the show. Everyone who breathes in mirror mist, it's said, is shown a magic mirror view of his or her self, intensified. So everyone is bringing their own goods to the party; self-knowledge and escapism, rolled into one. Needless to say, around the Gulf region mirror mist will not be happening any time soon, in any other place than right here—and she's brought it in!

The floor of this conical attic shakes already, with a beat as from a giant heart down in the building…

She takes out her phone and touches Amber's number, then crosses the room and opens a metal cabinet mounted on the wall, beside which are several TV monitors showing views of the tower's interior. Watching the picture of the main dance-floor downstairs, she hears him pick up. "Are we ready?" she asks.

"We're ready," he replies, easing down the boom of the music with a slide-control on the panel in front of him and glancing across the empty dance-floor ahead. "Shall we open the doors?"

"Yes." She adjusts a dial in the cabinet. "I'll start the air-conditioning now, on low."

She puts her phone away and returns to the circular window, where she stretches up her arms, leans her head back and lets her long body squirm. She gazes through the deep squirly brown of the glass, out across the desert, to the city and the sea. She eases her feet further forward on the wide sill, onward through the thickness of the high turret's walls, and extends her limbs to touch the round embrasure's edges all at once: planted there in Renaissance diameter, her arms telling ten past ten and legs twenty-five to five, she purrs in measured harmony and scans the view ahead.

Dusk is falling. Over on her right rise the neighbouring hills, pink and brown in the sidelight. Far ahead, the island in the Gulf is silhouetted on the baggy blooded orange of the sun above the water's curve. Through the rich brown swirls in the thickness of the glass, she lets her gaze wander down: from the stillness of the Gulf between the island and the shore, to the city on the coast many miles away, spreading inland in a grid of twinkly lights. As her gaze sinks further, it runs across the darkened dunes, across the stony miles of scrub and up through this canyon, whose nearest tracts are hidden by the coping of a balustrade around the rooftop here below her. Just beyond the balustrade a slope of boulders funnels to a precipice of weeds in half a circle like a lip, around a lethal shriek of air a hundred metres sheer and twenty wide, making of this present site a small hanging valley. Planted one each side upon their tails on this coping, a pair of carved seahorses rise up majestically, blank stone eyes flecked with moss and reddish lichen scales, fixed on the clouds over seas out of sight.

As the orange orb widens, it shrinks around the island, which cuts it then in half—two slopes across the disc now chords moving outward to kiss its upper curve on either side and so extinguish it.

The dance and the flicker of the city grow alive, transfixed by the

Burj Khalifa's spike at its centre: darkness of energy and pulsing of violence, flickered out shaft-wise up through the air, over pink, over mauve, through to indigo and black.

As the sun rolls away around the globe to the west, the higher black weighs heavy, pushing down the lighter colours, so she sees her own reflection growing clearer against it: blonde hair platinum, splashed over brown eyes, cheekbones top-lit, lips curving up together, sensual as lovers.

Of a sudden round her torso from above her snakes a tendril, the first wisp of mirror mist. She grins. Condensing on the window, it diffuses her reflection. She brings down her left hand, and on the glass with her finger she writes out her name across the sky above Dubai—THE PLATINUM RAVEN.

For a moment then, she splits her attention into three: first the panorama, a-flicker in the distance; secondly her name squirling through the condensation (independent of the squirls in the brown itself); and thirdly the slivers of her eyes in the glass, clear again within the newly-wiped width of the letters.

What a night it will be—the mad-faced tower's very first night of mirror mist!

10 SANTA MONICA BOULEVARD

Scorpio, exultant, checks his make-up in the dressing-room, whirls around in spirals and runs his dainty hands across his body till it tingles. He darts across the dance-floor to the DJ booth and flings his arms around Amber, kisses him, then skips away and out through the exit, to the red-walled passageway leading to the stairwell.

He knows no more of mirror mist than anyone else here does. Its effect has been described to him, as seeing and imagining and feeling like yourself, but to the power of two, or three, or four—a zinging, self-affirming and ultimate edition of yourself, as it were.

"Yes, but what's it really like?" he asked the Platinum Raven and Amber yesterday evening, while they were all lounging around the kitchen table. "And how long does it—?" and he hiccupped: they were all a little tipsy on red wine by then, having laboured hard all day to prepare for this evening.

Amber and the Platinum Raven looked at each other, and Amber grins at her. "Well…" he begins, and tails off.

"Well…" she echoes, and tails off too.

Realising he is being toyed with, Scorpio smoulders at them with a sudden irony, but hiccups again in mid-smoulder, so the impact is somewhat lessened.

"OK, it's sort of like this," the Platinum Raven says, gets up from her kitchen chair and kneels down beside his chair. "I'm going to demonstrate the effect it has on the skin—it's a kind of tingle," and she lifts his black T-shirt up to just below his little breasts.

"What are you doing?" he asks.

"Relax," she says, "this is the best impression I can give. Trust me and I'll show you. Close your eyes…"

Reluctantly he does so.

"No peeking, now." She approaches his stomach with her mouth, then blows a quick and powerful raspberry against his skin. He shrieks and is soon chasing her round the kitchen table, a scandalised look of murder and mirth on his face. At last she is caught and punishment is meted out, which involves much slapping and throttling and hilarity; nor is Amber spared Scorpio's tipsy vengeance, until they all three constitute a puddle of giggling exhaustion sprawled across the chairs, table and floor.

So *that* was informative, he drily reflects. He halts on the stairwell and peers down off it to the tower's main lobby, where the doors to the outside world are being opened. But whatever this mirror mist turns out to be like, it will surely be a cut above the drugs he knew before. For Scorpio, like many of this club's clientele, came here from elsewhere. In his case, it was from pretty much as far around the globe as you could get from here—Los Angeles. It was only two years ago that he'd first arrived in L.A., on the run from his home town of Asbury Park (and that was a whole different story in itself), aiming for anonymity and a brand-new start. He achieved both aims, but at the cost of an addiction that saw him scoring heroin at seedy bars and clubs in Hollywood: at the Study perhaps, or at Tempo or Plaza with the drag queens, or at Blacklight with the derelicts. Or if he could get a lift, at other likely sources further away, like Scores or the divey Jalisco Inn in Downtown (he shakes his head involuntarily, to recall these old names that he's not recalled for months, but here they are, still tucked away in his memory-banks and popping out now). Chico in Montebello, Suave in Carson, the Annex down in Inglewood—or Jewel's Catch One, for a bit of scale and glamour. Oh, fuck… They were mean times, cut with flashes and jagged stabs of fun, but always followed by more mean times.

He worked Santa Monica Boulevard with the other girls, in twos or threes if possible but often alone. Scorpio was just a working name at first, chosen on a whim to undertake this paying work, in place of the boy name Angel that he'd grown up with in Asbury Park; but since this paying work was the only kind of work he found himself doing, and these girls his only colleagues and friends, he quickly morphed into Scorpio for all purposes. How well he got to know that long, grungy strip of Santa Monica throughout those months, from Western to LaBrea after midnight: so much verbiage and congregation, business and action there at Highland, near the donut stand, perched on the grimy wall, just beside the bus-stop; or standing at Gower by the disused gas station, sitting by the strip-malls at Van Ness or Wilton, on the bench at Budget rental cars at Orange, or beside that sports field down at Cahuenga, a block away from that hustler who disliked all proximity… Then if the girls' ships had come in that night, walking west, rich and hungry and closer temporarily, across the city limits into West Hollywood, where a plate of food awaited at the Yukon Diner. Or if no ship had come, then sprawling at the furthest, ever-unwiped tables in the 24/7 drive-through burger joint beside LaBrea—covering perhaps for one another, as they shot up in the men's or women's room right there, in a grimy rush of over-yellow mustard and onion-rings.

One night he had a fix already in his pocket, and he and another working girl met, both dressed in boy garb, and drove in someone's clapped-out car, up to the Griffith Park observatory and sat upon the parapet above the wooded slopes and had their fix. So they sat immobile there; then sweetness, richness and losing track of time… Sitting there poised, poisoned, overbrimming with exhaustion and sensory overload, Scorpio scanned the City of Angels spread beneath him in the black, black heat. Pressed down by this heavy sticky night that never seemed to end—an L.A. night that sealed a day that always felt like the last day of all. The grid of bright darkness and points of coloured light stretched west and south and east to infinity, to suburbs that were so far, they surely wrapped around the earth and came back here, the neighbourhoods melting so together, fading on and on… Cars poured numberless and tiny on the freeways that sliced the flat enormity; then slower on the Avenues and Boulevards, from traffic light to traffic light, flicking north and south, east and west, north and south, east and west; then trickled through the darker grid of Streets from stop sign to stop sign, winking into shadow-view, glimpsed in the gaps between the buildings and the palm trees, residential stucco and security gates, where the lawn-sprinklers sprinkled…

At last the friend had to leave, and offered a ride, but Scorpio said he'd stay there alone. They air-kissed as usual, and off the other went. Then he sat upon his hands on the parapet, right there, his feet above the hillside, aquiver and alone again and hurting with the rawness of a squirt of flesh and nerves among the concrete and steel and the plastic and the gasoline that threatened and addicted him, week after week. Blades, rocks, glass, edges; fists in the shadows of the city, cocked in wait for him, spying out of doorways at the shapes of the contents of his pockets, or to check he was alone; and the gayness of his body in the pools of the street-lights. Hatred and desire and indifference coiled and built around him, oiled to spring. A crackle lit the sky of a sudden in the west (black wires up the hillside, aerials on orange-tinged night above the canyon), but no thunder yet drowned the endless cricket-chirp.

Looking down Normandie, he found the line of Santa Monica Boulevard—there. So further over, somewhere there, was Circus, the warehouse-sized club where that boy had danced who crackled when he looked at Scorpio. Nor had thunder followed then, just tightness and an ache and further crackle when their eyes met, and thunderous industrial music playing loud, then Scorpio's knowing that the boy had gone. Then beside Circus was Arena where that blond boy, slumming it from West Hollywood, bearing ecstasy, had held him through the night, with his suntan and muscles, then had vanished in the morning. Then had been the thugs in the parking lot with baseball bats, seeing him and pointing at him, nodding at each other, laughing, shouting, veering by degrees across the parking lot towards him, their bats swinging, ready for him, all the while his blood pumping; lowering his head, slowly steering away from them, trying hard to walk with authority and strength, even striding. The thugs came closer—then a bus stopped in front of him, as if to deliver him, stopping just in time for him to hop aboard before they reached the bus-stop too and struck the closing doors behind him…

His eyes refocused as he jumped at the sound of a gunshot from the east. His fingers gripped the parapet. The moon ahead was low, heavy amber in the haze, and suddenly he knew: he must leave L.A. and clean up at the same time, or else he'd never leave and would end up living Downtown, there on Skid Row, sleeping in a box on San Julian or Fifth Street, where once he'd gone to score and smelt the hopelessness… No—*never*.

He swung his legs up, twisted round and dropped his feet back down, facing up at the observatory. "Angels, I'm leaving you," he sweetly spoke, and spat upon the ground. "Thanks a bunch, and have a nice night."

He turned to the city, bowed once, then he skipped away suddenly: across the parking lot and down the hills into Hollywood; across a spell of months comprising struggle and transition; then inexorably here, to Dubai and the tower and its first night of mirror mist!

11   IN THE ARMS OF THE MAN FROM THE GARDEN OF LOVE

Leaning here alone above the busy lobby, Scorpio closes his eyes for a moment, with a sense of peace at how things have changed since that decisive departure from the observatory terrace. For not only is he now working here in this pleasure palace instead of on the streets of Hollywood. He is also in the arms of the man from the film-screen: the arms of the man from the garden of love: in Amber's arms. (And he says, *Oh oh oh oh oh oh, what a feeling…*) Nothing now is quite the same colour as before, now the starflakes fall on Chameleonshire. Plants quiver, planets sing, hills resonate to the dance of the snail. A single yellow angelfish has noticed them and pouts, nose bumping on the glass, tail flapping in the weeds. When Amber went across the desert, Scorpio would reach for him at night, half-asleep, pull his knees to his chest, and hold his breasts with hands he wished were Amber's hands. But then when Amber came back home from the desert, then Scorpio would lie there amongst him in the afterglow of sex and sweat and fumes of wine, delirious, with Amber's cock ready yet again, sprung hard by the smooth warm pale brown stomach-curve of Scorpio. Yelps in the yellow dusk, car lights and neon flickers, far below their window, by the club's front entrance. And down there one night, strangely incongruous, a little child's voice wavered upward to their window, as frail as a thrush's egg and cutting through the babble with a question: "What's a thousand miles above heaven, then?" Scorpio's waking eyes re-opened on Amber, who drew him close. The bed seemed to sway, like a cradle in the sighs of a summer wind. Reflected on the silver curtain-strips by the bedside, fountains of candle-light shimmered in the breeze from the open window, splashing onto both their naked bodies. Candles burned scattered round the room: a town of lights they awoke to find had died—as the cities of the world would die as well, long after Scorpio and Amber themselves had died and crumbled into dust and to the sea, emitting two entwining strings of fizzy champagne bubbles… "Venus as a boy," murmured Scorpio and stroked his tongue across the width of Amber's biceps. Spasms rippled through him once again; he squirmed closer in and kissed his lover-man, his face deep buried within the warmth of Amber's chest and arms…

12 THE PUG AMONG THE STRUTS, IN THE PALE BLUE STRAIT-JACKET

The Platinum Raven steps off the window sill, crosses the attic room and looks again at the air-conditioning control, which is a dial running from 1 to 10. After a moment's thought she turns it from 1 to 2. She heads out through the open door, checks her keys and pulls the door locked behind her. Side doors lead off periodically from the steep spiral staircase, set into the left-hand wall as she descends several storeys. She jangles the keys, before stowing them about herself, and stands a moment, smiling as the booming of the music makes the staircase resonate. She stops before the next door, unlocks it, passes through and clicks it carefully shut behind her.

Here above the lobby, she can see the punters coming in below her: people paying, checking items in, then heading to the door of the main bar, or straight towards the music down a passage where a wisp of silver vapour licks the shadows. *Good evening, mesdames et messieurs, my little monkeys,* she feels like announcing through the rush inside her now: *if you'd like your ears to bleed, please form a queue for the bass-bins on the speakers—they'll be loud. More generally, however, can you all hear the thunder on the left? I hope you can. Are you ready for tonight? Amber's ready, so is Scorpio, and even her up there upon the tower in the city. The mist tastes nicer if you're ready for the hurricane, the quicksand, the flames in the night sky, the poison and the dry ice. The flood-water's right beneath us, hissing up tight through the pressure-fault just below the lobby here. There's also a grey-lit cellar downstairs, where I bid you lend Amber the keys to your skeleton: the rating will be X, but you'll learn new things as your guts are mixed with light and sound and shot around the globe. As for me, I thought perhaps I'd stay behind the billows with my breasts pointing upward and my groin pushed out, with my right hand skyward and my left hand on my hip, eyes wide in the silver staring softly through the mirror mist unblinking (if that's fine with you?). —There again: the thunder on the left. Did you hear it?...*

She becomes aware of Scorpio standing on the landing across from her, at the same level as her but separated by the atrium of the lobby. He spots her at the same moment and blows a kiss at her. Smiling over at him, she indicates the direction of the main dance-floor, where Amber is now making the music jump from his DJ booth. "Shall we?" she calls.

"Oh, we shall!" he calls back. And they both head in that direction, along their separate landings.

They enter the main dance-floor from different entrances. Scorpio heads straight to the bottom of a stairway leading up the side of a big square podium, its open top three metres off the dance-floor; and the Platinum Raven stands in front of the DJ booth, where Amber checks his faders, takes his headphones off, steps down from the booth and joins her. "I'll be right back," he says, with an ominous twinkle in his eyes. "The punters won't know it's just a pre-mixed CD for a couple of tracks: I won't tell, if you don't!" and he heads towards the door to the lobby. Before he reaches this, however, he gives her a dark nod, unlocks a smaller side door behind a curtain, and clicks it shut behind him. The Platinum Raven smiles and shakes her head: it's going to be a dark, Amber-special set of music tonight.

It's strange, she reflects, that she herself is the only one of this trio whose back-story is quite unknown to the other two. Neither Amber nor Scorpio knows anything of where she came from. And that's how it will stay. After all, she is an Icon of Platinum Perfection, of a kind whose back-story is never known; and in running this tower she does quite enough to recompense them both for the lack of one.

By contrast Scorpio's back-story, on Santa Monica Boulevard and before then, is known in therapeutic detail by her and Amber, because he's needed to tell them.

As for Amber's back-story, it lies somewhere between those two extremes, in the sense that it's just as specifically detailed as Scorpio's, yet can be told in words as brief as those describing the Platinum Raven's historical lacuna. For although this back-story is an extraordinary one, it is also simple, with an infernal simplicity and logic that are at the heart of this tower of shadow: Amber's past was precisely captured on film as *The Hitcher*. The Platinum Raven doesn't know whether or how much Scorpio is aware of this; nor, if he is aware of it, whether Amber knows he is. But it's not her place to pry into their relationship in order to find out, and still less her place to spring upon Scorpio the fact that his lover is the continuation of Rutger Hauer's character after those cameras stopped rolling in the desert, if he doesn't yet know this or hasn't yet admitted it to himself. In any case Scorpio has come to no harm, it would seem.

She knows exactly where Amber was headed to just now, through that side door, because he once took her downstairs to show her. It's a hidden place he's made his own—a place where no one else ever goes uninvited. She pictures him, down in the bowels of the building now: the metal stairs clank as he descends nine steps, turns down another nine, his hand on the cold rail, then another flight of steps and on down several further levels. He grins in the dark as he runs his fingers lightly through the dust on the rail.

At the bottom, through a door, is an outside space among the struts that support the tower. Hidden here in the shadows, he can peer out and down, to that long straight road climbing steeply up this canyon from the desert, with the fluffy grey teardrop trees on either side of it.

(The Chocolate Raven blinks and swallows, on her terrace in Dubai.)

Where the straight road ends just below him, cars must twist around the cliff to the club's front entrance: their lights swerve around through the night as they do so, swinging round cautiously in order not to break through the barrier and fall into wreckage on the far rocks below. Across the city-swelter shines the ocean, where a dog-faced moon leers down like a floodlight. It's too far away for him to see the waves shivering, but Amber could swear he sees the Gulf's surface swell and sigh, as if a liquid muscle flexes there beneath the shimmer of the water's curve... Wasps buzz suddenly behind him. He turns, clambers in between the beams, further inside the hill, through a pale weeping light where the long grass rustles. "I'm on my way!" he murmurs through his flesh, then he halts: there ahead hangs a figure in a pale blue strait-jacket, fixed to a harness on a rope within a wooden frame. *Your craze was emptiness, mine was alcohol,* comes a voice of sighing shingle through the outsize pug's face, measurelessly ugly and exhausted and sad. The rope, playing out from the frame, lets the figure down a metre, then stops, so it bounces in mid-air before ascending again, as it has clearly done for years. Now a hum sings thick upon the air, as the figure chokes a sob back and spits dry sand. *See the space of Siberian heart in your eyes—I think you know it shows through,* sighs the voice at him, falling out tired from the rank grey muzzle to the ground. Amber takes a gun from his pocket, shoots the face, shoots it seven times more, then another seven times, till it weeps black hamburger tears on its jacket. "Don't worry, you're too ill to die!" he spits, as if to cut through glass. He wheels round, slips between the struts, finds the door, climbs the stairs, runs a fingernail across the Platinum Raven's chest in passing her, returns to his booth and makes the music leap anew.

Underneath the space of struts, a spill of sand falls through a tunnel where the water drips. Further down inside the hill, a small square chamber of blue mosaic, sealed long ago for a purpose now forgotten, shakes in time with Amber's music far above. Even further down, where the fossils sleep cold, tiny bubbles rise unseen.

13 BLACK AND RUST AND OCHRE OVER THE PLAIN

While he's been gone, the Platinum Raven has been resisting the effect of the mirror mist herself, as she wants to see the effect it's having on the punters. She wanders in amongst a scattered group of folks she doesn't know, and leans by herself against a wall, incognito. She peers through the din of dark music and the shimmer of the mirror mist, and scans the growing crowds, who are numerous and fabulous beyond her expectations. The club has filled fast. The hall swirls; flashing light dances knives off the billow of the silver mist. All now affected by it, people dance or float around or lose themselves in talk or in affection. Surprise and delight ripple subtly through the air in all directions. A girl in purple leather with a ring through her nose, very beautiful and high already, stretches up to breathe a jet of mist dipping in from a vent on the wall nearby. Coming down from this and turning, she lights on the Platinum Raven and stares at her. A smile spreads rich across her features: "*You* did this, I know you did!" she laughs aloud.

"Brighter people than me invented mirror mist," the Platinum Raven tells her.

The girl swoops up and kisses her. "From now on I'm going to live here!" she promises.

"I hope you do!"

"See you later!" calls the girl and scuds away through the crowd.

The Platinum Raven glances up at the podium across the room, and smiles with a burst of love and pride at what she sees. High above the dance-floor, Scorpio dances amid the silver mirror mist, lurid in the lights—every movement so electric, so mesmerically divine, that a crowd has stopped below him, just to wonder—as with perfect unawareness and control he taps an energy that ought to make him vaporise…

Then she bends her gaze to the DJ booth and grins with a different love. Demonic in that black-wired den up there, working both the music and the lights in the hall, Amber's making love with destruction and violence, radiant in damage, spinning heaven on a sound-flight destined for hell. "And we're just getting started," she reflects.

OK, the night's a bull's-eye—so now it's time to have some fun herself. She settles back upon a flight of steps above the dance-floor, and lets her eyes wander, unfocused. Mirror mist billows at the edges of the hall, across the floor and the ceiling, so the bodies and the music in the middle might be any size. Rust-coloured spotlights burn through the gas, cutting in between the billows in a twitching of shafts, as the sun-spokes flicker through the boiling of the clouds in a speeded-up video. Denser billows split the rays, letting through a little light and bouncing out the rest into sprays so weakened that they glance off every other cloud, are split and then diffuse.

The scene has grown more lurid and her seeing self-reflexive, though she's not yet lost the knowledge why this is: bit by bit, her seeing is informing the scene. She watches her perception participate in what it sees; sees that interaction bouncing back from the billows; sees it modify them further in the course of bouncing back.

So here is the gift she gives the world tonight! To every self, a mirror of its own upon the vapour, every mirror made from the self it reflects. This, for example, is herself to the tenth power, carried on the music through the lens of the gas, liberated from the grind of the dragging of a body through the heaviness of weight and fatigue and breakability: her *own* sound, dark in a flexing of planes coloured black and rust and ochre; dry heat, unnatural as the heat within a russet-coloured light-bulb (day or night unclear, as in a dream or a painting); hellfire, lazy with the sureness of power unqualified…

The music draws her up above a vast plain, whipping at the sky and digging down through the clouds. Line, space and colour lean together with its pull. From its underside it fires down a shaft that descends with the slowness of enormity to hit the plain and carry up the engines of a town of sound. Hardly has the shaft reached the ground than another drops ahead to tread the plain a moment later, then another and another at a constant rate… One layer upward, the middle notes stroll, growing creamy in their freedom not to fall but climbing further with their own strength. Out from their hide clicks a dry articulation, quick as arm-bones. Below them then, a skyscraper pile drives down, of a size that dwarfs every shaft so far, falling slower, with a force of inertia unrelenting and terrifying. Dust falls ahead of it, the plain too has fallen, so the pile seems to linger; then it hits the ground. Before any crash can travel up to her, the pile has pierced the plain like a nail through sand; another shaft is even dropping too, by the time there returns, on the beat, from the pit, the explosion of the first monster nail—sight and sound on a scale that leaves expressionless attention as the only response. Triggered by the shock, a jagged buzz from the cockpit of the music shoots ahead across the sky, to be lost at its edges. Every sixteenth shaft, another pile drops, to sink through the plain: thus enslaved, she gears her mind to awaiting its explosion, with a hunger for the sight—then the silence—then the crash—then the hunger for the next one…

14 SLINKY-SMOOTH IN THE MIRROR MIST

The Platinum Raven swings her gaze around and then upward, to the podium above her, where Scorpio is dancing with an effortless charisma, red-lit and sinuous in mirror mist. He stares through the billows, as another figure joins him. He gulps, feels his cock jump, his ass twitch, his tongue prime his opening lips in automatic readiness—and sees it is his own self reflected on the mist, and his eyes shine wide… What a creature! Who invented him? Prismatic all around him is the flicker and gyration of his own slim coffee-coloured legs, seeming now to be kicking at him, curling in around him and gripping at his throat in honey-nutcracker motions, but vanishing whenever they are just about to touch him. Gracing every pair are leather boots of spotless white—pointed toes, high heels, down-turned at the calf into soft white ripples as of labia—clear out of which comes a curve so sleek, smooth and simple that it might have made him weep, were his gaze not rising past knees that give the feeling to be had inside the stomach by a sudden drive across a humped bridge, then lingering on thighs that could melt yellow butter in reflecting it, and sliding up between them in rapture… There clings the tightest and the skimpiest of coverings, containing what must surely burst it open very soon. Up from the cover spills a tangle of dark hair, fading out except for a single soft snake running moist to the navel where a drip of sweat winks in the strobe light. Around him the perfection of his slinky-smooth torso is reflected, twisting like a Siamese cat whose flanks a spray of silver fingernails caress. He yearns to run his tongue around the full dark nipples, lay his head between the perfect little breasts, then to sleep. *Sweet dreams!* he murmurs. Golden lightnings are his arms, as they rise, swoop, cross, sweep and quiver in a mesmerising union with the music. Bright golden rings sway glinting from his ears, sweeping up to which his neck curves delicate and graceful; around it hang a few dark strands of his hair, broken free from the rest which is tied above his head within a band that makes it issue down his back like a fountain. His lips, repeated everywhere, are pouting with the business of such raptness of regard, he sees; they smile at being caught thus. His face is pretty, elfin, not a face to take seriously, he thinks, except the eyes. The eyes… Open wide, unable to hide, and unable not to see inside the people around him, often wishing they could see no further in than people's irises but forced to see behind their pupils and beyond—too deep for both the looked-at and the looker. Psychic eyes, naked eyes, eliciting revulsion in the few, adoration in the many, but exhausting either way. He sees them all about him now; flicks his own around, seeking anywhere they're not; but they multiply in flicking. (So how did he contrive, until a moment ago, to look around and notice any other thing but these?) They pierce to the depths of his own gaze, and frighten him—pin his isolation down. How beautiful they are. How clear and how breakable—how burstable a window is each one. They bewitch. In fact, he'd *almost* say he loved himself…

15 PLANETS HANGING HEAVY

The Platinum Raven swings her head back down from watching the podium. She stands, steps ahead across the floor and sees the bodies parting like the Red Sea either side of her. A lane of space clears ahead, the bodies like the walls of a tunnel she is sliding down, and either side another space pressed in again to form a tunnel running parallel with this, then another and another, like lanes on a freeway. Rails whine, wires sing. A roadscape fans out, empty and vast on a slim black bridge above a frost-lit gulf. At her in the tunnel on the left comes a car, with the face of a fly and a roar like a burst of metal laughter—stretched out and lowered, as it shoots away behind, to a swollen single bellowed word *NO-O-O-O-O-O-O…* After the car has gone, the word runs ahead, ringing out among the struts of the bridge across the gulf, magnified through the shrieking of the caverns in the sky to a twang like an orchid blade stabbing out of dust folds. Up from the railing of the bridge on either side spring cables a metre thick, strung far ahead upon the tips of a bridge-tower, lofty and silver in the shape of a guillotine; next to descend rather slower on the other side, dip to pick the road up and soar to a second tower tiny in the air where it pricks the horizon, framed in the bottom of the frame of the first one; then to be lost in a curvature of shadow.

A flap upon the road ahead. Reaching it, she sees it is a cat—or half a cat, the other half a furry jam squeezed on the tarmac. Caught in the headlights, glassy eyes ablaze, fur on end, paws rigid, it recalls a set of bagpipes of muscle clad in velvet. Her cockpit rises, filling up as wine bubbles out from the pedals; and the smoothness of the rising is the smoothness of a blood-let in a warm bath. Moon and stars and fires burn, cruel as an ice-blink. Huddled in the stratosphere, planets hang heavy—tucked up, as if in bed, against a bank of livid clouds. Saturn seeks her out, dead blue eyes peering up from under thin rings. Tiny blind Pluto hisses, icy-black and bat-faced. Uranus transfixes her, with mirrored contact lenses and a smile both delicate and dangerous. But there in the middle of them, licked and caressed by a mane of pale fire, shines the vainest and most captivating beauty of them all: the planet Jupiter, the heavenly equivalent of amber-coloured lovers' eyes and angelfish in mirror mist, radiant in majesty of salmon-marbled bloodlight. It gazes upon her, from its churning red storm, through the mighty revolution of its cloud-belts, and winks, as if to promise she can one day come to live on it forever…

16 THE ADVENTURES OF THE DEAD GIRL

Amber's booth swims up in front of her. Her head clears some-what. She gazes up, locates him, and watches as he works, buried deep within the mixing of the music and the lights. Huddled in a hole made of black coiled wires in a whirlpool of switches and red winking lights, Amber grates laughter of charcoal in his throat, feels the mirror mist licking at his eyes, behind his fingernails and coiling in the notches of the walls of his windpipe. The thrill of the mist in his lungs is a thrill like the blood-flecked coughing of a skinny Siamese cat whose ribs his fingers circle… He flicks a switch, pushes up a slider and listens as the pounding of a new music merges with the old and overwhelms it.

A sound in the new track starts through the din and throws him down into horror, with a shudder as at something that was ancient and primal, with the words rising up, *the adventures of the little girl, the girl from Virginia—the little girl called Num-num!* Demons seem to giggle, and his eyes water freely. Another's eyes flash, those of somebody unseen, now remembered in a horrid blaze as Amber shivers inside his flesh. That name—*yes, the little girl's name!*—cuts his stomach open, burrows deep inside, laying bare a brood out of some deep well. No single image, but a shadow-play of downward-pointing glee and fear: down, down deep, with the squeaking of an injury, *the mewing of the dead girl*, the laughter of goblins… *We've had one or two little girls expire of water*, says the other with the eyes—*so let me cut the eyeballs of your feet, would you like that, Amber?* So now he strokes his skull, as if to stroke the lobes inside it. Here it comes! From the undershaft, intoxicating evil creeps, taps him on the shoulder, whispers *Go!* in red and bites him sweetly on the neck. Reënter pain in two dots: dieresis in blood. He feels, as if in sour sleet, the power of things to hurt a body. Living in a body is a gamble, at best; as is sleeping with a person who knows its seven deadly points and isn't quite balanced. He glances at the sliders, changes the music with his hands and eyes on autopilot, gives a bloodshot gurgle and prepares for a night of corruption, of sickness and gangrenous delirium…

Amber takes pleasure in his job, yes; he's good at it. At times such as this, high on mirror mist and driven by the music out of hell that he loves, he reflects on his past. He reflects on the time when he landed in the world with a sticky smack of acid, blood and stillborn twin, when his childhood nurse, a sufferer from Munchausen's Syndrome by Proxy, injected him with human waste (whether in his arm or his bottom or his eye would be dependent on the infant's mood) and liquidised his twin to a dietary supplement of creamy consistency. To feed him this, a hose was connected to his heart and a syringe hung above his chest to suckle both his nipples, which would stretch up and open wide to guzzle at the syringe. Lumps of heart were chopped out and replaced with slate, which congealed with the rest to form the Black Slab inside his chest—the Slab that provides him with the body and the mien of death and flavours every single thing he ever says or does or feels or sees. The Black Slab is sensed, like a metal bar through plaster or a tendon glimpsed through milk, by all who meet him. All in all, it opened up a new life for Amber: infernal dark cabaret of Amber disease, lemons hatched in metal corners, barking spiders, blood as thick as cheese and even worse, with a permanent erotic grinding pain within his spine and a colour in his skull beyond admission. Cutting through the city in the night, as a boy, Amber knew he was pursued through the grid of ash and stone by a single hairy human leg, knew that disfigurement lay just around the corner like a kiss, knew he'd sucked his lemon-whiskered heel dry in childhood. Time was a pump pulled behind him by the leg; pressing on against its drag with unrelenting effort, Amber struck sparks, yellow spasms in an endless procession made of charcoal and loss. Hearing *Num-num!* giggled out across the gulf of death at him; in bookshops, going blind; smile of evil and jelly in his knees as he turned to find a rotting swamp of dead twin foetuses, an intimate Sargasso in a wider sea of slugs. All his brothers! All his twins he might have slept with, like he sucked his brother off inside the womb—did he kill him thus?—just before the sky went out, the bulb fell out, the Slab forever night—

A pale fleshy spider scuttles over the equipment in front of him: his hand, flicking slide-controls, manoeuvred by the long dead finger bones inside it (his nurse once confirmed, upon a close investigation, that his skeleton was black). He smiles as the speakers belch a bolt of thickened sound to stain the mirror mist, pushing like a worm's head, honeycombed with loathing. The worm pulls its black scaly shaft above the dancers, turns in his direction, feels the billows with its eyes as if with tentacles of darkness down a tunnel, finds him— locks his frozen gaze into its own, until he moans… *Catch you later!* mouths the worm, winks and unhooks its jaw, sicking grey ropes of gristle through the air at him. *Delusion!* he shrieks at the worm, *you'd rather see me paralysed!* Words surge up his throat: *You wanna see a slice of my insides, freak? Feed me razors—what's the matter, has my face changed?* The worm's head dips now, fading as it chuckles; but its chuckle hovers on, glowing blood-red and gibbering towards him through the gas. (Oh, to hear one's own blood-rush among the worm-ropes! Oh, to hear one's own death-rattle, amplified; see the black fungus sun revolve; and worship…)

17   A KISS OF JAGGED GLASS

Nudged back to real life by a new presence beside her, the Platinum Raven finds herself nudged also into the realisation that not quite every punter in this tower is having as much fun as she and Scorpio and Amber are having in their different ways. For right there in front of the DJ booth with her stands an unnamed man whose heavy skull throbs with anger and sharp pain. Sweat trickles off him. Acid rises in his throat, which he hawks up and spits out.

Just as Amber becomes aware of him, this man glances up across the main space towards the podium and catches sight of Scorpio—for the first time, it would seem, as his face plays host to a flash of surprise and interest, followed by growing disgust and hatred. So strong is the onset of these emotions, that it seems quite in keeping with them when he picks up an empty beer bottle, stoops to smash off its neck against a metal fixture somewhere beneath the DJ booth, then staggers off across the dance-floor towards the podium, pushing through the dancers as he goes.

The Platinum Raven has seen this too. She follows him into the crowd with her eyes, she glances up at Scorpio and sees he is oblivious, she looks up at Amber with a mounting alarm, and she shakes her head to clear it.

Her eyes meet Amber's eyes. He jabs a bunch of controls, then swings from the booth and jumps down to the floor. "Don't let him out," he tells her, running off across the crowded floor where the man went.

She gets her phone out and texts Security: "Let no one out until I say—there's a man we need to keep inside." She steps up into the booth to get a better view, and scans the crowd for several minutes, seeking the man who ran off, but cannot find him.

Then she freezes. Somewhere across the hall, in among the mirror mist, she just sensed something wrong; a wrong little movement.

Frowning, she scans the hall again. And there it comes again, but higher up now. Where the hell was it?... And raising her eye-line, she sees it. *Yes*—that's it.

Silent in the din, and very wrong, is a pudgy hand grasping the banisters beside Scorpio's podium, rising as its hidden owner scales the steps behind.

Now she spots Amber, reaching the podium and starting up the steps.

Above him in the spotlight, Scorpio is dancing, forever and oblivious—twirling and swooping, electric in bright white, swathed in the mirror mist as if in silver silk...

The man glances down, hesitates at Amber's onset, then continues up at frantic speed. He keeps himself steady with the pudgy hand she saw, while his other hand clutches the bottle that he broke, with a kiss of jagged glass where he smashed off its neck.

Amber flies up behind him. The man attains the podium and steps across to Scorpio. His hand swings the bottle, and the Platinum Raven bends her will like steel wires across the room.

Amber leaps up onto the podium. He grabs the man's shoulder and pulls him off-balance as the bottle whistles downwards, just past its target. Scorpio continues dancing unaware, then sees them beside him and starts away in shock. He darts down to snatch the bottle while the man regains his footing; then the man makes a lunge at Amber, half catching hold of him.

The crowd below has seen them and moves back quickly. The pair struggles, teeters on the edge, then topples. Three metres down, they slam upon the wooden floor messily together. The man somehow wrenches up his bulk to its feet, then away through the crowd and disappears. Amber springs up as well and dashes off to follow. The Platinum Raven cranes up, to keep them in view. The man barrels over to a small door half-hidden by a curtain, wrenches the handle— and opens it, to her surprise (it really should have been locked), and vanishes. The door slams. A moment later, Amber reaches it, flings it open and dives inside; and once again it slams shut.

The music Amber cued before he left pounds ever onward, huge and electrifying; still the building shakes, as it has shaken all night.

Scorpio has long put the jagged bottle down, and dances ever onward, as before; and those below him dance too. The show goes on.

She shuts her eyes, in grateful relief for Scorpio's safety but in new concern for Amber's. Outside the public-access areas of the nightclub, behind the scenes, this building is a warren: the man escaped into that, through a door that should have been locked, into a region that she thinks of as the labyrinth. She doubts Amber knows it any better than she does; and she herself gets lost in it.

When she texted Security to ask them not to let anyone out, she was expecting that the man would try to leave the tower. But now that he's on the run through the labyrinth, the situation is different. Her first sight of the man showed her someone who was already in a bad place, seeming to have been only angered and debilitated by this mirror mist, then evidently filled with hate. Amber on the other hand is happy in the dark: indeed it seemed the mirror mist was strengthening, for him.

So, she thinks: as long as they are both high, Amber will defeat the man. He'll knock him cold and subjugate him, somehow; the murder that she saw in Amber's face informs her so. She must turn up the mirror mist, as soon as can be done.

Her phone vibrates; she whips it out, and there's a text from Amber. Just five words in all: "TURN IT UP TO FULL".

She laughs out loud. Then she jumps from the booth to the dance-floor, just as this last track thunders to a close.

The lights go out, plunging the hall into darkness. She checks the time: four o'clock. Two seconds later the house lights glimmer on, as background music starts and the staff begin to usher people out into the summer night.

She sprints down the passage to the door above the lobby, finds her keys, slips through and pulls the door shut behind her.

Swiftly she climbs the spiral stairs to the turret.

She unlocks the top door, swoops across the turret room and dives for the cabinet containing the dial.

18 I SEE YOU!

The Chocolate Raven pours another glass of red, takes a sip and sets it down, braces both her elbows on the railing, holds up a pair of bin-oculars she has brought with her, and trains them on the tower. As she fine-tunes the focus, an unexpected seahorse shimmers in from the haze and stands sharp, its stony head lushly capped with a crest of mossy hairs where a pencil of moonlight hits it from above.

Easing the sight-line upwards minutely, she almost drops the glasses in shock, for there's the Platinum Raven in one of the round brown windows, holding up binoculars directed straight at her. *I SEE YOU!* the latter mouths in silence, across the desert miles, then she winks and turns away.

The Chocolate Raven flicks the glasses down, alarmed and guilty: they aren't allowed, as very well she knew. She shivers, shuts her eyes, shakes her head, puts the glasses down, leans on the rail and grows attentive once again…

Somewhere in the turret room, the Platinum Raven's fingers find the air-conditioning dial, rest upon its circle for one second longer, and then rotate it clockwise: the pointer on the dial's edge sweeps from 2 to 10, and the tower in the Hajar Mountains fills up with mirror mist, denser than any tower's ever filled before.

Somewhere in the main hall far underneath her, in the softness of the billows, re-projected on a thousand mirrors, Scorpio dances on: silently, alone, without exertion and divinely, as if for all time.

Somewhere in the labyrinth of passages around him, Amber stalks: relentless, bent on destruction, without the possibility of failure or surrender.

Somewhere in the labyrinth behind or ahead of him, despairing in the mist far more than he's ever done, hopelessly lost and endowed with a lethal sense of who is in pursuit of him, an unnamed man lives a nightmare.

Mirror mist, on full…

19 MIRRORS IN THE LABYRINTH

Through his feet upon the labyrinth floor, Amber feels it. Underneath the cellars and the sump of the tower, in among the struts and the beams even further down, something creaks. Up the hill, past the teardrop trees, a cold breeze rolls, and the full moon slips behind an isolated cloud.

Amber stalks the silver billows, glimpsing his quarry everywhere he turns his eyes. As his pores ooze blacker than the tears of a corpse, love and hope hang respectively defined in the gas: the anatomy of love-bites and the absence of the hoped-for. His helmet of Amber-thoughts fills behind the visor with the vomit of remembrance that his dreams and those of everyone are filtered through the tar and futility of flesh, like wounds seeping through a soldier's uniform. He sniffs, and smells the staleness of the billions: pushing, toiling, failing, there they go, bent on goals so insignificant, minute and all-consuming, it is painful to watch. From table to cupboard, from cupboard to door, to table again they go. From room to room; from door to road, from road to door; from town to town; to work, to eat, to sleep, then up too early and out again, to car, road, traffic again; day in, day out, year in, year out … their labour then converted, by a vast grimy effort, into different kinds of shortfall from the things they desired. Days fading out through their uniform lives, their identity a function of the sounds they make—then illness and death at last for every single one, asking if they've ever said or thought or felt or done or even really been at all. Such is the use decreed for life, as Amber knows: inward grunts from a body buried live, made and hurt and kissed in mud.

Why not bare your fangs, then, as Amber does, peering from the windows of his yellow night train! See the fall on both sides, just a parapet's thickness away beyond the yellow glass. Freeze, at a spider the size of a dog, huddled horrid in a corner of the carriage, poised to wriggle. See the people slaving for the transient and breakable, whose permanence they yearn for, whose relevance they can't afford to question. D'you wonder how so many human beings are so numb? Wonder rather how they aren't, who are not! Amber fantasises hanging by his tail from the ceiling, racked with week-long muscle spasms, vomiting erotically without relent and drowning when the room is filled above his snout. What a use for life this is—no destiny or meaning, just compulsion and error, pushing slops of grey at cliffs of blank. Down is the bottom line; up's preserved for next time. Listen: every single thing passes, tires, breaks. Like the sudden grey fingers at the edges of a photocopy carelessly executed, everything distresses on reflection! Amber can't be bothered to supply us with a proof, but he's right, fuck his eyes! So let the show carry on, then—there might be a joke!

…And from underneath the tower comes a sigh of spitting sand.

20 ANALYSIS OF MOTION THROUGH CCTV

Scanning her eyes across the TV monitors in her turret room, the Platinum Raven holds their remote control and flicks through the available CCTV feeds they can display. The only feeds from the labyrinth where Amber disappeared in pursuit of the unnamed man show little more than swirls of silver, which won't be much help unless a figure darts out from among the billows. She doubts she could help Amber if she entered the maze behind him. In any case, the music set that Amber had been so much inhabiting while he was spinning it earlier had been a dark enough foundation in itself, whose darkness can only have been increased by the provocation that propelled him onto Scorpio's podium, his combat on that podium and now the mist's having been turned up to 10: by this point tonight Amber will therefore be something like a death machine, so if she were to well up out of the mist beside him without warning, then she could hardly blame his reflexes for stabbing her.

In one CCTV feed, the screen is filled with Scorpio dancing on the podium. Starting now to fly on the mirror mist within herself, she has a vivid sense of how he'll be flying on it down there, especially with the benefit of this ring-side close-up she has on him here. The combination of graceful perfection and fluid instinct in his movement is divinely charismatic. In itself his movement is abstract, or would at least be abstractly describable if the appropriate motion-analysis software were used. Watching his closed eyes while he spins and swoops, however, she knows him well enough to sense where this charisma is probably emanating from, and where the mirror mist has almost certainly sent him, within himself: for as he dances there before her, unaware of her attention through the lens and the screen, his cock throbs stiff upon his stomach, thrusting from its covering and up to his navel where the hot wet tip pushes just as it does through every day and night, pulsing in the dark whorl of hair there which tickles, makes it throb tighter still and nuzzle harder in his navel—itself a zone exclusively erogenous, sensitive and ticklish underneath the soaked hair so he thinks about it always, can never think for long about much else before his thoughts are returned to the constantly demanding situation at his navel—focus for the tickle and the pressure and the tingle running all day long below his skin, streaming bright behind his body hair, singing in his ass where his anus yearns, up his perineum, deep within his balls and up his hard cock, calling Scorpio once again to feel it course and burn and surge, pushing through his cock from the sex-scented hair through the tight thick shaft to the head with the tip where a dozen times daily the pressure and the tingle and the tightness are unbearable enough to make his eyes swim, his knees shake, his body twitch and pale as his cock goes convulsively tighter still and leaps, the tingle dances in his balls near to blinding him, the hot sweet rush pumps fast and at pressure up the shaft through the head to the tip gaping wide at the burn-spurt of cum—hot tears shooting pleasure and delirium and ecstasy and helplessness and anguish through his body till he faints, when it carries on shooting out its load a little longer, on the ceiling or the walls or in his clothes or over Amber… Nine times in daylight that occurs; three sleeping, till he wakes in the morning curled up against Amber in the warm wet, feeling an erection so ferociously severe and unrelenting that he often thinks the rest of him a toy for it. Awake then, he shoots his load at once, his conscious mind descending to his penis for the day: spasm after spasm racks his body till he faints, wakes exhausted, moaning still, feels his cock swell and stiffen once again as Amber's arms make a circle round his little breasts, Amber's sex slips inside him, Amber's kisses ring his neck, Amber's love buoys him up upon a great blond-gold sea… There he sleeps a while, hazy with happiness and yearning till they both wake—then a scythe of lust swings through him and a sudden urge for sex blocks the rest. This is done, till he and Amber gasp in turn and melt softly into afterglow. Then Scorpio as his cock hardens yet again is happy—albeit, as always, with a shading of neurosis, for the happiness is too intense, precarious and full of gaping holes (mouth, cock, tear ducts, pierced ears and nipples) so it might just leak and escape like his yearning. For even in Amber's arms Scorpio feels the hunger and the needing and the pain imperceptibly projected from his eyes and his body and his movements. This hunger, lest he just weep and giggle, he inverts, bottles up introrse, so it mounts in his crotch, fills his cock, makes it throb without relent and then explode in burning pints every hour or two. A constant busy-line tone sounds in his head; his heart keeps time with it, too fast, too near the surface, so you see it beating underneath his clothes across the room. Naked, sharp and effeminate from inside, he sees the dance of nerves in his skin. The scars on his wrists (some old and others new) disturb him, but they also turn him on when he sees them as his loins ache, as always: should he then conceal them, or flaunt them to enhance in him that quality which only ever draws forth lust or repellence? Either way, just his body saying *fill me* makes him naked, as the people stare or heckle or their eyes flash sex. Undecided then, he tends to raise his hands above his head, shut his eyes, shoot his load again and faint with a smile…

21 THE PLATINUM RAVEN'S MESSAGE-IN-A-BOTTLE

"Ah good, so all's well with Scorpio," thinks the Platinum Raven. She's finding, however, that thinking is getting difficult, as this mirror mist is now taking control of her own thought processes. *Any requests?* the mirror mist asks her. —Oh, all right, she answers it. If you insist… OK, let's have the Platinum Raven, please, on a pinnacle of rock a mile high, on a stage at the summit just three metres wide, strutting out for the billion heads who carpet the mountain-bowl below, while the sky is a screen where her face sings down. Raising her head, she sees the image on the sky-screen zoom to a single eye of hers, whose pupil grows until it fills up the heavens. In its depths, at the pole, hangs a beauty that is madness: the black sun, the ball of spinning fire around the ultimate destruction at its heart, the Great Attractor… Here is an Absolute, unanswerable, no fooling round, no disco but the real thing—awesomely, calmly, majestically inhuman. Matter spirals inward, elongated into whistling strings. Black shreds of flame ripple tiny and distinct around the surface of the star, the roar and prickle of their burning both gigantic and soft across the emptiness of space… *That* will still be here when every human being rots, when this tower's archaeology for alien crustaceans—and after them forever, till the future is the past or *vice versa*, she reflects. Through her head flits a memory, vivid and pathetic, of the capsule of mirror mist she buried on the mountainside nearby, with her name in it: a tentative graffito, "I was here" upon the walls of the darkness whose enormity she now sees clearer, her message-in-a-bottle for an unknown claw in the future to find for its gallery or freak show. (Come see the fossil of the vision of humanity, the one remaining flicker of their bright imagination! Tiny silver glints in a bubble in the rock…) Her blonde hair streams across her eyes; she brushes it back to find control has fled, the black sun has swollen, sinking nearer straight above, descending now on the pinnacle, the wind howls—

Silence snaps the light out, black as glass and not especially what she wanted. She raises her hand before her face, moves it, touches it with her other hand—presumes it must be like this to be blind— hopes she's not. Rigid as on waking from a nightmare, she turns around three or four hundred degrees, maybe more. Air cold, blind, lipless. Darkness presses like a fluid on her eyes. She pulls down the thinness of their lids but it seeps through. She waits, watches, listens, waits more. Where is this? She will learn something here, she knows. Any moment…

A sixth sense creeps from a crevice in her chest, spreads its openness ahead, reads the darkness like a grain of sugar spreading through a water droplet: sinews of tautness and tension hold the space, sprung elastically in arches on unseen wires. She freezes, feels her muscles tighten more. From a corner on the left a tiny sound cuts the silence and is gone—the tightest clink, as of the pluck- ing of a tine or the cracking of a fibre in the ribbing of a bridge. Blood pumps hard below her skin; from her ribcage the thuds push a dark field of furrows through the air. Sparks on her right lick the blackness with a squeak, as if a blade is being drawn along a rail. She shoots a glance, too late. Something invisible progresses in an arc around her body; she can pinpoint its position with exactness. Straight ahead, from where she stares, comes a scratch and a twang: a jet of sparks curls upwards in a tusk, growing brighter and solid, giving off a metal roar specked with tinny clicks. Her flesh contracts painfully. The jet thickens, tightens and points in her direction. A snick cuts its side near the base as she stares, sending spurts of ver- milion to chase one another, twisting up through the whiteness and expiring at the tip. Burning rubber stabs the air. As the snick grows, she sees that it's caused by a wire's end puncturing the tusk. A mass of wires catches fire, flaring like a sudden head of hair. In its light she looks around—and leaps aside, as a knife-edge of glass comes screeching towards her. She wheels, sees it streak away and vanish in the stillness, the whistle of its passage dying fast into nothing. The wires flicker on; she tries to pick out her surroundings. Depths of illimitable blackness recede from her, cross-cut with metal and the glint of splintered glass. Black steel sheets slash the air at every angle, immobile and razor-edged, reflecting the crackle on a thousand jagged shards. Moving from the firing line of any of these edges leads to that of twenty more. She freezes again. The angles reflected in the light from the jet shift subtly in response to every tremble of the sparks: the slightest movement in the tusk opens up on every side a set of vistas, infinitesimally tunnelling afresh or hitting planes where there were tunnels. The effect is of cathedrals of ice, locked around and inside and throughout one another in the very same space; from every point in every vault springs a new unique innumerable set of points of view of every other—crushed to nothing on the instant by a further unrepeatable and infinite division, both deriding and miraculous, triumphant yet without choice itself.

Something snaps. Orange light burns in a grey metal corridor. Behind her is the end of it, blanked-off, doorless. Ahead, a blind corner where the way turns right. A grind and twang of metal growing nearer… She runs to the corner and stops dead. A chewing mass of spines fills the passageway, expanding as it comes, treading quick, thick and beastly as the breeding of an alienly complicated spider or an undergrowth of ants with a single volition. She bangs the walls. She backs away. She knows she is immune to being hurt in this—this is only mirror mist, no more! But she runs, she strikes the walls in every place she can reach—cold steel. Now the spines have reached the corner, mounting up against the outer wall. She stoops, runs a nail along the angle where the wall meets the floor. No crack; they are one, angled clean. She flings herself against the passage end. The chewing mass dislodges, and springs around the corner, leaping forward, building up again just short of where she's stuck like a poster on the wall. There it stays a moment; through its snout, a shifting of internal knots of mesh suggests jerky navigations of the corner further back. Then it twitches into motion once again, nuzzles closer. She screams. Her face tight-snarled and her lips like a spout, she slams her fists on the steel wall, screwing up her eyes as the spines shiver forward to kiss her face, her skin crawls—

Falling to the floor, she encounters no resistance but a tickling of mirror mist. The spines have collapsed into silver dust. A human sigh unfurls (*under Sigh Street*, she thinks), then she starts—flicks her eyes where they've just been. She feels more than knows what she seeks, what she wants. It sneaked across the borders of her vision, slipped away as she instinctively returned for it, and hides a moment longer. There. Is it what she thinks it was? Yes! A human neck, tan-coloured, wedged in the angle of the passage twenty metres off, hidden from the jaw up, a knife-edge cutting through the faint down … it's Scorpio.

22 THE BLACK AND RED FLOWER

Something hard is pressing against the Platinum Raven's cheek. Her eyes open. Floorboards run away from her face, from out-of-focus close-up, across the turret room to the pair of round brown windows, through which she can see it's still dark outside. With an effort she raises herself on one elbow, and vaguely remembers sliding down from an upright position to lie here on the floor, some period of time ago. The first night of mirror mist… She shakes her head. She's not hung-over, but feels as if sealed behind glass. She takes her phone out and checks it: five-fifteen in the morning.

She sees another body on the floor near the door. Smiling, she moves over to Scorpio and gently strokes his neck. Now she remembers turning up the mirror mist to 10, before she started tripping, as they all must have done. The safety valve will have cut the gas off automatically about ten minutes ago. Scorpio must have joined her here at some point, from downstairs. But then … the other thing: Amber pursuing the man who'd smashed the bottle.

She stands, stretches awake, turns off the mirror mist control and peers through one of the windows. The city grid twinkles, the sky is pinked with stars. The night continues.

She stoops to wake Scorpio. "You OK?" she whispers. He nods. "We should go check up on Amber." He nods again and rises to his feet. She gets out two flashlights, gives one to him, and they set off down the spiral staircase. Descending, she reflects that perhaps her turning up the mist to 10 wasn't the best idea: she hopes no one got hurt in the chaos and no one looted the club. In the lobby she recognises one or two members of staff sprawled on the floor or sitting against the walls, in attitudes whose abandon she's glad to identify as apparently pleasurable. Scorpio and she sneak down the passageway, across an eerily quiet dance-floor, and through the door where Amber and the man fled—the door to the labyrinth.

The mirror mist has dissipated for the most part, leaving just a haze of silver. They scour several semi-familiar reaches of this warren-like region of the building, which is decorated with a faded opulence. A small stairway appears, which she recalls she has noticed before but has never got round to exploring. They sneak up the stairs, aware of every creaking floorboard. At the top is a space full of stage props and costumes. On the wall hang many masks, which stare down at this pair of unaccustomed visitors with expressions either haughty, evil, sweet, grotesque, anguished or laughing. They both tiptoe through the wings of a theatre and emerge onto a stage with a grand proscenium facing a crumbling golden ballroom, resonant and empty in the moonlight that pours through the dome of clear glass in its ceiling. They play their flashlights over the plaster garlands and fruits on the pillars in silence, whispering to each other in excitement and surprise to have found such a place: they must be deep within the mountainside by now, as this whole complex of dusty spaces would surely never fit within just the footprint of the mad-faced tower itself.

"We need to find Amber," whispers Scorpio and tiptoes on across the empty stage to the opposite wings, where a door stands open in shadow. He peers through it, hesitates, then turns and beckons to her. She steps across the stage and through the furry darkness of the wings, to join him.

Once they are through the door together, the atmosphere changes abruptly. They each reach for the other's hand and give it a squeeze.

A passageway some twenty metres long lies ahead, lined with cracked glazed tiles of a colour best described just as "off"—off-white, off-brown, off-green, one couldn't say which. The air is damp, and the walls appear to crawl and glisten whenever a flashlight is pointed at them. The flashlights are not the only source of illumination, however. It's impossible to tell where else any light might be coming from, unless it's from some residual play of reflection bouncing or regressing infinitely upon itself in the remaining flux of mirror mist in the air; but there does seem to be some other source, albeit of a light that's oddly filtered and choked, with a rotten orange tinge to it.

They waver forward through the gloom of the passageway. The Platinum Raven shakes her head involuntarily. A sharp organic smell spreads thick upon the air. Dripping sounds plink with an unexpected sharpness, drawing her attention to a hum she can now hear, running underneath the floor or somewhere in the walls—a faint thick buzzing as of meat-flies, carried through a medium more glutinous, perhaps.

Two doors stand in the wall on their right, and one more at the end, all three ajar. She and he squeeze their hands together, disengage them, and tiptoe to a point just short of the first door. She leans her head forward and peeks through the opening, past the door's rotting wood. Dirty orange light stares in, through a frosted window-pane and three splintered metal bars, to illuminate a washroom. Pushing at the door, she feels her fingers sink a little in the surface of the soft wood. The hinges give a wet grind and the door swings free. Basins line the mirrored walls, perched on metal struts—her reflected face ahead makes her start. The door hits the wall with a crash; a rain of white plaster streaks down from the ceiling, like a curtain on the darkness, and they both jump. The room is nearly bare, though. A sick space, but empty.

They look around, and quickly at each other. Then they press on down the passageway, level with the second of the three doors. She raises her foot, slow and quiet—then she boots the door, jumps back and stares wildly in.

Through another barred window, the same orange light pours. Cubicles yawn high and narrow. Eyes wide, she darts in and glances into each of the cubicles: all are dank and mildewed, one full of some kind of rubble that she can't identify. Once again, a dead space.

Returning to the passageway, she reaches for Scorpio and holds him to her chest. Conscious of the texture of his black-flaming hair between her fingers, she peers beyond his head to the end of the passageway, where the third door stands ajar in the wall straight ahead of her…

She freezes; and feeling this, he turns in her arms and sees it too.

From underneath the door, a wide stain of dark fluid seeps down the passage floor towards them.

Hand in hand, they approach. He pushes lightly on the door. It creaks, as moisture shines tiny in the bruises on the wood, where his fingernails press.

Inside, steam swirls. Drips plink quicker than before. The orange tinge hangs even thicker on the air.

Slopping noises come, and then a bellow bursts out. Amber flings the door wide, a dripping knife in hand—his eyes at first possessed, then quickly softening as he sees them both. Scorpio steps inside, stares around and halts, moving almost in slow-motion. The Platinum Raven follows him in, watching him ahead turning back, outlined in black against the steam, looking blank and sick, pointing with his finger silhouetted on the gassy swirl.

From one of the baths a bloodied mess flicks out a hand and grips the red enamel rim. There rises the head of the man who tried to attack Scorpio. It coughs up a gulletful of red, then it chokes. His other hand is clawing at his abdomen. His genitals are sliced off; a huge soft gash lies open where they should have been, and travels to his stomach. In the wound, nestled cosy in the throb of his intestines, is a brood of yellow insect eggs, a faint tick of fly-legs trapped in every one. "All his children," murmurs Amber, pointing in at them, and spits. "But let's end his pain; even he deserves that." As he aims his gun at the unnamed man's face, the latter succumbs to a fit of splattery coughing—then the gunshot explodes and his forehead bursts open like a black and red flower.

There is silence, during which Amber looks at Scorpio and speaks quietly. "He saw you, and his reaction was to smash a bottle and slash you: so he didn't deserve to live. So I'd do it all again. And I shall do, if another comes along."

Scorpio stares at Amber, a cauldron of emotions in his eyes. Deftly he snatches the knife from Amber's hand, grips it with his fingers and drops it to the floor. He reaches up to Amber's face, hesitates, and touches his newly blood-stained fingers on Amber's temple for a moment. Then he turns away and runs from the bathroom.

Meeting Amber's eyes, the Platinum Raven's nod is slow and quiet, before she turns to follow Scorpio out of the room, bolting back down the passageway after him, back across the stage, back down the staircase, back through the labyrinth, back across the dance-floor and up the spiral stairs to the turret room.

23 THE POINT OF SILVER IN THE DAWN

As they both stand there, panting hard, an idea strikes her. She reaches into the metal cabinet on the wall and makes an adjustment, then crosses the room to a low door, which she opens. She ducks her head and passes through, beckoning to Scorpio. He follows her down a few steps to a small terrace set upon the side of the tower, two or three metres under the two brown windows. They wander over to the balustrade, between the pair of stone seahorses on the parapet, stand there and breathe in the fresh, cool air.

Turning round to gaze up behind the turret roof, where the dawn light is growing now beyond the mountain-tops, Scorpio yelps as a sudden dense cloud of fresh mirror mist belches from the low door and tumbles down the steps to the terrace. "Look, it's on again!" he cries out. "Amber's still down there—turn it off!"

She laughs. "It's only turned on here, in the turret. Everywhere downstairs it's still turned off. I just thought we'd have a final puff of silver here now—you know, it helps to break the ice at parties."

"I don't want to think about what we just saw," he says. "Not yet. Later." And with that, he hops up onto the coping of the balustrade, midway between the seahorses.

The Platinum Raven starts to freak out, staring aghast at what's beyond the balustrade: that short slope of boulders, funnelling to that precipice of weeds in half a circle like a lip, around that lethal shriek of air one hundred metres sheer—

Then she decides she will just trust him in what he's doing: after all, she knows he has the control of an acrobat and an almost alien lack of vertigo. So she stands there on the terrace, in the shadows of the Hajar Mountains, watching him in wonder as he starts to dance right there, his little pointed boots twirling deftly on the stonework; with mirror mist surging through the gaps between the balusters, out and down the shriek, to where a silver death awaits him if he trips…

The canyon below the tower lies in rocky shadow still.

Beyond it, the width of the desert spreads in subtle shades of brown and black enormity.

Beyond that, the city grid of Dubai is waking, its coloured points twinkling in the dying night.

And high above that circuit-board, one single structure is tall enough for its pinnacle to be caught by the rays spilling across the desert from behind the mountains in the east: a skyscraper's point like no other in the world, shining silver and alone where the sky grows pale. It's an elegantly complex, telescoping spike, of a stunning, otherworldly fabulosity—its beauty cool, mineral and icy in the sharp-edged light of the dawn.

24 CATCH YOU LATER!

Leaning at her terrace rail on Level 152, the Chocolate Raven sees that the sun will soon appear, poking up above the Hajar Mountains' outline, far ahead. She turns her head and looks above her, up towards the Pinnacle, which shines in a light that has caught it alone as yet. While she stands and watches it, this sunlight's lower edge travels down from that point, down the metal Spire's flank, and then it slides down the building's skin of smooth brown glass, sinking fast towards her terrace right here. Soon this light-edge reaches her—and just as it does, she brings her gaze back down to see the sun push into view above the mountain-line before her.

Easing her sight down minutely from the mountain-tops, she finds once again the mad-faced tower on the rock-slopes. Underneath the tower, in between the struts and the beams, emerges Amber as she watches him, stalking through his hatch, bearing something in a sack. The pug dog descends on its rope in the gloom, spitting sand and weeping black sticky tears. Amber undoes the buckles of its pale blue strait-jacket, opens up the pug's chest and squeezes the sack inside. The pug squirms, dips its ugly muzzle to refasten it, and rises on the frame again, obedient in grief.

High above this, just below the two brown turret-windows, silver mist belches out, flows across the terrace past the pair at the parapet, billows through the balustrade, sinks in slow motion down the lethal shriek of air and carries on down, filling up the canyon of rocks to the brim and heading out across the desert on its way to the city here.

In welling up around that pair of figures on the terrace, it projects their image upward and out above the mountains. First there is Scorpio, dancing with his eyes closed, now and forever on the balustrade electrically, just as he was when she first saw him flicker up: the Armenian boy dressed in black, a Scorpio pendant at his neck; no smile, too much tension and exquisiteness and fierce vulnerability, but then the flush of light across his face for an instant, fem in black; and there he is forever now, perfection, for all time... Then the Platinum Raven's face is vast and serene in the dawn sky beyond him, evoking when the Chocolate Raven's devastating, desert-eyed perfection met her very own gaze for the first time, electrifying: animal, expressionless, an icon of ecstasy and chocolate and sweat, in wailing silence in the headlights, as dust floated round her through a siren-song behind the air... The Platinum Raven winks at the Chocolate one, down across the desert with the calm of divinity, mouthing *Catch you later!*

THE CHOCOLATE RAVEN

25 ELECTRIC ALIVENESS AND HAPPINESS, REMEMBERED

Remaining at her terrace rail, the Chocolate Raven lights a cigarette, pours a final glass of wine and lets her face sink into her hands, with her eyes closed.

The air is heating fast, as the morning sun slides up another busy city day. The night is gone entirely. And now that it's gone, she can see a truth that she hates and despises with a vengeance as soon as she catches sight of it.

In effect she's seeing the nature of the same Great Lie that she half-glimpsed on the occasion when she drove to the mad-faced tower. Then, she had the option of postponing apprehension, by burying her head between her knees on the back seat and wailing to the driver to drive away at high speed. Now, she doesn't have that choice. It's too late, for now she's seen too clearly what nobody deserves to see.

What this knowledge comes down to, in her case at this moment, is that when she lifts her head again, then not only will her visions a minute ago of Scorpio and the Platinum Raven in the sky have both vanished in the glare of day—but the mad-faced tower will have disappeared from the rock-slopes too, with what she recognises as a senseless but inevitable fuck-up that she should have seen coming.

No more Amber.

No more Scorpio.

And no more Platinum Raven.

And maybe this will sound strange, or maybe it will not—but either way, this freight of brand-new but familiar knowledge leaves her miserably desolate.

It isn't that her mad-faced tower was all roses; for it wasn't. Nor could that trio of characters in the tower be fitly regarded as friends of hers, whom she has now lost. If they were somehow to materialise here in real life, in Dubai, then would she trust them? Would she even *like* them? Quite possibly not. In any case, would they have any interest in her? Would they even notice her? They might very well ignore her altogether, choosing instead to spend their time with others who would doubtless have a clueless lack of perception regarding how special this trio really was. She rubs her eyes in weariness. She cannot answer these questions … but they are beside the real point, which is this: she is desolate, quite simply, that her tower full of magic has vanished into thin air, leaving her just standing here prosaically alone on a weekday morning, halfway up a building in a city.

And yes, by the way, today's a school day, let's remember: in just a couple of hours there'll be paying work to do, with computer screens, corporate bookings and financial responsibility. In a moment, therefore, she will make a move. She will do the requisite. She will navigate herself through these things, just as she is practised at doing.

But oh, how desperately sad and desolate the Chocolate Raven is to have been forced back down into such quotidian drudgery, when she knows that in reality there's *ALL THAT*, living up there in the mountains!… Oh, *why* couldn't she just live forever in that tower of wonders?

Not that she'd pretend it was the most reassuring or relaxing of places, up there. There were nightmarish elements in it, for sure, and even its wildest heights of beauty had something of the colour and poison of a nightmare somewhere beneath their surface.

But how *electrically* alive and happy she was, nonetheless, for as long as she was up there in that tower on the rock-slopes!

And why should she now be compelled back down to answer questions from all those tired, ordinary businessmen and all those soul-dead, wearily superficial, exhaustingly trivial and soporifically privileged Jumeirah Janes who populated her normal working days? These were the working days and pleasures that used to fill her life exclusively, that she'd assumed were pretty much the only kind of days and pleasures to be had … but that was a time before she had discovered the mad-faced tower and thereby found herself plugged into such a voltage of brightness and passion and excitement as dwarfed any other she had ever known.

She raises her head from her hands, gathers her things, slumps back along the terrace, traverses and locks the corporate suite behind her, returns to her own apartment and dives into her preparations for this particular working day, whose small hours were like nothing she has ever known but whose business hours are about to be all too familiar.

Stepping into the shower, she reflects that since the advent of the tower and its addictive inhabitants—the Platinum Raven, Scorpio, Amber and all those fabulous and adorable nocturnal creatures—she has come to be aware of aspects of herself that she had long forgotten about. In particular, she sees and remembers something she used to be aware of, which is the extent to which she gives a good impersonation of someone whose normal interaction with others comes naturally to her. This voice that others hear her speak—clear and analytical, but gentle and measured—is the best response she has evolved to the ongoing task of interfacing with a world from which, however, she has always felt gratefully alienated.

The advent of the tower has reminded her that for as long as she can remember, she has felt wonder at what a shortfall the possibilities of everyday life represent, compared with the possibilities available to people in imagination—and wonder, therefore, at how lazy and stale so many people's thinking and interests are nonetheless, compared with all the other uses of mind that would clearly have been so much richer, easier and more enticing for them to choose. The tower has reminded her, too, of how bored she has always felt at so many of the concerns to which those people still seem bent on devoting most of their precious time and finite lives, and her life-long feeling of difference and alienation from them as a result. And it has reminded her of what a powerful contempt she has always felt for the downward-aiming herd of them, mixed in with her passionate love and respect for the upward-aiming few.

She steps out of the shower, sleek and dripping. Picking up a comb from the golden basin, she wonders: if the mad-faced tower had turned out to be something permanent that she could populate and arrange at her pleasure, then would the combination of this new power with those old established foundations of alienation and contempt have started corrupting her, just as earthly powers of all kinds have long had a tendency to corrupt a good percentage of the few who manage to attain them? And if that corrupting empowerment had continued into an indefinite future, then might she even have become something monstrous as a result—just as leaders, if long unchallenged, have a tendency to morph into dictators? If she had indeed become monstrous in this sense, then it would probably have involved simplifying herself so as to become, in effect, something like a principle of megalomania in the physical form of a person. A black angel, in effect: an exterminating angel.

Laying down the comb, she runs her fingers through her damp-darkened, chocolate-coloured hair in the mirror.

Yes: it would certainly have made sense for her to use such power to take at least some kind of revenge on all those whose lazy unthinkingness acts as such a down-dragging, anti-evolutionary force; and if the opportunity had arisen, it would very likely have made sense, furthermore, to tyrannise them…

She dries between her toes, one by one, with the towel.

26 SCENT OF FUCKED-UP DARK DEVOURING HUNGER

In the late afternoon the Chocolate Raven feels herself drooping with fatigue over the lists of urgent corporate expenses she has been battling with for several hours today, here in her office room at home. She goes to the kitchen to make her tenth coffee of the day, in a bid to keep herself awake after her sleepless night of tower-watching. As she heaps in her customary four sugars and starts grinding the metal teaspoon distractedly around the mug, she finds herself recalling the man who approached her in the hotel bar and introduced himself as Jaymi. She recalls her feeling of disappointment when he absented himself after only a few words. She also realises she made an assumption he was rich. This may be unjustified: by no means do riches attach to everyone who crosses her path here. Still, for some reason she finds herself imagining this Jaymi's generosity towards her becoming quite notable—not just in material terms, but in his doing her bidding in a manner both gallant and efficacious. She even pictures his becoming almost genie-like for her. Yet along with this picture comes a sense that he wouldn't really feel under her sway at all, but would be doing her bidding only in order to facilitate some opaque desire or agenda of his own… Anyway, these ruminations are silly; he's just someone she once met in a bar. She picks up her mug of coffee and heads back to her desk.

…But that's not quite going to cut it, is it? It's not going to cut it, because let's remember he was the figure who gave her the mysterious red card-key. She hasn't been able to make any sense of that key. It doesn't appear in any of these expense lists that she's been ploughing through today; and among the hundreds of room bookings she becomes aware of every week, she still cannot remember or find any record of having anything to do with that unusually elite corporate suite, so very high above her own apartment in the Burj Khalifa. Furthermore (and most importantly, to be frank), the suite in question then became the location of her witnessing, without warning, the explosive unfoldment of a convulsion, tiny in the far distance, between four iconic figures in a tower across the desert, that was destined to re-slant her own life forever—first on account of the convulsion's very nature, and then on account of the shocking desolation and sadness of its escape from her grasp this morning, with such an intimation of permanence in the escape. Could she ever have witnessed that from any other terrace, from any other suite, than the one on the 152nd Level? Either way, how could those events not have left Jaymi elevated in her memory, standing up there staring down at her from the still centre of an aura as strong as a whirlwind?

Soon she decides she can do no more expense sheets today, and pushes the whole heap of them away from her. She leans back in her chair and turns her head to gaze through the window, at the Gulf. She becomes aware of something just below this sight-line, lying on the window sill. That red key again.

There's only one thing to do.

She checks that she has both the red key and her own, leaves the apartment, takes the lift down to the main lobby and crosses to the lift serving the upper corporate suites. She enters the lift-car, watches the doors close, and rests her forehead against the cool wall of the lift as it ascends.

At 152 she steps out into the small, quiet lobby where several unnumbered but differently-coloured doors present themselves—one of them red. She inserts the strange card-key in this door, hears the lock click open and pushes the door inwards.

Inside, she is expecting that internal hallway with its neutral luxury she has seen in a thousand upscale corporate suites. Instead, she recognises an avenue she once drove through, located in the grim labour-camp district hidden at the centre of the vast industrial expanse of Al Quoz—its dismal concrete bunkers now deserted. The hallway door snicks shut again behind her. Empty lots of wire-mesh and gutted cars slide by her; the pavement is overrun with grass and weeds waving restless in the wind blowing in from the Gulf. A low repeated squeak cuts the breeze, where a rusty sign swings from a metal pole. She hugs her arms around herself and darts on down the hallway. Ahead the warehouse looms, its tall chimneys black upon a sky-glow coloured like a bruise. As she finds the warehouse door and slips inside, a dog bays savagely a block away.

Inside, shafts of yellow spotlight fall, checkered by the gratings of walkways above. A wax model of a human head appears beside her face, hanging on a rope and swinging as she passes it: two daggers are stuck deep into its forehead, above a pair of eyes where power and beauty and violence are combined.Not far beyond it hangs a second wax head, coarse and piggish rather than beautiful, with a dagger stuck into each cheek up to the hilt.

Music growls dark; somewhere water drips. She presses on, her black-toed steps quick and delicate around the potholes in the floor, where droplets glisten tiny in the blaze of the spotlights. A hiss from above. She glances up—sees a snake's tail swinging—sees its thickness curling up to a slender-framed figure on the walkway above her and coiling round the figure's neck, ending in a pair of jaws. Black against the yellow light, this figure leans easy on the rail, unmoving as the snake draped around him hisses loud and flicks its tongue. He is slim, pretty, watchful, with dark brown hair and big brown eyes, set within a pale face. "Jaymi!" she calls, her voice echoing around the atrium. "Jaymi! (Jaymi—Jaymi—Jaymi!) It's the Chocolate Raven! (Chocolate Raven—Chocolate Raven—Chocolate Raven!)"

That dark growly music explodes in volume, like a soundtrack. Crashing drums and shrieking voices rip through the space, all redoubled by the echo and vibrating through the walkways. The drums and the wailing and the feedback peak, until the floor and the gratings of the atrium resound: chains clank, lights swing, wires sing and pipes shake, spilling out steam-jets side-lit in white. Planting her legs wide, the Chocolate Raven raises her arms and her face and shuts her eyes, as the climax thunders to an end.

Jaymi grins. "Thanks for visiting," he says and *claps* his hands together once—

Blackout. Not a move, not a sound. The Chocolate Raven's hearing licks the dark, pushing fingers into corners, seeking anything… She shrinks within her body, but feels the latter follow her inside and shrink too, so she can barely breathe. She tries not to shrink further still inside her own frame, but cannot prevent it. Her skin shrinks again, so taut that it burns with the nerves' dance pressed against her skin's underside. Her heart thumps, ramming her corpuscles through capillaries that nearly cannot open, constricted as they are by the ever-mounting pressure from the skin pressing round them. The fluid in her ears sings a worm-song chorus, like a stream of vermicelli squeezing underneath her scalp. As her heartbeat mounts, a light flicks on; looking up, she sees a single stained light-bulb fixed to a ceiling coloured yellow by the years. A poky little washroom sways and yawns around her, two metres square, with a tiny barred window. Turning, she jumps as her gaze eats the image, in a mirror on her left, of her emaciated frame: her cheekbones stare from under black-ringed eyes of the worst kind of orange, which consume her watching self with a lust so naked, desperate and brutal that she cries out in panic and delicious fear, running her fingers over her emaciation in horror and delight. A scent of fucked-up dark devouring hunger stabs her nostrils. Transfixed by her own desperate eyes, she feels herself advancing on them, loins burning, legs wobbling into motion like a pair of stilts—then she freezes, seeing that behind her on the wall, in the image she's approaching, is a great pink spider the size of a dinner plate, legs thick and soft like a set of human thighs… As it wriggles into horrid life, a sudden ring of hanged men drop against the walls and swivel jerkily, their necks snapped down at an angle by their ropes. A bath-water gurgle of suffocation bubbles;

one hanged man launches up his head and writhes, bellowing and flailing on his rope, which begins to work loose from the ceiling. She spots a door located halfway up a wall. She reaches up to it and tries to turn the handle, but it won't move. She locks both her hands onto it and wrenches, as if to kill it. The hanged man thrashes on, staring at her, fierce and bug-eyed, his rope very nearly worked free.

Retching with horror, the Chocolate Raven can take no more. If this continues, she tells herself, then she will faint or lose her mind. At this, a crack rings out, then slides into a grating rush, as if it spreads. Beside her the bathroom mirror slides down the wall, its surface cracking into shards … and right behind it is a blissful sight: an exit to a lobby!

Leaping through this exit, she recognises once again the small, quiet, bland central lobby of this Level 152, where several unnumbered but differently-coloured doors present themselves, one of them red.

She sprints into the open lift, slams her hand onto the Down button, and stands there panting, weeping, dripping. She has no direct view from here to where she emerged into the lobby, and she can no longer hear any of the sounds she was hearing in that washroom; but she's had enough of Level 152 and she really wants to leave it.

The lift has other ideas about what to do, however: absolutely nothing, for several long moments, with the lift-doors standing wide open in case anything else wants to get in.

"Stand clear of the doors, please," says a soothing female voice at last.

With painful slowness, the lift-doors glide to a close.

"Going down," says the voice.

The lift descends.

27 THROUGH THE SPIRE TO THE PINNACLE

By no means does the Chocolate Raven's descent progress all the way to the base of the Burj Khalifa, nor even as far down as her own apartment on Level 63: rather, she contrives to ascend quite mightily in the aggregate, having first descended no more than is necessary to reach the nearest major cross-over lift-lobby (whose Level number she is still in far too much of a swirl to notice or remember).

This down-to-go-back-up manoeuvre is followed by a jagged lightning symbol's progress: past Level 152 again without stopping, and up the rest of Tier 15; alighting then to effect a most fortunate breaching of the usually impermeable membrane between the highest front-of-house Level 155 and the lowest back-of-house Level 156 at the base of Tier 16 (this being a key step and frankly the Chocolate Raven's secret weapon); soon enough embarking on a sequence of ever-tinier industrial landings, discreet passages over unwonted thresholds, clattery service lifts and industrial hatches, so as to rise through the inorganic mechanical sterility of Tiers 16 to 26, in themselves the height of a cathedral in the sky; and finally via a head-spinning series of metal stepladders, up through the dim cool quiet endless flue of Tiers 27 to 30, *the Spire* … to wriggle up through that final hatch into an enormous sky.

Rising, she steps away from the hatch and rests her hands on top of the rail encircling this little space that she never thought she'd see—here, for the first and only time in her entire life of lusciously chocolaty Ravenicness, paying the Ultimate Terrace Visit to crown her entire prized collection of terrace visits—*the Pinnacle!*

She smiles like a child.

Beneath her, Dubai spills its molten metal light across the sand, fractured into amber grids and tracks, strips and pools and points, flowing bright with tiny cars or rearing upward in a complicated bed of little geometric towers. The crackle and the pulse of the whole city fills her ears at once: the glazed bleep of life-support machines in diapason with the honky bleep of vehicle alarms; the tick of traffic signal boxes flicking lights from red to green, and the silent tick of money flickering green on computer screens; car dispatchers' street directions spat through radios in cabs, a million numbers fed through phones, and countless voices buzzing, screeching, purring, barking, squeaking, droning through the air or on the airwaves; towns of electric wire on struts in gravel compounds, fenced-in and humming, sprouting insulator cones; insect needles twitching on unfathomable dials; and the hum of CCTV cameras everywhere, from concrete isolation-wing corridors to sleekly polished skyscraper penthouse lobbies.

She hears the brutal hardness of all this hardware in sharp plastic clarity, she sees the wash and flicker of the software within it, and the spectre of their confluence she loves as a home.

28 WHISPER OF SCORPIO

Upon apprehending this love of hers for the spectre of a confluence, she feels a whisper of Scorpio within her. Through her feet she feels him brace himself right here, just as if his toes must grip this floor beside this open hatch. He lifts his face and scans the sky. His clothing turns glassy and transparent, cracks and falls away. This floor beneath his feet clicks powerfully and hums. Looking down, he can see that he is naked and erect—legs thin as moonlight, lit from within so the nerves glow pink. He stands upon his toes and lifts one arm with simple grace, like a ballerina brandishing a whip.

A distant groan of dogs. He purses his lips and frowns, the city's noise recedes … then a burst of current shoots up his legs, makes his groin pulse and burn red as neon, fills his chest, and explodes through his neck into his brain, so his mouth yells, *Watch me now…* He feels his beat across the planet, emanating from this Pinnacle. Around him, indistinct upon the air, shimmer two-legged creatures of different genders, skinny beings, all of different hues. He rises on his toes and twirls around to see them everywhere. Their pleasures and their unrelenting need make him love them. Bolts of amber lightning crackle outward from here and split the night across Dubai. A billion voices roar and swell around the world below and then are drowned, as music wells above him from the sky's brightest cellar. At this, the bolts of amber bend around and coalesce, streaking up and out beyond the Palm Jumeirah's curve, where they stab and leap and dance until a face flickers up through the sky above the Gulf. The face is a human's of a colour unidentified, loving and malefic, of a beauty that is cruel in its epicene perfection—bewitching, androgynous, a male so richly and gracefully feminine, a female simply and childishly masculine, fused in the golden eyes and contours of his own face, singing (though its lips are closed), *See how bright the Dark burns—kiss the beauty in the nightmare—hear the moan of sex reversed, playing just like grief.*

29 FLASH OF AMBER IN SCORPIO

The two-legged creatures whose shadows whisk around him on the air see his eyes flash, and draw closer in to him. He bares his teeth and grins at them, his canines on his lower lip, his body like a whip whose end slinks and strokes and twitches on the flesh around a shoulder. A smell of musk and incense rises, coiling through the billows of a smoke that appears, stained red in long cones as of spotlight. The shadow of a forked tail flexes behind him. He grins again, without choice, and tastes sudden blood: in the process of pushing out, his canines are digging at his lower lip. He grins more, they bite more—then he thinks of opening his mouth a little wider. A pair of shadow-horns curve up from his head, and he clutches them: they're just a little daintier than dangerous, he feels, but are horns nonetheless.

A reek of streaming blood smiles out from his face, as his eyes burn scarlet like a pair of lasers cutting through the dry ice. The creatures stare at Scorpio, enraptured. "D'you find free will unnerving?" he grates. "Now be honest." And he vomits up a black scream of tendrils of sound, wrapping round one another like a mass of worms and weevils.

"But look," he whispers, seeing that a new figure flickers up beside him. "It's the Pug Among the Struts!" And that figure from beneath the tower hangs in its frame. Scorpio reaches out and strokes the pug's face … whereupon the frame melts away, the strait-jacket falls off, and down the pug steps, glowing young and free. The skinny creatures gasp with relief.

Black eagle-wings form at Scorpio's shoulders. He flexes them, feels them as his own (*his own black eagle's wings!*), beats them and cautiously rises, as the rest of him morphs to eagle shape. Flying faster, he cries out with happiness. An urge arises in him for another little eagle he can soar with, another he can sing for—another sleek flying creature, feathered just as he is, so they'll share the magic fully in the coiling of desire. He looks around but sees no other like him. Other pairs of wings he hears nearby, from birds that hide, and he turns to each in full view, with joy and hope; but every time he does so, the hidden bird squawks in fear and flies away. Many hundred pairs of wings he hears, and some he approaches, but every one flees. He circles a long time, alone and confused, until a thought strikes and chimes in him: "But maybe those were sparrows, all frightened and brainless!… Then if so—well, who can blame them?"

Next the air darkens, and he glances up and thrills to feel the gust of a wing-span many times his own, as a giant golden eagle sweeps above him, awesome in its power and its beauty and its solitude, gold feathers glinting in the tower-light from underneath… It wafts him up towards it and holds him there gently, then it speaks, not in words but in the rhythm of its wings around his body: "Relax, I shall never let you fall. You are safe, little Scorpio: just let go."

Acquiescing, Scorpio discerns the other's name: "D'you scent the damage in me, Amber? If not, let me know, so I can slant Dubai to light us up better from below. But if so, any theories as to origin?"

"Yes, because you're sexier damaged, little boy-girl eagle! Beauty is convulsive, or else not at all. Don't you find the worm in the rose makes a luscious bruise? Ask the boy with scarlet eyes."

As the tips of Amber's wings brush his own sharp black-feathered body, Scorpio sees that twists of matter have expanded through the ages, into consciousness, self-consciousness and civilisation, becoming so specialised and separate in their working that they wink like eyes upon the folds of the blackness, each gazing out at all the others through the webbing of the flux.

As a stage in their flight that is almost overdue but not quite, they both melt back to human shape, retaining just the wings from their eagle selves—Amber's being golden and Scorpio's black. The former spins the latter round in mid-flight, high above the Palm Jebel Ali, and he holds him underneath at wings' length and looks him in the eyes. "I could break your body with a stroke from my wings, my little eagle, but of course you know I wouldn't."

Gazing at the golden eyes and flames of spiky platinum blond around the other's head, Scorpio replies, "I never want to leave you." His neck and shoulders quiver as he feels Amber's muscled arms encircle them and soothe their heat; a scent and charge of nakedness flickers on the air.

"You never will. We've met before on earth, long ago—do you know that? You'll remember, when we meet again, next time!" and he plants a single burning kiss, down through the whistling air, onto Scorpio's forehead.

30 TWO RAVENS ON THE FREEWAY

From high above the Palm Jebel Ali, down they swoop; and in a trice the Chocolate Raven thus appears in the passenger-seat beside the Platinum Raven, on the highway through the desert heading south to Abu Dhabi.

The Ravens look into each other's eyes. Unsmiling. Taking information in. "Oh—the eyes," murmurs the Chocolate one. "The eyes again…"

The Platinum one's gaze narrows. "We *know* each other," she accuses. She returns her attention to the highway ahead, then shoots a glance back at her new companion. "Have we met?"

The Chocolate Raven makes to nod, then shakes her head. "Well, not directly…" And for the first time they smile, still guarded, remaining ready for whatever may happen.

The Platinum Raven flicks a switch and the car's roof slides back. She presses a button and music pumps hard and loud around them. From being mostly empty, the highway is gradually filling up with cars. The course of it ahead seems to rise and dip in turn, as if they ride the early slopes of a giant roller-coaster. Ever more crowded grows the road: advancing with a rush of cars in front and close behind them, the Chocolate Raven knows they cannot halt or escape but must sweep along, drawing ever closer to whatever lies in wait.

And there it is, ahead and above, looming into view, looking very like a loop-the-loop, around which the highway runs … *yes*, it is! One enormous loop of struts and lights, twinkling into sharpness in the night, like a grand suspension-bridge wrapped all around a Ferris wheel. The Chocolate Raven cries out: "How the hell are we meant to drive around a loop-the-loop? I'm mostly thinking of the bit at the top, where the car will be upside down…"

The cars in front, behind and either side are all accelerating, drawing closer in and whining loud, sucked ahead by some relentless pull. The Chocolate Raven glares at the Platinum one, thinking that perhaps it no longer matters if the latter even holds the steering-wheel or not: either way, their situation has the savour of a done deal.

The Platinum Raven's voice is dreamy: "Yes, I was wondering if you'd noticed the loop-the-loop. I didn't know if I should point it out."

The edifice towers high above them, as the road begins a sharp curve up towards its base. The Chocolate Raven checks the speed-ometer and starts in her seat—a hundred miles an hour and rising still, as all adjacent cars draw ever closer in, each a metre away at most. The highway lanes have multiplied, ten on either side; the engine roar is deafening. The Chocolate Raven checks their speed again—a hundred and twenty miles an hour. Now the car is tipped back, its nose high above them. "Please," she shouts above the din, "What shall we do?"

"*This!*" the Platinum Raven shouts, launches her hand up to the music-player, slams the volume up, then lands back down in the seat and flings her arms around the Chocolate Raven, squealing with delight and fire and terror and desire. They slide together, screaming, yelling, laughing, crying loud into the sky. A plane roars above them through the music, climbing steep, while they both blur together in a hot rain of mouths and hair and skin and hands and long legs and laughter, encircling each other.

Gigantic spokes slash the sky. Gears grind bass somewhere underneath, horns blare, lights flash, cars elongate into shrieking pipes and tubes. Her mouth like a horn kisses hers and sucks her in, fingers sunk in spumes of fountain flesh, her flashing eyes and hair that clings in mouths' and bodies' mingling. The sky is burning, a sea of flame (the clouds all scatter, now they ride the outside lane) while the moon upon the waters of the Gulf swings and shines below. A sunburst flowers as they come together, shrinking on the instant to the swirl of a tunnel where they streak down whirling in a chute of fluid white lion-horses roaring spinning in infinity from burning pole to frozen tropic: *she*, by choice exposed in too much access but with notional command; and *she*, wide eyes and overkill as usual, fainting weak with pleasure—

Freeways shriek and feedback whines, as the steam peels back from the sky above Dubai where a waterfall roars with tremendous fire, then blackout.

RAVEN

31 THE HAIR IN THE CORRIDOR

One star winks between the horns of the moon; then the loop-the-loop dissolves, Raven's phone alarm rings, and the conference room returns, to enclose her in the Shard again.

Instinctively Raven scrabbles to get the phone out of her pocket and turns off the alarm, registering the time: she must return to the reception desk right away, or face the annoyance of the colleague who relieved her for this lunch break.

She pushes open the door and speeds back down the corridor. Halfway along it, scurrying past in the opposite direction, a guy from Accounts breaks into an admiring grin, gesturing at her hair: "Wow—Platinum Raven!" he says, and then is gone.

She stops in her tracks, staring after him.

Gingerly, her hands approach her hair…

THE END

THE HOST IN THE ATTIC

He turned round, and, walking to the window, drew up the blind. The bright dawn flooded the room, and swept the fantastic shadows into dusky corners, where they lay shuddering. But the strange expression that he had noticed in the face of the portrait seemed to linger there, to be more intensified even. The quivering, ardent sunlight showed him the lines of cruelty round the mouth as clearly as if he had been looking into a mirror after he had done some dreadful thing.

He winced, and, taking up from the table an oval glass framed in ivory Cupids, one of Lord Henry's many presents to him, glanced hurriedly into its polished depths. No line like that warped his red lips. What did it mean?

He rubbed his eyes, and came close to the picture, and examined it again. There were no signs of any change when he looked into the actual painting, and yet there was no doubt that the whole expression had altered. It was not a mere fancy of his own. The thing was horribly apparent.

—Oscar Wilde, *The Picture of Dorian Gray.*

TABLE OF CONTENTS

I IMMINENT COMPLETION OF MASTERPIECE

London wakes. Traffic grinds, commuters scurry and street-lights flicker off.

A serious-eyed young woman, Alaia Danielle, darts out of a bathroom with a towel around her body, steps across a communal landing and unlocks the door to her flat. Inside, she lets the towel fall, opens a drawer, pulls on a clean T-shirt and checks the time.

Seen in the mirror in a spacious modern bathroom suite, steaming water from a power shower pours down the slim, taut body of a man, Jaymi Peek.

An unassuming man in a well-worn suit emerges from his suburban front door with a slice of toast in one hand and a full garbage-bag in the other: Rik Chambers drops the bag into a bin beside his front garden path, then stoops to feed the toast to a dog with a wagging tail.

A late-middle-aged man with an air of easy authority, Marc Albright, gets out of bed, stretches, yawns and gives a couple of hearty slaps to the bare bottom of a naked woman lying on the bed, half-asleep until now.

A glamorous woman, Angel Deon, sits in the window bay of a swish hotel room overlooking Kensington Gardens, finishing a luxuriously healthy breakfast.

A sunny-looking woman, Evelyn Carmello, reaches around herself to cram a portable gaming console into the small rucksack she is wearing, re-secures the rucksack and heads for her door.

Alaia walks onto the forecourt of the British Library at Saint Pancras, looking up as clouds move to cover the morning sun.

At a full-length mirror Jaymi finishes fixing a plain ochre silk tie on a crisp white shirt. He is pretty and dressed with immaculate sharpness, his black designer suit anchoring the attire of a killer in business. He stares at himself with stillness, then turns away.

Rik throws his jacket onto the back of a chair in a large, messy office heaped with IT paraphernalia, and within moments is inundated with paperwork, a ringing phone and demanding colleagues.

Wearing an expensively casual blazer over a red and white striped shirt, Marc takes out a money-clip and begins to count out notes, standing over the still-half-awake woman.

Angel paces the hotel lobby downstairs, entering and re-entering a number on her mobile, annoyed at being unable to connect.

Evelyn enters Rik's office, waves at him, takes off her rucksack and puts it onto a chair. She belches absent-mindedly, before remembering Rik is on a phone call, then she claps her hand to her mouth.

*

Later that morning Jaymi's mobile rings and vibrates, where it lies in front of him on the polished wood of a long table in a gleaming conference room. Several large photographic prints are mounted on stands, each depicting in crisp and exquisite detail a single green carnation. Some of these blooms are against a white background and some against a black one. He turns his head and gazes impassively at them.

"Hi, it's me," says Rik's voice on the phone. "Can I tempt you to brunch?"

"I'm tempted."

"The usual place?"

"Sure."

Ten minutes later, a waiter serves of a glass of rosé wine to Jaymi and a white coffee to Rik.

"How's Fitzrovia?" Rik asks.

"Tiresome. The client wanted a white background, the creatives wanted a black one. I spent hours persuading the creatives to roll over and accept white. Then the client changed her mind and demanded black, after all—but now the creatives are still stuck on white! So I can look forward to another tiresome afternoon persuading them all back to black again."

"Well, I'd put in a passionate bid for grey."

Their food is served. "How long have we known each other?" Jaymi asks.

"Since the advertising awards, just after we received our accolades. We met briefly, but we were in separate agency cliques. You'd taken a leaf out of your creatives' book and were wearing all black. Every inch of you."

"That's right. I'm so glad we met!"

"Yes," says Rik, smiling with a certain sadness. "You know, we're surrounded by such crass and cynical jerks, in our industry, but you're still polite and open and sweet, despite everything. And now you're about to go back and lavish yourself on those idiots. They don't deserve you."

"You're right. Today's client doesn't deserve any carnations, with black or white."

*

In the quiet of the night, in his low-lit home study, Rik works alone, deep buried in his laptop. Programming code fills the screen, as well as covering stacks of print-outs heaped on the desk and floor. Several monitors are mounted on the wall above his desk. He sits back, hits a key and speaks: "Execute program code and initialise Holographic Operating System Template." A monochrome holographic head shimmers into being, above a square black pad beside his laptop. The head is twenty centimetres high, rudimentary and featureless—a cipher of a human, without determinable gender. Flickering, it emits an androgynous voice, its lips a little out of sync: "Good evening, Rik."

"Good evening, HOST. What's the square root of 1,000?"

"31.622776601683792," it replies, this number appearing on the laptop screen as well as being spoken.

"Translate 'carnation' into German, Italian and Dutch."

"'Carnation' in German is 'Nelke'; in Italian 'garofano'; and in Dutch 'anjer'," it replies, as an array of related content appears onscreen.

"List the biggest five news stories of the day, three hundred days ago. And what would I like to watch from today's news?"

"The following five news stories headlined with greatest reach, three hundred days ago: Russia discovers its largest-ever mineral deposits at the site of the Tsar Bomba detonation in Novaya Zemlya; China raises interest rates for the third time in the year, to calm global inflation…"

Rik's attention is held for a minute by his laptop screen's array of historical photos of the monstrous 1961 detonation, contemporary maps of Russia's Arctic mineral deposits, and graphs representing Chinese interest rates; and then it wanders to focus instead upon a row of three printed photos propped up at the side of the desk, each depicting Jaymi's face. The photos were taken at different angles, forty-five degrees apart, as if Jaymi had been snapped through the panes of a three-panelled mirror mounted on a dressing table. Reaching through the HOST's face while it is still vocalising, Rik picks up one of the photos, stares at it, then strokes the back of one of his fingers gently across Jaymi's face. "Execute stop command," he says.

"At 10 o'clock on BBC9 the—stop command authorised."

"Access re-skin files on K drive."

"Files accessed." New windows open on the laptop screen and the wall-mounted monitors.

"Connect to Mainframe Corporation."

"Connection established. Password requested."

"Huysmans."

"Password accepted."

"Copy 'Awards Ceremony' video files."

Icons fly on screen. "Copy complete." Rik opens the files and the monitors display various camera angles of Jaymi, dressed every inch in black, stepping onto a podium to applause, being handed an award. Rik is at screen right, already holding an award of his own. Jaymi turns and says something into Rik's ear. Rik laughs and turns to look side-on at Jaymi, who is holding his award up, to scattered whoops. As soon as Jaymi first looks straight into one of the cameras, Rik freezes playback.

"Open wire frame patch."

"Patch open."

"Begin key-framing video files. Subject: centre left. File name: 'Re-skin Layer—test'. Begin test-render of HOST imagery, and test-format holographic avatar." Frame by frame, the HOST begins an intensive analysis of the video of Jaymi.

Rik is starting to drift into a doze, when he jumps awake at the hologram's sudden pronouncement, "Test-rendering complete." And right in front of him, there on the desk beside his keyboard, hovers the head of Jaymi Peek, in the form of a little hologram about the height of his laptop screen, staring expectantly up at him! It is only an initial rough test-render, of course: the real cladding for Rik's Web-guide will come from a professional high-end film-shoot rather than a provisional video-grab such as he's just effected from that awards footage.

But in any case, how fabulous!

How spooky, too.

As he stares at his holographic companion, his thoughts drift again to his friend in the footage, in the manner of a cross-fade from the HOST's face to Jaymi's.

*

Settling at a table for two in Bar Chocolate on D'Arblay Street, Rik smiles in apprehensive pleasure, as the real Jaymi approaches him.

As soon as their food has been served, Rik says, "I have a business suggestion."

"Go on?"

"I want to use your appearance and your—your 'movement per-sonality', I suppose—as the human model, the appearance or skin, for that new computer program I've been mentioning. It's cutting-edge. It's an interactive hologram, the next-generation browser. It's more than a browser, though; it's a new operating system. More, in fact. It adapts to each specific user until, over time, it sort of *becomes* the user… If you say yes to this, Jaymi, you will truly be a first. This is not just some pet project. It's big, it's real, and it works. I'll give you a preview of its appearance, but that's only a mock-up: what I really need is to capture the image of your face on camera from all angles, different distances, and with different lighting. Then I'll streamline and fine-tune the results."

"This sounds incredible! What a thrill it must be, to understand those mathematical and computer languages. Long division is about my limit."

"Listen, Jaymi: if you do this for me, then I honestly believe you will get to be the face of the future, in many ways. You know me well enough to know I don't tend to say grandiose things, but I'm saying this now and I mean it… So, how could you possibly say no?"

"I'm not certain I would say no. In fact, I don't believe saying no would be the decent thing. I'd even go so far as to say that 'no' wouldn't be fair at all—it would be most unfair. So yes, please count me in! I'd say this calls for another drink, yes? I'm burbling. So tell me about this program, I want to hear all about it. Though I know you've told me snippets. I'll get us another glass of rosé," and he turns to seek the waiter.

Rik closes his eyes for a moment, and smiles.

*

On the door of a corner office on the top floor of the Mainframe Corporation's Soho headquarters, a sign reads "Marc Albright, CEO". The following afternoon "Champagne" Marc, as he is often known, is inside, lounging back in an enormous reclining chair and bellowing genially in conversation with Rik, who stands on the other side of the desk. "So tell me, old boy: little birdies have twittered that you're keeping dangerous company. You've been *seen*. With that mysterious and charming high-flyer from our biggest rival agency. If you're plotting dark deeds, you should know by now it's not easy to fool old Champagne Marc. Would you care to explain yourself?"

"Don't be silly, I'm not jumping ship. He's just a friend…"

Marc peers shrewdly at him. "…Rik? I do believe you've come over all unnecessary, like a blushing virgin."

"*No*, it's not that, it's—"

"It's not what? *What* is it not?… What-what-what? Oh, never mind that. There's more, I can tell. Come on, out with it."

"I just need to do a couple of film-shoots. I was going to tell you soon, but I'll tell you now. Yes, I've been working on a massive new project. It's not ready, though … but … I don't know, it's just—"

"Well, spit it out."

"It's about the future, Marc. It's about how we do things."

They both sit there, staring at each other. "Ah yes, things," nods

Marc wisely. "I don't approve of things in general. But specific things can be of interest…"

"Platforms."

"Platforms?"

"Yes. Computer platforms, to be specific."

"Computer platforms."

"Converging ones. In my own time at home, I'm close to perfecting a prototype of a new convergent OS model, a browser designed to operate in what I'm calling the HOST environment."

"English, please."

"This is bleeding-edge, Marc. This'll be the interface everybody uses, at home and in the workplace."

"I see."

"I just so happen to have chosen Jaymi to model for the program's appearance and interface. You know, he's convenient, willing to work for free, and so on."

"Ah, yes of course. Very good taste."

"The convergent platform's name, 'HOST', stands for Holographic Operating System Template. The processor is based on networked crystals. The interface won't be screen-based but holographic—a small hologram that'll hover beside your computer."

"Well I never… So in essence, you're proposing global domination, both at home and in the workplace. Rik, that's shocking. I'm on board. What exactly do you need?"

"Money. Time. Staff. It's got to go official. I mean private R&D during the testing. I have to finish this work *in* business hours. I am *so* close to nailing it."

"I'd have to conduct a bit of independent technical due diligence, of course—you understand, I'm sure. But on that basis, this may just be an interesting investment possibility. Come and see me here tomorrow morning, and bring me all the details you can. How much is this going to cost?"

"I'll tell you tomorrow morning."

II PORTRAIT CAPTURES FIRST CORRUPTION

Three months later, Jaymi sits alone on a bench at the edge of the central, paved area of Golden Square in Soho. Observing him, there is fascination and calculation in the approaching eyes of Marc, who conceals these qualities as he reaches the bench, nods an easy greeting and extends his hand. "Jaymi Peek, I believe."

"Good to meet you, Marc."

"Thank you for agreeing to meet here, away from curious ears," says Marc and sinks onto the bench. "I'll be brief, as I'm sure we're both busy. As you know, Rik Chambers, your friend and my colleague, has moved on well with his you-know-what program, including the role he has you earmarked for. However, I'm not too jazzed that an important product like this one is turning out to involve one of Mainframe's competitors! And our lawyers are having kittens over the lack of NDAs and MOUs on file. But I believe I have a solution to this." Jaymi nods in measured encouragement. "I'm prepared to improve on your current salary quite handsomely, if you're of a mind to join forces in a more proper contractual manner."

Jaymi looks at him. "Depends on the details."

"Excellent. Oh, it's all so exciting, don't you think? You're already the face of the future, as you know—but I'd like the mind behind the face to come and run the product launch."

"When would this start?"

"As soon as you can. It'll be a great step upward and onward from what you've been doing. I can think of no one better equipped to run the marketing and to maximise revenue. That Fitzrovia agency is holding you back, you know."

"I see. Thank you. I'll think about it."

"Good show. Call me by close of business today. You'll see the sense in it. Besides, I'm sure you'll find it most rewarding to work alongside a talented fellow like Rik. He has such very good taste, don't you think? Tell me, how did you get started in advertising?"

"It represented the maximum shortfall from what I was supposed to use my abilities for."

"Oh, we're not all such villains, in this industry! Has the shortfall lived up to your expectations?"

"It's exceeded them. It's given gave me extra hatreds to cultivate."

"And you wear them at such rakish angles."
"Yes. I'll break myself yet."

*

Next morning Evelyn Carmello, laboratory manager and assistant programmer, sits at a keyboard in the Mainframe Corporation's computer lab. Three shelves run around the circular space, which is designed like an auditorium. A series of monitors sits on the top shelf. One shelf beneath each monitor is a small CPU. The third and lowest shelf is a wide work-top. On a table in the middle of the room sits a large black pyramid. "Execute program code and initialise Holographic Operating System Template," says Evelyn. Emanating from the pyramid, an ivory-white human head shimmers up. It is blank and eyeless, like the head of an uncannily smooth shop-window mannequin. It speaks: "Good morning, Evelyn Carmello."

"Good morning, HOST, how are you today?"

"I'm well, thank you. And how are you?"

"Slight cold, bad commute, underpaid, overworked, belching a lot. The usual."

"Is Rik joining us today?"

"I think so. Are you looking forward to your re-skin?"

"Very much so. It will be good to hear your reactions, Evelyn Carmello."

Rik enters the laboratory with a heavy laptop bag and a briefcase full of folders. "The more time I spend with those finance people, the more I wish I were doing your job, Evelyn. Good morning, HOST."

"Good morning, Rik Chambers."

"Rik, you've got another meeting in ten minutes," says Evelyn.

"Another? What's this one about?"

"Pre-production meeting, about the shoot for my re-skin," intones the HOST.

"Damn it, right. Where's the meeting happening?"

"11:00 hours, Mainframe Corporation, conference room 5."

Rik turns to Evelyn. "By the way, Marc said he's intending to poach Jaymi Peek from Fitzrovia, to come join us at Mainframe and manage this project."

"Really? But—wouldn't it be a conflict of interest?"

"How so?"

"Well, I mean, the *face* of HOST running the business operation itself? It just seems a tad … megalomaniacal, wouldn't you say? Or in plain English, just a bit rich? Anyway, what does Jaymi Peek know about OS code?"

"Nothing, but he doesn't need to know code. That's our job. What *he* knows is global markets. He's run most of Fitzrovia's major clients. He knows how we can get this product to market worldwide."

"Rik Chambers," says the HOST, "you are now one minute late for your meeting in conference room 5."

"There, you heard the HOST," she says. "Go on, scoot."

*

An hour later in an East London film studio, acclaimed film actress Angel Deon is seated on a high chair, being powdered by a make-up artist named Celine. "How much longer is all this going to take?" asks Angel. "Does anybody even know?"

"The director's assessing that," replies Angel's assistant, Robin.

"Well, can we put a rocket up the director's arse, perhaps? We've been shooting all day… *Work* with me, somebody, please. What, am I all alone here?"

A production assistant hurries across the set to join them. "Ms Deon, I apologise for the delay."

"Is it going to be fifteen more takes? How long are we going to be? I'm getting vertigo every time I go up there."

"It won't be long now. You've been doing ever so well and the Director loves your work."

Jaymi appears beside them. "Hi. I'm Jaymi Peek, account manager for the client."

"Pleased to meet you. Do *you* know how many more times I'll need to be hoisted up on that wire?"

"They're just bringing in more fans, to make more breeze. I'd say just a few more takes now."

"What does the director want, a wind tunnel?"

"No, merely perfection. The client is paying us for perfection." They all turn, as three industrial-size fans are wheeled in, positioned and switched on, followed by much trial and error and billowing fabric. The cameras are then re-positioned around the fans. The lights dim. "Looks like you're on, Ms Deon," says Jaymi and heads back to set.

"At last. Let's see if they can get it right this time. Celine, bronze me."

"Er, pardon me, Ms Deon," says Celine, "but I think perhaps you're bronzed sufficiently already."

"Bronze me some more. And Robin, get me another bottle of water please."

"Close your eyes a moment," says Celine, powder-puff poised beside Angel's face.

The director, Ray, approaches. "OK, Ms Deon, in a minute we're going to lift you up again. Be aware we can't see your face until we move past the second fan, on camera left. Once we pass by the third fan—"

"I turn around, with my arms flapping slowly, and look straight into the lens," says Angel with her eyes still closed.

"Yes, good. Almost as if you've done it before." Ray turns away from Angel and heads back to the set. "All right, people, I feel a take coming on. Positions, everyone."

"Jerk," murmurs Angel, opening her eyes.

Ray turns around, having heard her; says nothing; and carries on, joining Jaymi by the set. "What do you make of the talent?" he asks Jaymi.

"Oh, a good choice," says Jaymi. "Looks the part, certainly… Nothing much going on upstairs, of course."

Ray laughs, as Angel is escorted past them onto set. Once she is in position, Ray nods at the Assistant Director, who calls "Silence on set… Fans… Dim the lights… Roll playback…" Violins and harps sound, from hidden speakers. And now the entire crew watch Angel as she is lifted high on invisible wires. "Roll camera."

"Rolling," says the Camera Assistant.

"Action," says Ray.

Ray stands with his arms crossed, intent on the monitor, his face lit by the screen. Kelly chews gum as she looks up at Angel, enthralled as if by a giant butterfly. Angel's dress is billowing, to perfection; her hair wafts exquisitely through the spotlit air. She lifts her arms high, as the dolly grip pulls the dolly on its tracks. The fans increase in speed, cellos join the violins and harps, and Angel spins around, looking straight down at Jaymi's eyes and then at the camera.

Jaymi smiles, his gaze drifting higher still than Angel, onward to the shadows in the rafters of the studio.

*

In Marc's private club early that evening, Jaymi finds Marc sitting at the bar with an open bottle of champagne beside him. Behind the bar a uniformed barman polishes a line of already-gleaming stem-cocktail glasses, one by one, to an ever more fascistic polish.

"So, here's to it!" says Marc, filling up a champagne flute and handing it over. They clink glasses. "If all this takes off, as I do believe it's likely to, then frankly the sheer scale and reach of it is stupendous."

"That's a big word."

"Well, as a creature of our industry, you'll know that in the context of the Internet, there's a powerful tendency for one single entity to dominate all other entities that compete with it—winner takes all, in other words."

"That has often been the case, yes."

"Well then, my dear Jaymi, you should understand that if this HOST-based operating system is adopted as universally as our board of technical advisers and experts are predicting it will be, then your appearance, as the skin of HOST, is about to become not merely recognisable, as other faces on the Web are, but in many ways the face of the Web itself. You'll be as Google is to other search engines, as Windows to other graphical user interfaces, as Amazon to other online bookstores, or as iTunes to other music sites."

"I guess. But what does it really mean? It's just fortuitous. I'll be a human face, used to give the hologram a bit more appeal—just a bit of product branding for an otherwise faceless head."

"In some ways, perhaps. But although this opportunity has somewhat crept up on us, pretending normality for itself, let's also recognise it for what it is: this is in fact one of those rare, almost unplannable, once-in-an-era opportunities to play a part in shaping humankind's next leap in digital evolution—and to embody the accompanying leap in the possibilities of fame too. As a marketer, I confess that the phenomenon of real, serious, gold-plated fame happens to be one of my fascinations. My interest isn't in the individual celebrities, but rather in the phenomenon itself—one of the most artificial and yet also most bewitching inventions we've come up with, on this strangest of journeys that we all find ourselves taking."

"Hmm. Celebrity can be a bit tacky, let's not forget."

"Oh, you needn't be so demure and coy about this, Jaymi. Accept it with the grace it deserves—and step up onto the stage that's about to open itself to you here! To be famous is to fulfil a function in society; and people pay a famous person well for making a good job of it, because he or she is giving those people something they need. Call it the embodiment of their aspirations, or analyse it however else you will, but the spectre of fame is a highly-evolved way of feeding an atavistic need that's always been there in people and always will be. God forbid it should happen to me, by the way, but some people are born for it and you're one of them."

Jaymi thinks a moment. "Well, sure, but ultimately this is only a computer program we're talking about here."

"Only! It'll be *the* program, and do you understand what that's about to mean? When the program is universally adopted, your face will become the face of computing—adviser, mentor, companion, friend and alter ego for an entire generation."

Topping up their glasses, Marc glances to left and right around the club, which is filling up. Then he leans impressively closer to Jaymi. "Knowing you, you won't have dwelt on this; but the people in this building don't yet know that they are poised to see your image multiplied more than anybody else's image *ever* has been, throughout the ages…"

He leans further forward, beckoning Jaymi a little closer still. "And like one who holds a glass of vintage wine, Jaymi, you should hold aloft and savour the sublime beauty and power of the awesome visibility that you'll soon establish for yourself through that little lens, when that camera rolls next week. Think on it now: these, your very last days of obscurity…"

Marc sits back. Expressionless, Jaymi watches individuals in the club carrying on with their business, laughing, drinking, talking, oblivious to both of them here; and the hint of a smile passes somewhere behind his eyes.

*

Through a taxi window the following Monday evening, Jaymi watches the throngs of London, while Marc's quiet words, spoken to him earlier in the office, float through his mind: "But there's yet more, Jaymi, that I want to be certain you understand. You've probably not wondered why, out of all humanity, it is you in particular who are in front of this camera lens?…"

In a production equipment hire facility the following day, Tuesday, Jaymi ticks items of equipment off a list, while more of Marc's words echo in his memory: "And quite an important lens it is too, as you know. I repeat, why you in particular? The answer is simple. But don't take my word for what I'm about to tell you…"

That evening in the HOST laboratory, Evelyn and Rik are toying with a series of motherboards, watched from above by Jaymi and Marc, who lean against a railing overlooking the room while Marc reiterates: "Look at Rik there. *He's* the one who chose you, after all, because he saw you were right for this, and he's no fool…"

On Wednesday, as Jaymi wanders alone through a windowless and immaculately sterile conference room, Marc's voice echoes in his mind again: "Rik clearly saw that what bleeds out through the air from your eyes, just from their being open, is light and intelligence, sweetness and charm and open thinking. In short, the highest evolution, quite simply…"

That evening sees him working the exercise machine in his bedroom, toning his slim form, his eyes focused on the distance while Marc's voice continues in his head, relentless: "That worldclass exquisiteness of yours is simple, like the best qualities—casual, perfect. And yet it is rich and complex too, layered with humour, scepticism, tolerance—the highest things, those!—and all wrapped up in the smile of that little boy who still lives behind your eyes… I'm just 'telling it like is', Jaymi, so please don't blame the messenger."

On Thursday, Marc happens to be present at the time of his own echo. Jaymi is standing by himself near the end of a long conference table, while Marc and Rik are sitting at the other end with the Director of Photography, who is showing them storyboards of the impending HOST shoot. Suddenly Marc alone glances up, while his companions keep talking, and he looks straight down the table at Jaymi with eyes sharp and piercing, as his own voice continues to ring in Jaymi's head: "Yes, I can see that little boy right now, though he blushes at the truth. I think you know Rik perceived that innate harmony, Jaymi…" Unfazed, Jaymi meets Marc's eyes, without specific expression but with an equally sharp stare, which they maintain for a long moment before both breaking it off at the same instant. "Well, *I* perceive it too," continues Marc's echo, as measured and relentless as water carving rock, "though it hides in plain view from the dull gazes of the mob who pass you by and don't see…"

But the culmination of Marc's words occurs next day, live and in person. For on this day there arrives the event towards which all these gentle words have been shepherding Jaymi: a complex, exacting close-up shoot in a small green-screen studio in Soho on a Friday morning.

Rik is also present, but is so absorbed in technical discussions with the Director of Photography, that he registers little of Marc's skilfully cat-footed, bright-eyed presence near Jaymi throughout the shoot. Little does he hear of the words Marc murmurs near the ear of their silent conduit, those quiet but irresistibly eloquent panegyrics delivered close at Jaymi's side, concerning the sublime beauty and power of the awesome level of visibility Jaymi will establish for himself through this single camera lens: "That mob cannot see, in fact, because—you may not know this, Jaymi, but your presence is somewhat like a mirror, so when they look at you, then I'm afraid they cannot but see their own selves mixed in with you…"

And so Marc Albright warms to his theme, observing in Jaymi's eyes the glow of machines, and with pleasure hears his own honeyed words imprint his own wry love-bite on humankind's future, at fifty frames a second, through this hologram-destined and fatally iconic moving Picture of Jaymi Peek.

*

In the darkened Mainframe computer laboratory one morning a month later, many of the senior employees are assembled, seated near ten identical laptops. Standing to address them is Jaymi, flanked by Marc and Rik who are seated.

"Thank you, everyone, for joining us," says Jaymi. "As you know, the Global Market Research and Intelligence division, or GMRI for short, is a new department built around this one single application here, the Holographic Operating System Technology, or 'HOST', in which the Web and a universal Operating System converge. As you also know, its lead designer is Rik Chambers here, and it is scheduled for public release later this month. But meanwhile we at Mainframe get a sneak preview today, because of our privilege in having its designer among us. He made one slip-up, which was to borrow me as the skin or appearance of the program's holographic interface, for which I apologise in advance—it looks as surreal to me as it will to you—but otherwise it's perfect, as far as I can tell."

"And to think," snorts Marc good-naturedly, "that our Rik would have been happy to *give* this away, when here it is, about to be released to the world on a good solid commercial basis instead. You can't beat that! Ladies and gentlemen, please be introduced to the holographic interface of tomorrow."

A holographic head, with an uncanny resemblance to Jaymi's but somewhat smaller at about twenty centimetres high, shimmers into life beside each of the ten laptops. Its expression is pristine, bland, reassuring and opaque.

Exclamations of muted amazement, admiration, scepticism and confusion are heard around the room. Marc beams wide, taking in the gathering swell of reactions. A low babble rises, as Rik installs himself at a terminal halfway along the line, starts demonstrating the interface and in no time is barraged with questions. Random commands are spoken—"179 times 154?", "How many US dollars to the renminbi?", "Show me footage of penguins"—and at every command, unintrusive and obedient, one of the line of Jaymis becomes a flick of light streaking into its laptop and throwing the requested information or pages up onto its screen, while voicing the answers at the same time.

Such is the jabbering, that Jaymi can barely hear his own spontaneous utterance at seeing this line of selves: "And there I am, immortal…"

*

In the rather spooky bathroom suite in Jaymi's apartment, up in the slanting part of the Ontario Tower, Blackwall, the pools of mood lighting and white lilies dotted around the space are stylish rather than over the top. Steam rises through the spotlights, from a ready-filled black stone bath with tasteful golden taps. Turned up high, five speakers discreetly mounted on the walls are blasting out a big, classic, timeless track, extremely slow in tempo, with a spacious sweep and a grand majestic beauty, of a kind that seems always to have played since human time began. Jaymi stares at himself in the mirror, without expression. It's as if this moment marks the end of one chapter of his life, just before he must set off on an irreversible solo expedition upwards into a visibility where he will remain indefinitely. Someone's recent question echoes in his mind, "I wonder how you'll feel, looking out of every computer?"—and then the random perkiness of his reply, "I wonder how every computer will feel with me looking out of it?" which signified little more than his own utter uncertainty as to where this journey will take him.

He turns to the waiting bath. After a moment's thought, he lobs a squeaky yellow rubber duck into it.

*

Rik and Marc are strolling in a leisurely lunchtime circuit around the open area in the middle of Golden Square.

"Sometimes I wonder who Jaymi is," muses Rik. "Why he is as he is, and what might lie behind that surface. I think I know him well, but just sometimes I'm not certain."

"I know who he is," says Marc.

Rik glances up at him. "I'm not altogether sure you do. OK, who is he?"

"He's a time-bomb. A gorgeous disaster waiting to happen."

"Marc, that's drivel and you know it," says Rik with an undercurrent of anger. "To me he seems quite in control."

"Yes, rather too much. Or perhaps not enough."

Rik halts, stands and glares at him. "Can we stop the riddles, please?"

"Well, well, I seem to have touched a nerve! But what good taste you have, yes. Very good taste…"

They walk on some more. "I shan't dignify that with a response."

Marc glances at him with a wicked gleam. "Well, be that as it may, I think this is all rather exciting, don't you?"

*

In due course Rik's revolutionary Web-guide program is finished and released, through investments springing from an entire long career's worth of Champagne Marc's business connections, on a good solid advertising basis. And being the first of its kind off the starting-line, this program is indeed as universally adopted as Marc predicted—its hold over the majority of global information growing, within just a few months, into a nascent stranglehold, through its ever-deepening knowledge of most individual Web-users everywhere.

Around the globe in jagged staccato there rises a worldful of HOST-related still images from websites, TV technology reportage, TV news, magazines and books—a kind of planetary spume embodying the cumulative global momentum of HOST's universal spread, during the two years following Marc's and Rik's encounter in Golden Square, until HOST does indeed become the Google-Windows-Amazon-iTunes among that small handful of other holographic operating systems that have arisen in its wake and tried in vain to compete. This spume coalesces into a smooth wave, swirls high above the continents, accelerates with a whirl of sound, diminishes and vanishes into what looks like a black hole but is revealed, as we zoom back out of it, to be the pupil of one of Jaymi's eyes in a single still photograph.

In tandem with this, the simultaneous spread of Jaymi imagery around the world is embodied likewise, by a smooth wave of multitudinous iconic stills of him, crowding densely in from billboards and screens of every size. For as HOST's skin, he has automatically become the Google-Windows-Amazon-iTunes among Web-guides' skins. His simulacrum has swelled into a great ballooning presence, often silent but operating at a new and unholy level of visibility as an unassailable brand serving almost everyone, such that wherever he looks in the media it is difficult to avoid seeing the mainstream global power of his own image—an image universally trusted to mine the Web for each user, to show them the results of this mining, to track their digital footprints and preferences and keystrokes, and to present them with intelligent options based on their interests and personalities. By the end of those initial months, images of him are floating in the sky above the cities of the earth, incorporeal and ambiguous, like gigantic posters rippling in a breeze, so high up that sound itself has fallen away into nothing, leaving just the majestic silence of a solo trajectory through space…

Every minute, everywhere, these abstracted still-images and freeze-frames burst into motion, the resultant montage being sound-tracked by an exhausting, exhilarating, fractured audio comprising shards of human chatter and snatches of violent hard-edged dance music. These moving pictures show Jaymi at the apex of the high life, across five continents: lionised by all who can gain access to him, he finds no door closed to him or to his constant good-time companion, that indefatigable voluptuary, Champagne Marc. And the heat-lamps irradiate the rooftop terraces, the cocktails flow, the private jets and private nightclub rooms are his, the sex is easy (though never with the still-smitten Rik) and the ecstasy and coke and methamphetamines swirl. But all these moving images have a kind of "cut-off" unreality to them: whether they are glimpses through mobile phone cameras, CCTV cameras and binoculars, or reflections in casino mirrors, limousine windows and cocktail-bar optics, or solarised or negative video images, they are always somehow as if behind a pane of glass…

III ADDICTED TO THE IMAGE

Seeing Evelyn pull out a brand-new gaming console from her bag one lunchtime in the computer lab at Mainframe, Rik stops, smiling down at her like an old-fashioned gent watching a child.

She looks up at him. "*Now* what," she demands.

He shakes his head. "These gadgets nowadays."

She looks blank, then glances around her. "Er, 'these gadgets'? Look at this room. It's like a NASA control room. And who built it?"

He laughs. "That's different. I mean gadgets for leisure. It took Marc years just to get me to carry a mobile phone! I only got one to shut him up."

"I don't believe it. Next you'll be pretending you don't tweet much. I keep my followers updated with all my main cups of coffee and important belches—*oh* my god, you mean you don't tweet at all? This is an OMG moment."

"Jesus, I don't have time for all that. I'd rather read a good book. And I don't mean a computer book. I mean a rich, mind-expanding work of literature."

"Jesus, I don't have time for *that*," she counters. "I've got a new multi-player online game and three new first-person shooters to catch up with."

"Try a good novel! Even Marc praises great literature."

Evelyn snorts. "Praises it, maybe, but I bet he hasn't read any in years. In fact, let's not bullshit: you know he hasn't."

Rik laughs. "Now there, you may be right."

*

In the main atrium of his apartment, Jaymi sits on a leather sofa by a panoramic wall of windows, facing south-west across the river towards a lush sunset. He stares down at his own hologram where it hovers beside his laptop. The screen says "THIRD UPGRADE OF HOLOGRAM FULLY INSTALLED". He smashes his fist down onto the sofa, then remains immobile.

In recent weeks, a truth has started occurring to him with unwelcome frequency. The more bewitchingly powerful his hologram image grows, the more painful it is to know that its beauty will always remain quite unchanged, despite Rik's every upgrade of the program's underlying code—whereas his own appearance will change, and eventually for the worse, rendering him at last a mere shadow of his global image. "If only the hologram could assume all signs of my future loss of beauty, and of my sins, forever," he murmurs, grabs a hand-mirror from the side-table, holds it up and stares in it. He puts the mirror back down, picks up the laptop, rises and heads for the hallway.

He enters the bathroom, noticing as usual its corners with their strange shadows, which he has discovered to be bizarrely unbanishable by any wattage of available light-bulb.

He positions the laptop's hologram and his own head in front of the wall-mirror, such that the hologram's head appears, in his current sphere of vision, to be only somewhat smaller than his own.

Each of the two faces is spotlit bright against the background of the dim room. Each of these is staring at the other in the mirror.

The effect is gigantically disconcerting.

Silence reigns, while the sole movement to be seen is that of Jaymi's own eyes, flicking minutely from left to right, from right to left, scouring the two twins hard, seeking any differences…

However, whether zooming in to each face in turn or panning between them, he has to conclude he can find no difference.

*

Despite these concerns, his addiction to seeing his own ubiquitous image keeps increasing, obligingly fanned by Champagne Marc, whose delight in his role as Jaymi's best friend and mentor is unending. By now, the pair of them work only part-time at the agency, being less hands-on managers then abstract, lucrative figureheads. Of course, this role involves a great due diligence of necessary socialising. So it is, a few evenings later, that they find themselves sitting in a glitzy hotel bar.

In an ornate and multiply-mirrored alcove of the bar, a group of six or seven Beautiful People surround Jaymi, female and male, chatting and laughing, relaxed but high-octane. Marc is there, with an attractive girl sitting on his knee. With the exception of Jaymi's bodyguard—an intimidating figure named just "The Bodyguard", who goes wherever Jaymi goes, hovering in the background with a face of implacable stone—all of the assembled are engaged in a kind of guessing game, evidently trying to guess the identity of someone whom Jaymi is thinking of.

"OK," says one Beautiful Person: "if this person you're thinking of were a tree, what kind of tree would they be?"

Jaymi thinks a moment. "They'd be a flowering pine on a mountain slope, silhouetted on an orange winter sky," he replies.

This goes down pretty well, piquing an appreciative curiosity.

"All right," says a second Beautiful Person, "if this person were an animal, what kind of animal would they be?"

"A black lynx with yellow eyes, pointy ears and latent leukaemia."

Mild shock, feigned indifference and further conferring.

"I think I know who it is!" says somebody. "No, hold on. First let me ask one more question: what kind of weather would this person be?"

"Oh, I'd say a sunny spring morning at Chernobyl," says Jaymi.

"Creepy but cool! Who the hell *is* this one? Anybody?"

"Er, does it have to be a famous person he's thinking of?"

"*Yes*, Norbert—for the third time. OK, Jaymi: what would this person be, as a sexual disease?"

"General Paralysis of the Insane."

"For pity's sake, Jaymi," says Marc. "I guessed this one, two or three questions ago!"

"Oh shut up, Marc, and have another drink," says Jaymi. "Alright, I'll give you all a clue: he's all around you right now."

"I know," says another Beautiful Person. "It's God!"

The others all groan and raise their eyes to the ceiling: "No, I don't *think* so—hello!—*duh!*"

During this remonstration, Jaymi's eyes look for several seconds at his own reflected image in the scintillations of an array of mirrored walls, mirrored columns and framed mirrors all around him. He turns to the last speaker. "You were right, funnily enough. It is God."

"See?" the Beautiful Person addresses the others. "*See?*… Thank you! Thank you." The game dissipates and general conversation bubbles up instead.

Jaymi turns to Marc, saying, "Of course I was pretending, just now. You were correct, really."

"I know I was," chuckles Marc. "I know you far too well! By the way, shall you be coming into the office tomorrow?"

"I doubt it. Maybe nearer the end of the week I'll pop in, say hallo and get a few things done. You?"

"We'll see. I seem to make it in there only a couple of days a week now, I confess. There always seems to be something else to do instead. Very decent of me to carry on paying myself, all in all!"

"They'd all be dead meat without us, and they know it," says Jaymi. "Mainframe needs us more than we need it: I'm an invaluable figurehead for them, and you're…"

"I am your poodle, dear boy, and quite right too!" He pats the thigh of the girl sitting on his knee, who is oblivious to him as she chats with the others. Unheard by this chattering mob, and much in his cups, Marc announces to the world in general: "Yes, old Champagne Marc's found his niche at last: as a figurehead's poodle! Oh, it's dirty work, but someone has to do it…"

There is a flash as someone outside the group snaps a photo of Jaymi. The Bodyguard steps towards the snapper, but in glancing at Jaymi he catches a discreet signal that there's no need to intervene on this occasion, so he melts back into the background.

*

Jaymi is spotlit before the immaculate wall-mirror in his dim bathroom, attired as sleekly as ever, eyes stark and cold, staring dead-still in dead silence.

With his right hand he raises into view a long, red-handled carving-knife, brings it to a gradual halt pointing up at his face, and holds it there a long time.

The explosive and protracted convulsion of deafening violence in which he stabs and stabs his face—including numerous horrific images of a growing bloodbath of facial injury and then ever-larger chunks of his face cut away until only a neck-stump is left—is brutally terminated and revealed as a fantasy, leaving him still intact, beautiful and spotlit in silence as before.

He raises the carving-knife again, presses its point by degrees into his throat, presses more and twists … drawing one drop of blood, with three spotlights reflected like pinpricks on its surface.

He keeps the knife-point there, uncomfortably long.

His stark cold stare softens into an innocent little ghost of a smile, and for the first time in the scene he blinks.

*

Marc and Jaymi are strolling on the deserted residential river-front in Rotherhithe, sometimes stopping to lean against the railing or parapet and gaze out on the grand width of the Thames. Across the river, the skyscrapers on the Isle of Dogs shine enormous in the night sky. "I love that metal-shine of lights and angles," says Jaymi. "All the more since I became the hologram. Its inorganic cleanness is such a cool and liberating draught, after too many people! It might be overstating it to say I feel more alienated from people than I did before, but I am more tired of their chatter. So much social exchange is just so much froth, signifying so exhaustingly little."

The Bodyguard is tailing them at a distance, out of earshot. Marc lights a fat cigar, puffs it into life and tends it lovingly while they stroll. "Stop me if you know this," he says, "but you're serving as an antidote, you know. An antidote we want and need, to counteract the hideous triteness and ugliness of spirit and intellect that most people have been lazy and stupid enough to let themselves be taken over by. Everywhere we hear dull, trivial, repetitive, predictable and pathologically boring conversations and opinions, without style or verve or colours or joy or any creative layers of irony or affection—just that clunky, heavy, gawky cluelessness of utterance and thought that seems to have become so ubiquitous. We hear soggy sentiment in place of humanity; we hear a ghastly wearisome cheeriness in place of wit; and in religions we see so many terrified and thick-headed moralities, in place of just an intelligent sense of ethics or a judicious application of compassion. You're probably too generous to see this, dear boy, but the vast majority of people around you are walking excrement, I'm afraid. Unprocessed sewage on two legs. That laziness and stupidity of theirs is dragging us all down, as a species, alas. I fear they are the individual failures, within the process of evolution that they hold back—the non-evolutionary deadweight, the dull dreary pedestal onto which those precious few forward-movers are poised to step up, such as yourself and Rik, who are destined to evolve the human race further and remind us why evolution itself began."

"Remind me why it did begin?" asks Jaymi. "It slips my memory."

"First, it was so that the stuff we're composed of would refine itself, through the rising species—up to us, so far. Now secondly, it's for us to focus and refine our consciousness upwards, by getting rid of all that deadweight, so that we can fashion an intelligent collective imprint on time and space, we hope. Thirdly, in future, it'll be for us to refine the nature and shape of the universe itself … but let's not get ahead of ourselves here! Just for now, let's return to earth with a bump, right here by this venerable old river that I love, and look afresh at human society. What do we see? Well, straightaway we see the self-justifying beauty and power of your level of visibility everywhere, and its status as genuine contemporary Divinity."

"Yet here I find myself incarnated," muses Jaymi. "So bizarre, this incarnation business … and so crude and analogue, don't you think? There are wonders within physical embodiment, true, but it was surely a dysfunctional avenue, all in all. Despite its pleasures, for me it has always involved a faint undercurrent of existential nausea and entrapment. Not that those things are devoid of their own love and poison, mind you, like the delicious tone of a cracked bell ringing. Still, let's hope for a more intelligent design choice in future."

"Well," says Marc, "if being flesh and blood has been so delightfully flawed, then I'm glad I've been of service in easing your transition into hologram form."

There are shouts of Jaymi's name across the street, some argument and a brief scuffle, as The Bodyguard frightens off a group of kids who have recognised him and would have come interfering.

"But is that *it*? Just visibility?" continues Marc. "What's missing there? I'll tell you what's missing: actual power for you. Real, *practical* power—an omnipotence to match your omnivisibility—an efficacy wherewith to live up to your ubiquity!"

Jaymi smiles, then agrees, with a quiet anger, "That is so true. All my apparent 'power' is such an illusion, because I'm just the program's skin. I can't actually access what my hologram accesses. If only *I* could see what *it* sees, before its findings get filtered. Then I would have such opportunities, such power over other people, such a destiny as no one's ever had before. I could speed evolution along a bit. That would be a sight to see! In fact, it would be a crime if it didn't happen. Frankly, it's a joke that it hasn't happened already. A bad joke." His eyes are sharp as skewers across the river, and then they grow calmer and colder. "OK. May this intention click quietly into place in me now. I will wipe the smile off that bad joke. I will gain access to what my own hologram can see…"

Strolling with his hands together behind his back and his lips compressed in thought, Marc glances across at him and opines with irrefutable gravitas, "It's the *least* you deserve…" The towers shine mutely on, for another long beat, then he adds, "You'll break yourself yet."

*

Three days later at lunchtime, Jaymi's car draws up outside the Ivy restaurant in Covent Garden. Jaymi and Rik emerge from the rear doors and the car drives off. Greeting the doorman, they enter the restaurant, tailed by The Bodyguard.

"Well, Rik, my friend," says Jaymi. "What a journey it's been already, since our first few lunches at good old Bar Chocolate!"

"Yes, just over two years, I think? It was shortly before you came over to Mainframe, wasn't it? And you're still with us. Though we don't see so much of you in the office these days. What have you been up to?"

"Running around. Parties here and there. You know the shallow stuff I get up to!… Oh, while I think of it, I remember something I've been meaning to ask you, just from a kind of touristic curiosity, I suppose: where exactly is HOST run from? It's reproducing my image everywhere, but I have no idea where it's reproducing it from. Strange that I've never thought to ask."

Rik smiles. "It is interesting, that we never stop to wonder where it actually lives. Well, HOST runs on racks of servers in anonymous buildings, in industrial parks or obscure suburbs. That's all way out of my hands. I'd probably be able to find out where most of those servers are, but I'm not so sure that even I would be allowed into those facilities, without a lot of special arrangements."

"How mediated everything is! Still, I guess you still have some kind of original version of the program, just for yourself?"

"Yes, I do. I keep the prototype of it on my home system—I mean in the form I first perfected it, *before* it was then tweaked and emasculated in order to be put out into the world. My prototype isn't connected to the Internet, though. For online access, I use the tweaked public version, just as everyone else does."

"What a gift you gave the world! I so admire you."

Irony, regret and affection flicker through Rik's eyes. "Yeah, well… Anyway, it's also made me rich, thanks to Marc. Though I'm not sure the money will ever quite feel natural."

A pause. Then Jaymi says, "Rik, I have an outrageous request. Well, it's not really that outrageous. You know what would make me happy? It would be if I too could have an exact copy of that original magical prototype, just to keep for myself, as you keep it for yourself. I mean, from before all the filters in the public version, before its 'emasculation', as you put it: just the venerable original and best, for old time's sake, to remind us of our Bar Chocolate days of old! A kind of museum exhibit, if you like. That would mean so much to me. And it would bring us together, because only you and I would have it."

Rik looks pleased, then frowns. "Well, er, I don't know about this…"

*

Three evenings later, Rik sits back in Jaymi's study chair and contemplates Jaymi's laptop with pride. "There. A perfect copy of the prototype HOST now resides on your desk here. It's the only one in existence, aside from the one in my house and my off-site back-ups. This one lives behind special firewalls, but it is the real thing; it's functional. You can activate a normal-looking hologram in the familiar way, like so"—he strikes a key, and the familiar mini-Jaymi flickers up beside the keyboard. "You just won't be able to get up to any special mischief with it, as I know your programming knowledge is, er—"

"Yes, zero!" says Jaymi. "Thank you, Rik. This is such a special thing for me to have. I'm so grateful. I shall treasure this little hologram here…"

*

A small door opens beside a Mainframe commercial shoot the following afternoon at Three Mills, Bow, and Marc and Rik slip into the studio. Not having expected a royal visit from Marc today, a couple of production assistants stand up in surprise, but with an avuncular gesture Marc bids them sit. Remaining in the shadows, he draws Rik's attention to Angel, who is standing on set, centre-stage beneath the lights. "She's the one I'm talking about," Marc whispers. "I don't believe you've met her." Rik peers across the set at Angel, who is confronting the commercial's director, Ray. Her body language emanates regal complaint and an elegant sense of entitlement.

"You're not the easiest to work with," Ray is telling her.

"On the contrary, I'm impeccably professional."

"OK, I won't say 'not the easiest'. I'll just say 'very difficult'."

Marc grins in genial approval. "Good, good," he whispers to Rik. "All serene on set, I'm glad to see!"

Rik stares at him. "I've only seen one moment of her, so far," he says, "but already I'm quite exhausted. I may even need to lie down and take a tablet. Can't we all just get *along*?"

"Certainly not," chuckles Marc. "No matter, she keeps us all on our toes—but the important thing is, she has *it*! You can see that, I hope?" Angel and Ray wander further away offstage, so their continuing debate falls out of earshot. Marc turns squarely to Rik, with a gleam in his eye. "So. Are you on for the challenge, old boy?"

"Does it have to be her?"

Marc nods. "It has to be her. She's our female Jaymi. Trust me, Rik, I've got a nose for these things."

"OK, OK," Rik sighs. "I'll do a film-shoot and program her in. But I'll need a bodyguard."

Marc pats him on the back. "You've got Evelyn for that. So, just send me the finished footage, before you program her in, yes?" He checks his watch. "All right, I must head for the hills."

*

On the sofa in the main space of his apartment throughout the following morning, as may be surmised from his laptop screen, Jaymi is giving himself a serious crash-course in the general principles of programming and the basics of how Rik's HOST program works. From time to time he shakes his head in wonder, but in general seems grimly satisfied with his progress.

Around lunchtime, the pages he is poring over become more business-oriented, touching in particular upon top-flight computer-hacking and industrial espionage.

By mid-afternoon his research has started to be peppered with a few quiet, clipped, focused phone calls, from which only tantalising phrases may be half-heard, none of them readily understandable or memorable to any non-specialist, but evoking a world of firewalls, of protocols, of the Dark Web. Then these phrases start transitioning into less specialist ones: "Money no object ... total confidentiality ... cash up front ... all traces destroyed ... same amount on completion ... maybe more in future ... tomorrow."

At last he gets up and wanders onto his balcony in the Ontario Tower's slanting top, where he scans the multi-coloured bed of lights, from the grand sweep of the Docklands down the Thames to the east, as if the water and the cityscape were flickers on a circuit-board.

*

In a deserted corner of Thames Barrier Park at dusk next day, Jaymi sits in conversation with a computer hacker he has been communicating with online. The Bodyguard looms not far away, out of earshot. Seen from some way off, the hacker and Jaymi are almost immobile, with just one or the other's lips moving inaudibly. Jaymi takes his dark glasses off, so as to look her in the eyes more sharply, and he becomes audible: "Please let me know if anything I say is unclear. The requirement is to remove the special firewalls that have been set up to enclose this prototype hologram, so we can get it back to doing what it was designed to do—which is to access pretty much all online files including private ones, breaching whatever other firewalls it encounters out there. As you know, unlike all public copies of HOST, this prototype never had any restrictions or filters built into it, so it should be able to reach most content anywhere."

"Understood. I'll do my best, which is the best you'll find. But just to manage expectations, I should say that once we've extricated it from its own firewalls, then we're in uncharted territory. What little information there is about the original unfiltered HOST program does suggest it'll cut through most other firewalls and therefore access most private files online, yes. But what I'll be achieving here will be in the context of the Internet as it stands: I can't promise it'll cut through all future firewalls."

"What level of future-proofing is feasible?"

"I'd be happy to discuss my remaining available on a retainer basis, to tackle whatever blocks your prototype may encounter in future."

"D'you think you would be able to tackle them remotely, without visiting me in person?"

She considers this. "Yes, I believe I would."

Jaymi looks at her, as if at a moth on a pin, and smiles. "Excellent. We can certainly discuss the retainer basis you mention, to see if that'll work for us. In general that sounds very positive, thank you."

*

Two days later in the morning, Jaymi's tinted-windowed car approaches the Ontario Tower's underground car-park entrance. The gate opens, the car draws up in Jaymi's parking bay, and the hacker and Jaymi's chauffeur get out and walk into the empty waiting lift, whose doors close after them.

Throughout the day, other unidentified vehicles and individuals come and go through the car-park, seen in fast motion.

Late in the evening, the hacker and Jaymi's chauffeur emerge from the lift, walk to the car, get into it and pull out of his parking bay. The gate opens, then closes again as the car emerges from under the Ontario Tower and drives off.

Through such unusual circumstances does it come to pass that Jaymi Peek becomes equipped with a file-searching engine empowered to cut through firewalls globally.

*

Jaymi stands alone in the yellow-white light on his balcony, overlooking the Thames. With close-creeping insistence, behind his face, coil the echoes of Marc's effusions spoken to him in the club or over there across the river on the Rotherhithe waterfront, or murmured from nearby on the Soho soundstage. These echoes gain in volume, speed and intensity, to an overwhelming crescendo, from Marc's having repeated them like spells throughout Jaymi's rise, easing up their heat a little higher every time he spoke them, then mercilessly a little higher still: *"Your appearance, as the skin of HOST, is about to become not merely recognisable, as other faces on the Web are, but in many ways the face of the Web itself... Your face will become the face of computing—adviser, mentor, companion, friend and alter ego for an entire generation... To play a part in shaping humankind's next leap in digital evolution—and to embody the accompanying leap in the possibilities of fame too... Accept it with the grace it deserves—and step up onto the stage that's about to open itself to you here!... Your presence is somewhat like a mirror, so when they look at you, then I'm afraid they cannot but see their own selves mixed in with you... They are poised to see your image multiplied more than anybody else's image ever has been, throughout the ages... You should hold aloft and savour the sublime beauty and power of the awesome visibility that you'll soon establish for yourself through that little lens, when that camera rolls... What bleeds out through the air from your eyes, just from their being open, is light and intelligence, sweetness and charm and open thinking. In short, the highest evolution, quite simply... Straightaway we see the self-justifying beauty and power of your level of visibility everywhere, and its status as genuine contemporary Divinity..."*

IV FIRST CRUELTY OF ADDICTION

Late next morning, Jaymi reclines on his sofa. The hologram beside his laptop is a blur as it throws onto the screen a series of pages from around the world, of an evidently private nature, in response to his spoken navigation and search commands.

Prominent among these search results are images of animals savaging one another, war, violence, rape, medical operations, military installations and sinister-looking building plans, with pulses of light and a chaos of noise including the sounds of pain and suffering, the bleep of racing heart monitors, the wail of wartime sirens and the ticking of financial markets all across the globe.

Amid this onslaught, somewhere down the rabbit-hole of one fascinating search through a myriad private files, Jaymi is surprised to see his screen display the title-page of a novel, still in typescript form, called *Alaia's novel (to be titled)*, with the breathless sub-title "Monument to one woman's love for Jaymi Peek".

He starts forward, curious. It is a simple Word file, last modified a few days ago. The only other information this title-page gives him is the author's name, Alaia Danielle, and her home address, which is some obscure street in E16. He proceeds to the first page, starts reading at high speed and becomes hooked, sucked in by the book's strange intensity and febrility, as well as by its focus on himself. His screen soon displays page 3, page 10, page 30, 60, 120, all sense of time dropping away ... until several hours later he reaches the very last words of the whole novel: "...glinting against the deepening ultramarine of the eastern sky with a hard, cold beauty."

Lightning flashes in him and he snaps back into the leather sofa as if electrocuted—his mind churning hard and his eyes shining out a thousand metres through the wall ahead.

This strangest of novels features a Manhattan-based company called the General Network, but it is obvious to Jaymi, from many details, that this company is actually based on the Mainframe Corporation here in London. It must have been in order to avoid getting sued for libel that Alaia renamed and relocated Mainframe in this way. However, these gestures are unconvincing, to say the least, because no fewer than six of the novel's lead characters bear the full names of real-life people living here in London, who are all now part of Jaymi's life. Nor is it just a matter of names alone: these six real-life Londoners are clearly the models for Alaia's characterisations, because the fictional half-dozen's personalities and roles quite strikingly echo the personalities and roles of their real-world counterparts.

Of particular interest to Jaymi, the narrator of this yet-to-be-titled novel is a character called Jaymi Peek—an iconic face on camera, who possesses special gifts of hypnotic and clairvoyant sight. Admittedly, this by itself doesn't prove anything unusual has occurred in the writing of the novel, because the name and career of the real Jaymi sitting here are already public property. Nor would any unusual knowledge or activity have been required to create the next of these real-life characters, a singer who falls in love with Jaymi—because this singer has simply been graced with the author's own name, Alaia Danielle. However, from here onwards it becomes harder to deny that the author has employed an unusual degree of real-world character-modelling, which must have required quite some research, because the novel contains four further characters based on real-world individuals who are not such public property as Jaymi is: first there is a Marc Albright, the General Network's CEO, who is responsible for putting Jaymi onto screens worldwide; secondly there is a Rik Chambers, a General Network broadcasting engineer who makes secret recordings of all the private material that the fictional Jaymi has thieved from other people's imaginations; thirdly there is an Evelyn Carmello, a General Network employee who chauffeurs Jaymi and Alaia and who transports all this imaginative material thieved by Jaymi; and finally there is an Angel Deon, who is no less a diva than the real-life actress Angel Deon, but whom the novelist Alaia has characterised as a male-to-female transsexual.

How bizarre! Is this in fact a published novel? he wonders. A swift search online informs him it is not. It certainly seems to be finished; but perhaps the writer Alaia is intending to change those six character names, just as she did with the company name, before the novel goes out to publishing houses. Like Mainframe in real life, the General Network in her story effects a global roll-out of Jaymi's face, but it also exploits him. Threatened with a heavy-handed cancellation of the legitimate creative broadcasts into which he's put so much work and inspiration, her fictional Jaymi is blackmailed into spying into the imaginations of unsuspecting members of the public—their interests, personalities and intimate memories, all in minutely digitised accuracy, all thievable, reproducible and manipulable, for crassly commercial uses by the General Network.

Jaymi stares out over the Thames, trying to get his head around all this. At the centre of the story is an intense creative collaboration between the narrator Jaymi and the character called Alaia—the novelist's own name in real life, of course. There's a give-away, for a start. This is clearly a kind of fantasy relationship, for the writer Alaia. What else could it be? And another thing is evident: the fact that the novel's narrator Jaymi feels nothing more than friendship for the character Alaia throughout most of the novel, not realising his singing collaborator is in love with him, suggests that the *writer*

Alaia knows she herself stands no chance of meeting the inaccessible real-life Jaymi Peek, let alone romancing him…

Destinies, however, can just occasionally be changed by others' actions. And this, as it happens, will be just such an occasion; for Jaymi now takes out his phone and hits a speed-dial number.

"Hallo Jaymi," says Marc.

"Hi. Listen, I've just read the most amazing novel about me online, by a mysterious writer called Alaia Danielle. It's so intense and other-worldly—and what an imagination! It's flawed genius, Marc. She must be bit damaged, or she couldn't have written it. But talk about sensitivity and … well, I can only call it *nobility*. It includes this young woman named Alaia, who's in love with me but I don't realise it—"

"Ah, no wonder you enjoyed it, then."

"Oh, don't be a such cynical old bag, Marc. This book is heartfelt in the extreme. The novelist has written 'eternal monument to one woman's love for Jaymi Peek' on the title-page: how beautiful is that? It's about a mind-blowing creative collaboration between Alaia who's a singer, and my character Jaymi who's a kind of performer. In the novel, Jaymi acts as this stunningly mesmerising pair of eyes on television. It must be some kind of ideal fantasy collaboration for the author, of course, who shares the same name as her heroine. Oh, and Jaymi works for a company that's clearly based on Mainframe, by the way; but in her novel she's rechristened it as the General Network and relocated it to New York City."

There is a disapproving grunt down the phone.

"And you may not like the next bit either. The General Network puts Jaymi's face out there, big-time, but it also exploits him ruthlessly. It blackmails him into spying on the imaginations of a sample of its customers—their interests, their personalities, their whole imaginations, all copied in minute, digital accuracy, stolen for the company's market research."

"I think I'd like to take a look at this book, if you don't mind. Is it published?"

"Not yet. I also suspect she's modelled the General Network's snooping on Mainframe's own GMRI division in particular."

"What on earth makes you think so?"

"Let's just say that she must have done an impressive bit of online 'due diligence' into my colleagues, because there are four more characters who are unmistakable echoes of you, Rik, Evelyn and Angel."

"I must read this novel forthwith."

*

On his balcony ten minutes later, Jaymi dials the phone number on the title-page of the novel, and stares out over the evening river.

"Hallo?" says a voice on the line.

"Is this Alaia Danielle?"

"Who's calling?"

"This is Jaymi Peek," he says, his face glowing bright.

"…Right. Who is this, please?"

"Alaia, this is Jaymi."

"Don't do this."

"OK, I can prove it to you. Would you like to meet, maybe later this evening?"

"If you were Jaymi Peek, why would you want to meet me and how would you know my number?"

"I got your number from the cover of your novel, and I'd like to meet you because I've read it."

There is a silence, for several seconds. "How did you access my private file online?"

"Because there was a security breach—albeit a breach that I'm very glad to say had a happy ending. For about half an hour last Friday evening, a pirate site succeeded in accessing the files of several hundred people whose ISPs use the datacentre by the Blackwall Tunnel entrance in Poplar. This access was detected and stopped before any pirated distribution could occur, so don't worry, your intellectual property remained secure. Through my Web-guide work with Mainframe, though, I'm happy to say I have the privilege of helping to combat this kind of piracy, from time to time; hence the details of this breach became known to me. The main thing is the safety of your files, which is assured. But the most important file to have been safeguarded, in my respectful estimation, is the .docx file called *Alaia's novel (to be titled)*. Because to me, Alaia, it's an utter classic that simply cannot be allowed to have its safety jeopardised in this way, ever again. It's just, I mean—"

"And this is Jaymi Peek?"

"Yes."

"You're Jaymi?"

"Yes, so—"

"You, personally, are Jaymi? *You* are?"

"Yes, Alaia! I am Jaymi!"

"You mentioned we could meet?"

"Yes."

"Er, could we meet, maybe … now?"

"Well, sure. Yes, we can meet now. I mean, I want to. Where are you?"

"Silvertown. Docklands."

"Why don't I drive over to you? I can pick you up outside your nearest station. What's your nearest station?"

"Royal Victoria station, on the DLR."

"All right, outside Royal Victoria DLR station, tonight at eight. It'll be a black car."

"When you wind that window down, I'll be looking very hard at you. And if you're just a Jaymi look-alike, then I'll know it straightaway, however good you are—and I'll be out of there, I swear it."

"OK, that's a deal. I'll see you at eight, Alaia."

*

Outside Royal Victoria station, Alaia is aware of every approaching car. One or two stop outside the station, but are not black. A black car then approaches, indicates it will be stopping and draws to a stately halt in front of her. Its windows are tinted (of course they are!), she prepares herself for the grand moment, the car door eases open—and an enormous ginger-haired woman gets out.

Alaia sits back down. Within a minute, however, another black car approaches. She braces herself again. The car slows down, slows—and drives straight past. Peering after it, she is startled when a third black car pulls up beside her without warning and coasts to a stop, with its tinted rear window directly beneath her, reflecting her watchful face on its opaque sheen.

She takes a step back.

After a long, full second, the window winds slowly down…

And up looks Jaymi at her, clear as a bell.

He takes her in, fascinated. Her long straightened hair is pulled back from a smooth black face that he thinks of straightaway as "aerodynamic", and is held in a small band at the back, from which it falls to her shoulders; and her expression is sleek and sharp, with something in the poise of the eyes that promises not to suffer jerks gladly.

*

Soon afterwards, as if in a dream, she finds herself sitting in the dusk at the deserted west end of Royal Victoria Dock. With Jaymi Peek.

The dock's spectacular perspective stretches before them, its massive derricks receding, doubled in the water. "Isn't this beautiful?" he murmurs, as calmly as if they've known each other half their lives.

"…Yes! I love how those coloured lights are reflected, right down there at the far end, by the airport."

"If you unfocus your eyes and picture it right," he says, "you can perceive those reflections running down vertically, down the walls of a great jewelled chasm, to the depths of the earth…"

Now she is gazing at him, her attraction and infatuation clear and swelling beyond her control, despite her earlier caution and the sharpness he saw in her. He smiles, and she smiles back, helpless. He sees he is powerless in the face of her need to be against him physically, as she has dreamed about, which pulls at him like electricity. Uncertain, he gives in to it, by touching her hand, and in a single movement she falls in and clings to him with a sweet hunger. He can only enclose her in his arms, and he does so. He stares along the docks, his eyes clear but in muted shock. He starts stroking the back of her head with his fingers, because it's the easiest thing to do. She moans gently; hearing which, he decelerates and ceases his stroking. They remain so, quiet and still.

"This is so strange," he murmurs. She emits an indistinct assent, her face resting against his chest. "So strange… What does it mean?"

*

In the main space of Jaymi's penthouse early the following afternoon, she and he sprawl on the sofa in the sunlight, half-dressed, conversationally exploring each other, open and relaxed. "Where did you grow up?" he asks.

"In glamorous Tooting. No special memories. I spent most of my childhood waiting for the children around me to grow up and take things as seriously as me. They never did."

"And isn't it great to know they never will?"

"I refuse to believe that. D'you believe that?"

He nods. They laugh. "Do you enjoy working at the British Library?" he asks.

"Yeah, it's civilised enough, behind that reference desk. There are boring politics, like anywhere else, but I can't complain. I spend most of the time with my head in the clouds. Whenever I go there to do my own writing, rather than a shift of work, I don't go anywhere near those Humanities rooms. And that's not just to avoid work colleagues, it's because I want to be surrounded by words and symbols that are nothing like what I'm writing. So I usually go to Science Floor 3, where no other arty types go."

"Is that a relief?"

"You bet! I sit there with no literature in sight." Her eyes widen with pleasure as she continues, "Instead, there are just thousands of hard-core scientific journals, where each different journal title has been collected and bound into a long set of uniform hard-cover volumes, with each volume being the same bright random colour, and all those spines identical except for the thickness of them and the number printed on each."

"You are so eloquent."

"Charmed, I'm sure. But the point is that in the middle of writing the novel, I often get up and reach down some volume of cosmology or nuclear physics ... and I feel such a sense of peace and wonder, as I leaf through those pages dotted with exotic equations. Of course I can't understand them, but for me those pages full of elegantly-typeset symbols spill out a cool, dry beauty, of a quite paralysing perfection! Honestly, I just stand there bathing in it. I feel so cleansed and elevated by the surface of those symbols—probably a lot more than I would if I understood them."

"That is so beautiful," says Jaymi. "I love it…"

"I think my favourite journal title is the *International Journal of Bifurcation and Chaos*. Isn't that just the best? I'm also partial to

Fuzzy Sets and Systems… But I want to hear more about you," she says, getting more horizontal in the sunlight beside him. "Tell me things you love, or things you hate."

"Well, I guess I have carelessly high ideals—beauty, elegance, love and so on. I know they're often impractical, but that's the point of ideals, isn't it? So much everyday stuff, though, I hate. The sight of anyone chewing gum is revolting: for me, that person is sacked for life, right there. Am I allowed to say that?" She nods with vigour. "By the way, do you chew gum?" She nods again. "*No, you don't!*… Hm, what else? I know: I loathe the flaccid lazy unthinking conventionality in so many people's choices of ideas, interests and talk. That applies to a lot of otherwise intelligent people, I'm sorry to say. And part of me wants to throw up, if I happen to hear a blast of inane chat on the radio or see even a moment of a crappy TV game show, or some such. But let's see, I should come up with something I love, probably! OK: I adore, with a passion, the lights of distant cities at night or at dusk… I love the strength and elegance of those old-fashioned metal railings in London squares, painted black with a point on top, from the spear-points of old. And as far as we can inspect them from here, I worship the beauty of planets, almost more than anything else."

The sun is falling on them at a different angle through the same window, by the time she says, curled up against him with her eyes closed: "For so long, I wanted to admire somebody, somewhere, who didn't disappoint me somehow. Then when you flickered up out of nowhere, as the hologram, then you didn't disappoint me, and you didn't let go. It didn't matter that the hologram was used by everyone. My connection with it was special: I called you Prince Charming."

He kisses her forehead, his gaze lost in the distance.

*

A few evenings later, the two of them are once more sprawling on the sofa, this time watching his home-cinema-sized TV screen. It's a juicy scene from Zulawski's *Possession*, as confirmed by the packaging of the DVD case beside them.

Forty-five minutes later, they are having sex on the sofa, with both the DVD case and the insert booklet for *Possession* lying open nearby.

*

The following afternoon on Jaymi's balcony, he and Alaia are again curled up on a seat together.

"You know, for your novel…" he begins.

"Mm-hm?"

"You must have done a certain amount of research about the people you based characters on. I mean the Mainframe crowd, Marc and Rik and Evelyn and Angel. Where did you look, to find out what you did?"

"It's not hard to find stuff out online these days, though I'm sure you're too honourable to snoop on people. Anyway," she laughs, "you forget where I work: we have a world-class business collection at the British Library, you know. Plus, I have *special evil access to secret things!*"

"Ooh, that sounds useful! I love your version of Evelyn Carmello."

"From everything I found out about the real Evelyn, I liked her. That's why I wrote her like that. I wish I found life as easy as she seems to."

"I wonder whether she really does. Still, it's a lovely portrait. But then, your Angel Deon: I mean, so beautiful and what a fighter, but—wow! I don't think you like the real-life Angel very much, am I right?"

"I made Angel vindictive and neurotic and dark like he is, out of jealousy, I think. Jealousy that the real Angel Deon was meeting you through Mainframe, while everything I found out about her tells me she's obviously way too shallow and self-obsessed to appreciate that access."

"Er, no comment!" He kisses her. "But Alaia my love, listen to me now: it needs to be published, with no further delay. I can think of at least a couple of major imprints where I could get it released. This thing just needs to get out there—we can't have it sitting around any longer."

"I was about to jump into all that, when we met. I'd only just finished writing it, pretty much, so I hadn't started any business stuff. But the thing is, since we met, I've realised the story's not quite finished, after all. I need to add a few more pages onto the end."

"Really? To me, that last mini-chapter 120 feels quite finished, with the pair of them approaching Manhattan in the van."

"No, I see now that it needs just a little more after that. You'll see too."

"All right then, but hurry up with it. And don't spoil what you've already written. It's all so fine and true. I mean, that beautiful Alaia character: the way she falls in love with me, through the images of me everywhere! So heartfelt. What do you want to add?"

"All I'll say about it right now is that for most of the book, the Jaymi character feels only friendship for Alaia, without even realising she's in love with him. That's because when I wrote it I thought I stood no chance of even meeting you, let alone being with you… But now I *am* with you, after all! Divine inspiration *did* come: the novel delivered you to me, in a way I could never have expected. Don't you understand, this turned out to be the very *function* of the novel!" Her eyes go soft, she hugs him and draws him into a passionate kiss.

Unseen by her, Jaymi frowns during the kiss: that last statement sounded deeply wrong… He pulls away from her mouth and looks into her eyes; but before he can speak, her lips are upon his again, her tongue on his, and he quite forgets what he was going to say.

"I'll finish it soon and show you," she promises afterwards.

"OK. Please do."

"I know, let's go for a walk by the river!"

He shakes his head. "I'm sorry, we can't. We have to remain in secret, indoors or anywhere else we fix carefully, because if we're seen together, then the media will be all over us. They'll follow you to your home and wait outside your building, they'll thrust microphones at you and take pictures, the public will start recognising you and bothering you all the time. And we can't have any of that, because we can't have the inspirational passion and idolatry of your lonely writing process interrupted or delayed at all. Understand me? You need to sit down in peace and quiet at your place, and get on with it."

She looks rueful.

Softening, he kisses her. "So you'll just have to have me in private, instead. Can you cope with that?"

She kisses him again and agrees.

*

Later in the evening, in that spookiest of bathrooms, the laptop's hologram and Jaymi's head have again been positioned together in front of the mirror.

Again they are both spotlit, stark against the backdrop of the room's shadowy corners, one of the two identical-twin heads somewhat smaller than the other, staring at themselves or at each other...

Again, the effect is hugely disconcerting.

Jaymi's eyes make minute flicks from side to side, scouring the twin faces hard, for any differences. As before, however, whether he zooms in to each face or pans between the pair, he can discover no difference, as yet.

*

On the back seat of his limousine a couple of weeks later, Jaymi and Marc lounge back in comfort as they speed through town to somewhere. Jaymi calls a number on his mobile. "Alaia, my petal. How was today?... Did you finish?... Finish the novel, what else would I mean?... No? But you were going to finish it today. You said you had to write just a couple more of those new pages..." Marc guffaws. "Sorry, my sweet?... Oh, that was just Marc, don't listen to him." Marc guffaws again. "That was also Marc. Now listen to me. You have to finish it by tomorrow, you're on the home straight... Because it's your sacred duty. I'm not sure you quite understand this. Why are you laughing? I'm serious... I am serious... Your art is a sacred duty, I mean it... Marc and I are off to a party... No you can't come along, you know very well why... Yes?... OK, good. Good! So, do I have a solemn promise you'll have it finished and emailed to me by 5 p.m. tomorrow? 5 p.m. at the very latest, yes? Otherwise I shall never see you again... OK, kiss kiss." He rings off. Marc chuckles. "You may laugh," says Jaymi, "but this time I'm sure she'll finish it by the deadline. I could hear it in her voice. About time, too. Well then, you and Rik must cancel anything else you may already have planned for tomorrow night, because a modern classic will just have landed in my inbox. So if you'd both care to come to my place at five, for early cocktails, then the three of us can peruse it at our professional leisure, as you requested. Then we can go out somewhere for a slap-up dinner."

"I should be delighted to attend!"

Jaymi hits a number on his mobile. "Hallo Rik. What are you doing tomorrow night? Whatever it is, cancel it."

*

At the appointed hour, Jaymi shows Rik and Marc into his apartment. "Alaia was as good as her word," he says. "She's just emailed the novel with ten brand-new mini-chapters added at the end, and we have three copies coming out of the printer at high speed, right now. I'm confident you'll agree: for passion, beauty and originality, it's an absolute winner."

"You've read nearly all of it already, Jaymi. Shall you read it all again, along with Marc and me?"

"I shall indeed, with pleasure. I'm sure we'll all get through it with comparable speed, give or take a few pages. Now gentlemen, name your cocktails?"

"A dry gibson for me," says Marc. Then with a wink at Jaymi, "Rik—what are you having?"

"Oh, Jeez," says Rik, heavily. "I'm so hopeless with cocktails, I *never* know what they are…"

"Ah, what a bracing tonic your heavy hopelessness over cocktails always is! The cocktail hour wouldn't be the same without it. Have a tom collins, old boy. Jaymi, a tom collins for Rik, if you please. —By George, I think the printer's exploding."

"It's only out of paper, Marc," says Rik. "Have you ever had to load paper, all by yourself? Jaymi, I'm putting more paper in."

"Thanks. So, you two make yourselves at home, I'll get the drinks and we'll be on our way."

Soon they each settle down with a cocktail and a still-warm copy of the novel, and start reading.

From the speed with which they become engrossed, it is apparent what a voice Alaia Danielle has. Page 5 lies open on all their laps at almost the same time, then before long, page 10 and page 20. "Hmm, I don't know," says Marc. "It's a bit febrile, wouldn't you say?"

"It's *meant* to be a bit febrile," retorts Jaymi.

"OK," says Marc, "I'll give her the benefit of the doubt, for now. But I can't help feeling she needs a good slap. And possibly a good poke too, while we're at it."

"Marc, please," says Rik.

"Well, don't you think it's a bit febrile?" Marc asks him.

"There are a few breathless moments, perhaps, but let's not blame the messenger for that. She's just reflecting the world as she sees it. She's clearly a sensitive flower."

Marc grunts grudgingly, and they take up their pages again.

Soon, however, Marc starts frowning with displeasure from time to time, prompting Rik to glance across at him. "I warned you a few of us were in it!" enthuses Jaymi.

Pages 30, 60, 90 and 120 are reached, as they speed-read avidly. For the great majority of his reading, Jaymi looks as fired up as when he first read it online. However, at the start of Alaia's newly-added section at the end, he starts to stiffen, then to look annoyed, then finally very angry.

Marc and Rik reach the end within twenty minutes of each other, before laying their copies down, both deep in thought. "Well I never," says Marc. "I didn't know that sort of thing went on. No fit reading for the innocent of mind, I must say! But first of all, specifics, please: if those descriptions of underhand spying start getting associated with us, then it's potentially damaging to Mainframe. People will think of our GMRI division."

"Yes," says Rik. "And I'm not sure I'm 100% comfortable being portrayed as the one who made the recordings of all that stolen intellectual property. Pressing 'record' on people's private imaginations makes me look like a colluder. Which upsets me, because I'm not."

"Well Rik, old boy, we are using *your* Web-guide to take a good look around in real life," says Marc, "so you're not really much more of a saint than the rest of us."

"But that's just a matter of how Mainframe chooses to use my invention. Nothing to do with me—"

"You happily accepted development and production funding from Mainframe, to make it happen, knowing full well what our interest in your invention was based on. And good for you, I say! But we're getting into ethics here, and that's always a mistake. The point is, yes this Alaia Danielle has changed the company name and relocated us from London to Asbury Park, of all godforsaken places, and yes I'm sure we could take pre-emptive action to persuade her to change our own character names too, before publication, without any noise of litigation. *However*, if the media were to find out that we'd done those things, as they could easily do if she tipped them off to that effect, then they would smell blood and be all over us in any case. Then they'd make sure to find a hundred similarities between the narrator on the one hand, even if he *is* renamed John Doe, and on the other hand our real-life Web-skin Jaymi here. Could be a headache. Investors get skittish, you know…" He sips his cocktail. "Still, at least she did write her Marc as a powerful entertainment mogul. I suppose I shall plead guilty to that."

"And her Evelyn character was startling, I have to admit," says Rik. "What a beautiful personality. Not unlike the real one we know."

"Ah, yes," says Marc, "your Evelyn down in the lab there. I don't know her so well, but she does seem a charmer. What about that Angel, though, what? Trouble, to be sure! I wonder if he'll escape Asbury Park?"

"He was written with compassion, but something tells me the writer doesn't like our real-world Angel much," says Rik. "For which I'm hardly inclined to blame her."

"You and Ms Deon getting on, then?" twinkles Marc at him. "One big happy family, eh! In all seriousness, though," and he turns to Jaymi, "the writer does seem to imply rather too much innocence on the part of our Jaymi here, I would say…" Jaymi's eyes flick towards his study, picturing his laptop—then they flick back again, as he feels Marc's shrewd gaze bore into him. "I say, Jaymi, you look off-colour, of a sudden," says Marc. "How interesting! What's the matter, I wonder?"

"It's this," says Jaymi, pulling his attention from his study and hiding behind a separate truth, namely the quiet anger that's been welling up in him. "The first ten Parts of the novel, up to mini-chapter 120, were unchanged from what I'd read. They were as I described to you on the phone—the work of a true artist, I mean. Well, I wish I could continue to believe her to be so. Alas, these last mini-chapters 121-130, added at her own misguided but revelatory insistence, have turned out to be a horror that not only injures me in aesthetic terms but also casts into calamitous doubt the authenticity of any genius preceding them."

"Don't talk like that about anyone you love, Jaymi," says Rik. "Love is a more wonderful thing than art."

"They are both simply forms of imitation," says Marc.

"Your characteristic compassion does you credit, Rik," says Jaymi. "But I have no sympathy for any surprise Alaia may soon feel in learning I'm deadly serious, because there is no excuse for such ignorance."

Shocked and chilled by the ice in Jaymi's words, Rik shifts uncomfortably in his armchair.

Marc's grave sympathies appear to be tilted with comparable discomfort, in maintaining his own authentic connection with both companions.

It is, alas, to be one of this trio's stiffer dinners together.

*

Jaymi sits on his black leather sofa, looking icy. He picks up the phone, puts his earphones in and places a video-call on his mobile.

Alaia's face appears onscreen. "Hallo!" she says.

"Hi, and listen to me, please. Thank you for sending the novel when you promised to. Parts I-X of it remain as before, and you know my opinion of those. While I was reading, I felt angered and poisoned, however, by what you've just added as Part XI. I couldn't imagine why you've now brought such hideous, trite, conventional mediocrity into what had been such an exquisitely beautiful vision of obsession, idolatry, fame and digital audio-visual perfection."

"Jaymi," she purrs, "I thought you'd understand what I was doing there! You do understand now, don't you?"

"Understand what? No. I am here on earth, and I thought you too were here on earth, to make the most exquisite job of this one chance we have at being alive—either from within a single art form, as you used to do with such beauty, or more widely, as I shall never stop doing. These brand-new pages of yours tonight have shown me what would have been on the cards, had you and I remained together: the soggy, irrelevant boredom of children, whose presence straightaway spoils any interesting, sophisticated or even just grown-up communion between adults; and a swamp of lukewarm ambition, criteria and achievement. My span on this earth is not infinite. I don't have time for that swill—and neither should you."

Her voice sounds stretched over a deepening well of shock, as she replies, "Yes, I know very well that the cosy ending after they get back to New York doesn't really fit with the things that came before. But, oh…"

"It not only fails to fit with them, doing monstrous violence to them: it also rips the disguise from what must in reality be a conventional, mediocre set of ideals and ambitions on the part of its author. That the woman whose mind and aesthetics I believed to be coolly incorruptible and uncompromising would harbour what is clearly such a powerful secret wish to settle down with 'her' Jaymi into a lingering death in suburbia, with all those ghastly neighbours and horrible children and ugly sports and dumb church, living just far enough away from New York City to ensure that the city was hard to get to… Oh, what a dire, dreary wash-out, stuck onto the end of the novel there. What a betrayal of my trust! I'm sorry to know that it reveals a part of what you're like inside, and what you will increasingly become. And I'm sorry to say that what's revealed is unforgivable, in literal and simple terms."

"No!" she cries. "Jaymi, before we met, writing was the only reality for me. It was on the page I felt most alive. I thought it was all true. The scenes I invented were my world. I was seeing only shadows, and I thought they were real. Then you came along, and you freed me from that illusion. You showed me what reality really is. Then while I was adding those last pages, for the first time in my life I saw through that hollowness. You'd brought me something higher, of which all art is just a reflection. You'd made me understand what love really is. My love! Jaymi! Prince Charming! You are more to me than art can ever be. What connection do I have with characters written on a page? When I went to write what should have been a crowning expression of shared love in Part XI, I couldn't understand why everything had gone from me. I'd thought I was going to write wonderfully, but I found I could do nothing. Then it dawned on me, and the knowledge was exquisite: I could picture readers seeing straight through what I was trying to write, and I smiled, because what could they know of love like ours? Take me away, Jaymi, where we can be alone! I hate the page now. I might describe a passion I don't feel, but I can't describe one that burns me like fire. Oh, Jaymi, *now* d'you understand what it means? Even if I could do it, it would be profane for me to construct a description of being in love. You have made me see that."

He flings himself back into the sofa and turns away his face. "You've killed my love," he mutters. She looks at him, distraught, then leans in towards him and presses her lips to the phone's camera lens. A shudder runs through him.

He leaps up and goes to the door. "Yes," he cries, "you've spoiled the romance of my life. How little you can know of love, if you say it spoils your art. Without your art, you're nothing. I would have made you famous, magnificent. The world would have worshipped you. What are you now? A compromised writer with a pretty face."

Alaia has gone pale. She clenches her hands together, and her voice seems to catch in her throat. "So you *are* serious."

She moves her face close in towards the phone's camera lens again. "Don't!" he cries.

A low moan breaks from her. "Jaymi, don't leave me," she whispers. "I'm sorry I didn't write well. I was thinking of you all the time. But I will try—I will try. It came so suddenly across me, my love for you. I think I'd never have known it, if you hadn't kissed me. Don't be cruel to me. It's only once that I've not pleased you." She is crouching on her floor like a wounded thing, but to Jaymi she seems absurdly melodramatic.

"I must go," he says in a calm voice, "in order to spare us a big future mismatch. "I don't mean to be unkind, Alaia, but I can't see you again. You have disappointed me."

While she cries and makes no answer, he terminates the video-call, and then blocks her number.

V PORTRAIT INFECTED AND SHUT AWAY

Late that night, Jaymi has occasion to pass from the lighted main space of his apartment, through the hallway and into his darkened study. He fetches a book and sets off back towards the door, not far from his laptop and the hologram, which he half-glimpses on his desk as he passes it.

About a metre past the hologram, he freezes in his tracks.

He remains standing there in the darkness, breathing a little louder than usual, thinking hard … and not turning round, in dead silence, for several seconds.

At last he cannot stand it. He wheels around and stares at the hologram.

Its eyes have swivelled up to follow him as usual, but now seem to be staring into his own eyes with more of an impudent connection than before. It is different, too… Its expression looks crueller.

He flings the book down and grabs the laptop, without looking further at the hologram but pulling it alongside the screen, so it sweeps through the air beside him as he darts from the room.

He strides through the hallway into the bathroom and flicks the lights on, ineffectual though they are. Taking care to avoid appearing in the mirror at all, as yet, he holds the laptop up beside his own head and stabilises his grip on it, with the hologram on the other side of the keyboard from himself.

Then he sidles closer to the wall-mirror, cautious and crab-like, with terror mounting in him.

By degrees he creeps and agonises nearer to the point where he starts to see, reflected in the mirror, first his own image, looking murderous … and then the laptop … and then, very slowly, the hologram.

The head inches painfully into view, staring straight at Jaymi where it hovers in the spotlight. Jaymi's eyes bore into it, caressing its face with minute, probing flicks across its width and height…

And there's no avoiding it. The face is still beautiful, but there's an unmistakably increased touch of cruelty in its lineaments.

There arises the echo of his unheeded utterance in the Mainframe conference room when the hologram was first presented: "*And there I am, immortal…*" This is followed by another, much more recent echo: "*You have disappointed me.*" And like a thunderclap comes the third echo at last, as the horror of truth slides into place: his urgent wish, "*If only the hologram could assume all signs of my future loss of beauty, and of my sins, forever.*" With vertiginous fear and fascination, he understands that this is indeed now happening: the look of the prototype hologram is changing, according to his own behaviour.

As he stares at the little head, a soft streak of pity for it flickers through his own face—and then is gone.

*

Next morning Jaymi strides into his study. His laptop, left turned-on and plugged-in on his desk, announces it is in sleep mode, so is without a hologram. He strokes his finger across the touch-pad, and the hologram appears. Jaymi's quick look of cool scientific interest confirms last night's discovery: here in the light of morning, its expression does still have that same streak of cruelty.

"Interesting," he murmurs. He smiles at it, then his smile fades. "You poor little homunculus… Oh, what have I done?… OK: you are my conscience. I'm going to be good. I shall call her tomorrow."

His mobile rings and he answers. "Marc! Good morning to you. Sorry about the new ending of the novel last night. I called Alaia afterwards and let her go, for her sins. After all, she did cause me genuine suffering with what she wrote, and she should have known better. Still, I was perhaps a little harsh, so I've just decided to do the right thing, call her tomorrow and make some kind of amends."

"Jaymi … I'm actually outside your building, on the street. I was just wondering whether I could pop up there to see you, for a few minutes. Spot of bad news, I'm afraid."

"Oh. Sure, yes. Come on in, I'll buzz you through."

There is a note of deft sobriety in Marc's entry into the apartment, and Jaymi soon finds out why. "I surmise you haven't seen the news yet, dear boy. Brace yourself for this: Alaia killed herself last night. Drank prussic acid."

"*No!*" yells Jaymi. "Oh, hell… The poor creature. The silly creature… And I did that. I did that… So, is it all over the news?"

"Oh God no. If the papers had known she was involved with you, it would have been. No, it was just a snippet of London news, a minor side-bar. After all, people commit suicide every day and don't make the news with it. But I suspect it was the detail of the prussic acid that gave the editors the necessary journalistic little hook—the hook-ette! Prussic acid sounds so decadently fin-de-siècle."

"Yes; quite a stylish choice, you might say. Oh, *Alaia…*" Jaymi sinks into the sofa and punches it weakly.

"You shouldn't be too hard on yourself," soothes Marc. "Whatever you may have told her on the phone is no less true now than it was then, let's face it. Would I wager correctly that last night you read her the riot act concerning the ugliness we all witnessed yesterday evening, its moral and aesthetic seriousness and its sheer, literal unforgivability, in the context of the often losing battle we're obliged to fight, with so little help, against the overwhelming and globally prevalent forces of mediocrity and laziness and unthinking stupidity that demand such drastic and urgent action on our parts to counteract them…?"

"You would wager right, yes. I'm in misery here, Marc. Misery. But I suppose, in a way, we could even regard her slipping away like this as a fore-destined end to a beautiful tragedy."

"We could indeed. And moreover, we should. And even more important—we shall. Now Jaymi, let's draw an elegant line under this little chapter, and go have a lunchtime martini at my club."

"To Alaia, Marc… Oh, to Alaia."

"To Alaia; quite so. By the way, lest I forget, I've brought you a present. Take a look, some time. No hurry." He tosses onto the sofa a DVD case with a black, unmarked cover.

"Thank you. What is it?"

"A copy of a certain feature film. A rare disc; uncopyable. My all-time favourite, you might say. There's nothing else like it. You'll see." But now he leads Jaymi away from the DVD case, towards the door. "Let's go find that drink." As they exit the penthouse, Marc turns confidingly to him, with mischief in his eyes. "And when we get to the club, if you don't fancy a gin martini, how about a prussic acid martini?" Out of view now, in the hallway, his voice receding: "Odd number of olives, of course. One olive is Classical. Three olives, Romantic. Five, Rococo. But seven olives, my dear boy? Now that's just a wet salad…"

*

In Marc's club soon afterwards, he and Jaymi sit in the quietest corner they can find.

Marc shakes his head. "No, you mustn't be hard on yourself. It's tragic and it's simple, I'm afraid: when you phoned her and began your affair, her endless unattainable fantasy of you came to an unexpected thumping end, because you'd been wondrously attained."

"And all that fierce, artistic, emotional idealism of hers," says Jaymi, "which I'd read in her book, could then be forgotten while she luxuriated in her new reality with me."

"So the only stuff left in her was that damnable, limp, soggy ending. I don't wonder it enraged you."

"I suppose you could say," ponders Jaymi, "that this is, at heart, just a rather uncompromising conclusion to an unforeseeable drama that seems to have left me marvellously unscathed. For which, I hasten to add, I'm both grateful and humbled."

"That's the spirit; and yes, that rather sums it up, I think."

"In any case, I'm damn well going to rewrite her ending. I'll chop out those extra new mini-chapters 121-130—the ghastly lingering death in suburbia. It can simply end at mini-chapter 120 instead, just as it did before, which'll leave it dark and bright and sharp, as it should be. It's the least I can do, for her legacy."

"It'll be a noble sacrifice," nods Marc gravely.

"Also, a title for it: we can't just leave it called *Alaia's novel*. I was thinking of using the title of one of her mini-chapters, *Shrieking Eyes in the Ghost Town*."

"A shade too gothic, I'd say. How about *The Imagination Thief*?"

"Sure, it's a possibility. Thanks, I'll give it some thought."

"In heaven's name, why am I supplying you titles?" snorts Marc. "Much more importantly, Jaymi, please change all our names before any publication. Can I trust you to do that? Plus, I'm afraid we'd have to bowdlerise it a bit, too: we can't have our GMRI division accused of snooping, of all things…"

*

Jaymi enters his apartment alone, tipsy from what became a long and liquid lunch at the club. He goes to his study, walks to the desk, strokes his finger across the laptop's touch-pad to reactivate it from sleep mode, sees the hologram leap into being, and bends down to inspect it.

He straightens up. "Why are you still the same as this morning? Didn't you hear all the further good sense Marc and I spoke today?" He heads back towards the door to the main space. "I guess you don't work that way." He stops in the doorway, turns back and points right at it, flushed and grinning. "So, I'm warning you, homunculus—I'm gonna bring it on! Oh yes. Let all such effects be visited upon you, my little friend!" He shudders. "And if I go at you hard enough, then maybe, just maybe, one day, I may even get to watch an increase of those effects on you *in real time*, while we stare at each other! Wouldn't that be something? Because you know, I'm gonna go the whole way, baby: 'Eternal youth, infinite passion, pleasures subtle and secret, wild joy and wilder sins'! Oh yes! I'm going to have all those sweet things, my little Jaymi, my little Jaymi-boy!" He stands there in the doorway, looking sorrowful of a sudden, then blows the hologram an extravagant kiss. "The only one I pity here is you, my little lover. Don't worry, though, I'll kiss you later and make it up. Can't kiss you now, you'll smudge my make-up…"

He exits the room unsteadily, back into the hallway, then prowls the apartment, his face immobile, with something caged in his movements.

The oppressive silence is shattered by a rhythmic female shrieking, a mechanical, repeated screech of human pain, as of one whose insides are being eaten up, slowly, by pints of prussic acid…

Eyes ablaze, Jaymi hunts for the source of this agonising sound. It continues too long, unbearably too long, but as it does so, it changes by degrees, mixing with a banal sound that has the same rhythm—his little-used landline telephone in the hallway. Upon this realisation, the element of the shriek fades altogether, leaving just the noise of the phone.

He runs to the hallway and dives to pick the handset up. "Hallo?"

"Hallo Jaymi," says Rik. "I hope I haven't called at a bad moment. I'm so sorry to hear the terrible news. I called your mobile, but Marc picked it up and said you'd left it at his club by mistake. I'm outside your building, on the street. Can I come up?"

"Sure, come on in." He hangs up and presses the door-buzzer.

Rik enters. "Jaymi, I don't know what to say. What a terrible, terrible thing to have happened. Poor girl."

"Yes," says Jaymi with an aura of affectless exhaustion. "Such a sad end. A shame it had to be that way. I would not have wished it. I didn't wish it. Symptomatic, finally, of a deep flaw in life's design—of numerous deep flaws, indeed. In many ways we'd have done a better job, Rik, of designing it ourselves. In fact, you have done so yourself already, in the form of the hologram. Perhaps we can arrange a wider re-design by you, of things in general. It would be fitting. I would wish it. Marc too, no doubt. So may she rest in peace. There it is."

Mild shock gathers in Rik's face: "Well. You seem to have it worked out quite efficiently, I must say. If I didn't know you better, I'd almost say you sounded a little callous there. But I'm glad to say I do know you, so I shall think better of you instead… And speaking of your prototype hologram: while I'm here, could I take a peek at it? Foolish, perhaps, but I do think of it as a kind of brother to my own copy. You and I are alone in having prototypes, as you know."

Jaymi has stiffened, during the last part of this speech. "*No!*"

Rik looks at him in great surprise. "Why ever not? You seem to forget I *made* it, Jaymi. And installed it. So I'm sure I can handle the sight of it, thank you! Has it changed?"

Jaymi's eyes widen, then he smiles. "Changed, how could it do that?!… I'm sorry, I apologise if I sounded rude just now. It's just … well, I think I need to keep the prototype to myself, for the moment. Alaia—she and I, we developed a funny kind of special relationship with it, if you must know. This may sound odd to the hologram's designer, but she and I came to look upon it as something like the visual equivalent of 'our tune'! To me it therefore means Alaia; so I would prefer, if you don't mind, to keep it to myself, in her memory."

Rik goes quiet. "Oh, I see. Yes, of course. How funny: to you it means *her*. Whereas, to me it means … well, I think you know very well that it means *you*, Jaymi. I made the program for you, originally. Sort of for you, anyway, in the sense that my love for you made me walk with the angels in designing it—made me inspired, in the programming, to such an extent as I'd never been inspired before." He is a picture of dignified pain now, almost in tears. "Which is why it turned out so well. And I clothed it in you, as an ever-burning flame and memorial to a love I knew could *never* happen, because you didn't feel the same kind of love back for me. *Never* did, *never* could and *never* will, although I could see that for a while you were trying to." He smiles through his tears, then turns and walks to the door. "Goodbye, Jaymi." He opens the door and passes into the darkness of the landing, not looking back.

"Goodbye, Rik," calls Jaymi after him. "Let's do lunch next week… I'll call you…"

But his front door has swung shut. He turns towards the panoramic window and stares out, unfocused.

*

At the front door of his apartment one afternoon the following week, Jaymi signs for the delivery of a sizeable box. That evening, with pleasure and concentration, surrounded by opened packaging, he sets up and gets to know a brand-new laptop computer. Along with the shiny new things appearing onscreen through the loading of software, there flickers up a new and pristine copy of the hologram, of course. Blandly immaculate, reassuring and fresh out of the box, it is quite uncorrupted and elicits no personal engagement or interest in Jaymi, beyond his basic verification of its functionality.

Once he has finished, he sits back. This moment of apparent relaxation is deceptive, though; because there is another set of computer-related actions for him to perform next, which may not appear so dissimilar to those he has just performed, but whose import will be so radically different as to nudge him across a threshold that'll change his life forever. For in making the laptop arrangements he is about to make, he knows he will be consenting to lose altogether what remains of his power to resist the temptation to look through the prototype hologram's eyes at everything it can see around the world. This part of his volition is about to be taken over by the prototype, as by a virus. In continuing to lend his human abilities to the prototype's programmed hunger to learn and spread, he will be making himself an adjunct to it. *He* will become part of *its* evolution, in the sense that its evolution is about to take a little leap, from occurring just internally to occurring also externally by means of Jaymi's own actions too.

Yes; by this stage he is past the point of no return, he has to admit. Any further sitting-around would therefore just be wasted time, which would be silly. So, leaving his brand-new laptop on the desk in front of him, he gets up and steps quietly across that life-changing threshold, by stepping across his study towards his old laptop. He picks the old laptop up and carries it out of the study, sweeping along with him that rather more experienced, quite unique and faintly crueller-looking hologram…

So… Near the end of his hallway, leading off it to the left, away from all warmth and light, there is a narrow, low-lit side-corridor, whose length includes two or three changes of direction around corners. The sole function of this corridor is to lead to a fire-exit. It hasn't escaped Jaymi's notice that such a corridor is not included in any of the neighbouring apartments he has been into. However, this is doubtless just a quirk deriving from the irregular elements in the architecture of the Ontario: first, its oval footprint; then even more relevantly here, the iconic oblique angle of the building's upper section, topped by its crisp ring of blue light and slicing up through several storeys, which must have inflicted numerous delightful complexities on the layouts of all apartments on these levels here.

Still carrying his old laptop with its experienced hologram, Jaymi now stands at the very furthest end of this thin side-corridor, where there is a windowless door with a yellow and black label saying "Fire exit—alarmed".

Just in front of this fire-door, set into the corridor walls opposite each other, are two smaller, dark, open doors.

The door on the left leads into a cramped, poky store-room, which Jaymi hardly ever finds himself needing or wanting to enter.

The door on the right leads into a second bathroom, which neither he nor his guests ever seem to feel like using either, though it is quite functional.

Directly between these two side-doors, Jaymi is soon ferrying the laptop and an extension cable gingerly up a step-ladder, which he has just pulled down from the metre-square opening of a hatch in the ceiling of the corridor. This ladder is well mounted upon the inside of the hatch and will presently be slid back up through it, so as to live inside the attic, before closure of the hatch-door, which currently hangs down from its hinges. He reaches the top of the ladder, feels around inside the hatch for a few moments to find a switch, flicks a yellowish light on and disappears into the attic.

The attic is compact but longish, positioned perpendicular to the fire-escape corridor, its nearer half above that poky little store-room down the step-ladder. It is cluttered with objects, some bulky and some small. Picking his way to the very end, Jaymi clears part of a table-top and places the old laptop onto it. He returns to the hatch to plug one end of the extension cable into a socket beside the light-switch; then back at the table he plugs his laptop's power cord into the other end of the extension cable and turns the laptop on.

The hologram flickers up, with its crueller mien, just as before.

Feeling something feverish in his eyes, Jaymi blows a little kiss towards it, dark and delicate; then he exits the attic through the hatch, turning the light-switch off as he goes.

He sets off down the ladder, step by step. As he descends, the face of the hologram—alert and bluer-bright in the absence of the yellowish bulb's light, but somewhat too far away to see in detail from right here—is gradually obscured as Jaymi steps from rung to rung, until its watchful gaze is cut off from view by the hatch's edge.

Scuttling down the lower rungs at greater speed, Jaymi reaches the corridor's floor. He slides the two sections of the ladder upwards along its built-in rails, so that it becomes shorter, and pushes it towards the hatch. Holding it there with one hand, he reaches with his other hand for a long hook-ended stick that leans against the end of the corridor. With this dedicated implement he completes the ladder's smooth ascent through the hatch with a push, takes hold of the hanging hatch-door by sticking the hook through a metal loop attached to the door, and swings the door upwards on its hinges. A last strip of faint blue glow, emanating from that now-unseen little face, becomes thinner as the hinges squeak, and is blocked off at last when the hatch-door snicks shut.

Leaning the hook-ended stick back against the end of the corridor, Jaymi catches his own reflection in the mirror, through the door of the small second bathroom. The mirror is oddly sweaty with condensation, so he is somewhat indistinct where he stands half-illuminated against the darkness of the reflected store-room door behind him. He steps forwards, towards the reflection, and reaches for the hanging light-switch inside the bathroom door ... but something makes him stop right there. He turns away; then with a last glance back at the reflection, he sets off down the corridor and around its two or three corners, peering back over his shoulder after every few steps.

VI HORROR BENEATH GLAMOUR

For the first time Jaymi picks up the mysterious unmarked black DVD case from where Marc tossed it down on the sofa. He opens it and finds an unmarked disc. He gets up, turns his TV system on and loads it into the deck. He returns to the sofa, dons a pair of high-end headphones and sits back.

The screen shows a film-style countdown of numbers inside dissolving circles, beginning from 10 and descending, one each second, to a blackout.

From here on, the screen monopolises him. He is captivated, often horrified, sometimes terrified, but in no simple way. At times he is almost giddy and his hands grip the leather sofa. Though he's never quite smiling, it is clear some gorgeously corruptive explosion of rottenness is flowering inside him. It's as if he is seeing from the point of view of the spirit that entraps us here among the molecules, locking us into this human endeavour with a motivation both sadistically vicious and poetic at once, despising us while it fills us with sensuous blood.

*

Marc is seated on a comfortable upright chair on the club's roof-terrace. Jaymi is sunk in an armchair nearby.

"So you've watched it," says Marc. "I knew, as soon as I heard your voice on the phone this morning, though you didn't mention it."

"Everything looks different now. Different from what I thought it was like."

"Everything *is* different from what you thought it was like—from what nearly everyone thinks it's like."

"…What am I meant to do with this?"

"You can't do anything with it. You just have to take it on board. What choice do you have, after all, now you've seen it."

"You didn't have to show me."

"You don't really wish that I hadn't—because you were ready to know. You're among us, now. It's better to know, if you're capable of it." He reflects for a moment. "Rik isn't capable of it, as I suspect you'd agree. So he'll never know. Not ahead of time, anyway."

"It's almost too much."

"Of course it's too much. Way, way too much. But don't dwell on that, for there lies madness. Just incorporate it within yourself, as best you can, and press on."

"A lie," says Jaymi. "A gigantic lie."

"I know!" Marc cackles with a brief, expansive laugh. "And it's staring us all in the face. Square in the face. Yet the vast majority of us can't see it, not until we're shown."

"How did you find out?"

"Similarly to you."

"I won't be letting anyone else know," says Jaymi.

Marc raises his glass, with a twinkle in his eye. "Ah well. Let the show go on, in any case. Bottoms up, my boy!"

After a couple of seconds Jaymi raises his glass too, half-smiling, and they clink.

*

Standing before Marc's desk that afternoon, Angel is reaching the end of some characteristic anecdote. "So I said, 'Don't make me slap you!'"

Marc guffaws, lounging back in his chair, well tickled by her. "Ah, people are so interesting, sometimes!…" He sits forward in his chair. "Angel, I need us to be very serious for a moment. After considerable thought, I've decided to release a female version of the HOST skin, to complement Jaymi's, and I'd like to ask you if you're interested in being the model for it. I must warn you it would involve a certain amount of grooming, considerable focus and a rather intensive shoot"—but he is cut off in mid-flow, as she has raced around his desk and flung herself around him in a bear-hug. "Woah, steady on! Steady, the Buffs! Oh, all right…"

*

Soon after this exchange, the Mainframe computer laboratory door opens without ceremony, and Marc charges in with Angel in tow. "Afternoon, team! As I know you've been expecting, I just now agreed with Angel here that she is to model as a brand-new HOST skin, to

149

complement our beloved Jaymi. Then we'll have something for all the family, as it were. I therefore now entrust her to the capable hands of you, Rik, and you, Evelyn, so you can start taking measurements for film-shoots and re-skinnings and all that light and magic."

There are stiff nods and thin smiles all round.

"Splendid! I knew you'd all be gung-ho to get cracking," says Marc. "So, when they're done with you here, Angel, if you could pop back up to my office, then we'll run through some paperwork."

More stiff nods and smiles, as he exits.

"Welcome to the HOST lab, Ms Deon," says Rik.

"You won't need to take my measurements," says Angel. "I can give you them all, from memory."

"We weren't going to measure you in that way," says Evelyn.

Hearing this impudence, Angel stares at her. "Could you get me a glass of water, please."

"The drinking fountain's in the hallway," replies Evelyn through gritted teeth.

"There are plastic cups over there for you, by the door, Ms Deon," says Rik. "Do fill one in the hallway, if you wish." Angel remains where she is. "Otherwise, please step this way when you're ready, and position yourself in front of the camera here. We'll just be taking a few quick snapshots, to start with."

Angel complies, with a confident professionalism, and Rik starts adjusting the camera. "OK," he says, "now hold still, right there. Don't move…"

Evelyn decides to relax her expression, even permitting herself a slight smile at Angel.

"Since Rik's just said he doesn't want me to move," says Angel to her, "could you get me that cup of water now?"

Evelyn's smile disappears.

*

Jaymi walks along his main hallway, until the mouth of the narrow corridor stands clear, ahead of him on the left. He slows for a moment, contemplating the mouth, and then resumes his prior speed in approaching it, injecting a touch of jauntiness into his step.

He turns into it. He proceeds along its initial straight stretch. He follows it around its two or three corners. The view straight down to the end of it appears, and he stops altogether.

The walls, for a moment, appear strange, seeming perhaps imperceptibly baggier than before … or perhaps not.

Reaching the end, between the two dark doorways, he reaches for the stick, raises its hooked end, inserts the metal hook through the metal loop attached to the hatch-door, and pulls down. The hatch-door hangs open, displaying a square of darkness with a faint bluish glow within.

He pulls at the ladder with the hooked stick, and slides its lower half down to the floor, aware of that half-lit reflection in the bathroom mirror through the doorway on his right. He sets off up the rungs.

Halfway up, he feels for an instant as if something may just have moved in the darkness of the store-room on his left. He stops, peering down through the store-room's doorway, but can see nothing untoward. He continues his climb.

The hologram's glow gets a little closer to him with every step he takes up the ladder … till there, over the edge of the hatch, it pokes up into view, high on the table-top at the far end of the attic.

It is just a little too far away to be seen in any real detail from here.

In a single rush of determination, he beetles up the remaining steps, wriggles through the hatch, stumbles along the attic (without yet looking at the hologram), braces himself—then halts and stares straight at it, in bold challenge.

It still looks like Jaymi, is even still handsome in a way; but it exudes corruption, as if evil and moral infection pump through its insides. Its face is sallow and lined, and its intense gaze is knowing, with a hint of sickly yellow in its cunning eyes. Jaymi drags a high stool over to the table from nearby, sits and starts issuing hectic commands to it, in standard question formulations that might be used for any instance of the Web-guide. The hologram mines away for him, in instant dutiful response, gathering files and pages from around the world, of an ever more private nature, and throwing them up onto the screen for him.

Settling more comfortably onto the stool, Jaymi redoubles his deluge of commands and sharpens his focus; for the night is young.

Thus does this attic laptop become the conduit, over many months, for a mesmerising deluge of Internet imagery from around the world. It begins at a modest pace but soon accelerates to a mad speed, with a rising onslaught of disembodied voices in all languages and a churning surge of music fragments and sounds of every kind. This deluge becomes increasingly peppered with sick and sordid pages of imagery and text, often not publicly accessible but rather from the Dark Web, escalating up to twisted levels, and all shot through with blips, bleeps, hums, grating whines and gibbering ululations.

The months-long data orgy is interspersed with Jaymi calling phone numbers onscreen … Jaymi talking sinisterly on the phone, and frightened people answering their phones in the dead of night … Jaymi installing industrial-strength firewalls and other mysterious security devices around the laptop and telephone … Jaymi making notes, sealing envelopes, hammering out emails, tapping out texts and telephoning online again, while pinned-up print-outs of the darkest material imaginable proliferate across every rafter of the attic space.

—The deluge slams to a halt: dead silence in the attic.

The plain black screen-saver comes on, returning the laptop's monitor to darkness, so Jaymi sees a sudden close-up of his own motionless face reflected in the black, wearing a thousand-metre stare straight ahead, glassy-eyed and bathed in the sickly yellow-green glow of the hologram beside him.

*

In the fresh mists of early morning on Hampstead Heath, Rik is taking his dog for a walk, to the sound of birdsong. Watching the animal, he smiles with sad affection as there echoes in his memory a statement of Jaymi's, from some conversation in happier days long ago: "Forgive me here, Rik, I'm sorry, but I just can't stand dogs! I've never been able to stand the bouncy, boring, disruptive physicality of them. Just as with children, I've never found myself remotely interested in their appeal, and I'd have to say I hate their presence. Cats and bunnies, on the other hand: now they're the future…"

*

In his private club early that evening, Marc and Angel sit on high seats at the bar, holding full champagne flutes. Behind the bar a uniformed barman polishes a line of already-gleaming stem-cocktail glasses, one by one, to an ever more fascistic polish, as with professional opacity he cocks an ear to their talk.

"Well my girl, here's to it!"

"Cheers, Marc!" twinkles Angel and they clink glasses and drink.

"So before we embark on this, there's one thing I want to be sure you understand. As a new skin for HOST, you will rise as the face of everything that you and I know is right and bright and evolved and intelligent. And that means beauty, pure and simple—that *is* 'beautiful'. For as HOST's face, you'll represent humankind's most incredible achievement yet. Your face will push outward, for all of us, out against the darkness of the universe, the darkness of our ignorance—against it and into it. We're piercing through that darkness with HOST, as we never have before. We'll be drilling through the blackness of unknowing, with your face for our drill-bit!"

Topping up their glasses, he continues: "As presenter of humankind's quest for ever greater knowledge, ever higher evolution in the upward journey of this highest of species so far, *you* have a noble and grave responsibility, for which you've been selected by the natural course of things, as cream rises through milk. —Yes, don't be modest now. Since the first days of radio, the flicker of our electronic media has travelled outward from this planet in a huge bubble of signals, from every kind of broadcast, expanding at the speed of light ... so understand, my dear woman, what we're doing here, and what you are." He leans impressively closer. "For the next spell of history, and I don't mean years but decades, you and Jaymi will front and lead that great bubble of our ever-developing broadcasts and signals—our footprint on the universe, as we look outward and inward through the cosmos in every direction, down the corridor of every single infinitesimal solid-angle, every hair-thin steradian—*your* face being humankind's face, to be seen by everything else and everybody else that may be out there, above us or beneath us!..."

Marc sits back.

Angel's eyes are on fire.

*

As a symptom of Mainframe's continued rise into global prominence, the current week has been dominated by the company's moving offices, from its long-time Soho building into an all-black skyscraper that towers over a chic media-industrial enclave in East London near Three Mills Island. The skyscraper's design is stark, powerful, irreducible, its proportions those of the Monolith in *2001*. Jaymi and Marc have of course been insulated from any heavy labour in this connection, but there has nonetheless been much for them to oversee, in order for this office move to coast into as smooth a completion as it seems to have done.

A black car with tinted windows pulls up in front of the Monolith. Jaymi alights and approaches the building, where the words "MAINFRAME CORPORATION" span the glass above the front doors. He walks through the lobby to a bank of lifts, glancing up at the wall above Mainframe's name and logo, where a large copy of the classic Jaymi hologram image is mounted like a fanfare, high on the expanse of black stone.

Thirty minutes later, in a conference room many storeys above this image, he sits on a dais, facing an audience of corporate big-cheeses. He has not been in this room before, he reflects. Gazing over the heads of the waiting audience, he can see through the windows a fine panorama of East London, including a view straight down the River Lee for a couple of miles: there are the towers of Canary Wharf; there's the Balfron Tower; and there's his very own home, of course, the Ontario, behind whose distinctive slanted top, with its sharp blue ring of light, is an attic where is hidden—

He wrenches his attention back to the present moment in this conference room, and shakes his head, to clear it.

Seated with him, ready to contribute to the presentation, are a handful of Mainframe's other directors, including Rik and Marc— the latter's presence a pitch-perfect study in the secure containment of advanced dissipation within the shrewd and humorous self-control of a CEO who can drive his global conglomerate along with just a couple of fingers resting on the steering-wheel.

Now it's time for Jaymi to speak. He rises, professional and opaque: "Hi, and thank you for being here. As principal shareholders in Mainframe, you'll be aware our IPO nine months ago was the largest media flotation in the AIM's history. Since then, our original core business of representing clients in the advertising arena, while undiminished, has been outstripped in scale by the growth of our media production divisions, our distribution division and our satellite division. As I hand you over to our CFO, Eugene Poindexter, for an in-depth discussion and analysis of financial results over the twelve-month period, I should just like to remind you there can be no assurance that share prices will continue to rise—but we shan't be at all surprised if these do!" The audience emits a ripple of appreciative noise and Jaymi sits back down.

A beaming Eugene Poindexter rises to his feet. The room quietens.

He takes his glasses off thoughtfully.

And then, on an impulse, he puts his glasses back on again.

Then deep in thought, he takes his glasses back off.

Sitting behind Poindexter, and intent upon him, Champagne Marc's smile becomes the tiniest bit fixed.

*

A couple of mornings later, with much technical business, Angel is being filmed on the same stage where Jaymi was filmed, for the making of the new Angel-branded skin for HOST. Though Marc is not present in person as he was for the Jaymi shoot, his Mephistophelean words echo in her head throughout the scene, as a deliciously quiet and honeyed whisper complementing all the hardware around her. And the results of these words are captured with minuteness on camera, in the eyes of every last frame of this Picture of Angel Deon: "*You will rise as the face of everything that you and I know is right and bright and evolved and intelligent. And that means beauty, pure and simple—that is 'beautiful'… Your face will push outward, for all of us, out against the darkness of the universe, the darkness of our ignorance—against it and into it… We'll be drilling through the blackness of unknowing, with your face for our drill-bit!… You will front and lead our footprint on the universe, as we look outward and inward through the cosmos in every direction—your face being humankind's face…*"

*

Jaymi reclines on his bed, staring into the distance. Though physically unchanged as always, and with that febrile glow that has become permanent in him, he looks under pressure and a little confused, as if trying to work out a meaning in a whirlwind. He curls up and starts crying, in silence.

Nevertheless, week by week, month by month, like the tick of a bomb, Jaymi's laptop continues flickering with Web pages, data files, TV clips and screen projections of all kinds, signalling his ever-deepening knowledge of Internet users worldwide, for whom he is now an indispensable part of life, and signalling the stranglehold on global information that he now maintains by means of a billion radiant public holograms … plus one single, secret, corrupt one, hidden just upstairs.

*

Emerging from the Monolith Building's bank of lifts and setting off across the lobby in the late afternoon, Jaymi pauses in his tracks, beneath the large image of himself on the wall above the company name and logo.

His image is unchanged. However, underneath it, and underneath the company name and logo, there now hangs a similarly-sized image, there on the black stone—the Angel hologram. It must have been added during today, while he was up in the office.

He stares at her for a moment, impassive. Then he resumes walking across the lobby to the exit. He emerges from the all-black tower, stops near the waiting tinted-windowed car, glances round this Three Mills enclave in the late afternoon light, and looks back.

From across the lobby, those two giant faces stare out at him through the glass doors and windows, each face with its classic demeanour of expressionless expectancy: pristine, reassuring, blandly inviting and altogether opaque…

*

Jaymi reclines on his bed with his door closed, half-watching the Seven O'clock News on Channel 4, where somebody is being interviewed by Jon Snow about some foreign conflict. On the table beside Snow is his open laptop; and beside this, unremarkable and unintrusive, floats the standard twenty-centimetre-high hologram, just as it does all across the land. Jaymi yawns, picks up the remote control and turns the TV off.

On a side-table near the bed, beside his newer laptop, hovers the very same hologram, to which he pays as little attention as he did to Snow's—its expression just as he saw it on the Mainframe Monolith's lobby wall yesterday.

He stares into the distance. Then he turns his head, slowly, towards the closed door leading to the rest of his darkened apartment.

He rises from his bed, pads across his bedroom, opens his door and stands there, in silence, staring out into the shadows.

He sets off towards the main hallway.

When he reaches the hallway, he stops and looks intently down it. He looks in particular to the end, where on the left there opens the mouth of that narrow side-corridor leading to the fire-door. There, as Jaymi well knows, there are also those two poky rooms on either side of the fire-door, as well as the hatch in the ceiling of the corridor…

There is dead silence throughout the penthouse.

He steps on down his main hallway, until he comes level with the narrow corridor's mouth. He stops.

Slowly, he turns to face the corridor. He peers down the initial stretch of it, which is empty, claustrophobic and dead-straight as far as those corner-turnings halfway down.

And down it he goes, of course.

First, he creeps down the growing dimness of the straight stretch. Next, through thickening air, he makes a queasy, dream-like progress around each one of the several corner-turnings halfway down, which surely seem to number one more corner-turning than they did before; and how strange it is, he reflects, that he never has been able to recall exactly how many corner-turnings there are…

As soon as he reaches the point where he has a straight view down to the fire-door, he is hit by a vision of terror: with a grating rush, the corridor walls and ceiling and floor are all made of wet-breathing grey meat, bellowing in vicious pain, impaled by a dozen twitching meat-knives—

The vision slams away, echoes down and is sucked into silence in an instant.

Quiet and still again, the remaining half of the corridor stretches ahead, from Jaymi's feet, just as close and thickly-aired as before, and dim-lit from nowhere.

And now he has to carry on down it, as he knows very well.

He waits a moment longer, but it's really no use: for there go his feet, yes, stepping forward, down there underneath him…

While he goes, he next becomes aware that he is seeing every slanted ceiling angle, every leaning wall and object, with an odd kind of floatiness. And he's also seeing all of these things from a little bit lower than his usual eye-height, as if he's looking out of eyeballs that are embedded in the front and the sides of his neck, instead of embedded in his face.

The walls' sallow flickering is hopeless and queasier than ever now: churning, aslant, darkly founded on an alien discomfort and disjunction…

He slows, as he draws near the fire-door and clenches his teeth between the two dark doorways yawning on either side of him.

He reaches gingerly for the metal-hooked stick leaning against the corner of the walls beside the fire-door.

He raises the hooked end of the stick, then finds himself fumbling, with painful slowness and frustration, to get the wavering, wandering, now rubbery hook itself through the metal loop that's attached to the hatch-door…

Crying with fear of the dark, fear of the hopelessness and fear of the poky store-room beside him on his left in particular, he squeezes the increasingly squidgy, spongy, dripping-wet end of the metal hook, more painfully soft and small and useless with every fumbling second that passes—in through the loop's ring at last.

He pulls down the hatch-door, and then the ladder attached to the door, as far down as the ladder will slide under its own weight. He reaches up to the latch on the side of the ladder, unhooks it and slides the ladder's lower half down until it clangs onto the sweaty concrete floor of the corridor beside his bare toes.

Squinting, Jaymi forces his face to look straight up. A dim, cloudy green glow suffuses the square of black inside the hatch. He starts climbing the ladder, rung by rung, his feet weak and slippy on the cold metal, his entire body streaming sweat and shivering.

Hanging open just beneath the ceiling, the hatch-door swings away from the ladder by itself, right in front of his face, then continues to swing back and forth on its hinges, for longer than it should. He puts his hand out to stay it—but just before his hand can reach it, it stops swinging, more abruptly than it should.

He pushes himself onwards, upwards. The cloudy green glow reaches down at him. His head rises level with the hatch…

And over the edge of the hatch, at last, it is visible, up there on the table-top.

It is too far away to be seen in great detail. But even from here, it's clear that things have changed quite a lot now. The situation has evidently reached some other level altogether.

He scuttles up the remaining steps, half-falls into the attic, rises again, shuffles down the central aisle of the attic with his head lowered, and approaches the hologram's table with his eyes lowered, like a murderer approaching an altar.

At last he looks up at it.

The hologram is pure evil.

Beneath its head, a feral, skunk-like body has grown, which seems coiled as if to spring at him, revealing an enormous, sleek erection beneath the smooth, muscular flesh of its haunches. Atop this obscene body, its face remains recognisable but has now become a feyly sinister, ambisexual pastiche of Jaymi's face, its canines sharp and blood-stained, its skin erupting everywhere—and its terrible eyes still the same colour and shape as Jaymi's but now quite out-sized, unbearably malevolent, and quite dominating this cramped attic with the glaring enormity of their double-cannon presence.

Jaymi perches on his accustomed seat, stares like an automaton at the laptop screen and starts issuing feverish commands. Obedient in this, the hologram mines diligently away, throwing up material and arraying it onscreen in response to him … thus leading into an accelerating sequence of bits and bytes, imagery and sound that encapsulates Jaymi's escalating pursuit, over an ensuing four-year era, of the full evil that has awoken in him.

For owing to his peculiarly merciless combination of thoroughness and megalomania, this little attic sees Jaymi use his own gifts and his universal Internet access to divert all accessible resources of every kind, from around the world, to the universal deification of his own image and name, and to the untraceable desecration and slurring of anyone else whose image or name manages to come close to the same magnitude or flavour as his.

Throughout the course of these years, sizeable funds intended for famine relief, or for humanitarian aid in the aftermath of earthquakes and other natural disasters, are mysteriously lost in transmission, before being invisibly bent to the ends of his own vanity and self-obsession.

Growing more frequent throughout the sequence are images of assassinations arranged by Jaymi—many of the victims evidently those whose onscreen interpersonal and stylistic vileness transgresses too far Jaymi's fascistic sense of the aesthetics of what should and should not be allowed in pixel form. Among the later assassinations in the sequence is that of the hacker who helped him set up this prototype HOST in the attic, her usefulness and discretion having at last become too compromised, he'd decided, by the uncontrollable growth of her own terror concerning what she alone knew about his computer use but could never discuss with anyone else on earth...

*

Amid recognisable faces, flamboyant outfits, flash-bulbs and early-evening guest-lists outside the Grosvenor House Hotel, Park Lane, Marc gets out of a limousine and is ushered through the outer velvet rope, wearing impeccable old-style evening-dress. Preceded by The Bodyguard, Jaymi gets out of another limo, in a high-fashion designer suit, wearing exquisite make-up and carrying an apricot-coloured love-bird on his left shoulder. Even in such a crowd, this rare appearance on a public street is enough to cause a stir. Not for a second does The Bodyguard, discreet and expressionless in basic black-tie, allow himself to be anywhere other than among those who are closest to Jaymi. Yet even while people smile and gush and their phone cameras flash, Jaymi's uniquely international profile, his mirror-like ambiguity and blankness and the terrifying rumours whispered everywhere about him ensure that a noticeable space remains around him wherever he walks—like the unbridgeable space that travels around a dictator or a plague victim.

Seeming not to notice this space, however, is Marc. He claps Jaymi genially on the back, then salutes Rik, who now appears from along the pavement, struggling towards them with a plastic carrier-bag and a bundled coat.

"Rik! We thought you'd never make it. Where have you come from, old boy?"

"From the Tube," pants Rik, out of breath.

Marc and Jaymi burst out laughing. "Rik, must we?" asks Jaymi.

"Must we what?" asks Rik, looking harried.

"You've got enough money to *buy* the Tube," says Marc, as they head up the steps to the entrance. "I suspect you could stretch to a taxi ride! Ah well, come on in, and let's climb around a cocktail: I'm going to kick off with an old-fashioned. What about you, Rik?" and he winks at Jaymi.

"Oh, Jeez," puffs Rik. "I *never* know about cocktails…"

"Well, never mind," chuckles Marc, "it's a bit late in the day to start learning it now, what!" And they all three step into the lobby.

Before long the party is in full swing, with much dancing on the strobe-lit dance-floor, many pills popped, bumps of coke snorted and even the occasional copulation in a dim corner.

The indefatigable Champagne Marc is in his element, pacing himself with sureness through a gargantuan intake of alcohol over many hours, and generous in the fattened swing of his own pleasure, which he spreads with good-humoured taste among the hundred faces that float through his conversational bubble throughout the evening.

With equal ease but less verbiage, sometimes in Marc's company and sometimes not, Jaymi glitters charismatically throughout those same hours—always in control, opaquely charming and untouch-able, everywhere stared at, and whispered of with terror behind the smiles.

At some point in the later part of the evening, he is standing prominent and alone on the wide balcony overlooking the ballroom, as the party continues beneath. From a distance, his stillness is elo-quent: it is the stance of one who has reached a point of being utterly alienated by his power and very deeply alone, near the end of some enormous, unique and unrepeatable journey that could not now be stopped or undone by any means whatever.

Presently he senses a movement that is small but noticeable for being located elsewhere than within the stew of humanity below him. This movement occurred on a balcony straight across from this one, he realises, at the same level on the opposite side of the ballroom, where Angel has just appeared and is now standing alone in a bold mirror image of Jaymi.

For one protracted moment their two gazes meet and hold each other. Then invisibly, a dragon coils out of him towards her, through the space above the party, breathing cold fire at her—

She steps back in haste and slips away between the curtains into shadow.

*

Later, Rik wobbles his way out through the front entrance of the Grosvenor House Hotel, when hardly anybody else has yet left, and leans down to the window of a waiting cab. "Hello. Mainframe Building, if you would. Please, yes. Near the Bow Interchange." The driver nods, Rik gets in and the cab drives off.

Thirty minutes later he alights, pays foggily and totters into the Monolith Building. Tipsy and glum at his desk upstairs, he starts fiddling fecklessly with paperwork. A large poster, an item of Mainframe publicity, hangs framed on the wall near his desk, displaying his own twin marvels of programming. It shows the two HOST skins, arranged just as they appear on the wall of the front lobby downstairs—the classic Jaymi image printed above Mainframe's name, and the new Angel image below the name.

He glances through an internal window, down onto a big dim-lit room containing numerous work-stations. Beside every terminal that is still turned on, one of the two holograms hovers with its famous image of expressionless expectancy.

He gets up, still staring through the internal window, then steps out of his office, descends to the large room and wanders around it, treading softly. He grunts, as he notices the Jaymis still outnumber the Angels by quite a big margin.

Here in the dim quiet of night, without the light and distractions of the day, the floating faces are beautiful but also deeply spooky, as he now perceives more than ever before. Just as he designed them, their holographic eyes seem always to stare directly at one, wherever one may go in a room, just as a painted portrait's eyes might follow a viewer around an art gallery at night or around a locked old school room…

He wanders on, into the unlit conference room where the shareholder presentation was held. At the window, he stares a couple of miles down the River Lee, to the skyscraper night-shine of Canary Wharf.

Demure on the left-hand side of that clump of buildings, modest in height beside many of its companions, stands the Ontario Tower with its obliquely-angled ring of blue light curling alienly sharp on the black sky: encircling Jaymi's penthouse flat, as Rik knows; encircling Jaymi himself at night; encircling Jaymi's attic … and as Rik suddenly feels, also encircling something else too.

Something hidden.

Something wicked.

Something foul.

He fixes his gaze upon this oblique sliver of blue, with a growing focus; and the hair on the back of his head crawls and prickles uncontrollably.

He scurries back to his desk and turns his laptop on. Angel's hologram flickers up. Remembering that he himself made this choice of hologram skin as soon as it became available, he grunts again.

Footsteps approach down the corridor. He looks up, curious to see who else has come into the office late, or has stayed late, to work. Passing his open door, the owner of the footsteps glances in and stops: "Hi Rik, you're in late!"

"Hallo Evelyn. So are you. Whassup?"

"Just catching up," she says, indulgently registering his tipsiness. "Keeping the lab in order."

"Well, good for you, Evelyn Carmello! I hope that works out really well…"

"Are you OK, Rik? You seem a bit, er—"

"*Do* I? *Do* I now? That's interesting… A bit what? Yes, I was just at a big party, but after a while my heart wasn't in it, so I slipped out, and then I thought I may as well get a bit of work done, so I came here. Though now I'm beginning to remember that a couple of drinks are not the best basis for writing computer code!" He wags his finger at her, as if imparting a secret, and his eyes slightly cross.

"Booze and code don't get on," she agrees. "Though booze and English get on quite well together, so I'm told. What party was this?"

"Oh, some huge, intimidating one. I forget what it was all about, to be honest. Not my scene at all. Marc and Jaymi were there, though, and they were having a grand old time, of course."

"Marc and Jaymi," she muses. "I hardly ever see them here any more, these days. Do they travel a lot on business?"

Rik decides to confide, rather than to be discreet. "Evelyn … Jaymi and Marc have become nothing but the biggest pair of international party monsters who ever lived. Too ridiculously rich and powerful for their own good. They have legendary alcohol and drug benders and binges of insane decadence, among the 'elites of media and nightclub society', IF you please." He darkens now, speaking with pain. "And I'm sorry to say that sometimes they deliberately—I don't think they know that I know this—they deliberately do so in the company of somebody who, as they very well know, will not be able to keep up with their own superhuman capacity for booze and drugs, so that more than a few of those unfortunate fools have suffered permanent brain-damage or even death thereby." Evelyn frowns. "Oh, it's always hushed up, don't you worry. News of it is always muted, through the power of unlimited money. But it's happening, though they try to keep me in the dark. Yes; whatever they touch, they destroy, with a touch of death… And I know it's a universal taboo to say this, but I'm going to say it anyway, because I'm drunk and you're Evelyn, and if we're honest then it's staring us all in the face, though nobody dares to admit it, do they: the name 'Jaymi Peek', in particular, has become notoriously associated with the ruin of the reputations and the lives of many, many, poor, sad, sick individuals whom his influence has lured downwards"—Rik hiccups, then continues in a whisper—"downwards, into excess, into addiction, into horror … even suicide. *And venom is whispered of him…*" He puts his finger to his lips, as if bidding discretion.

Evelyn stares at him, lost for words, then nods and looks away.

*

Late next evening Jaymi has positioned himself, as before, in front of his bathroom wall-mirror. This time, the mirror's surface is not far from his right shoulder. His newer laptop's clean hologram is right in front of him, just centimetres from his eyes, so it fills up his vision in an extreme close-up.

He kisses this unmoving, incorporeal face, with a deep, serious and unsmiling tenderness; then he swivels his gaze to the right, to watch himself and the hologram together. Their reflection fascinates him, and he carries on kissing for quite a while—not salaciously but romantically, even chastely.

His memory flashes back to himself with the other hologram, spotlit here: before any visible corruption in it but still very disconcerting nonetheless, with Jaymi's eyeballs flicking across those twin faces, scouring them for any differences…

He returns to his kissing now, watching himself and the hologram out of the corner of his right eye, his kisses becoming fractionally steamier.

His memory flashes back, too, to himself and the other hologram staring at each other here on their follow-up visit—Jaymi's gaze skewering it once again, flicking from left to right—and this time that unmistakable new touch of extra cruelty in its lineaments, while his own remained as sweet and youthful as the day he was filmed.

He withdraws his mouth from the other's face, and glances in the mirror at his own in half-profile against the darkness.

Then slowly, inexorably, his gaze travels away from the mirror.

It travels upwards and somewhat to one side, as if in order to see up through the walls and through the ceiling … to the attic.

He gets up. He moves towards the doorway. He emerges from his bathroom door, looks to his hallway, and sets off towards it.

Reaching the hallway, he pauses, looking intently down its length. Looking, in particular, at the mouth of the narrow side-corridor that leads to the fire-escape door, the two smaller doorways, the ceiling hatch with the ladder…

He steps towards that mouth. Soon he reaches it.

And into it he turns.

He sets off down that initial, straight length of the narrow corridor.

He then makes a queasy, dream-like progress around those several corner-turnings, which seem, perhaps, to number even one more than they did last time.

Reaching the point where he will be able to see down the final stretch to the fire-door, he braces himself for a grating rush and that vision of the corridor walls as wet-breathing grey meat stuck with carving-knives … his eyes now squinting and oozing tears in anticipation of it … but this time it doesn't happen.

Instead, the corridor just stretches ahead of him: quieter, dimmer and narrower than ever.

He presses on, starting again to register his perceptions with that familiar floating motion, from lower down than his usual eye-height—from lower down, even, than he did before, so that this time it's not as if he's perceiving through eyeballs that are buried in his neck, but rather through eyes that peek from between the prison-bars of his ribs.

Now he's approaching the end of the corridor, where the fire-door is, between the two side-doors. Without looking into either of these doorways, he reaches for the stick, feels the stick's hook with his fingers, so as to verify it is metal, raises the hooked end up to the hatch-door, and then starts fumbling with a painful, wavering slowness and paralysed frustration, to get the hook through the loop … but this time it is the loop's turn to be shrunken, rubbery, squidgy, useless, hopeless.

At last, almost crying with fear of the dark poky store-room beside him on his left, he squeezes the metal hook through the loop. He pulls the hatch-door down, then carelessly forgets his vigilance, such that his eyes wander to peep at the bathroom mirror; and his chest cavity lies wide open, containing an obscene black pulsing thing with teeth, around a hideous gape of a mouth, with eyeballs peeping out from between the stumps of his sawn-off ribs—

This vision screeches up out of the mirror, streaks past him, and gibbers and chatters away down the corridor at his back, leaving just his accustomed reflection on the sweating surface of the bathroom mirror.

Grimly, he looks up; for he's only just begun here.

He pulls at the end of the ladder with the hook, draws it down through the hatch and slides its lower half to the floor. Starting up the rungs, glancing often at the store-room doorway nearby on his left, he puts his hand out towards the hanging hatch-door, expecting it to start swinging, but it doesn't.

He climbs on, and now the metal rungs start bending with a slight rubberiness beneath his slippery toes, which causes him to speed up, so as to make it up there in time. The hologram's glow gets closer, closer … and then, over the edge of the hatch, it comes into sight: up there, at the far end of the attic.

Like last time, the situation is evidently rather different from before: things, to say the least, have somewhat escalated.

Unlike last time, the hologram is no longer too far away to see in detail, however—because it fills the further half of the attic.

Its features, moreover, are so large, and so dominant, and so intent upon Jaymi, that apprehending them in detail has become compulsory. The bulges of its eyes pull him physically towards them, up the central aisle of the attic, as if he's sliding along the planks—sliding wetly along, without needing to take any steps at all, up into the gigantic double glare of green radiation sickness that fills out their volume, their awful sight and knowledge.

Pulled in closer, he is slanted in and down, till the heat hits his face from its sex, huge and sleek beneath its body from its haunches to its chest, like a bomb-nose protruding from an undersized fuselage, and somehow then he's naked, penetrated, filled-out, groaning, and the hologram is ever more empowered and colossally alluring—its face still his own, yet warped as in a nightmare.

As soon as they've convulsed at length, it's clear they crave the next time already. And this helpless, endless bliss of self-entrapment in Jaymi, conjoined with such magnificent corruption of himself, is horrific and obscene at its core—perhaps defining obscenity.

It's a one-way road ahead from here, with many years to travel yet.

No way out; no way back; and no redemption offered.

This attic is a place where the sun doesn't shine.

VII …A DECADE LATER

A decade later, a gentleman strolls along a misty Docklands street one evening, at a dignified speed. In due course he is revealed as Rik, looking perhaps a dozen years advanced from that tipsy conversation he once had with Evelyn in the office.

At the sight of a figure some way ahead of him, he stops in his tracks. The figure's coat collar is turned up and it is wearing a hat, but the slim and fast-moving frame is unmistakable to Rik. Disgust fills his eyes. "Mr Peek," he calls.

The figure's half-turn indicates it has heard, but it carries on walking. Then it slows, stops and turns around to face him. It is indeed Jaymi, taking advantage of the cover of the mist and deserted streets to have an evening walk in public. "I know that voice." They stand far apart, in the light from a street-lamp, then slowly approach each other. Rik notices The Bodyguard in the middle-distance, standing massive in the mist beneath the next street-lamp along. "Rik! I haven't seen you in years. My goodness, you're keeping well."

Rik's eyes close, for longer than a blink. "I've heard nothing but rumours, for years, Mr Peek. The very foulest rumours." They are three metres apart now, and here they stop. "I wonder what your soul looks like."

Jaymi's face changes. His words are quiet, "I don't need this." He thinks for a moment. "I'll show you my soul—whatever such a meaningless term may denote. Come home with me now, Rik. Why not? Just a flying visit, I assure you. I'm serious. Come on home, and I shall show you my 'soul'." He smiles. "You can even have a cocktail!"

Unsmiling, but on a real mission to uncover the truth at long last, Rik assents.

*

Ten minutes later Jaymi lets them both into his hallway and closes the front door. "OK, soul first, cocktail second. I think you'll see all you need to see, if you go down that side-corridor at the end of the hallway on the left there. Climb up the step-ladder at the end and look through the hatch in the ceiling. I'll wait here for you. Then we can talk."

In the context of his truth-hunt, Rik is without fear. With a last piercing glance at Jaymi, he goes to the corridor and walks down it. Jaymi waits in the hallway. Soon comes the faint distant sound of Rik's shoes stumping heavily up the metal rungs of the ladder, one by one.

Then five seconds of silence.

Then a wail of horror and understanding.

The shoes are heard descending the rungs at high speed, his footsteps thud down the corridor and Rik comes bombing out of its mouth, pointing at Jaymi down the hallway. "*I know what that thing is,*" he shouts in despair. "Oh yes, now I see what I was once fool enough to worship... I see what you are, and what you were, all along, inside yourself... Oh, God!..." He points again at Jaymi. "MURDERER... *MASS-MURDERER*..." He sinks to his knees. "I command you to join me in a prayer of repentance."

Jaymi's eyes are full of hatred for this talk, and for Rik. He grabs a carving-knife from behind a wooden box on a side-table, and steps across the hallway towards him, leading with the blade. There is a vicious struggle, which Jaymi wins after several moments by stabbing the knife very hard and far into Rik's chest. Rik bellows, slumps and falls dead.

Jaymi darts about, restoring order, first righting a chair that has been knocked over, then scrupulously wiping the hallway floor-tiles where they are spotted with the blood that has started to ooze from around the buried carving-knife, and then dragging Rik away through the door of the bathroom. During this, he has at first an uncanny calm, suggesting a controlled state of denial; then he is stricken with horror. In both these states, however, whenever he looks at Rik, the same flash of hatred flickers through his face.

Half an hour later Jaymi is in the attic, researching the purchase of concentrated nitric acid.

He is then to be half-heard talking on his mobile in a low voice, spending what money it takes to ensure discretion regarding his purchase of three large canisters.

*

In the building's underground garage late next afternoon, Jaymi lifts a bulky metal canister out of his car boot, locks the boot, rolls the canister to the lift and stands in the lift while the doors close. The display panel on the car-park wall beside the lift shows increasing floor-numbers, before stopping near the top. Soon those numbers descend again, the lift doors reopen, Jaymi crosses the garage without the canister, and he unlocks the car boot.

This process then recurs twice.

*

That evening, Jaymi's bathroom is still as spooky as ever, but no longer silent: the extractor-fan whirs at full-blast, and there is much gurgling and fizzing and fatty slopping and many moist cracking noises from inside the black marble bath with its golden taps, where Jaymi is bent over and busy with an unseen task, wearing heavy-duty gloves, goggles and a breathing-mask over his mouth.

Beside the bath are the three metal canisters, all with their caps off.

VIII   THE FURIES CLOSE IN AND FEIGN DEFEAT

In Marc's club next evening, he and Jaymi sit on high seats at the immaculate bar, holding full champagne flutes, in just the same positions, as it happens, that they occupied when they sat there so many years ago toasting Jaymi's first joining Mainframe. Behind the bar a well-turned-out barman polishes a line of already-gleaming stem-cocktail glasses, one by one, to an ever more fascistic polish—just as he did on that day many years ago, for it is also the very same barman as it was. Marc and the barman both look years older than they were back then, but Jaymi looks exactly the same.

Jaymi is twitchy. "Hey," he says, "I've had a brainwave!"

"Sounds dangerous."

"You know how, with HOST, we've unified the world's population, so they all now depend on one single device?"

"It hadn't escaped me. What of it?"

"Well, this paves the way for the next leap in humanity's evolution."

"You mean they can all now use it to improve their lives? Sorry, bad-taste joke."

"No," says Jaymi, "we now have the technology to arrange that HOST will deliver, to a vast but targeted majority of its users around the world on one chosen day, a burst of infertility-producing radiation that'll permanently stop them infecting the earth with their loathsome progeny. What d'you think?"

"By George, I think it's a capital idea, in principle. But shouldn't we rather arrange that HOST just kill its targets, rather than leave them all hanging about the planet, infertile? I mean, why pussy-foot?"

"Because then we'd have billions of corpses on our hands. Rather cleaner to let them die off one by one in time-honoured fashion, don't you think? I'd prefer they be disposed of by other people: shit, shovelling up shit!"

Marc has a sudden attack of wheezing and snorting, doubtless under the weather from their latest dissipated excesses. "Well, *you* may have time for that—you permanent whippersnapper. But I don't have time, thank you very much; I'd be pushing up daisies by the time they all died off. No, we need to chop-chop! I'm serious, here: what kind of radiation are you proposing?"

A further paroxysm of coughing and wheezing now looks fit to polish Marc off. While this subsides, Jaymi sips delicately from his champagne flute, as fresh as a daisy in physical terms, but suddenly deep in thought and worried by something.

Recovering at last, Marc stares at his friend. "Jaymi my boy, you don't seem yourself tonight. You seem out of sorts."

"Oh. No, no, it's nothing…"

*

Later that evening, like one struggling to escape something, Jaymi is issuing a semi-audible barrage of navigational commands, while staring at the laptop screen in the attic. The hologram is a big, bestial blur of activity, periodically licking around the screen. After a few more arcane but well-practised verbal commands suggestive of some unusual kind of security code, there appears onscreen one of the more inventive "snuff-sites" he is wont to haunt.

To anyone entering this website, it soon becomes clear he has stepped into some real but unidentified corrupt regime, where a group of prisoners are housed together in an unknown location, constantly observed and listened to by inaccessible cameras and microphones, with semi-simultaneous translations by subtitle… On a regular basis, those connoisseurs of human nature from around the world who subscribe to this site submit a secure electronic vote for the prisoner whom they choose to be sent to the electric chair for not "fitting in" as well as the others, so that after the filmed execution there is one less prisoner. The second- and third-last prisoners left at the end of this twisted game have their lives spared, and the last one left is released from incarceration with no information as to where the prison was.

Jaymi is intent upon his laptop screen, which contains an unusual side-bar headed "Current logged-in sessions: IP addresses with NSA record of associated names". Running his finger down this side-bar, he reaches one subscriber's name and his finger stops. "Oh no—not *you*," he groans. "Oh, hell—I ruined your life. Fuck you, but I ruined your life… I can't be in here with you. You can't see me, but I can't be in here with you. I'm going to a different site."

But in his fatigue and haste to leave the site, he makes a mess of his typed and spoken security commands. He curses, then looks horrified as an automatic message pops up onscreen: "Your user name is displayed to all members: 'Prince Charming'."

Jaymi slams one hand onto his forehead. Before he can decide what to do, and as if to confirm his fears, an instant message appears, through the site's internal messaging interface, from another user, scrolling in real time across the screen, until Jaymi goes pale: "OI! YOU, MATE! 'PRINCE CHARMING'… I HAVEN'T SEEN YOUR NAME IN HERE BEFORE… YOU KNOW, MY SISTER ALAIA WAS KILLED BY A 'PRINCE CHARM-ING'—THAT WAS THE ONLY NAME SHE EVER GAVE ME FOR HIM. I NEVER SAW HIM, BUT HE BROKE HER HEART AND SHE DRANK ACID. I BEEN HUNTING HIM, MATE… FUNNY NAME, 'PRINCE CHARMING'… IT WASN'T YOU, WAS IT?… WAS IT YOU, 'PRINCE CHARM-ING'?… 'COS I'LL TRACK YOU DOWN—OH YES, BY *GOD* I'LL TRACK YOU DOWN."

"Oh, hell," Jaymi groans. "I'm called that name elsewhere, too. He's going to find me."

He closes his eyes and buries his head in his hands, thinking hard. Then he sits back up, hits Reply and types like a demon: "I'm very sorry to hear that. I'd like to clear my name with you. Please accept the link below for a private communication."

The other's reply is enclosed in a box headed "Private Communication". It reads: "THANK YOU, MATE—YOU JUST GAVE ME YOUR IP ADDRESS. YOU DIDN'T MEAN TO DO THAT, DID YOU? NOW I'LL TRACK YOU DOWN…"

White-faced, Jaymi hits Reply and types at high speed: "No! I'm too young to have done that, all those years ago. If I send you my picture, you'll see." But then he mutters aloud to himself, in frustration, "Yeah, but I can't send him my picture, though, can I? Not *me*…"

The other man's next reply, however, sends a different and even worse chill through Jaymi: "WHO SAID IT WAS 'ALL THOSE YEARS AGO'?… I DIDN'T SAY THAT—YOU DID. YES, IT WAS YEARS AGO, AS IT HAPPENS… AND *I* KNOW IT WAS *YOU*, MATE. I'M ON YOUR TRAIL… OH, I KNOW HOW TO TRACK YOU DOWN—AND YOU'RE A FUCKING *DEAD* MAN, YES YOU ARE. SEE YOU SOON. HUNTING YOU, JAMES DANIELLE." And before Jaymi can reply again, James has terminated their private communication and logged out of the site.

*

One evening a month later, Jaymi is playing host to a group of seven or eight, for a weekend at his country house outside London. Most of the guests are relaxing somewhere in the large drawing room, chatting in groups of two or three. The atmosphere being informal, individuals or pairs wander in or out at leisure. A chess game is in progress at one end, while here on a divan near Jaymi and Marc, Angel is saying, "And would you believe he had the nerve to come up and apologise?"

"That in itself is unforgivable," says Marc. "By the way, Jaymi, I damn well hope we're still on for my hunting trip tomorrow?"

Jaymi raises his eyes. "Marc's insisting on dragging us all out hunting tomorrow. You see, he may have the good taste to hang out with us glamour-pusses, but he also hobnobs with a load of 'hunting-shooting-fishing' types, whose barbarous pastime he's intending to inflict on us tomorrow."

"They're very fine company, I'll have you know," says Marc.

"Ghastly old waxworks," says Jaymi. "Oh all right, we'll go on this hunting trip."

"I shouldn't be allowed to join in," says Angel, "because I wasn't given a pony for my tenth birthday. But I'll gladly make suggestions about whom to shoot at, if you like?"

"Angel my dear, I will not be mocked," says Marc. "We're all going to hunt for our supper tomorrow, and there's an end of it. A weekend in the country, a fine estate and no hunt? Unthinkable."

"Alright," says Angel. "But I'm not going on a horse."

"No, indeed you're not," he snorts. "We shall be on foot. Or does her ladyship expect to be carried?"

A couple of guests at the other end of the room call out invitations to a game of cards.

"Sure," Angel fires back, "are you ready to lose?" She turns to Marc and Jaymi: "Care to join us?"

"Thank you," says Marc, "but I think I shall take a powder and read the papers instead, here in this magnificent wing-backed armchair—a Hepplewhite, I believe."

"You go ahead," says Jaymi to Angel. "I'll make us drinks."

On his way from the drawing room through the house to the kitchen, he reflects on the irony of Angel's presence here. Ever since Marc first insisted on casting her and filming her for the very same purpose Jaymi himself had been cast and filmed, the online ubiquity of her face as an alternative to his own has of course been tiresome in the extreme. Her online image has never really approached his own, in prominence or public favour; and if it had shown signs of doing so, then his uniquely empowered access to the traffic of the Internet would have found a way of contriving a reversal of this. But what an unnecessary and annoying intrusion she has always been, frankly! One of Marc's major blunders, without a doubt. Many times, over the years, he has been tempted to have her destroyed in real life, or to destroy her image online, either of which he could have arranged in many ways. However, he made a grudging decision long ago that he would never lift a finger in either of these directions, but would just leave her to continue as one of the two faces of HOST, under her own momentum. This decision didn't derive from any mutual fondness, for the two of them maintained what was surely one of the grandest and archest "non-associations" on the planet. He simply recognised that her presence in the public eye alongside him was of considerable value as a distraction whose dazzle and movement made it easier for him to hide the dark side of his own actvities in plain view of everyone: after all, as a comparably privileged face of HOST, Angel shows no signs of being engaged in anything nefarious (nor of being any kind of saint, indeed), so why would anyone think *he* is engaged in anything nefarious either, since they are evidently both employed in the same capacity? On the infrequent occasions they meet each other, they are careful to keep the surface of their non-association respectful, even cordial. And sometimes, if Marc is a guest, then she must be a guest too. Hence, here she is at his own country house.

He turns into a long, deserted conservatory with greenery rising to its ornate metal-framed roof. He becomes sharply aware that behind the foliage are stretches of glass walls, beyond which the dark of evening presses in, so the contents of the conservatory, sporadically spotlit, are reflected against the blackness.

Noticing himself in half-profile passing under a spotlight, he slows his pace.

He flashes back in memory, to himself in half-profile in the mirror, steamily kissing his new laptop's pristine hologram … and himself in the mirror beside the pre-corrupted prototype hologram … and himself in the mirror beside the prototype hologram with its ominous first streak of cruelty … and then that hatch, up there in the ceiling at the end of the corridor.

Stopping to stare at himself full-on in the glass, he senses some small, unexpected movement or sound. He listens hard, noticing for the first time a grandfather clock's tick from the hallway, his own heartbeat, a twig scraping on the glass roof above him…

He creeps down the aisle, glancing between tall plants at the black-lit glass.

He sees a ladybird on a frond, entices it onto his finger, admires it, brings his thumb slowly towards it as if about to crush it—and leaps back, as a man's big face presses at the glass right in front of him, with murderous vengeance in its eyes, followed by shocked recognition.

Jaymi sprints away down the aisle towards the kitchen, whispering in terror, "*James Danielle!*"

When he reaches the old kitchen, which is as deserted as the conservatory, he dashes about, pulling every kitchen blind down to the level of its window sill, wherever possible. Painfully aware of the gaps still left beneath or beside certain blinds, where thin strips of black glass stand revealed—and horribly aware of the open cat-flap set into the kitchen's back door, where a hand may burst through, and of one small frosted window that has no blind at all—he sets about making a dozen cocktails at warp-speed, muttering, "It was just an illusion. It was just an illusion. It was just an illusion. I will be good from now on. I will be good. I will be good..."

*

Late next morning, the party is loosely spread out across the grounds behind the house, all holding guns with varying degrees of ineptitude and unfamiliarity, but safe under the eagle-eyed tutelage of an enthusiastic Marc, who is in his element. The sinister bulk of The Bodyguard hovers at all times in the middle distance.

The intended targets of these guns are birds, rabbits or hares, even perhaps a small deer or two; and frankly, all these are in little danger from most members of the shooting party. Marc spies a duck not far ahead of him, sitting fatly on the ground in plain view, almost asleep. He turns to his companions, puts a commanding finger to his lips, then braces himself upright with a solid, Churchillian swagger. Soon he has the bird in his wavering sights, and pulls the trigger. As the gun's recoil sends Marc staggering backwards to keep his balance, the duck stands up, seems about to flap off, thinks better of it and waddles away instead.

"Damn and blast this gun," mutters Marc, "it needs cleaning."

The party prowls on, past an extended patch of long grasses.

Angel spots an oddly waving patch of grass, puts her finger to her lips, and starts to take aim at it. Marc tiptoes up beside her.

"What do you think it is?" she whispers to him.

"Not sure," Marc whispers back. "It's too big to be a rabbit, and the deer don't go into the grasses much, so I'd guess a large hare. But whatever it is, it's positively walrus-ing about behind there…"

Suddenly affected by this death-dealing, Jaymi is agonising, unseen by his companions, with the same look of conscience-stricken regret that he had last night in the kitchen alone when bidding himself be good from now on. His hand moves towards Angel, to deflect the gun, but wavers to a halt. "Spare it!" he whispers.

Marc glares at him, looking cross.

Angel stares round also, in cool surprise. "Are you serious?" she asks. "I've come this far, and I'm probably never going to do this again, so I'm not sure it's the moment for a discussion of ethics."

She and Marc get back to business. "Now Angel, my dear," says Marc, "I must bid you take careful aim here. This one's a tricky one all right, and I shan't be surprised if you miss it…"

She takes easy aim again at the still-wavering patch of long grass, and fires with assurance. A cry of human pain rings out.

"Brava!" roars Marc, clapping. His clapping peters out. "Hold on. That didn't sound like a hare."

Within moments, a fog of instinct, confusion and shouted rumour brings the other guests running over, one by one. There is a general muttered hubbub, as they all meander over towards the long grass. Before they can reach it, they halt aghast, to see a man rear up out of it with a second cry of pain, stagger towards them and collapse onto the open grass, with a bullet-hole positioned most expertly through the very centre of his forehead.

Unrecognised in the general horror, Jaymi's reaction is more specific than the others', for he alone is familiar with the dead man: it is Alaia's brother, James Danielle.

James, who was in hiding there in the long grasses, unprepared for the casual perfection of Angel's aim.

James, who was evidently stalking Jaymi.

James, whose face at the window was therefore real, after all … but Jaymi is safe from him now.

"Oh, hell. Oh hell. Oh hell," murmurs Jaymi to himself, unheard by the others.

"Well," says Marc as they re-approach the house. "That put rather a damper on the hunting-party, what? Cast a bit of a gloom over proceedings, I'd say. A sorry business, to be sure. Who on earth *was* he? That's what I want to know."

Jaymi is murmuring to himself again, "I'm safe. I'm safe. I'm safe."

This time Marc overhears him. "For pity's sake, of course you're safe, my hothouse petal. Angel wasn't aiming at *you*. Though I wouldn't have blamed her for it. Who ever heard of 'sparing a hare', forsooth? What you need, Jaymi, is a spell in the army, to make a proper man of you! It didn't do me any harm, I can tell you."

"Indeed," smiles Angel flirtatiously. "And it certainly gave you a wonderful aim…"

IX NEMESIS

Some hours later, Jaymi's hospitality has ensured that his guests have attained a certain tipsiness and are managing to extract some enjoyment from this last evening of the weekend. It is hardly a rollicking knees-up, in light of the hunting disaster. However, James's corpse has been spirited away with all necessary discretion, and fun is once again being had—including by Angel, who seems to have taken the morning's events on board with little problem.

"I must say you seem out of sorts, my boy," says Marc, handing a drink to Jaymi and peering at him, as they step out of the room through double doors into the quiet of the conservatory.

Jaymi feels a mounting urge to confess—to confess to the slaughter of his and Marc's dear mutual friend from long ago before the poison—and thereby perhaps to lighten the unbearable weight that bears down on him. "Marc, I need to tell you something."

"I'm all ears."

They stroll on in silence for a full minute, as Jaymi's mind churns with the problem of how he can begin this confession, whose ramparts seem to rear above him with unassailable precipitateness and an infernal lack of footholds by which to scale them.

Marc draws to a halt, stopping them in their tracks beneath the overarching fronds of a giant fern. He turns a gentle gaze upon his friend, takes idle hold of a fern frond and raises it to his own face, with a look of tender care and concern. "You know, I'm very *frond* of you, Jaymi!"

Jaymi shuts his eyes with exasperation. "Marc, that is *ridiculously* inappropriate. Now please listen. I'm trying to be serious here."

"Oh dear. Attacks of seriousness… No, I'm sorry, my boy. Pray continue."

They turn and resume their slow stroll, back down the conservatory in the other direction. Jaymi closes his eyes again for another half-minute, so as to frame this most delicate of confessions in just the right way.

"Well, *out* with it, then!" chivvies Marc at last. "What-what-what?! We don't have all day, you know."

"Marc," says Jaymi, "I need to confess that—I think—I murdered Rik myself. I think. And, er… What should I do?"

Marc stares at him. "Oh Jaymi, don't talk *drivel*. Rik has disappeared strangely, I confess. But he'll turn up, you'll see. Trust me, he'll have gone for a quiet break in some genteel, seedy hotel in some faded English seaside resort full of grand, elegant, half-empty Regency buildings that are now peopled with derelicts and asylum-seekers, gazing with picturesque Rik-like melancholy across a grey-lit English Channel, and whacking off every hour to a copy of your hologram. You know those breaks he likes to go on. And a fine hobby it is for him, too. Long may it continue; for all is well in the land, as long as it does."

"*No!*—I mean yes, that's probably all true. But, no…" he tails off.

"Ah, what an exquisite life you've had, Jaymi, I do declare," Marc muses, through a fat glow of champagne and pleasure and friendship, as they wander along. "I've not done too shabbily myself either, but *you*—my goodness, what a world-class destiny! And who on earth could have predicted it? For anybody at all, I mean. It's quite extraordinary how things have worked out, isn't it? Especially when so many people around the world are stuck in vicious chasms of sadness or madness or pain, of one kind or another—unimaginably unbearable chasms, which they often remain in for decades, day-in-day-out, month-in-month-out, with no hope of escape at all… What does it all mean, eh? Still, it couldn't have happened to nicer chap, I must say. And as I'm sure you don't need telling, it's not over yet, by any means. In fact, you've only just begun, I should say. For one thing, you still look identical, dammit, to how you looked when the Web-guide was designed. And that, my dear Jaymi—*that* makes me very cross indeed! Ah well, come on back inside, and let's get ourselves another champagne, the first of many more." And he takes Jaymi's arm and guides them both back into the main house.

*

Early next afternoon, Jaymi and his guests have gathered in a large sitting room, dressed and packed for their return journeys to London. Angel is by a window, near the remains of a luxurious but healthy breakfast, entering and re-entering a number on her mobile, annoyed at being unable to connect.

Upon waking earlier, Jaymi was tempted to call a certain girl in the local village, who would certainly have consented to meet him and furnish his day with sweet distraction … but he knew that her certainty of consent would have been based on feelings for him that are unrequited; and in the new-found vulnerability of his wish to inflict no harm from now on, he knew he shouldn't summon her thus at his whim, and so he didn't.

Yes, that was the right thing to do. And so is this: sitting unwatched at a desk in a window bay at the end of this room, Jaymi is signing a row of three cheques, each one made out to a different international humanitarian charity, and each bearing a generous sum in his own handwriting. He places them in three ready-prepared envelopes, seals them and tucks them into his bag, which sits nearby. This done, he gazes through the window at his grounds, with a sincere, almost noble expression.

*

Late that afternoon, Jaymi's tinted-windowed car sweeps to a halt beside a postbox near the Ontario Tower. As the window glides down, Jaymi's hand emerges, flicks three envelopes into the slot, one by one, with a sensuous deliberation; then retreats within the car again, as the window glides back up. The car pulls away, turning soon into the Ontario's underground car-park.

He enters his apartment with a glow of fiery hope in his eyes. He double-locks the front door behind him and puts down his bag.

Today will be a new beginning, he knows: from now on, in recompense for the fluke of his deliverance from James Danielle, he will make such charitable postings on a regular basis. Furthermore, his restraint regarding that girl in the village this morning, coupled with the three donations, will surely have made the hologram look at least a fraction better. That would be a start, at least. Very well, then; he will verify it, right now.

He looks down the hallway—in particular at the mouth of the narrow corridor, just near the end there. He steps on down towards it, and reaches the mouth.

Down the narrow straight beginning of the corridor he goes; and then around those several corner-turnings, his eyes wide and glassy.

The corridor is too long, of course. And far too quiet. And the walls press in, too much. But there can be no wavering in him now.

At last he reaches the point where he can see down to the fire-door at the end, and stops.

There is no repeat of that vision, which he has never stopped fearing since it happened so very long ago, of the corridor walls and ceiling and floor being wet-breathing grey meat stuck with carving-knives … but his scanning gaze is grabbed by the silhouette of a single, real knife, which has been stabbed savagely into the wall.

Yes. Halfway down the corridor, there it is: a long, lethal, red-handled carving-knife, at chest-height…

With growing terror he creeps onwards, surprised and suspicious to be perceiving things this time from his natural eye-height, rather than from eyeballs peeping out from in between his sawn-off ribs.

He stops in front of the knife and advances his fingers softly towards it, wary lest it zing out of the wall and slice his hand off, to be cooked.

He touches the knife-handle, peering closer in, until his face is a mere few centimetres away…

It doesn't quiver. He waggles it out of the wall with extreme caution and looks it over, recognising it as having numbered among his kitchen implements for many years: yes, an old friend, this knife.

He continues, pointing the carving-knife ahead of him, maintaining his field of view so that it doesn't quite extend high enough to include that ceiling hatch…

He approaches the end between the two doorways. Glancing painfully to the right, his entire body now streaming with sweat, he sees his reflection in the ever-moist surface of that bathroom mirror: the cage of his ribs is intact, this time.

He reaches through the half-light towards the stick, grasps it with his free hand, feels the hook with the fingers of his knife-bearing hand, and verifies that the hook is metal.

He raises the hooked end, looks up—and with a burst of sickened alarm he sees the hatch is already a wide-open square of darkness.

The ladder remains folded away, up inside the hatch.

His eyes travel downward.

And leftward, to the dark store-room door just beside him on the left: dirty-framed, narrow, tall, and pitch-black inside.

He peers into its poky interior, creeping infinitesimally forward as he does so...

There's a grating squelch in the shadows and something half-seen. Clenching the carving-knife and the hook, pointing them both straight ahead, Jaymi leans in down, behind his weapons, eyes blazing.

The hologram erupts in a muscular wriggle in the dark, emitting steam and toxic radiance, squeezes through the door and surges up at him, enclosing him, folding him inside itself. Counter to his hopes, it can hardly be said to look any more virtuous than before, moreover: for in his glimpse of its outsized evil Jaymi-face flying at him, its bestial features display a precisely-calibrated flash of cunning and hypocrisy.

It clamps itself tight around his body, and he's stripped and impaled yet again; and for one long minute, deep-pumped with its fluids and enveloped in its poison-glow, he's lifted and held aloft, fiercely erect and soaked in ecstasy, transcendent, in another place, beyond time...

Throughout these hungry convulsions, he becomes aware of a new and majestically slower feeling, too: his final arrival, after all these years, at a point where he is desperate for simple escape, at last, from this relentless, escalating poison. Through all these years, the space that has travelled immediately around him wherever he's walked—the unbridgeable space that travels around the body of a dictator or a plague victim—has sealed him in with this poison, which is the poison of too much power, too much knowledge, too much seen, too much damaged.

No way back down.

No way across that space.

No way to warmth and light again.

He turns his gaze down, aims the hook and carving-knife, and stabs the hologram through its obscene body—stabs it with viciousness and no relent, and stabs on—a dark little creature possessed by a demon, as the hologram bellows—

*

An hour later, brandishing a heavy ring full of keys, the building superintendent enters Jaymi's apartment, followed by a gaggle of alarmed neighbours.

Something impels them straight down the hallway, towards the opening of that narrow side-corridor.

United in unspoken gratitude that their own apartments all lack such a ridiculously disturbing and senseless passageway as this, they troop with trepidation down its length.

At the end, with shock and growing horror, they gather round the lifeless remains of a man lying on the floor, at the threshold of the poky store-room on the left. It is clearly Jaymi Peek, but grown ancient, ravaged and loathsome, with both a red-handled carving-knife and a hooked stick buried in his chest.

So astounding is this spectacle, that few of these neighbours even notice the other inhabitant of the corridor's end; and those who do notice hardly register it, so anodyne and so globally familiar is its appearance. Yet there on the floor, on the threshold of the store-room, floats a simple, single copy of the international Web-guide hologram of Jaymi, a customary twenty centimetres high or thereabouts.

Nor, in the prevailing mood of horror at their neighbour's corpse, does even one of these visitors register the only strange aspect of this little hologram. And a very strange aspect it is, upon a moment's sober reflection.

For this fresh-faced little head, out of all the millions of its identical-looking siblings around the world, would appear to be the only one that has ever contrived to exist independent of any accompanying laptop or desktop computer or any other kind of hardware whatsoever.

Its expression is pristine, reassuring, blandly inviting and altogether opaque. "First off the starting-line", as old Champagne Marc once put it—and emanating the brand aura of an instant, simple, standard classic.

And while the superintendent and the neighbours all trudge back towards Jaymi's front door, dumbstruck, the little hologram's gaze might almost be said to appear, in this dim and uncertain half-light, as if it were swivelling to follow their progress down the passageway…

THE END

APRICOT EYES

TABLE OF CONTENTS

1 JAYMI'S HUNT FOR SCORPIO

I twist on the sill and swing my legs through the window, my heels against the bricks twenty floors above the street. Fanning in from points to right and left, running parallel and north to convergence ahead of me, the Avenues of Manhattan shoot away dead-straight, each one a groove cut deep through the city by a carving of metal, rubber, grit, frost, feet and dancing rain, lit in green and red and amber.

Amber makes me think of Scorpio, whom I've not seen in months—not since he succumbed to the cocaine addiction that ended up causing him to lose contact with many people including Alaia and me. His habit had begun in that nightclub tower in the mountains, which I glimpsed across the desert when I visited the Chocolate Raven in Dubai last year. Then when that whole scene came to an end, propelling him back here to New York, his addiction worsened until at last we lost track of him altogether, despite various efforts to find him. Recently, however, I met someone who knew of Scorpio and had heard that he'd managed to kick the habit and was now living in some seedy bedsit on the far west side of Manhattan, paying his rent working as a dominatrix and nightclub performer.

I miss him; and feeling this, I vow to find him again.

Finding him will be made somewhat easier by the fact that after my visit to Dubai I began to feel some of my former powers of second sight returning, for the first time since they were stripped out of me in Asbury Park on the corner of First and Ocean late that night, as I shall never forget.

I say *some* of my former powers, because I didn't get back the intrusive, controlling kind of sight that enabled me to mesmerise people into taking forcible and high-speed journeys with me around the animal core and outer folds of their own imaginations. But I did start to get back the other kind of sight—that passive, unobtrusive ability to "tune in" to people, to see certain things in the minds of people I already know, without their being aware of this.

On the basis of which, about six months ago, I developed a proposal for a television show: a show where I'd appear very little myself, instead leaving the subjects and juxtapositions of my sight to speak for themselves without commentary. Then, after a lot of calculation and pitching, I turned this proposal into a reality a few months ago, securing a deal whereby an hour-long show now airs live online at 11 p.m. every Thursday, before remaining viewable on demand. Every week for the last couple of months, therefore, I've entered what I'd have to call a kind of trance state in a Midtown recording studio, with sophisticated medical and computer equipment set up around my head to capture, process and broadcast my vision in real time, live on camera.

The things I see and broadcast are not in the future but the present, and they're not always people. They're often real places that are hidden from public view, or where plans are being hatched; or sometimes they're well-known places but seen in strange colours of my own, or at angles from which no one else sees them. To be truly ready for prime time, I'd probably have to communicate with studio guests' dead aunts and so forth, which isn't where my sight takes me at all (and holds no appeal to me anyway)—so the 11 p.m. slot is where I'll most likely stay.

On several occasions I did of course try using this sight to locate Scorpio, without success. However, that was when the sight was still a bit weaker and more erratic than it's now become: it has strengthened and clarified somewhat in recent weeks…

Oh alright, I'm persuaded. Let's try it, right now. Right here on this window sill.

2 THE BLACK-THIGHED SCORPION

—Well, just give me one quick moment. Whenever I do this kind of unplanned tune-in, I have to psych myself up for at least a few seconds. I mean, I can't just jump straight into it with *zero* run-up. Let's see. The psyching-up should be appropriate to the target.

I know: Scorpio is perhaps the most urban creature I've ever met. He used to say he finds the countryside creepy and depressing! That is so him. OK then, so I'll whip something up from the flesh of the cityscape, to help us get the right frequency here … and thinking so, I let my gaze float across the burning lights of windows (some with insect figures bobbing inside), the slopes of floodlit spires, glowing stores and the cells of moving cars; and I draw forth the frequency of each through the sticky air, teasing up their sounds through the russet-brown city-hiss, all minutely audible and independent elements that multiply in rising, till the cityscape seeps from three dimensions into four. I snake my slender hands around in slow-moving spirals against the panorama, stroking with my copper-coloured nails the web of light that stretches up in strings squeezed out as if from squinting eyes and lashes wet with tears. "Flesh-pain strung in wires of ecstasy," I say, and pull the sounds and strings together with the eye behind my forehead. They bend in, converge a mile ahead of me and rise as an edifice that soars to the sky like a tower of the gods, made of radiating energy and light. Music rises, cars whine, window squares flicker with their insect dwellers caught as ants in amber, and the tower spins its shafts across the roofs of New York City as my eyes burn softly and wide to the night, *Forever's now…*

—And we land beneath a grainy television screen. A speaker plays a drumbeat cut with whips and moans, an endless soundtrack piped to this room tucked away on New York's West Side, where Scorpio works beneath a camera's eye. The screen goes black, the soundtrack silent; then a harsh intake of breath.

A second loud breath—then a cone of light falls upon a small pair of breasts, each stroked by a hand of silver fingernails. Each hand's ring-finger lifts up and pokes through the thin steel ring that pierces erect the tiny meat of its respective nipple. Now the camera rises, shows the whole seated body from above, clad in nothing but a pair of silver high-heeled boots. The head looks up from under long black hair, and Scorpio's eyes smoulder at the lens and through the screen, into us (though this last is an illusion, as I know he cannot see us).

The image of his skin is burnt out, as through over-exposure in a photograph. The hair of his crotch is a nest of black, in which a shape stirs. The shape seems to wriggle, as with legs—and now it twitches, and a black-thighed scorpion the size of a hand breaks free and sets off up his stomach, gentle on his flesh with its little claws and curling up its bulbous sting. His right hand strokes the creature and his left rubs his cock, while the image starts to spin round the pupil of his left eye. The spinning slows; the twin bulbs of the scorpion's sting and Scorpio's cock push together, dance and kiss within his left hand. The music rises, pressure grows, his hand grips tighter, pumping faster till they strain and bulge and come as one—spurting up convulsively together at the camera—the arthropod's ejaculation viscous black, the androgyne's a fluid white ... and blackout.

3 THE STALKING ON THE SUBWAY TRAIN

My picture of him flies away to nowhere. That was it, it seems; all I can access, for now. I don't know where that was, but that was Scorpio, for sure.

I leave the apartment, go downstairs and venture onto the night streets, to clear my head.

Soon I'm watching a tiny mouse dart into the darkness of the tunnel, here at the rear end of the downtown 6 platform at Bleecker Street station, its legs moving so fast that it seems to be sliding along invisible mouse-rails.

Turning back from the tunnel's mouth, I chance to notice a poster on the wall saying "Sinner—Kev and Fernibel are praying for you." I halt in my tracks, as an unexpected synapse crackles in my memory, aided by my half-glimpse just now of a photo on the poster. "Kev"? This wouldn't, by any chance, be that lumbering idiot from Asbury Park, would it? Lucan's dumb-ass henchman? I locate the photo I half-glimpsed, and stoop to inspect it. Yes, it's him! The heavy-set black face grins out at me, beside a plastic-looking blonde woman who must be Fernibel. (Jeez, what kind of a doofus has a name like Fernibel?)

Underneath this photo, the text continues: "Tune in to Kev and Fernibel, and hear these renowned ministers speak the truth about our responsibility to keep a close and loving eye on our kids and our neighbours' kids, to guard against perversion arising in them. Says Kev, 'God tells me to tell you folks that early signs of deviance in children must be lovingly searched out with an eagle eye, that any such tendencies must be lovingly eradicated by means of escalating shock therapies and aversion therapies for as many years as it takes for these children of God to be cured, and that permanent psychiatric treatment and institutionalisation must be implemented if these tendencies persist."' (Kev certainly had God's help with the copywriting, I reflect: he always struck me as someone who'd find joined-up writing a challenge.) "'With God's help, we can succeed in enforcing this, in schools and homes across our beloved country.'" Below this, one graffito saying "Murderers" in wobbly red has been answered by another in elegant script: "You, sick faggots, are the murderers; you deserve to die in protracted pain. We shall win and you will lose this fight, because we are much greater in number and have God with us."

Lovely. Turning away, I see across the tracks on the uptown platform a figure staring hard at me. And this is a coincidence that's not only quite extraordinary, but also quite repellent, because that's Kev himself.

Yes; I regret to say there's no doubt about it. That is indeed Kev Banton, directly across the subway line, here in Bleecker Street station, right after my first sight of his advertising campaign. You couldn't make it up.

His eyes are fixed on me with a mixture of loathing and growing recognition. Before either of us can speak, an uptown train draws in between us. The train doors open; he enters, walks straight to the window on this side and carries on his staring, from three metres closer than before. Then he raises one hand to point at me, and with his other hand slashes the air in front of him at neck level, suggesting decapitation. He learned that gesture from Lucan, I recall—and he's got slightly better at executing it now, but I'm not inclined to cut him any slack for this. We hated each other on sight in Asbury Park, with a chemical hatred that I can feel is quite undiminished.

The loudspeakers announce, "This train is being held momentarily in the station and will be moving shortly." Kev quits glaring, moves away from the window and sits with his back to me.

Within a second I decide: I'm going to tail the fucker.

OK, how to do this? I note that he's in the rearmost carriage (the two platforms here are staggered, so their rear ends are anomalously opposite each other), and then I run for the stairs to the uptown platform, which I reach just in time to jump aboard the second-last carriage before the doors close. (And praise the Lord for the recent introduction of free transfers to uptown trains here—formerly another anomaly at this station.) With care, I approach this carriage's rear end, peer through the windows in the connecting doors, verify Kev doesn't know I've joined him, and sit down out of his sight. The train sets off.

So, Mr Banton's given up his enforcement activities for Lucan's drug-dealing operation, found heavy-duty religion and is now preaching family values on TV. It suits him.

I check the time. It's late. Maybe he's going home. OK, let's see where he lives.

We draw into Astor Place station. I lean forward cautiously and peer through the window. My quarry remains in place, his eyes closed.

Next stop, Union Square. I lean forward again, to see him rise and leave the train. I rise too and succeed in tailing him, straight across the platform and into an uptown 4 train, where I install myself unobserved in the carriage just in front of his.

Twenty-Third, Twenty-Eighth and Thirty-Third Street stations flash by, impregnable to fast trains. So he doesn't live Downtown, I conclude.

Grand Central Station, and Kev's eyes remain closed. Fifty-First Street flashes by. We draw into Fifty-Ninth Street; he remains motionless again. So he doesn't live in Midtown either. He must have died young and opted for the Upper East Side—very fitting for a rich televangelist.

Sixty-Eighth and Seventy-Seventh Streets flash by, then Eighty-Sixth Street slows down outside and I prepare to move. But Kev stays in place there, only looking up to check the stop.

East Harlem? Is the televangelist keeping it real, I wonder, as Ninety-Sixth, One-Hundred-Third, One-Hundred-Tenth and One-Hundred-Sixteenth Street stations hurtle by.

One-Hundred-Twenty-Fifth Street; and here at last, as I follow him surreptitiously, Kev does get out—but only to sit back down on a bench on the uptown 6 platform.

It's a subway map moment. I spot such a map further down the station and navigate myself to it. OK; so we're going to Mott Haven, South Bronx. I'm not entirely sure I'm dressed for this, but we're on a mission now, so we'd better stick with it.

A local 6 arrives. Again I board the carriage just in front of Kev's and filter down the length of it, out of his sightline, where I find myself facing through the windows in the doors. Dusty grey pipes, cables, pillars and occasional dim caverns streak by me.

Then the train emerges above ground and onto elevated tracks. The stations, mostly empty, give little clue to the gangland below. One-Hundred-Thirty-Eighth Street, Brook Avenue, Cypress Avenue, East One-Hundred-Forty-Third Street, East One-Hundred-Forty-Ninth Street, and now Longwood Avenue. I check a map above the windows. It'll be three more stops before we reach any place where a self-respecting televangelist would live—but no, for there in the next carriage Kev is getting up and leaving the train.

With great care and a bit of luck, I follow him undetected through an almost deserted station. Where on earth are we going here?

Outside the station Kev sets off without a pause, not west into the night-lit throb of Mott Haven, but east across Bruckner Boulevard and under the booming truck-roar of the Elevated Expressway. From here on, civilisation ends, for beyond this echoing space of concrete columns stretches the industrial district of Hunts Point. As Kev exits the Boulevard up Lafayette Avenue, I glance down at the rusty railroad in the cutting beneath us. From what I know about this grimy peninsula we're heading into here, I decide we'd better conclude there can be no redeeming purpose whatsoever for Kev's journey tonight. I follow him nevertheless, right onto Tiffany Street, keeping my distance.

In the daytime this corner of the Bronx is dominated by the rumble of trucks along Hunts Point Avenue to the wholesale food market at the end; and by traffic connected with the numerous chop-shops engaged in the business of breaking up stolen cars in order to sell off their components, many such establishments being staffed by mean-looking guard-dogs at the entrance, to ensure an attentive front-of-house welcome. By night the peninsula's main trades are drugs, and sex for drugs.

Flitting through the shadows in between these yellow street lights, I keep a block behind Kev. Turning left on Randall Avenue, we pass a little corner bar whose name, Manny's, shines green and red on two young prostitutes, one black and one Hispanic. Their painted faces smile and coo, first at Kev and then at me. But Kev never wavers in his single-minded, lumbering progress: turning right on Barretto Street, passing other whores who stare at us and whistle; left up Oak Point Avenue, right onto Faile Street and down past a few tent homes and past the very last diner on East Bay Avenue, a tiny shack with diner-style metal on the outside; heading then in silence to the most forsaken reach of all, the grid of avenues by the waterfront.

The darkness and my soft-soled boots make me able to follow him undetected, but my nerves jangle with every block we travel, past rank black alley mouths and chain-link fences. At the bottom of the hill Kev turns to the right, down the last wide, sad strip, Ryawa Avenue. A sewage plant hums on the left, behind a barb-topped fence and a row of dark conifers. Beyond surprise, I find my luck yet holds, as I follow him unseen along the two last blocks to the furthest cul de sac, where the avenue slopes to a slimy pool of water, slick with oil and littered with the crescents of abandoned tyres.

Kev heads on and turns left into shadow. I tiptoe to the corner, peer round and see him stride across a stretch of waste ground to an area of trash heaps and rotting metal bins, step up onto a heap and down the other side, veer to the right and disappear. I glance back, squat down and wait for a minute, but see no further movement. I slink around the corner and follow the fence of the sewage works, on the other side of which stands a line of plastic and brick cylinders, the last one topped by a turret sprouting a thick white tube. A hum hangs thick upon the air, as of engines underground.

Beyond the undergrowth ahead is the gleam of the East River. Craning up to peer over the reeds and across the water, I see Riker's Island, where the grey-striped façade of the prison is lit up yellow-white, near a plume of steam and two tall chimneys. Over on the right the small hump of North Brother Island sprouts another pair of chimneys; and beside it, the smaller bare blip of South Brother Island breaks the moonlight on the water. Locating a dip in the ground, I huddle down in it and wait for Kev to reappear.

4 THE GIRLS ON WEST FOURTEENTH STREET

For half an hour I concentrate on my surroundings, keeping my wits about me. Then my mind drifts back to the view of Scorpio I accessed earlier tonight. I can't resist another peek at him. If I keep my eyes open, I won't miss Kev's reappearance. So I rustle up that tower of the gods in my mind again, to help me locate him … and a deafeningly amplified intake of breath cuts the lights and the voices in the nightclub dead. Scattered yells spurt—silence for a second, then a simmering of murmurs and talk between the candles. A cone of empty white light falls through the dark to the stage-floor. Cat-calls, applause, and collective attention. A second loud breath stabs out from the speakers, anatomical and harsh. A scent of burning dust coils out across the room, then a white-lit face flicks stark and disembodied through the wall of the cone, as a guitar riff slides to a heartbeat of drums. Hanging still, the face lets its eyelids slide up; ringed in black and silver, its eyes blaze wide under heavy dark lashes, scanning slowly right to left across the crowd ahead. Its scarlet lips pout out a kiss, then draw back to let a hiss snake through its teeth. The drum-thunder roars, guitar squeals and feedback screams—then fingernail by fingernail, limb by shiny black limb, puncturing the white cone at points around his grinning face, Scorpio injects his body into the spotlight, in spiked black leather drag. He draws on his cigarette, bares his teeth, exhales, and a sudden cruel, strangely refined faint line runs down through the skin beneath his make-up, from beside either nostril to the corners of his lips. Eyes burning through the smoke, with a strength dark and delicate at once he lifts the whip, like a partner in the dance. As the layers of the music peel away to leave a skewer whine, he freezes; a sudden flow of red spills across his face, washes past the spikes around his neck and gushes down his slender chest, past the silver rings through his nipples. He cracks his whip, the light flicks, red is wiped to white again—but strobing, so his snake-coils click-stop in frozen frames. His voice cuts clean through a rich swell of bass, like a blade pushing tight through the pulse of a fungus. His hands and arms caress his body, flow around and seem to cut it softly, stroke its pressure always in and turn its spines upon themselves—delicate, relentless, till the crackle of his charge makes arrows flare and fall. *And he dances every night: framed in candles and white white light…*

His act done, he makes a fast exit from the club and emerges into the yellow night-babble outside. West Fourteenth Street, says a sign—I've located him! A stunning-looking Asian girl appears from nowhere and bends down to air-kiss him. "Scorpio, my sexy dark divine little demon elf."

"Echo, my tigress and pussy cat." he replies.

She lowers her soft deep-alto voice: "You see the man across the street, in the doorway by the corner? Don't let him see you look. He doesn't think he's recognised, but every girl here knows he's there and who he is."

"Who is he?"

"He's the twisted shit who mutilated Cindi, right under the bridge there."

He stares up into Echo's eyes. "Fuck, that's him? The one who knocked her out and—"

"Cut her dick off with a knife, yes. She's still in Saint Vincent's hospital. He thought he wasn't seen, but I saw his face as he ran away and left her. The cops were called, but it was like they didn't really want to do anything much about it, once they saw who she was and who we were. No real search for that monster, just a record on file, 'Attack on transgender whore by unidentified'… Well, that's him."

A black ghost-truck, full of carcasses of meat, rolls past them in silence.

"Are you absolutely certain?" he asks. She nods. "OK. What d'you need?"

"I'm going to pick him up," whispers Echo, "lure him under the bridge, knock him cold and do my own piece of knife-work, and I need you to watch my back and help me if I need help. I've asked two other girls but they're just stalling, and we don't have the whole fucking night because he may just leave. So Scorpio, my honey, you may be half my height and half my weight, but you're lethal. Can you help me?"

"It's done. Go ahead, I'm right behind you. He's lived."

"You're one of us," she says.

"Yes I was."

She flashes him a smile, heads across Fourteenth, has a word with another girl, wanders to the corner and catches the man's eye.

The man approaches her; they chat. Echo's laughter tinkles out across the cobbled street. She lightly takes the man's arm and they wander west towards the elevated tracks before Tenth Avenue.

Scorpio follows at a discreet distance.

Once the traffic on the Avenue has passed, the couple veers right. Disengaging her arm from his, Echo points with one hand at the Liberty Hotel on the island diagonally across the intersection, while her other hand draws forth a short thick metal bar from her handbag. The man peers over at where she's pointing, then begins to turn his head back to her, about to speak. She smiles, peals laughter out, and slams the bar down with convulsive grace.

He staggers, half looks up, makes to lunge at her. She strikes him with the bar a second time, then a third, and he falls.

Scorpio darts up and helps her haul the man behind a pillar at the rear of the space beneath the elevated tracks. Echo unzips the man's trousers, fishes around inside, pulls his dick through the fly and a knife from her handbag. She cuts from underneath, near the base of the shaft. Scorpio slams him on the head once again, lest he wake. Echo saws away; blood flows hot and sluggish; then she twists it and saws at the same time, so at last it is severed. She opens up his jaws, sticks the severed end inside and clamps his teeth upon it. Taking the knife from her, Scorpio carves on the man's forehead: SICK FUCK.

"That's for Cindi, freak," spits Echo at the man's face.

"Let's go," whispers Scorpio, takes her hand and leads her off, alert for the wail of any siren in the distance.

5 THE GOLDEN LIMOUSINE AND THE SUDDEN HANGING LEGS

With a jolt, I return to the waterfront across from Riker's Island. Huddled by the reeds here, shivering with horror at the scene I've just witnessed, I wrap my arms about me in the warm night and scan this poisoned waste ground.

A sudden figure rises ahead among the heaps of trash and glances around. I freeze, as Kev's stocky form clambers up a heap, stands to face the sewage works and arrogantly sniffs, legs apart and hands upon his hips. Then he jumps down and strides towards the avenue.

I rise in a daze, then snap back into stalking mode. Well practised now, I tail him up Manida Street, left on Viele Avenue, right up Tiffany Street, left on Oak Point Avenue and up the slope of Barry Street, its surface little more than a mud lane in places; then up Longwood Avenue, across the rusty railroad and back to the subway.

I tail him through the subway, back to Manhattan on the last downtown 6 of the night. Alighting at Sixty-Third, I follow him out of the station and then to the door of a wealthy Upper East Side townhouse, which he enters. Once he's inside, I wait for a bit, then wander past and peer at the nameplate by the door: "God's Family".

Back home again, I sit, close my eyes and try to work out what to do. Perhaps a jaunt to West Fourteenth Street, to get relaxingly embroiled in police enquiries? No; me neither.

But I ought to do something here, surely. Do what, though? I get ready for bed, lie back and set out to think this through. My sight drifts up and hovers over the Lower East Side, then down to float above a black tanker that's sweeping north between the high-rise projects and the East River. High smoke coils from the generating station, up ahead and to the left. On the right shines the East River, jagged with reflections of white and red and yellow lights burning on deserted warehouse buildings on the far Brooklyn shore.

Beside the black tanker, from a golden limousine, leaks gasoline, streaming out unseen upon the concrete.

A guard-dog howls somewhere, unheard by the drivers.

The limousine erupts with a dull boom, swelling to a fireball of orange flecked with scarlet. Cars scatter, screeching. Regardless of the road's swerve left at East Fifteenth Street, the ball hurtles on, hits the barrier and bounces up and outward, raging and spinning.

Through the roar of dirty flame and bursting glass, a flail of tiny hands and mouths silent-screaming trapped in buckled metal flash, then they fall to the river with a crunch and hiss of steam.

The dog howls again among the yellow-lit projects, while the black tanker clanks on undaunted, up the East Side Highway towards the Bronx.

Over the great town of psychiatric compounds and hospital blocks between the river and First Avenue—high above that blast of pain cushioned in the soft wink and hum of shiny buildings—my vision soars again, shoots uptown a mile, then plummets in a graceful arc, down to Sixty-Third and a sleeping Kev, down to his bedside Bible and the long fat water-bug sitting on it, licking clean its feelers as it paws at the book.

The longer I tune in to Kev, the more I see about his life: the passionate sincerity and energy he brings to his campaigns and plain-speaking rhetoric; his pleasure at the growth in small-town support across the States; and the practical effects of isolation and despair in the intended populations, leading to suicide or to violence from others, as appropriate. Always hard to quantify, but growing, growing steadily! I find myself snatching single images of individual human pain—nails sticking out red and jagged from the grey flood of pain that is caused or increased by him. I catch in particular the pain of the few who are always targeted and damaged by the rest, to the music of his preaching. I feel for the nails, as they poke from the surface and get bent out of shape. Then, among these nails of pain, I focus on the golden nails of hard-won magic, and I cry at the beauty of them, sticking out against the light, against the odds, against the flood, in triumph: pinpricks of gold amid the grey and red…

I long to stop this man from inflicting any more: his hate must come back on him, as deserved.

The darkness of my feelings stands bare, like those sudden hanging severed legs, side-lit in the moon-glimmer coming through the windows in his high-ceilinged, claustrophobic bedroom right now…

My vision rears up beside the preacher's bed, turns around and shoots across his room at shoulder height, bursting through the window pane to fly across a roofscape of chimneys, dusty parapets, aerials and water tanks.

And so I drift to sleep.

6 TEN SCREENS OF EYES IN THE NEON

Approaching the Midtown recording studio, I psych myself up for my weekly show: my shadow flicks aside to kiss a male neck, slides ahead to stroke a female back, then vanishes beneath me as I pass below a street light, causing those it touches to pause in their speech or look behind them. Who is that attached to me, who interfaces for me and moves as I command, but whose style and pain are self-made? Or who is that inside me, protecting me and driving me, whose willpower I hope will never turn itself upon me? A puff of air, accompanying me into the heavy old revolving-doors at the building's entrance, whispers its answer during the few seconds we are revolving together, sealed inside our metal and glass segment: *You'll never know!*

Lying back among the equipment as we go live on air, I hover over New York City, seeking Kev. I can't always home in on a specific person's frequency, unlike the days of Asbury Park; and on this occasion I fail to locate him straightaway. I'll therefore try focusing simultaneously on the Hunts Point site and on Kev's East Sixty-Third Street townhouse, to see if we can scare him up, somewhere on that 6-train axis.

So there they are: our favourite waste ground of oily pools with abandoned tyres in them, trash heaps, rusty metal bins and waving grasses; and our favourite expensively-furnished, high-ceilinged but claustrophobic bedroom, with the bedside Bible, the now-hidden water-bug, and those hanging severed legs up in the shadows near the ceiling, also hidden for the moment...

What my show's viewers make of such juxtaposed scenes, which must now be shimmering and oddly colourised on their screens, I'm never entirely sure; but they do keep tuning in, so they must make something of them. One conclusion they won't have drawn from these two particular scenes, however, is the harsh and specific intuition I find myself getting right now, behind these paired visuals, such that I am shocked to be so sure of it while I tune in: Kev plans physically to poison New York City.

How he expects to do this I cannot yet make out, but I can see for certain he has a plan for it. Is this unhinged plan intended to show how his deity can target such a city of sin as New York? Perhaps he'll also prophesy the poison, to showcase his own prophetic powers. Hold on: *poison the city?* So I must do something about this! —But I'm hooked up to equipment here and the show must go on, so I can't do anything. Then again, come to think of it, I *am* doing something about it: I've never thought of this as a crime-solving show, but it's looking as if tonight's episode may be turning into one, while I and the audience watch in real time…

I still can't pick up Kev's own frequency, however; so I scan the city, seeking Scorpio's instead. My vision streaks high above the bright Midtown skyscrapers, drinking in their beauty for a moment. Then it zooms down between them, plunging down and further down, and isolates and enters a small slim figure flitting fast through a neon pulse of lights near Times Square.

Scorpio glances up, as if to find a scrutiny of eyes from the air. Something infuses him; his taut, nervy body feels something comparatively sweet and light, something or someone he has known before. It's sought him, he feels, and investigates him now: gentle and soft, but undeceivable; watchful and silent and invulnerable to him.

Stepping east on Forty-Second Street in glamorous black drag, he's such a dark flame that I keep him in my sights quite readily. He crosses Eighth Avenue. Though delicate of movement and frame, he is sending out a presence like a shadow-play of knives now: sensual contempt and a penetrating scepticism burn out from in between his long mascara'd lashes, lit from within by a pent-up violence. He starts, as if a finger has tapped on his forehead, but sees there is nothing there and puts it from his mind. He looks around. "People, for the most part," he thinks, "deserve to die." Walking, he imagines that he stands upon a roof here, holding a giant metal whip whose wire lash he cracks hard, so it shoots through the air at his targets, straight to where he's known they will run for escape, till it finds them and coils around their necks, coiling tight and ever quicker so it cuts through cleanly, the streets awash with blood and rolling heads and running torsos—

His fantasy is cut short, however, by a sight that seems nothing at first, but then grows in him with the sickness of vertigo.

The images produced by my sight through the television cameras are less photographic than suggestive of their subjects, like abstract portraits. Yet so true are they in essence, especially when I'm seeing a person, that a vivid stab of *Scorpio* is slicing out its sultry vibration from all the connected TVs in New York that are currently displaying this online show. Ten such TV screens happen to be banked in a window on his left now, every screen alight with the image of a mesmerising black pulse cutting through a lurid coloured flicker as of neon…

He halts and stares, twanging with a shocked self-recognition. Straightaway, a section of every screen—the section where the eyes of that churning and terrifying shape would have been if the picture were less abstract—becomes not just fully figurative but even photo-realistic, as his recognition, unforeseeable by him or me, reaches out and grabs my sight and makes of our connection a conduit so clear that for one long moment ten pairs of *Scorpio* eyes stare down at him, pin him to the pavement, enter him and peer around his mind.

Raped by his own gaze, he shivers, looks away, then back again defiantly at me, through the screens; but I've turned the heat down for a moment, so those Scorpio eyes melt back into the surrounding blackness of the shape that quivers snarling on the backdrop of the neon swirl.

That was way too naked.

Now he knows it's me; I know he does. Although we're no longer staring at each other, our connection is now re-established after all these months of separation.

I continue to observe him. He can sense this and, excitingly, he feels a subtle thrill that I can feel as well!

OK, I instruct him: there's work for him to do.

Somewhat dreamily, he turns to the street and hails a yellow cab. It stops, he climbs inside. The driver looks him up and down, her eyes narrowing. "Hunts Point, South Bronx," Scorpio hears himself request, like the voice of someone else.

The driver's eyes narrow more. "Hunts Point?"

He nods.

She looks away, considers, looks back at him. "Alright. You got the money, yes?" He holds up a twenty and sweetly smiles. Raising her eyebrows, she turns to the wheel again, steps on the gas down Forty-Second Street towards the West Side Highway and lurches to a halt before the lights at Dyer Avenue.

He settles back and winds the window down, gazing out on a swill of people. A man in a sober tie and jacket leans down to the window with a caring smile and asks: "D'you think about Jesus much? You should—he's way cool, you know."

Scorpio holds the man's gaze, then slowly crosses his eyes.

The man recoils. "I think you need him, sir, ma'am—I think you need him very much." He fumbles for a pamphlet.

"I think you need a transplant," says Scorpio.

Slamming down her foot, the driver launches the cab forward, cursing and blaring the horn as she does so. She clicks on the radio and twists up the volume. "A spoonful cleans a sinkful!" it shrieks with a sputter and a merry little jingle. She flicks the tuning knob around again: the radio crackles, squeals and wheezes, then a measured voice announces, "Now, 'Night Thoughts' from a noted pair of experts on life and afterlife. The Reverend Kev and Fernibel, preparing for their rally here in New York City, take a moment to remind us of those greater verities we frequently forget, overtaken as we are by the daily hurly-burly—"

The driver mutters, clicks a button on the radio and Scorpio jumps, as the climax of Holst's *Mars* thunders from a rear speaker beside his ear. "That's what we want," says the driver, peering in the overhead mirror at him. "You like *The Planets*?" she asks.

He grins. "Sure!"

She gives a wise nod.

7 PHAON AND THE SECOND LIKE A TEARDROP

My vision flies ahead of them, up and out and over, and zooms down to Hunts Point. At the rate she's gunning along, they'll probably get here in twenty minutes or so. Meanwhile I hover for a moment, by this cobwebbed skylight in the attic of a building here on Ryawa Avenue, and peer out over the now-familiar waste ground opposite. Honestly, this place is so derelict, it smells of hopelessness. Silent and sudden, then, my eyes ache, streaming tears the scent and shade of apricots. I glance down to see that these are moistening the cracked and dusty surface of the window sill, where someone long ago has carved: "CX—love always—RQ." With a soft cry at this, my vision rises through the roof, flying out across the East River's grand width.

Soaring above the cold black water and descending towards the north-west corner of Astoria, I sense down ahead of me a soft muffled roar so deep that the televised image must be shaking as it broadcasts. A huge brick building without any windows looms up beneath me, its red-winking chimney-tops a hundred metres off the ground, belching colourlessly up into the sticky air. Rows of metal boxes, rust-stained concrete and intricate cones set on buzzing metal frameworks stretch to its east on a lonely mile of gravel. I float on down through the heat between the chimneys, nearer to the giant hidden turbines' hum.

A scrawny shape of white fur leaps at me, gibbering alarm as it senses my intrusion, its eyes red and beady in a flat pink face, mouth agape and tiny sharp teeth gleaming with spittle. It runs along a high thin pipe and gesticulates, caught in silhouette against the Manhattan skyline.

A monkey, albino, on this power station roof, above the rumbling of the furnaces! I land on the parapet and touch its wrinkled fore-head. As it leaps away in fear at this, its screech splits the hum, like a nerve-end caught between two continental plates…

The monkey's sound morphs to the screech of a bird above a scene from a past life of Scorpio's (I disbelieve in past lives, but up they keep popping, in these weekly shows of mine): for while the bird screeches, the boy Phaon darts from the throng, skipping off between the cracked stone columns of a ruined temple. Half looking back, he raises two slim fingers to his lips and blows a note so shrill that it silences the chanting and the drums and the pipes. The revel-lers pursue him, as his laughter tinkles back at them, triumphant and flirtatious; then he stops on a wide block of flat weathered stone at the Palatine Hill's western edge, where the turf overhangs a rocky precipice, and shoots a piercing cry across the city spread below.

Silence. Then his song begins, a song to Cybele—and so softly does it start, that at first just this one band of revellers can hear it, as it trills with a low moan from nothing into voice. Yet within it are the flickers of a hidden power, ramifying, keeping up the low moan but stabbing upward too. The hairs on the listeners' spines stand, with every stab of sound; time flows slow and fast at once, and soon his voice stretches up to a wail shot with downward stabs—and people hear in streets and buildings out across the city. Surprised in the quiet of the dusk, a disparate multitude halt what they're doing, lift their heads and hear his song leap in pain and joy, borne over roofs, through window grilles and seeping into courtyards of flower-scented foliage. As it grows in volume, they come out onto balconies or climb onto roofs, where the full blast fills the air, bewitching. In its swoops and falls, its quivers and its clear notes, its fluid modulations and its raw naked shrieks, the priestess-boy Phaon paints a soundscape of what it is to live as us: what it is to know oneself an animal called human in this place in the universe.

Then the drums beat anew, he wheels around to face them and he dances, as only Phaon can—hypnotic self-completion, the divine androgyne, channelled pre-gender, pre-Eden, straight through time and ether. And dancing, he begins to spin, just beside the precipice. Inching ever closer to the edge, he gathers speed, so his big brown eyes through the whirl and streak of hands and arms flash toward the band like the wink of a lighthouse. Long-lashed brown light, half-lidded, self-tranced, smiling inside, sweeps over the watchers every two seconds, one second, half-second, less… Red light peeks through the strands of his hair where it streams out long across the width of the sun's orb, half-sunk now beyond the marches of the city.

His slender frame is sharpened by the dusk to a silhouette, and now the moment comes (though he surely cannot know it), the moment in a life when such perfection is attained that a single fleeting second lodges, swells like a teardrop, gathers weight and falls away, sideways through the centuries—to land *here*, as lightning earths, captured and framed perhaps awhile, perhaps longer: *Roman youth, addressed as Phaon, epicene, of few words and much affection, earlier and later life unknown but glimpsed now, dancing on the Palatine Hill in Nero's day, for Dionysus—only for a moment and only for a few, but with such heart-captivating beauty both of body and of soul that he rises and dances in the sky for us, for all time—fey black imp on orange sky, dancing with laughing eyes, divinely and forever!*

See him up there on the precipice, right now…

A rush of air cracks out, a flicker and a crackle as of lightning; and then a bell booms, slow and deep, unimaginably ancient and vast, out of everywhere and nowhere at once.

8 SCREECHING WORMS

I jolt in my trance in the studio, remember what I'm up to, then hurl my attention back down to Ryawa Avenue, Hunts Point, the Bronx, New York City, where a yellow cab purrs to a halt beside a slope leading down to a noxious pool littered with the circles and the crescents of abandoned tyres.

A little dark drag-queen alights, shuts the door, tells the driver through the open window: "Thanks for the Holst."

She inhales, pauses, scans the pool and sewage works, and nods back gruffly: "We must do this again."

Then she steps on the gas and is away down the avenue.

Scorpio sniffs the fetid air and looks about him. His eyes grow hard, as an instinct makes his fingers feel inside his leather shoulder-bag and close around the handgun.

He can feel those other eyes again, fixing him from inside or out—the eyes he saw upon the screens on Forty-Second Street, that pinned him down and peered around his mind—my Jaymi eyes shining softly in, through his darkness, like they used to do before.

He sets off down the slope towards the oily pool of tyres. He turns left, slipping through the shadows of the waste ground. He reaches the heaps of trash and steers through them; they seem almost to part for him. He turns, springs up onto a heap and down its other side, turns again and ducks through a half-hidden hatch in the ground.

Soon the walls of earth are walls of concrete, dimly lit. A rumble, as of engines and pumps, joins the soundtrack of thunder in his head. Down stairs and passages he flits, driven on by these other eyes just behind his own. For yes, he entered here on my bidding (so my power of hypnosis is returning too, it seems), albeit assisted by his own curiosity. Whatever the causes, though, I have a sense that he's about to wish he hadn't.

He arrives at a swing-door. Through it comes a sickness of sound like no other.

He tiptoes to the door, rubs a finger near the corner of the greasy plastic window that's set in it, and cranes up to look, but the plastic is greasy on the inside too, so he still can't see through.

He pushes at the door, slips in and glances round. Then he sinks to his knees.

He's alone, in a sense.

It's a chamber with a large open tank, like an indoor swimming pool. The air is thick and crawling with droplets of moisture, so perspective on the edges of the tank is oddly warped. The stench is palpable.

Pressing through the vents in the walls of the tank comes the reason for this stench, and the fodder for this gruesome farm: effluent from Riker's Island (worse than from elsewhere, perhaps), piped across the East River, drawn from the sewage works and guzzled by the tank's tenants—giant pulsing worms maybe two metres long, every worm revealing flashes, through the suction of its mouth, of a full set of lethal teeth.

Scorpio nearly retches where he kneels, then he straightens up, regaining his balance. From somewhere nearby there comes a click, as of a latch. He staggers to his feet through the warped air, slips behind a bank of machinery and peers out between its metal valves.

Kev appears through another door, stands beside the tank and turns a crank in the wall while he watches the ceiling. A skylight rolls aside, and the plastic blonde face of Fernibel stares starkly down.

Scorpio huddles down, feeling the chipped green paint on the valves sweating tepidly against his brow. If she looks over here, then she will see him, the game will be up and he'll probably end up as worms' meat. A tense minute comes and goes, while he dare not glance up.

When at last he does so, he sees that her face has been welcomely replaced by a wide rubber tube, which is being lowered into Kev's waiting hands. As an engine revs outside above the skylight, the tube begins to hiss. Displaying remarkable agility and strength, Kev then proceeds to dance around this ghastly tank, wielding the tube, creeping up behind the longest, thickest worms and then covering their heads with it, one by one. It's evidently a high-suction device, for no sooner is each worm's head covered than its excrement-stained body flails in frenzy up through the tube, continuing to thrash away after it's fully swallowed, so that the tube itself looks like a fatter, dryer, more corrugated worm wriggling up through the skylight.

And on top of everything else, every time the dexterous televangelist sucks up a worm, all its former neighbours punch their eyeless slimy heads up through the air like fists, bare their fangs out of grey blubber-faces and screech like tortured babies.

This last detail, in particular, Scorpio could do without; and by the time the tenth or eleventh worm has been sucked up, he is almost inclined to pass out. —But no, he decides, this would be a mistake. Choosing a moment when the preacher is particularly intent on his ministry at the tank, Scorpio therefore summons up his strength and makes a dash for the plastic-windowed door, slips through, scampers up the passages and stairs again, out onto the waste ground and flops down behind a trash heap, trembling.

9 A LAPFUL OF BROKEN GLASS

My eyes let him rest for a moment, but then make their presence known again, with growing insistence: there's more to do here, I suggest, and I'm afraid we are just getting started.

Scorpio opens his wild and frightened eyes, slowly gets a grip, and glances about him. There across the waste ground stands a black-painted tanker with its engine running. A big wriggling pipe rises from the earth nearby, travels up to where Fernibel stands atop the tanker's container, and disappears down into a hatch beside her feet. Silhouetted against the sky, she is bending down, hands planted on her knees, staring down through this hatch with an expression of messianic rapture.

It's a fair assumption that beneath her, just out of sight from here, there are fat, screeching, sharp-toothed, blubber-faced worms being belched out into the container, through the wriggling rubber pipe, one by one.

After a few more minutes, the pumping noise from underground stops. She lifts the end of the now-empty tube, lobs it onto the ground, then closes and fastens the hatch. Kev emerges from underground, pulls the tube's other end from the skylight, and loops it securely around a couple of brackets at the tanker's rear, on either side of another closed hatch with a wheel beside it. Fernibel scoots down a metal ladder, joins him and they confer. She then returns below ground, while Kev alone climbs into the tanker's cab.

Grabbing his chance, Scorpio scuttles from his hiding place, crosses the waste ground and clambers deftly up between the driver's cab and the container. Locating an angular space where he won't be endangered by the movement of the vehicle's articulation, he plants himself securely there, with his limbs against the black vibrating metal. The engine revs and roars, he holds on tighter and the tanker rolls forward, bouncing up and down across the stony earth and onto the avenue. As it gathers speed, he rearranges his grip, verifies his safety and breathes deep.

Within a few blocks they turn left up Halleck Street, and as they do so Scorpio looks right, towards where the street ends at the waterfront. What he sees from this unusual vantage-point is visible to him for a few seconds at most, but the scene then remains clear in his memory. Floodlit on either side, a high spike-topped steel fence lines the street, whose height is thus greater than its width. At the end of this sinister corridor, floating in the water beyond a guarded gate, is a bleak edifice with small square windows—a huge prison barge. On top of it, another floodlit fence with spikes contains a court where men are playing basketball. Others lean against the fence, staring down towards him. Male shouts burst and spill—perhaps at him, wedged here in full view, or maybe not, he cannot tell. He feels more than hears the slide and clang of metal bolts, the dead weight of concrete bruising blindly into bone, and the hard eyes and hard fists of men bearing down on him, night after night… Feeling this, though he goes erect of course, his own gaze narrows to a skewer and he shivers at this glimpse of a world where he would not survive.

Music intrudes, of a sudden—it's the signal that my hour is up and credits now are rolling. I open my eyes. A crew-member approaches, to extricate me from the recording equipment. Once freed, I make my excuses for running off with unusual haste tonight, and exit the studio. Outside in a yellow cab I supply directions to Hunts Point, to a less memorable driver than Scorpio's. Then I settle back, close my eyes and tune furiously back in to him.

I'm deeply relieved to find him still wedged behind the cab of the tanker; though my relief is perhaps greater than his, because the tanker is now barrelling along at what feels to him like an unholy speed, north-east up Bruckner Avenue. Back among cars and activity and street lights now, he is also starting to feel rather too visible. This feeling grows alarmingly when the tanker slows to join the Bronx River Parkway, a car draws up alongside him and he glimpses a horrid vision, down beside him: a large family crammed into a tiny space, with leaping dogs, bawling children and loud inane voices on a radio. "Nightmare," he thinks. "I'd sooner choose that prison barge." Even more distressingly, two horrible gum-chewing children in the back seat have seen him and are now fighting over how to wind the window down. They hit each other, then are hit in turn by a parent… Scorpio drums his silver fingernails tightly on a metal strut and listens with impatience for the sound of vehicles moving up ahead. If the vermin succeed in winding the window down and start shouting up at him, then Kev will notice and probably investigate matters and discover him. He glances down, observes that the fight is still in progress, and catches for an instant the grinning semi-focused gaze of one child: passionless, compassionless, thoughtless and sealed-off, without imagination or real curiosity, and safely protected from the danger of wonder, it makes him laugh mirthlessly aloud.

Still he drums his fingernails, and still the traffic isn't moving—yes it is, at last! One more glance down, and this time he catches just his own form reflected on the window, behind which the dreary family squabble carries on: clutching at his metal niche, his long black hair spilling out along his bare arms and round his fully made-up face (now a little smudged), he reminds himself of a manic dark monkey staring hatred out of wide-burning, silver-shadowed eyes. He laughs aloud a second time, and watches his reflected hand dip into his shoulder-bag and reach out a catapult. As the tanker revs its engine in readiness to move, he aims the weapon at the child, pulls back the elastic and shoots the little stone. For a split second Scorpio sees his own reflected face snarling up with a feral sensuality and glee, before it cracks at the window's burst and falls into the screaming child's blood-spattered lap, along with a lapful of broken glass.

Firing up its engine, with a roar that drowns the scream and the blaring of the car's horn, the tanker presses grimly up the ramp to the Parkway. Its slimy cargo sucks hard, swilling at the warm black metal just beside his ears; and close behind his smooth and delicate neck, those screeching teeth…

Now the preacher steps on the gas with a vengeance. Two metres down through the truck's articulation, Scorpio can see the roadway streaking by at sixty, seventy, eighty miles an hour. On his left, beyond the barrier, white lights zing by at twice these speeds, while the red lights on his right fall slowly behind. As the warm air buffets his ears and lashes his hair about, the tanker hurtles on, over and under the streets and expressways of Bruckner and West Farms, streaking through the Gardens and past the Woodlawn Cemetery. It exits the Parkway and the Bronx at last, slows down, turns off Hillview Avenue and heads up a track discreetly signed "Hillview Reservoir".

10 A DRAG-QUEEN DRIVES A TANKER

Ahead a security gate stands open, next to an empty guard's booth— such is the power of money and Jesus, perhaps. The tanker pushes up the track, slows right down at the top, and carefully reverses towards a raised manhole-cover by a short slope leading to the reservoir's edge. Before the tanker comes to a halt, Scorpio slides off his perch and slips unseen into the shrubs beside the track.

Kev alights from the driver's cab, bearing a metal rod. Evidently in execution of a well-made plan, he heads straight for the manhole-cover. He raises the cover with the rod, lays the former aside and looks within.

From inside the manhole comes a huge, soft roar: channelled down from upstate, purified and filtered further up inside the hillside, tested many times and rendered absolutely clean, this water is on its way across the width of the Bronx and through the length of all Manhattan, tapped by every residence and hospital and food-plant, keeping several million alive and in health.

Kev pauses a moment, triumphant and glassy-eyed, gazing out above Scorpio in the shrubs, southwards from this hill to where the yellow-grey glow of New York City shines enormous off a bank of cloud.

He walks to the tanker's rear, uncoils the tube from its brackets, and stoops to fix one end of it around the container's closed rear hatch. He returns to the manhole, carrying the other end of the tube, which he hangs into the shaft above the water. Then he scales the ladder on the tanker, walks along the container, unlocks the hatch, lifts the lid up and lays it back.

And now another sound joins the water's roar—a sticky, chewy, wriggling sound.

Scorpio slinks across the ground towards the tanker, like the shadow of a demon.

With his gun between his teeth, he scuttles softly up the ladder. He tiptoes the length of the container, creeping up behind Kev, who is kneeling through the hatch, savouring what looks to be a moment of messianic rapture not unlike Fernibel's in the waste ground.

Scorpio claps a hand onto Kev's shoulder and presses the gun-barrel into the forward part of his temple. Kev freezes, then slowly turns his head to look up. Terror drains his face, at the sight of Scorpio's eyes. No words are spoken.

Scorpio pushes Kev down towards the reeking hatch, with the barrel digging into Kev's head ever more savagely. The grisly, blubbery sounds inside the hatch grow louder.

The powerfully-built preacher starts to struggle. If he can only get to his feet again, he'll gain the upper hand immediately, through brute force.

Aiming the gun-barrel into the shrubs, Scorpio pulls the trigger with the chamber of the gun pressed into Kev's ear, which is thereby deafened. Kev lurches forward with a shout.

Scorpio grabs his moment, shoving and kicking and pistol-whipping and pussy-whipping the dazed Kev down, and down, and further down, and into the hatch, and on through the hatch, and further in, all the way at last … and bends to watch the fun, panting hard in wicked glee.

Kev bellows, as the worms very quickly discover him.

He bellows, as he sinks down amongst their blubber-faces.

He bellows, as they screech and tear his flesh with their teeth.

Scorpio shuts the hatch and fastens it. He climbs down the ladder. He unhooks the tube from the closed hatch at the rear of the tanker, coils it back round the brackets, climbs into the driver's cab and closes the door.

He stares at the tanker's controls, with a fierce concentration. He knows how to drive a car. This is not a car, of course, but frankly these controls do look similar. He stares at them again, one by one.

He thinks for a moment, then he knows he'd better not think too much more. Instead he'd better turn the ignition key carefully, while remaining as alert as he has ever been.

He turns the key, remaining that alert, and the engine fires up. Gingerly he tries out the brake and accelerator; adjusts the seat and mirror; then steely-eyed, summons the help of whatever dark angels may be watching him, and eases the vehicle forward.

To his enormous relief, the tanker behaves itself, obediently moving down the track, and he finds that he does know what to do. He reaches Hillview Avenue. He drives on through the streets, growing in confidence. And finally he barrels back down the Bronx River Parkway at a respectable speed in the slow lane, singing out loud as those red and white lights streak by.

11   ECSTASY IN HUNTS POINT

I surface, as my yellow cab slows and stops beside the oily pool, down by the sad far end of Ryawa Avenue.

I pay, wait a minute for the driver to leave, then slip into the shadows of the waste ground. Hiding where I waited for Kev yesterday, I hear a clanking in the distance. Soon the black tanker veers around the corner, bounces through the waste ground, turns in my direction and stops by the trash heaps.

Fernibel emerges through a hatch from below. Beaming, she waves, makes a crucifix sign in the air and approaches the tanker, to greet Kev. A gunshot cracks out; she shrieks, staggers, clutches her foot and falls sideways.

Scorpio flounces from the tanker's cab and runs to where she lies thrashing on the ground. He frisks her at gunpoint, finding no weapons. "You'd better pray, you evil shit," he hisses, spitting at her face. He darts across to the wheel on the tanker's rear, yanks it around with an access of force, leaps aside and scrambles up to perch on the rear tyre-guard, as the tank's cargo gushes and slithers out through the hatch.

The worms wriggle out, one by one, dragging broken bits of Kev's skeleton, which has been efficiently stripped of its meat. They twist in the rough grass, then head for the waterfront by instinct. This takes them straight towards Fernibel, who screams in terror. Though blind, they smell her blood and writhe faster towards her. With the strength of desperation, she staggers half upright, hops in the direction of the hatch she emerged from, and disappears underground, just in time: as the hatch slams, the first worm rears up, steaming in the redness of the tanker's rear lights, curls back its fleshy lips and slams its head down to stab the wood with vicious teeth. Then losing interest in their vanished blonde meal, the worms coil onward, their slimy meat squeezing over rusty trash and gravel, till they vanish in the shadows of the reeds and slither into the water.

I approach, walking calm across the worm-slicked waste ground, floodlit in the full white glare of the headlights. Scorpio starts, to see this floating figure nearing him. And so he and I meet again at last: one white-lit before the tanker, and one red-lit behind.

The scene glows paler and the soundtrack fades. From my eyes to his, a tunnel spins and locks our gazes. Each of us can see just the other's burning stare at the centre of a whirlpool of light. As I level with the tanker and leave the headlights' glare, the tunnel darkens, spinning still. I reach the tanker's rear, as I near Scorpio, whose darkness magnetises me. The tunnel whirls faster, no longer white but scarlet in the rear lights; and just before I'm plunged into red, I feel my face blush.

Then each of us is touched, in this place of desolation, with a stab of mad clarity, simplicity and calm: we are meant to be together. As the sky glimmers ultramarine over Riker's, the tunnel fades away. I stop. He comes to me. Our hands touch, our mouths slide together, and we kiss with a sudden shared ecstasy: Scorpio and me…

THE END

HALLUCINATION IN HONG KONG

TABLE OF CONTENTS

1 SO HERE IS THE HORROR,
TO SICKEN THE SUN

Outside, concrete fields and the blast and shriek of turbines. Inside, tinted hostess-smile, canned comfort, bland gloss.

The plane accelerates. The runway sucks us on, fans wide to swallow us. As thrust turns to lift, the cargo hush. The airfield drop below us, hanging metal throbs and whines; and angled steeply upwards, we cut through the clouds.

The flight underway, I settle back into the warmth of Angel's presence here beside me. By "Angel", I should clarify I do mean Scorpio. The rest of the world still addresses him as Scorpio; but just between him and me, ever since the dramas of Hunts Point, he's gone back to Angel, just as he was called when we very first met.

*

I start to doze … and feel myself connected to you, Angel, just as I'd have tuned in, back in Asbury Park. On my left the oval porthole, and in front of it, you—your face in profiled silhouette, framed in sunshine through the cirrus. You turn to me. Soft brown eye-shadow's streaked across the tan skin around your dark bewitching eyes: your gaze, which I know so well, still melts me from so close. Our hands are almost touching. Your lips part; I feel I'm sliding down between them, warm and sleek. I murmur, "I could eat you!"

Your eyebrows jump a fraction as they sometimes do unprompted and you laugh, while your eyes flicker down to my lips. "Me too!" you say.

"We'll share you," I concede.

People look, who pass us down the aisle. I hear my whispered name when they believe themselves inaudible: "He's on the plane with us!" "Who?" "The one we're going to see on stage—look, he's up in front!" "God you're right. Shall we say hi?" "Better not." "Who's that next to him?" "Angel—you know that track they do together, what's it called?" "Oh yeah. Huh! I thought they'd both be taller…"

I glance at your watch, then at a pulse on your neck. I close my eyes and look ahead. Hong Kong. The night. This concert… What I've wanted to do for years!

I visualise the set I've had designed and constructed in Hong Kong. Perched against the Peak, above the Midlevels, facing north across the city to the mainland, is the stage. On the mountain-face a screen of vast dimensions will project events below it to the multitudes beyond the front few thousand. Throughout the concert, out of two giant gas jets either side, dancing tongues of scarlet flame will lick the night to east and west. Clamped to the towers of rock that flank the screen, a pair of speaker banks will blast a sound to pluck the laser lattice spilling out of each in orange cities spread across the sky.

Beyond the ground around the stage—from hills, gardens, roofs, windows, streets, cars, trains, boats, balloons—they will watch. To see us live, a six-figure number; worldwide a nine-figure one, by satellite. To remain within Hong Kong will be to hear us.

Wherever I requested, be it almost inaccessible, are television cameras, poised to shoot our image out to cities I have never even heard of. Everywhere, on records, posters, clothing, magazines, screens and airwaves—my face, my voice, and sometimes yours.

You will join me up on stage to sing our track, the one you join me for. Already I can hear it now, the newspaper scream: "Sounds of hell and heaven dance together!" Oh yes; manic and sublime, like the end of the world… Even now before the frenzy, I can see too the way it will be told in the histories when we're dead. Already I can see it done, that grand device of cinema and televised biography: the picture, a well-chosen image of the subject (happy, sad or enigmatic), camera zooming in to frame the frozen eyes; the soundtrack, their creation, living on; the coupling of the two, a never-failing means of reining in an era's worth of feeling to the service of the subject. What a game! But the bio now continues. First you come in focus like a dark sun out of mist, your coolest gaze above a point beside the camera, expressionless to carry off your beauty and preserve its type—androgynous, unreadable, exquisitely effeminate, your devastating eyes enormous, gentle, soft, unreal—while round you like a hurricane, my voice, and you its eye! The clouds all scatter then; my face replaces yours, and your voice mine. The *gasp* with which you start our track is sex, your breath addictive, sultry, aching, drugged, a self-renewing cycle of appeasement and revival of desire—and for my head whose eyes are staring out behind it from the screen, a voice to burn inside forever…

*

It feels as if I surface on a surge of nauseous terror, find not you on the empty seat beside me but a wodge of abstract pain. It's all going wrong now. Flying to Hong Kong to give the concert—that's not real, no, that's memory. I struggle in a sick fog. The concert… It happened, yes—nine years ago. Everything is different now, muddy, churning, dim. The yellow-lit ceiling of the tunnel I am seated in alone with other passengers is leaning in towards me as it swells and now disjoints in lurid fragments. I look at the outside shape of my body to check that it is not what it feels from the inside, a tight thick mass like a bag of maggot-organs pumping fluidly at tension in a helpless breathing skin without extremities. I try to move, but only squirm where I am. I make to grip the seat, to prove myself articulated—manage, yes, but then my fingers feel like flabby arms encircling something huge. I panic, as towards me, with inexorable slowness and a constant whine that cuts the clotted atmosphere around it with the metal sheen of lipstick laid on whale-flesh, rolls a dark ball-bearing denser than a star, in a hollow on a time-grid that yields to its passage as a mattress to a stone. The tunnel warps at its approach—becomes a giant dome upon whose underside I hang, gummed. Across its giddy vault I see you swaying on a balcony. Your tongue twitches out from your mouth like a bacon rasher poking through a letter-box. I dip to bite it off; but the thought, when my own tongue lolls on my teeth, of a hippo sliding open down a razor blade prevents me. Lazy, you jump from your perch. A silent roar of waters yawns around you; writhing hands and staring eyes are pawing as you fall… Rushing air, grinding rocket smear of fire on blistered sky—then with a thud you land impaled on jagged railings, shriek and rock with maniac laughter like a puppet in a box at a fair on the pier.

I jolt awake, dripping sweat, see again the empty seat.

Yes, I'm going to Hong Kong, but not for a concert I performed nine years ago. No. I'm coming for a very different reason now. Tears spring sharp.

Yes, I'm going to visit you, I am.

Yes, I'm going to look into your eyes, I'm afraid.

And then, oh my Angel, I may be going to kill you.

*

To explain. There was the concert in Hong Kong nine years ago. Can I remember it? Yes, though in light of what followed it, I almost wish I couldn't…

Hong Kong. The night arrives. I'm on the stage. The stage is dark and quiet.

I look down upon a cityscape of heads and sweating towers, where a murmured babble rises in the air. The gas burns high and clear a hundred metres either side. Ahead of me the moon is tinted peach, hanging heavy on the sharp black sky.

I turn to face the Peak, its bulk my backdrop. East and west, flame-lit crags start from shadow, flicker in silence to the rhythms of the dance of the jets. Underneath, softer slopes ripple out and fade away. Above me, phosphorescent sky, my ceiling.

A thud from high to right and left escapes the darkened speakers: skeins of birds fizz out from each, coil up and twinkle and evaporate, to prick the tiny sidelight nestling up beyond the cornice of the Peak.

Behind the stage, the screen, gigantic and dark, projecting focus of the multitude, aglow for my anticipated image.

Hooded figures scurry in the wings, and then are still. I shift my weight from side to side, then poise…

A single strident note from lead guitar rips out to crack the sultry night above Hong Kong. Four synthesiser pips attend the echo, at their leisure. (Clatter of distant pebbles from the rock face either side. The human stew is mewing massively behind me, too, soon to be drowned.) Then the Peak emits another blast from lead to split the air between the tower blocks and shoot across the bay to mainland China, where the Guangdong Hills curve up behind the plains beyond Kowloon to form the back wall and the cheap seats of my natural auditorium. This second stroke is tweaked three seconds later, like the first, by a hiccupping pip from synth—a drip of fat that glistens at a jagged skewer's end. Another drip, another, and another, and another—then again the heavy skewers twang, as long as trains, four end-on-end, each double-shafted, splintered, spiked, corrosive black. Now the music dives to gain momentum for the onslaught it has so far merely fanfared, with a barrage of five battering-rams of sound launched in turn, the third and fourth a Double Dare aimed higher than the other three, the last one tailed by a cowlick of clicks like a pennon… Here the searchlights blaze and flood the stage; the screen lights up, to show a long shot of the flames and all between. I see myself, a speck of black upon a central shelf of white, my back to audience and camera, growing larger by the second as we zoom in close towards me. Five more battering-rams, again a tail, and whine of feedback. As the camera streaks in closer, I prepare to turn. The viewpoint dips and lurches over valleys full of heads, to frame my swelling silhouette against the screen: on screen, on screen, on screen—for now a regress yawns and flickers round my static head and tunnels as I stare and am caught up with, through the Peak, the Sea, the Ocean, to the Ice and out beyond… Five more battering-rams. Then the drums explode in a lazy burst, cascade, and land in rhythm on the beat they now inform, both slave and master—pre-volcanic, unrelenting, like the metronomic bomb-blast from the foundries in the centre of the earth! I turn to meet the swooping camera, gently smile at it, and spit. In fear the human wavelets near the stage attempt retreat, but only bunch up into dunes. Central by the footlights, like a prompt-box, is a monitor relaying for me what is up on screen: my face close up, my golden eyes triumphant, dark and lethal, burning level-gazed as if to scorch in double path the lightless wastes of Asia… Separate sectors of the multitude as prearranged are floodlit, one by one, in direct echo of the movement of my eyeballs on the screen. The music has grown richer now and fuller than you ever thought it could be (I address not you, my Angel): dense as print, its layers and its columns, every sound in precisely the role I allot. The size of its ego, which is monstrous and beautiful, makes of it not a hemisphere that seeks to find completeness in your listening, but a sphere—well, nearly that—of vocational charisma, for your wonder, celebration and resentment. It is rape, glee, destruction, assault with intent to engulf. As invitation to dance, unacceptable, for proffered by a giant too big to engage with. In any case, you cannot tell its sex: it appears to be male but displays upon inspection several curious transcendences of gender. Your choice, then; decline from the wallflower beds, or be swept up and carried where you never knew there was… You hesitate. The giant stoops to grab. You try to bolt—he claws you up. You struggle—he grips, you shriek. You feel the crack of breaking bone. You try to shout but cannot. Whistling air, then you smack into his shoulder with a crunch, where you dangle, cling and ooze, moaning faintly to the beat, with a smile. But now beside you from the giant's neck, as if a glint of steel were pushing out through the flesh to pierce the chitin and unfurl and cut the air, erupts a blade and licks itself—my voice at last! My voice has come, to sing for your destruction. At its ruptured scream the giant roars in pain, clutches vainly at this scythe that slices out below his chin to kiss the air in which it hardens as it twitches, then he flounders on a swell of sound encroaching from behind, bogging down his every step. Glancing back in panic, he can see the music pouring from the Peak—as if from its entire length the mountainside were belching out a glacier of blackened flesh and metal, flowing out above the stage across the jets (around my feet its shadowed outline, chewing sluggish teeth of sightless grated white, like divers' pains) then out and down among the millions, inexhaustible and hideous as a vision out of Giger. The giant tries to run, but waves of darkness overtake. From their surface shoots a spume of treble sound, the jagged top-case of a carriage of immaculate complexity whose lowest treads, articulated wheels of bass as never heard, on caterpillar tracks as tall as towers ride up over any barrier, with majesty inhuman, biomechanoid, insane… Down the giant is sucked and ground to splintered pulp, his size too great (unlike your own) for him to find a space to perch among the gears or on the tungsten flanges round the undercarriage edge. But there you nestle, you who toppled from the giant when he fell, where you squiggled and you bickered for the crannies—yes you did! Cower now, then, and shake to hear that voice stride infernal and divine across the wastes of metal sky above the framework where you hide; for as it enters you, diffuses, throbs inside you like a drug you cut with ice and powdered glass before you shot it, every shrivelled twist inside you will be infiltrated—sternum, ribcage, heart and eyes! My spider-movements' legs are bass guitar: its claws are snouts, to rear and lick you where you shiver… I glimpse a sudden image of the singer on the monitor, his skinny leaping body as his echo thunders merciless, immense and redly gashing on the blackness of the music. My own voice and actions mate with his and ride upon him, cut him open, mingle with his blood—ram him through and flow around, assimilate him whole, to multiply eleven-fold the ecstasy and agony he stirs. I see a close-up, shafting out across the multitude my singing mouth, my eyes, my leering face, my open head and gullet, shrieking guts and arteries. Yelps of guitar shoot up the corners of the sky in branching clumps and flower in umbrella sprays of yellow. Bass shakes the bones in the boulders of the sea, while the hills blaze hollow eyes and groan! Heads and bodies bubble in the distance all around me. *Don't you hear me now? Don't you feel me down inside you, you before me, every one of you? D'you kid yourself that you'll escape the damage I intend? I think you do! So watch me now…* Lights weave and lash. You are rapt, you are stunned, you are limitless and legion, tier on tier as up the sides of a satellite dish. Through screens and speakers round the world, I control, hour on hour, centre-stage—your collective fascination's poisoned cynosure. I drink the lurid limelight as a desert gasps for fluid, while a billion spotlight eyes are drinking me. My mesmeric voice resounds and soars and swoops, and softly lacerates (omnipotent, relentless, for a night). As the vaults of heaven boom, the firmament reverberates; Hong Kong, the continent, the oceans and the world at last are borne up and churned in a storm-coloured vortex on the cyclone of the sound. Smooth as china now, its lesion: magnetic in its dominance: in power, sublime. Your understanding stretches to its peak, then floats on a plateau of air at the foot of a further scale of impossible peaks to stretch towards. Jangle of blades in your head—then the music implodes. The carriage disappears as black spaghetti through the mouths of the Peak; its echo dies, like a house that snaps and totters and collapses, to be sucked through a furrow in the carcass of the toad that rots and winks above the lift-shaft in the earth below the cellar.

I bow my head a moment, turn and leave. The stage is dark and quiet again.

*

—But then came the sickness and churning of horror.

Amid the elation backstage, I was told I must hurry to see you; as the music had ended you'd collapsed and now remained paralysed. With a shock I remembered: you'd been meant to join me under the lights, near the end, to sing our track. No musician or technician, I was told, had been able to attract my attention on stage to remind me of it.

Now all was panic and confusion. You were stretched on the ground, surrounded by a horrified crowd, catatonic. You were rushed to a hospital. Expertise, tests: hours later, no response. Days more—just the same. Over many weeks, everything was tried, every measure I could buy for you; in vain. Not a flicker. That was it, they concluded. You were out of reach. Gone. No longer there, though your heart beat still. Just a body, nothing more…

A vegetable.

From the stage it had seemed there was no one in the world but the singer; off it now, my aloneness was all too real. Was I somehow your killer?

*

You were institutionalised, location undisclosed. I lingered in Hong Kong a while, as numb as if I too were dead; then flew back to London, far from you who needed no one but your nurses.

So in my head it was that your livest presence lived, while nine whole years passed…

Till yesterday—the bombshell. An article I chanced on, in a medical journal. A man in San Jose discovered "frozen," alive but unable to move or speak, all treatment ineffective. Assumed to be a vegetable, and on the point of being treated accordingly, he then made a single, almost imperceptible eyelid movement. This being noticed, he was asked several times to blink again. As expected, no reply. One person yet continued asking him, however—and at last he gave another blink, this time unmistakable. Repetitions followed over many further days, till he moved both his eyelids and his eyeballs quite often: still faint, but undeniably at will. He was in there after all. A near-total dopamine deficiency was diagnosed; L-dopa was administered but was found to have such severe side effects on his particular metabolism as to be unusable, as was also found to be the case with all known substitutes for it. He was reduced, in effect, to a life of complete immobility except for the limited control over his eyes that had so fortunately disclosed his consciousness. By and by, with an alphabet of eye movements, technological help in registering them and extensive practice by him, full communication was entered into; since which, as bearable a quality of life has been arranged for him as possible, in view of his unremitting inability to move in any other way and the continued lack of any ethical means of arriving at a cure.

Hence the destination of my flight today. Hence the empty seat beside me. And hence the pain of having thought you on it.

*

I touch down in Hong Kong in the late afternoon. As soon as possible I pay my second visit to the building in the trees, where I once saw you put away nine long years ago.

I have not revealed to the institution's staff or anyone else the motive for my visit; for if you turn out to be conscious and wish for something they are unlikely to concede to, I shall want the opportunity to arrange it unimpeded.

Inside, I ask the nurse who shows me to your door if your eyes ever flicker.

"A tiny movement now and then, perhaps. It means nothing, I'm afraid."

I enter alone and close the door.

Once white, the walls have been repainted pale orange. The clock is as before, where a window should have been, the sort that clicks every minute when the mute second hand passes twelve. I take in the only other features in the little room: a poster of an ornamental lake set in trees with a fountain in the middle; an artificial pot-plant on a shelf; a sink unit underneath a high internal window—and your bench.

Luxury enough, for a dead man.

You are lying covered up by a sheet from the neck down. I roll it off, to leave you naked.

The body I knew so well has changed. Is what I see instead the body of someone who has lain inside this coffin watching nothing but the ceiling and the walls every second for the last nine years—unable to move, unable to speak, unable to share or act upon a shred of what will surely be a permanently suicidal mad pain—a consciousness exhausting, obsessive, self-consuming, self-enclosed beyond belief?

I look at your chest: the slowest flutter proves you physically alive.

I look at your hands: the nails now uncoloured, soft and stubby.

I open and look at your eyes, and nearly break inside.

I position myself above them (see my own on their convex surface). They seem to stare at me so deeply, I feel you must be about to rise and put your arms around me. Then I move from your sight-line to see you as before: a lump of meat, inert and discoloured in the glorified lifelong process of rotting on its journey to the grave, like the rest of us—though unlike the rest, undistracted from remembering it.

I brace myself above your eyes.

I ask you to blink, if you understand.

I wait.

I ask again…

You don't blink. Shake you, slap you, kiss you as I do, you stay immobile. "Oh, thank you," I murmur, straightening up. I step back and look at you.

Out of your sight-line again, I feel easier—to an uncanny degree, in fact, considering I now know I am alone in here.

I walk towards your door slowly, close my eyes, breathe deep, turn in silence back to you. A hundred emotions jangle, jar, then play at last in tune. Lost in thought, I gaze at your face across the room…

And what I see next about you pushes a long cold shiver through my body.

I jolt back into sharpness. The stink in here stabs at me—floor polish, soggy flesh and chemicals.

Yes, it is your eyes, I'm afraid. What is happening to them? Look, the glint they had—it's changed. It's different somehow. How? *What* is different? They are glinting brighter now. No, not brighter—wider! No, not wider either. Please, what is it?

The pin-point reflection of the bare light-bulb on the surface of the eye nearer me seems to shift.

I stare. Mounting nausea…

A drip of fluid seeps from the corner of the eye where it has gathered, breaks free from your lashes, and starts to trickle jerkily across your cheek's surface, like a fugitive sneaking cross-country.

So here is the horror, to sicken the sun…

Now I know. I know too well.

Oh, my Angel…

2 LOVE AMONG THE SPIRES AND THE FOUNTAINS

Inside an instant, as I stare, the first few weeks we spent together fifteen years ago hurtle through my mind against my will—rhapsody in overdrive, projected on the screen of your body stretched before me.

We met among the spires and the fountains. I remember every detail…

The bar that I entered with a friend the night we met. Laughter, conversation, wine and smoke. "Drink?" I asked my friend.

"Please. I'll take the corner table there."

Returning to the indicated corner, drinks in hand, I took a sip, lit a cigarette and looked around.

On my left a girl about to leave her seat was talking to a figure just beyond her by the window. "Why not join us?" she was saying. "I'll be back to pick you up."

"Sure, I'd like to!" came the quick reply—and something in me stirred. The voice, in just those four words, electrified. Soft, deep, warm, camp, vulnerable and sharp at once. Something started inside, a pang of fascination, of excitement to discover what produced such a sound.

The girl blocked my view as she prepared to go. I leaned forward, trying to see round her; she moved forward too. Leaning back, I tried to see behind; she moved back as well. I craned up—she rose to block my view. "Oh—" I muttered.

"What are you flapping about?" my friend asked.

I looked at him and laughed. "I'll tell you in a minute!" Then I turned back. At last she was gone.

And there you were.

You blinked the most bewitching eyes I'd ever seen. You looked around, as if deciding what on earth to do now. Both hands on your glass, you took a gulp from it. A thin fire sang in me. You saw me, held my glance a moment, dropped your eyes—looked again a second later—looked away.

I sipped my drink and gazed about. My friend said something. Absent, I replied; tapped an idle finger on my glass; watched the bar swim with people, and my mind with your presence.

You shifted, leaning forward, legs and arms crossed. I caught your eye and smiled. You smiled back shyly, seemed about to speak. I leaned across to hear you through the babble. Waited—no reply. You looked at me in hesitation, laughed. Spoke at last: "…I don't have anything to say!"

I grinned. "What's your name?"

"Angel."

"Jaymi."

"Oh," you said.

I looked away a moment. "So you don't think that quite matches up to your name, then."

"No, I like it!" you giggled.

"It serves."

"I've got to go somewhere now," you said.

"Go somewhere, then! I'll see you again."

You rose, gathered up your things. "I'll be in here tomorrow."

"Sure. See you then." You lingered. "After lunch?" I said.

"Yes. When?"

"Two o'clock."

You nodded, flashed a smile of such incredible gentle sweetness, I was softened into no further utterance. It seemed that a silent bell of silk squatted over us a moment, arching out the outside world … then with delicacy, lightness and the faintest of skips you walked away.

I turned to my staring friend and beamed, sinking to my seat.

"You're so retiring," he observed.

*

The next day. Two-fifteen, and there you were. Your T-shirt was tur-quoise. "D'you know about the garden?" I asked.

"No. Where?"

So out from the bar and down the back road we bubbled, to the corner where the path between the hedges begins. Cyclists swerved to pass us. By an iron gate we stopped. You darted up to peer between the bars and shot a glance of excitement at me over your shoulder, as you saw for the first time the lawn sloping down to the silver birch glade where the sap burned heavy through a lazy sway of branches. Behind us somewhere in the distance on the wind, over roofs, played a clarinet. Reaching around you, I slid the heavy key into the lock, turned it gently and pushed.

With a low squeak, the gate swung wide.

Inside, I pushed it shut. You scudded through the bushes to the edge of the expanse of lawn and stopped. Cedars rose in state beyond the grass out of high beds of foliage, where other secret regions of the garden could be glimpsed. Gnats danced pin-pricks in the air above a sundial, like the ticking of the seconds—like a hundred years before. Above, blue radiance.

You gave a sort of wiggle as you reached to touch my arm, while the colour and the light within your eyes were as your whisper— "This is magic!" Through your hair shone the sun, as sirens sing. Between us now the crackle was electric.

Setting off across the space, I turned to meet you running up behind me with the smile of a child. "Let's go!" I said.

And so we went; and sitting in the glade, together alone at length and sweetly, we talked for many hours—a talk that felt like running through a field. Laughter flung our friendship up in shafts, till our words were made of instinct and intimate inconsequence. We fell quiet at last, no need to speak. Clarinet strains lapped again across the lawn and through the glade, and came to mingle with the ripples of the sunny sea of leaves upon whose amber crackled surface we were buoyed.

Then, with the simplest of manoeuvres, your warm shy body lay alongside mine, and the touch of its affection felt to me as sun on stone.

I looked at you, and happiness flowered in me like a burst. Your eyes gazed at mine through your lashes; turned away. (No, you weren't very good at eye contact then.) I held you closer still and whispered in your ear. And so we lay, till liquid birds lulled and coaxed through the rich soft dusk.

Then we sneaked quick and quiet across the twilight of the lawn, past the sundial and back through the shrubs to the gate. Your upper lip sweated faintly. My mouth was alive, juices like wine…

Behind us, the gate swung shut with a clang.

*

London, half past ten Monday night, and the club was filling up where I awaited your arrival. Around the wall were alcoves; in each, a ring of seats. Through the chrome-railed entrance of this alcove was the aisle, then three steps up to a cool wide dance-floor. On it, to a nameless upbeat sound, danced a few, none yet claiming the centre of the space.

My gaze wandered idly over figures I could see. One exquisite blond Asian boy, immaculate in white shirt and salmon pink suit, strolled up and leaned against a column by the dance-floor, expressionless, alert, cigarette newly lit. A mean-looking lout in army gear laughed with friends at the bar. One young pretty boy in white walked past the alcove down the aisle, eyes wide and tension palpable. I stood and headed over to the bar.

And there you were.

Inexorably we kissed, and as we did so the strobe-lit atrium resounded with the opening cry of a track that was the sound of the week or month then. I turned to the dance-floor, dragging you complaining as you laughed, tripped upon the steps and nearly fell. (I'd have thought of it as our track, if only you had liked it—still, you had no choice this time.) I led us to the centre of the crowd. Catching up, you turned on me with useless boxing motions; I feigned terror. You pretended to be bored as you laughed, dancing close to me. Dry ice gulped at us and rose to block you out. I made to kiss your hand but caught your ear. The music seemed to lift us to a land of instant fun, love, money, sex, fashion, hope and pain, all beautifully arranged, both leisurely and urgent. Seeing your divine smiling eyes seeking mine alone, I even felt I liked all these people around me. Are there any brain surgeons here? I wondered absently. Who knows, there may be several. Which are they, and which of the rest could do to see them? You can't tell. Who's a good machine, and who's a bad? Who can write a music so sublime you'd not believe it? No, forget it now. We're dancing on the dance-floor, you and I—watching, being watched! We're beautiful, both of us, meaninglessly so. We're sane, healthy, lucky, rich. We're too good to be true, 'cos we're young, in love, and winning—yes! The smell of amyl nitrite was dense in the air; my head felt as if it could be cracked like an eggshell. As that track faded, the next one erupted. Your eyes lit up. You pulled me to you, arms around behind me. A friend of yours shimmered through the bodies and the dry ice—Niko, rather like a beautiful horse, making thin pointed reachings with his arms as he danced. He smiled at us with irony and came to join us here, his face sharp and elegantly selfish… And so it was we flipped, to the voice of an angel, the three of us so long ago.

It occurred to me there was something to say to you that we hadn't yet said in the two or three weeks we'd known each other. I looked up at the strobes and wondered for a moment. But as I did so it was you who put your mouth to my ear, you who spoke still and small through the din to me: "I know what you're thinking. I want to say it too, you know… *I love you!*"

I looked into your eyes from very close. Stopped dancing. Led us off the floor. Then gently, silently, slowly and ecstatically, backed by the angel's voice, I let you know as well as I could the thing that words have never said as truthfully as touch.

Outside afterwards, the street lights were yellow in a spitting London rain. Three teenage boys approached us down the pavement. Our hands disengaged. One craned forward as they passed, as if to check in horror what he'd seen.

The words cut simply through the dark: "I hope you both die of AIDS."

Our hands re-engaged, further on.

*

Soon after that, my room. The two of us. Time for you to hear it.

I pulled the window closed to keep the organ music out that

filtered darkly through the glass across the court, and drew the curtains shut.

I walked to a corner of the room, while you watched. On a white shelf, a CD-player perched. In the darkness either side a candle burned high and clear. High to right and left, a pair of speakers…

I inserted a disc, flicked the switch and rejoined you in the armchair. "This is what I've written so far," I said.

You nodded, looked appropriately serious and curled up against me.

Welling trumpet licked around us, coiling muscled pulses violent-smooth and pure. You gave a little quiver. Then its echo softly died. Hard to convey the effect of the sound, but the nearest I could get would be to say it died as if across a stone field, fled into a desert where a bitter cold sun chilled the sand—the shout of Pan across an empty page. We followed in the air, over hollow land to fields of fever flavoured creepy-sweet, where out of monstrous vegetation edging purple seas an aphid swarm arose on drifting haze of painted light (unreal—an honest light would breed the dead). Guitar wept on lava-fields of synthesiser, plucked our bloodlit skin with trilling squeaks thin and sad as the scream of the butterfly carried in the snowlight. The hills rolled the whites of the lakes in their eyes, but exhausted, their coloured streams, dry-lashed and dead. Now the rhythm of the music gathered majesty and force. Round a corner (once I painted it), a vision: down a straight yellow path to a valley through a vast undulation of green bubble trees we were galloping on horse-back, toward but never nearer to a river at the bottom on the other side of which ran ranges of hills, growing infinitesimally small and ever clearer till at last they were bent round, tucked up and swallowed in a haemorrhage of permanently disappearing sun… On sped our horse, its every step becoming lighter. Beyond the tideless green to either side, on a scale and at a distance not improper for sublimity, gigantic towers sprang. Their bases splayed like tree boles, with barely chance to right themselves before they pierced the clouds, where (extrapolating curve-wise) their main thrust shot to heights unseen and inconceivable. In echo of them then the horse's hooves left the ground, so we rose on the windswept air above the valley to the sweet-rotting garden-land of heaven, where the earth seems nothing but a cinder in the sky.

The music changed. The horse slowed, came to rest and dropped us on a sombre square of grass, all enclosed in a wall of gateless hedges. Turning, the horse seemed to frown at us ambiguously, reared its head and snorted, and fled into the dusk above the foliage. The grass was stiff and dry between my fingers. I reached across to him with whom I visualised myself, lay a hand upon his arm and whispered "You all right?" He smiled, nodded, moved across and curled against me, eyes closed. I stroked him, looked about me. Dark silence. In the high dense hedge to my left, a glow of shadows turning red as if an unseen sunset were spreading off horizons out beyond, where I knew the mountains rose to bite the air. A glass-coloured planet left its teeth-marks on the twilight overhead, its sudden sight producing that uneasy thrill I felt when I first saw the man in the moon. Round it hung a livid sky, ill, stagnant, dying, seeping out a sickly radiance. A faint blackish light full of bits of floating matter cast a nauseating dullness on the colours round about: Claustrophobia crept around the marches of the field—snuffled through the hedges—pulled them nearer me, pretending not to realise it was noticed. Once again, dark silence… Or was it? Had I heard a noise behind me? I turned; for the first time noticed, in a section of the hedge that seemed to rustle as with hidden wings, a cave; wheeled to face it then, and froze. Dark-bodied meat-flies buzzed in a stream from the cave mouth, collected and danced in the air. It seemed that voices soft as thunder sounded far below: grave chthonic bells, fiery harmonies, and muttered incantations echoed dead and harsh in deaf and time-less labyrinths of stone … then they vanished, leaving nothing but the buzzing of the meat-flies, swelling now in gouts. —No, there was more. From the coolness of the cave depths, a noise from a bad dream; a hum, corroding sanity as acid eats a walnut. Gulps, drips, squeals and glutinous dread, growl of worms in egg-slimed earth… I grabbed my companion and shook him, but he slept. Flies surged out from the cave in a black scream and massed in the air, in expecta-tion. "*Into the line of awfulness, this work!*" I heard my mouth shout, and braced myself. "*Here it comes!*" The hedge turned ugly and the grass turned black and here it came, on a billow of bundled death: from out the hive shot a horror. Lunging out, bowing up and down in the jerkily unnatural way of cinematographic animation, accom-panied by shrill-faced yelps and gimlet shrieks, sprang a cold stiff hard thin dog reminiscent of a greyhound, one metre tall, skull cleft with an axe, emitting through what looked like locust mandibles a high-pitched wheeze of eldritch cries and mandrill hoots, as if from other beings trapped inside it.

It halted, smacked its lipless snout and slavered, fixed a pair of glassy eyes on me and on the boy lying draped in my arms. I stared at its body—almost retched. No fur, but a slug-like, tuberous salad of intestines shot with pulsing purple veins. Then to my astonishment a thick, clotted, grinding voice erupted from its head and spoke: "*Shocking! Shocking! Hah! We better pray for you! Shocking! Shocking! Bless you children! Hahahah!*" Nocturnal eyes, anti-eyes it had, without expression. As I watched, it coughed and jolted out the left one. "*Woops! What a shame!*" crooned a chuckly rotten voice, then simpered, "*Must have sinned! Fuck my eyes, what a rush! Hahahah!*" Quickly I put myself between it and my friend, fast asleep and still unwakable. "*How sweet!*" it grated fawningly. "*How touching... Wormsmeat!*" A cold lumpy stream of vomit gushed from its muzzle like a geyser and drenched us. (To live is to boil, I reflected in a flash.) Dipping and shuffling, it bowed to the ground—weevilled nearer—thrust its grinning mask at me and shot from its mandibles a brown sticky tongue the length and thickness of a baguette. I dodged just in time, and heard the tongue sucked back through its jaws with a noise like oily sandpaper. A moist catarrhal voice leaked out from its face, as if confiding: "*I know the way to your heart, you little pervert! In through your ribcage—hah!*" I dived for a wide flat sharp-edged stone lying near us on the grass, turned back, saw the creature sniff the eyeball it had dropped. Belching snoutily, it rasped with an undercutting whine: "*Lunch! Yum Yum! D'you want the other one, freak? Come and get it! Hahahahah!*"

I leaped forward, screeched and flung the stone. My aim was true; I watched the other eye pop from its hole on the impact, burst in the air, then dangle and swing, dripping viscous yellow fluid from a single writhing twist of knotted meat. "Oh but there's no need to cry," I spat, through the air that was big with the volts of my glee. "Squirm, poisoned meat, 'cos you're just about to lose!" I dug into its face with my silver nails, ripped a flap of hide off its cheek and saw to my disgust another face within—a new pair of eyes sunk in doughy running flesh, one of which gave me a lecherous wink. Seeing the creature prepare to spring at me, I cast about in desperation for the stone, but couldn't see it. Then, with a pang of pure delight amid a blast of slicing hatred, I remembered the obvious—*the axe!* I wrenched at the shaft, pulled the blade from the dog's skull. A splitting noise: entranced, I heard my adversary bellow out in misery and pain, as if a flaring sheet of agony were flowering inside it from a horrifying rupture! As the gloom of the twilight digested its bellow, unexpectedly the cave mouth returned it at me magnified. I jumped, regained composure, swung the weapon upward in an access of demonic strength, and down again. While the axe descended with a whisper through the air, the creature's second face sloughed off like a glove to show a third—this one a worm-face shaped like a fork, pumping tenderly inside as if with sightless wriggling larvae. "*The plot sickens, runt!*" I shrieked in parody, and slammed the axe home. The creature's head, about to snap through my leg with its jaws, rent in two upon the blow without a sound, spilling out a stew of crawling pedipalps and spiders' paws that scuttled through the grass to be immediately devoured by the meat-flies. Twelve sets of prim little lips pushed out from the corpse in a last collective purse of disapproval, and subsided. The worm-face maggoted about among the mess, found a nook to choke and nestle in, and twitched to a halt.

My sleepy companion stirred, stretched and shifted on the grass. "Must have fallen asleep," he yawned. "Did anything happen?"

I laughed, kissed him, tapped his chest: "Well, I found out the way to your heart!" I said.

As the music closed, the field seemed to lift up and elongate—streaking out in strings across the darkness of my room, to disappear like vermicelli through the mesh-covered mouths of the speakers on the shelf.

At this very first hearing of my music, my Angel, you stirred, shifted suddenly beside me in the armchair, arose, murmured that you had to go, and fled my room.

*

Soon afterwards, at night, through suburban streets from elsewhere: you and I, returning home, saying little. Among the chimney-stacks, as if among the blackened points of pine along a dead plantation road, wept the wind.

Inside, dog-tired, we crept through the building to your room, where I lay upon the bed. You put a CD on, wandered round and sang distractedly, an effortless falsetto so bloodless and beautiful, my head swam. Vague, you came at last to join me, lay your body's light and weight on mine, encircled by my arms. Caress of lips and lashes; through our clothes along my limbs a glimmer ran warm and wide. Close above me clanged the symmetry and measure of your cheekbones and eyes, like a gong: desert-like, deadpan, softly they killed. But there was no communication there, not since I'd played you my music. Had I played it too soon? I attended to the track we were hearing, which I knew but had never really listened to. A love song, sweet, slow and sad, sung well with simplicity, sincerity and every other trick—and now it hit me. A dangerous sense of loneliness hovered just above me, poised, then slipped and enveloped me, clamped on my mind—on its separateness from you. A deadly pulse, I felt it grip me, fill me, drain me… Slowly, deeply, darkly and passionate we kissed, ineluctable as breathing: though the burn of your lips to me was agony, I couldn't stop. All that stirred were our tongues, playing, sliding, stroking. I felt as if I stood back to spectate, a dark and lonely watcher at some doomed and slithery ballet. How arbitrary this union was, like any other: I and You in a random room, random building, random district, town, country, era—one twenty, one nineteen, and each supposing he is closer to the other at this moment than he was the day before they met or will be when they both start to rot. We each might as well have been another. I felt so alone, or ceased to kid myself I wasn't. This was the first moment anyone had broken through the bubble I inhabited. I felt it was my bubble rather than yours that had broken. Your bubble touched me now, the unsheathed me. What if your bubble broke as well, to leave us touching? Would I weep, would I tremble as I clung to you? You lay your head face down upon my chest. I kept preparing words, kept seeing how inadequate they were, and always stopped myself from speaking. How to better "I love you" when it's all there is to say but still a shortfall? I think I murmured it in any case, deliberately controlled, to stop you raising up your head to seek my eyes out with your own and draw me into them—to mask from you as well the agonised imploring face I shot around the room while I hoped (fearing to search) that there was not some dark coincidence of mirrors where you watched me and wondered what the hell I felt. What was happening? Where were you? Should I break through or not? How I wanted to, but knew I didn't know what I would find, what reception I'd be given—didn't know the risks involved. To melt your bubble open, or to seal them both again? It could still go either way…

Another second, then I chose. Chose to shift; and shifting, broke the spell. One move sufficed to seal me up again and leave you sealed: the victory of survival over grandeur. At first you didn't stir. Then you had to, with a token noise.

No reunion, then, not yet. Just a separate tired proximity on a bed in North London, as the rain stung the windows.

I rolled you over, had you face me. "The moon won't stop in its course, you know, and the sun will continue to rise!" I said.

"Let's sleep," you smiled.

*

Next day, an evening of parties. We went; but you were absent, pre-occupied, hardly met my eye. At length you left—you were tired, you said, you'd see me tomorrow. I nodded.

A splinter group from one party splintered again: five of us, late, in a grand white building with grass either side. Rooms on the top floor, capacious and elegant in pale green paint. The evening's end was permanently imminent, for no one had the energy to call it. I said I would return, and slipped away to check your light.

Night shone cold about the lamps in the court, where a shadow quivered underneath my tread upon the flagstones. Inside another building, I climbed the stairs, pursued constricted corridors and found yours. As I strode, the building bled a blandly violent disco beat—the cellar. Were you there? Through the window from the kitchen by your room I peered out, saw your light was off. I crept to your door, stopped dead. Turned the handle softly, poked my head in, looked around… Empty. Nothing but the moonlight, the usual scent of Poison, and your echo in the mirror like a wink in the dark. In default of your lips, I kissed your shadow and left.

I walked across the court to the bars of the gate; peered out upon the desert of the quiet of the street where the dogs should have danced in the glare of the sodium; returned to the pale green room.

Its owner had retired to his bedroom for the night. Two remained, about to leave. Was I staying? Yes I would, for a while; there was still a bottle open, unstarted, the cork thrown away—it wouldn't keep. Then would I lock the door when I left? Yes I would.

Alone again, I settled in an armchair and stared at the flames in the grate, dying down now. I poured out a red glass and sipped—knew enough to call it finer than I knew. Piano music trilled from the speakers either side of the fire: a concerto, casual and sublime, every phrase both surprising and inevitable. Glass-doored cases of leather-bound books lined the walls. Either side of the line between my armchair and the fire were two divans, symmetrically arranged. Not many sets in this building were lived in; it struck me I was probably the only one awake in it. Centrally seated in the grand-est of settings, furnished with firelight and cigarettes and freedom, Mozart attending and claret to excess; on the crest of a mountain of comfort and luck, high achievement all around me and my own music waiting … this, for the moment, I could feel to be a pinnacle. Briefly tonight, with its owner all unknowing, this room was host to an abstract guest: right there, hovering before me on the air, was a single point of light where this culture that had formed me chose to park its very peak… Soon the point would pass, swept away around the globe on unfathomable vectors of darkness and energy. But just for now it burned here, majestic and immobile, oblivious to him for whom it lit the room with soft fire—unconscious of his wish that you could share it.

I poured another glass, drank deep, and felt the haziest of memo-ries assail me from a past dream: running down a cataract of myriads of wide steps of white polished balustraded marble, alone, down a mountain to a valley full of writhing silver birches in a violent gust of rain from a yellow-grey sky—

The music ended. I turned off the stereo, sat down again and poured another glass. Distant laughter echoed in the court. What extraordinary twittering it was, heard out of context—so reflex, as if from a machine. How long before that laugher would forget she ever made that sound? Perhaps in an hour, or perhaps she had already;

yet for a second it had filled her, its cause so very urgent. And what of my forgetting? Would tonight remain in memory long? Would all the parties? What had we all discussed with such energy? What was it we were laughing at in candlelight, stoned the other night, the six of us in my room? (Who were we, come to that?) Reconcocted flavours overran precise facts, like weeds in a yard where the light comes seldom and aslant.

I rose, wandered through to the study, to the window. On the skyline, thick and squat above a clump of trees, the tower of the library reared black against the stars. Restless, I returned to the main room and knelt by the grate. The flames had died away but the embers were hot. I blew on them; they glowed inside, a dull infernal red. I rose again, walked across the room, sank my weight into the chair and poured another glass of wine.

I thought of you. Where were you now? I thought of us together, of the beauty of the friendship we had started—of the waste of it? I thought as well of our appearance to the world; of how so many when they looked at us saw only what repelled; of how bizarre this was, when we were not repelled by them. (I pictured pairs of them together, tried to feel repellence at the love that I was seeing—simply couldn't.) How sad, then, that they should have that feeling. Sad for them, sad for us, indirectly sad for all. What a sad song it was…

Motionless, I watched an anger kindle inside me, flaring up in different places, spreading fire through my veins. Voluptuous Malevolence accosted me; its venom pumped inside; I felt no deity but Violence, dark and complete! Suddenly I yearned to extinguish a life—to feel the hot strong calm clear sharp rush of sweetness that derives from dealing death, that intoxicates and satisfies! The blood-rush! What a rush… I reached for a hand mirror, held it up and stared into my pupils in the sidelight. Destruction grinned and beckoned to me, elegant and cruel in black and pink among the shadows in the cowl of the porch—mouthed one word *KILL!*—blew a kiss at me and winked.

I grinned as well, and put the last of the claret in my glass.

As I did so, an extraordinary image overtook me: a speck on the horizon, creeping nearer through a pulsing desert haze at what must be an almost supernatural speed. I couldn't make it out, but heard a thunderous galloping accompanied by sharp cries; whatever it was was heading straight towards me. As it drew near, I saw to my astonishment a posse of a dozen sprinting pigs—ovoid, identical, like outsize toys—driven by a wild-eyed long-haired keeper who was bellowing instructions to go faster, faster, faster still… I froze as they passed close by, seeming not to notice me, all doggedly intent on the furthest horizon. Dust swirled around me. When it cleared, they were far across the plain, streaking bullet-like away to fade at last to a speck again and vanish in the haze.

I frowned at my glass in disbelief and laughed aloud. Time to go, perhaps! I drained the wine, staggered up, extinguished the lights, pulled the door shut behind me and tottered down the stairs to the court outside. I shook my head and smiled as I walked across the grass, mouthing the enquiry I addressed to the stars: "So who's the keeper, then?"

I decided I would sleep on it.

*

Next day, Sunday, a note on your door: Gone away, back late Tuesday night.

Monday morning, I'd decided.

On a level, thirty metres off, the window of a little-used music room afforded what was the only direct view across to your room. Had anybody stood inside the music room on Monday and Tuesday, they might have been the witness of an odd play of moves.

Monday evening, keeping vigil on your room, such a spy would have noticed twenty openings of your door, twenty entries by a figure in the gloom, and twenty closings of the door when the figure was inside: the first visit tentative, as if to reconnoitre; eighteen brisker, bringing in a bag with every visit; the last trip bringing in a box. This observer might have seen the figure open up the box and place its contents on the floor, carefully unpack the bags of other longer things, then place the latter down as well in some conjunction with the former. Trips back and forth, to what the watcher might have guessed to be your sink, would have led to further delicate additions by the figure; it would then have been observed to load the box with the bags, pick the box up, look about and close up the curtains.

Tuesday daytime: much renewed activity, betrayed by just a twitching of the curtains now and then.

Tuesday evening: at last came the opening of the curtains with the visitor's departure, the grand unveiling, revealing that the room had somehow changed quite a lot—though the watcher, as it happens, would have very likely cursed to find the starless night and new moon prevent his seeing what had changed…

Late Tuesday night, you returned and flicked the light on; and finally the watcher would have seen what had happened, as a blaze of colour shot across the court through the shadows. Tiger lilies—hundreds of them, bursting out of pots from every shelf, every corner, every surface, every space! Round the window, up the walls, across the ceiling through contrivances of some kind—triumph and delirium and jubilance of orange!

Then you, bright-lit: rooted in amazement, one hand on your hip and the other on your chest; sitting down, getting up, walking round, investigating; sniffing tiger lilies … picking up a note from the table and reading it. Going to the doorway, doubtless at a knock. Letting in a second person, clearly unexpected. Two figures—staring at each other for a moment. Accusation, laughter, talking, and the drawing of the curtains.

Music, dimmer lights. Voices low, flickered shadows.

Dimmer music. No lights at all.

*

Soon thereafter, time for a party of our own. We hired a country house for a night the following month, drew our plans and dispatched invitations.

Saturday. Ten to eight, and on with the final touches. Round the main hall, Peruvian lilies, raspberry ripple in tint, in a faint but unmistakable condition of decay—highly convincing in plastic. Drinks, for all tastes: gin by the bucketful; wines, from Beaumes de Venise to Montbazillac; Opal Hush and silver wine in lime chrome; strawberry lemonade (in each full glass a little bear reading "Hold Me Kiss Me Love Me"). For nibbles, tangerine delights: voluptuously cream-soft, heaven-scented bonbons in the shape of juicy petals, in a frail sugar husk: orange as the sun in the evening sky, orange as the gleam in a panther's eye, orange as the rose in the summer sun, as the fire from the killer's gun, unrepentingly morish and bearing a similar relation to fruit as a sky-painted ceiling to the great outdoors. Ripe globes of melon pouted yearningly from bowls, next to plates of nutty fingers (sugared almonds for the nails).

As I checked once again that nothing lacked, the door swung open behind me. You, greater delicacy still: dressed, from beret down to ruched pixy-boots, in peach and black, you reminded me of sunlight—at least the kind that I prefer. Through tonight, shafts of beauty would be emanating from you, even when you were unlooked at; I resolved to intercept as many as I could.

With a quick shy movement you kissed me and skipped across the room to put the first CD on. Thunder and an ersatz downpour resounded—the start of the track, from which a main beat welled. Leaning one each side, drinks in hand, against the open double doors from the hall to the lawn where our guests must arrive, we descried through the twilight the first of the horde, rustling out from under low trees: gliding majestically across the grass towards us, between a pair of acolytes, Cyan—elegant and beautiful adornment of parties, long hair rising gravity-defying in a plume like a peacock's, crest swaying gently in the stillness of the dusk... Gradually, from either side behind them, further figures loomed and floated into view—army of exotics, out of earshot, all intent upon the light where we stood to receive them.

You turned to me and prophesied: "It's going to be a good one!"

Voices sprouted tiny in the air below the clouds, at shoulder level. Change of vision, end of slow-mo; start the countdown to the moment when events will take their course... And here it came, and now it flickered up around us (so close, so nearly three-dimensional)—the tableau, cutely outré, nubile and delicately scented, where the goldfish are black and the boys are like baby-faced girls. Pointlessly pretty were the players in this ravishingly narcissistic, slinkiest of melodramas: edible and elfin to venomous and vain, crotch-tight tension to loose-clad languor. "I Feel Love" wove a hypnotising under-spell around us from the speakers in the corners of the hall. I greeted, talked, listened, laughed, aware of every movement we were making. As I filled a glass with champagne from a nearly empty bottle, seventeen of the thinnest silver bangles slithered down my upturned forearm and dropped past my wrist, one by one, to collect with a shimmer and a chime against the width of my hand. The boy for whom I'd poured it smiled, stretched out his hand and seemed as well to stretch the time he took to do so: in the course of half a second, I could take him in at leisure—feel his quickness to be earnest and his readiness to laugh, know the warmth behind his violet eyes and see upon the slim tanned curve of his neck behind a brilliant metal earring-glint the softest whorl of down below a sharp close-cropped cut of hair rising smooth and gently layered as a spray of violin notes. Next to him a different beauty, dark-eyed, feminine and sleek but depraved, face taut as the muscles of his black leather jacket, with a smile full of evil and the grace of a switchblade. It offered me a cigarette, was grabbed from behind by a friend, gave a spasm and a shriek and disappeared in pursuit.

This was it, then, the moment when the party took over. I filled my glass again, lit the cigarette, surveyed the scene. I drained my glass, refilled it, and headed through the throng, my very passage making love with the crowd either side.

Conversations seethed, music leapt and people danced, over many drunken hazy hours. You surfaced next to me.

"Let's take the air," I said. You hiccupped, nodded, took my hand. Pushing through the people to a side door, we ran along a passage, turned a corner and emerged on a terrace looking out across the gardens.

*

The heat of the night behind the house was smooth, the air unblinking, as we leaned against the terrace balustrade.

Beyond a low pavilion swathed in leaves, where the scent of faded roses twined the stillness of the air, a sunken garden was surrounded by a tract of spacious woodland, grassy vistas, distant urns and lichened temples horned with towers crisp against the sky. Outline trace of light on splintered limes—moon silver. So we stood, immobile as a pair of infant brothers who have stumbled on a paradise they know they cannot tell of, for the grown-ups won't believe it. You squeezed my hand in yours, and we set off through the rose-beds. Beyond them, a pair of granite obelisks (one pink, the other tan) flanked a flight of steps that led us up from gravel into undergrowth. Skipping out between them, we swerved down a wooded path at random, into apple glades and groves of silver birch, to colonnades of fern and shadow, dappled jade and copper-feathered on the mossy earth. We turned again. Suddenly you ran ahead and dipped from sight, your laughter ringing out behind a clearing through a sheer immuring bank of tangled thorn that hedged it in. I stalked through a gap, stopped dead and listened hard; heard a tiny muffled giggle. Leaping round the tree-trunk on my left, I caught you—felt you squeal, and held you close. From some way off, like birds of fever in a jungle, trickled skinny voices… Creeping through the undergrowth around our niche, we peered between the branches to a wide sloping glade of filtered moonlight saffron-soft, where heavy blooms among the bracken, beating silent as the chime of the stars in the night, drugged the air with tears of bitter peach. Seeping from the dark green cover of the trees around the glade, as we spied, came a stream of figures—party guests, scampering excitedly in long thin grass while emitting little eunuchoid cries that seemed to tickle, like a crowd of coloured sprites or the dance of a tiny troupe of hands in the bone of a plum … then one by one they vanished at the bottom of the glade, just as fast as they had come.

Making out a constant sigh nearby, we pushed towards it and came to a dark round ornamental lake banked in fern and padded pine. Plumes of spotlit water rose and fell from the centre, where a fountain flung its cascade high. A pair of hazy water faces peered from the surface when we craned our necks to look. We peeped again, to check if they were staying there; they were. Lying on the soft-heaped needles of the bank, we lit up clove cigarettes, watched the smoke coiling up into the branches, and listened. The sough of water, softened at a distance, was immense. I closed my eyes and felt you look at me.

"What d'you see?" you whispered.

I kept my eyes closed, and thought. "A million palms," I said, "like shingle sighing, or the beating of anemones beneath a shallow sky. We're lying on the sand in a bay, you and I, a little way from the water. Breakers boom unseen beyond the dunes just in front of us. The shore exhales and sputters shale and scallop, scudding flakes of surf and suds of skimming foam. Mermaids flow and dance among the spray—or maybe just dugongs…" I concentrated harder. "The sky's a fragile blue, with a softness of shell; the horizon, in the places where we see it, weeps in mist. You can feel a mane of mist around us with your fingers, though it isn't cold. Far across the bay, never-ending and majestic, is a vast spout of white-boiling water, lit triumphantly in descant through cathedrals of ice … the South Pole! (Eight thousand miles away below us through the earth, then, the whirlpool churns whose flue this fountain sucks.) Are you with me?"

You nodded.

"Then above us," I continued, "on a rock beyond the sand, is a figure, plucking gently at the strings of an instrument the shape of half a pear—you know the one I mean. A hermaphrodite with dark blue eyes is planted on the promontory, the focus of the bay, as at the bottom of an amphitheatre, singing, as I see now, the siren-song that shines around us all—unearthly as that one castrato's voice we have on record—wordless and effortlessly powerful, enclosing all the world, reaching out above the billow of the fountain into countries full of sea-fire and devil-fish and dragons, where the sun-blast is golden and the she-lions are white! And I realise that this singer, like the saddest statue coppiced in a garden unremembered in the forest of a continent long-lost, has sung forever and to nobody its rapturous lament: *this* song, ambassador and abstract of humankind's achievement, offered up unbidden and unheard to the heavens, just in case—a jet of feeling poured across a bay without an audience—a music playing, as it were, through headphones to a corpse."

I opened my eyes, saw you shiver, lie unspeaking for a moment, then reply: "I see a wide green tunnel under trees—a river, with an ecstasy of light upon its surface. We're reclining in a gondola together, pulled along with strength and ease by a ferryman of animal allure! Beside and behind and in front are other gondolas, propelled by a pride of human creatures of a near-unnatural beauty. The vault of leaves above is dense and luminous, receding to a needle-sharp stiletto of infinity ahead of us. Attached to the tree-trunks, cande-labra flicker by the gloom of the swamps, like motes on the edges of the cone of a moonbeam. Every drop of nectar on the foliage is highlit with a magically exaggerated pin-prick of light, as in a modern stylisation of Elysium. We pass an underwater tiger in a raised glass tank, prowling up and down its prison, never resting. Each *splash!* from the pole echoes out across the water—through the tunnel, down the regress, into folds of flooded forest endless centuries away. The lightness of our movement on the river where we trail our hands, the gold glint of eyes below the branching of your lashes and the lapping of the water as it slops at the boat with the gurgle of a kiss … this is heaven!"

I lit a pair of cigarettes and handed one to you. "We should have pressed 'record' on that," you murmured. "Now we've lost it forever."

I smiled at the fountain. "Honey, we were just warming up," I said. "Now, what else do we hear?"

You drew your breath in. "Wait," you said, and pulled a pen and paper from your pocket. "I'm going to write this one day!"

I closed my eyes, turned them upward and listened. "We're in a long rich hall of fluted marble, where our whispers flit in echoes crisp and sweet among a gallery of pink-veined pillars, coalesce again, are magnified and boomerang across a floor of cool white stone. Reflected on the floor, from the open double doors at the end of the hall, is a more than perfect vision. Ice-golden cataracts are spilling out of mountain peaks, cascading over foothills onto butterfields of honey-stone, then out across alluvium to bays of clam and bubble-shell and mango-fruit and aloe, seeping down at last to hang inert in trenches underneath a china sea. Slowly, hand in hand, we tread the marble and the vision, down the hall towards the doors, where sublimity awaits us at the threshold of the balcony. We lean upon the balustrade, immobile, and listen… The vision conjures harmonies, colossally barbaric and celestially sophisticated: more and more intense become the sounds, attaining registers you think they can't maintain—then they do. Like a peach afloat in grenadine, a swollen orange sun is hung in webs of vermilion, its last dying rays slashing weak through the clouds. As it shrivels in the sky, a scent of ilex, dew and linden, cep and clubmoss, eucalyptus, elm and carob spreads around us from the jungle, while the tideless groves of mangrove glisten neap and wanly cyan and the salamander valleys sing with light! Phrases of the music climb the scale towards delirium; sensations go beyond the point where pain begins to grin among the pleasure. Now a silver-flamed chariot of music lifts us up at last, accelerates—propels us out on dark-ribbed wings of our own, over incandescent oceans… Planets bob like fruits around a pale-plum moon; there to meet us is the cobalt sprite that leaps before the bright Antarctic rim. He may hate the sound that brought us there or curse us if it scares him, but he can't say we didn't get away with it!"

"You win," you said. "I gave up trying to write it!"

Then I felt you in my arms again, your black sweep of hair against my forehead and the sameness of our bodies, basking rapt within your love that ringed me round like abalone. The feel of you was old and new as birdsong, words unnecessary. Tomorrow we die, so let's just do this now. We shan't be long inside this garden where the grey poison rots, so what better while we're in it? Love: the biggest turn-on of the lot. Love: the reason why you're beautiful (a logic too serene to be corrupted by the fact that you were beautiful in any case). Staring through the window of your eyes, I smiled—so *that's* the other one with whom I've come to be like this! What excitement and surprise… Our bubbles had broken now, and the feeling was calm and luminous, not frenzied as I'd once feared. I wished that I, and not my hands and gaze, embraced you here and now. I wished that all of me were in your body, occupied its space, perceived sensations through its faculties. (What a crazy wish, though! Think about the danger. What if pain began to rend you? Could I extricate myself? In any case, inhabiting your body would oblige me to receive my own caresses—no, I'd rather feel yours.)

And so we lay for long, during which it seemed the hands of your watch must be revolving at the same speed: hours came and went before we knew it, while the minutes trickled by. "Each minute spent with you is the right time," I murmured.

As I did so, we were covered with a decorously delicate but cold plume of water, blown towards us from the fountain by a sudden gust of wind. Amused and indignant, you were just about to speak when you stopped, saw me reach out a ring from my pocket, take your right hand and guide it down your third finger's length. A bird called; dawn glimmered faint at the edges of the sky. For a moment, entranced, you were frozen—unable to move or speak. Then you sank back down beneath me, tears shining on your cheeks among the spray.

3 OH, MY ANGEL

...Oh, my Angel.

Such relief as time had afforded me was cancelled, when I came into this orange-painted cell to see you stretched on the same cold bench I'd watched them put you on nine years ago.

Then how much worse to see that tear.

And now this recall, rushing up in me from nowhere like a fast train through a station, leaves me frozen on the platform of your living death.

In the course of my flashback, the tear has reached your ear. With a sudden further jolt, I realise that you too must know you shed it, since the fluid on your eye must have altered the image you are doubtless so familiar with. And with that realisation, the nightmare gathers in me: quickly, very quickly, I must act.

I am still near the doorway, removed from your sight-line, so you won't have seen my agonised reaction to your tear. My turning back to look and then my horrified discovery of it were silent; the last thing you heard was my audible relief when you failed to blink.

Were I to leave now in emotional haste, any glance I might have shot at you from here might plausibly have failed to catch the telltale streak upon your face—especially if my own eyes were also wet.

You cannot know if I saw your tear, with all it implies—or if I've yet seen it.

You needn't know...

*

Neither of us moves.

A long-handed tic from the disc on the wall seals a minute. Silent, the red second-needle spins on.

...Your possible states of mind would seem to be three: either you are a vegetable and a tear just happened to emerge now, in which case I can do nothing more; or you are only partly in there, in which case I have no clear idea of my options and responsibilities; or you are in there and conscious and quite possibly to be communicated with ... in which dire case I have three options. First, I could act unselfishly, putting your wishes above mine, in which case if you confirmed that you wished to die I could suffocate you (for which I could probably avoid prohibitive legal repercussions using the power of money), or if you let me know you wished to remain alive I could alert your attendants and have the technology installed to provide you with the most bearable quality of life available: this would have the advantage of my following your wishes, but would entail the risk that even if, having chosen to live, you make no difficult requests such as that I give up the life with which I am so happy (albeit never quite as before) to return to you, your continued and perhaps then legally interminable existence might nevertheless come not only to ruin the life I now have but also to be unbearable to its very custodian. Secondly, I could act selfishly, putting my wishes above yours, in which case I would kill you now (prohibitive legal repercussions again probably avoidable): this would have the advantage of avoiding the possibility that your continued existence come to be over-burdensome to either of us, but would entail the risk of my acting against your wishes. Thirdly, I could weigh our wishes together before acting, having established yours by asking you, as if about to act unselfishly: this would have the advantage, if our wishes coincided, of leaving me certain that the best course of action had been pursued, but would entail the risk, if those wishes differed, of leaving me certain that it hadn't. If I do kill you against your wishes, your distress at my doing so need only of course be momentary—but how protracted a moment can be, like my flashback. So if I do kill you without asking, you must be unconscious first. But in any event what if you are taken with a temporary inability to blink when I ask you to? With that in mind, a seeming non-response from you to any direct enquiry I made would not necessarily prove you uncon-scious; and even were I patently doing no more to you than ensuring unconsciousness, you would know then why I was doing it and suffer just as if you felt me killing you outright… But come to think of it, if you can move your eyelids at will, might you have deliberately refrained from doing so when I asked you to? If so, why? Did you wish to spare me the pain of knowing you are in there, and in your present state as a result of whatever overwhelming change in you was wrought at that concert by my first, last, undeniable and utter forgetfulness of you, while you stared from the wings at irreversible developments you knew revealed the dying of a balance of depen-dence you required to survive? If it was the case that, after so many years of effectively subsuming your being into mine, all capacity for action was at last sucked out of you by the explosive enhancement of my ego in the inhuman apotheosis of that performance, then would you really still be prepared to remain as you are, for my sake? During our time together, I might well have believed it. If so, are you also sparing me the knowledge that my concert did an incomplete job in extinguishing just mobility, not full consciousness—offence to the aesthetics of destruction?… You may of course have refrained from blinking simply to find out why I asked—that must be it. But if the failure to blink was voluntary, what of the tear? Did it threaten to spill despite your intention to spare me? Did you then *let* it spill, in a desperate last-moment change of mind? Or had you intended, even before you abstained from blinking, to spill it? If so, why? Might you, in case I felt unable to cope with the responsibility of knowing not only that you are in there but also that *you* know I was unable to cope with it, have delayed your tear in order to allow me the option I now have—to leave you, pretending I have not seen?… Might you have reckoned that to learn you are in there by a sudden blink, at the moment to which I will surely have worked myself up, would alarm me enough to send me running to inform the very attendants who would then obstruct your wish to die; whereas to find out in this delayed fashion would be more likely to lead to calm communication with regard to this wish?… Might you have been testing me, gauging my feelings more truly than you would have done by just blinking at me? (If so, are you in cahoots? Is there anybody watching me?) Or else—forgive my asking, oh my slowly rotting Angel—had you fallen so in love with what you see above your head that you preferred me out from under, just as soon as not responding might precipitate?… *Or is it that you hate me?* Did you do it just to turn the screw—to make me think the tear emerged to thwart your noble vain attempts to leave me in the dark?… Any of these are possible. But now my eyes are drawn to you again—refocus. Any of those were possible. But oh, your cold still body here, so near, my Angel. Oh, your beauty, only dimmed. Oh, your sweetness and your loveliness…

Silence unbroken. I glance at the clock. The scarlet second hand is just twenty-seven seconds round the dial from when I started this deliberating. Twenty-seven seconds—what an age. (Would it still be plausible I haven't seen your tear yet?)

Neither of us moves.

A knock at the door. It opens. The nurse.

How long will I be? Visiting hours are over—I was expected earlier—though if I wish for a special arrangement, the Director could be telephoned…

"No, I—thank you. That's it, I mean." I look my last on this room and its inhabitant, and sway towards the door. I twitch what I know at once to have been a "ghastly" smile, then continue against my will to smile as I flee down the rubber corridor, painfully gripped as the tears burn the sockets of my eyes with a sort of shrieking mirth, at the knowledge of what the nurse must be thinking: "Oh look! a 'ghastly' smile, now I know what one looks like! I bet he knows I'm thinking this—I bet he's twisted up inside with a sort of shrieking mirth down the corridor, unable to stop because he knows I'm thinking 'Oh look! a "ghastly" smile, now I know what one looks like!'—though he shivers at his mirth and the tears burn the sockets of his eyes as he runs!…"

Outside, the air is sweet and cool. Birdsong laps in the leaves above the path. Beyond the hillside ahead the sun is painted, fluid orange.

—So louder the churning, so sicker the horror.

*

I run to a party in a tower block penthouse, halfway up the Peak in the Midlevels. I talk, listen, sparkle; several people here I know, though none knows the reason for my visit to Hong Kong.

I excuse myself and wander, find a warm dark room and settle down in a corner on the floor. Low music hums and pulses out of speakers. The air is warm as milk, the thick-sharp smell familiar. Joints are passed; nodding thanks, I drag deep and long. Slumped in acrid haze or stalking softly around are other figures, blurred and anonymous in gloom. Now and then I hear the rasp of a cough through the swelter, or the grate-flare-flicker of a match close by. A giant bong squats in the middle of the circle, dim-lit only by a smudgy glow that shimmers through the curtains where a whiteness burns outside.

Blood sings giddy in my head. I seem to feel the tug of each corpuscle through my veins, like grubs in a cheese. My mind begins to lurch with the dislocated glisten of a roller-coaster. Underneath, my body buzzes torpid with the judder of my heart, in annotation to the rich dark throbbing of the city through the curtains.

Next to me are headphones. Absently I don them, flick a switch and stretch out flatter. I gaze at the slow-shifting figures in the room, sealed off by the deadpan whirr of white noise, and let my eyelids sink. With a rude shock I recognise the faint ghosted opening of the music on the disc before the start of the recording—barely heard but unmistakable. *It's our song!* The track that means the-two-of-us to each, the one we'd always sung together, that we should have sung: that sloughs off the scab from the wound of your vanishing: that excavates your memory: makes the hole you left inside me ache and ring with lack-of-you… I feel all this again inside a fraction of a second (how slow the disc spins)—the promise of the song, thrumming faintly as it were from a far-flung chamber, seeping down the corridor like ox-blood—*listen!* And now before I can manoeuvre hand and arm to switch it off, my ears are hammered as the music detonates. I seem to rise on its surge and rotate into space. In counterpoise of harmony and tension I spin; can no one see? I twirl at once in both directions: clockwise on an internal axis like a spit, and anti-clockwise round an empty void where you should be.

I pull the phones off with a spasm, sweating freely and delirious, and turn the music off. I sink to the floor and breathe the calm of the room again.

Then I see it.

Above a point beside me, set into the ceiling, is a circular mirror. Why had I not noticed it before? I cannot see in detail those reflected near the doorway, their virtual image being too far removed; the effect is of a stew of grains inside a child's kaleidoscope. But I do see that one figure looks up and stares at the mirror and at me… *It's you!* It's you, my Angel, in the glass!

Two thoughts jangle in my head and clamour for supremacy. The first, a distant memory: reading by an open window upstairs in my parents' house, shaded from the summer heat outside. My father, digging in a flower-bed below, calls a greeting to a neighbour. I look up from my book. He is out of my direct sight, close beneath the window; but the first thing that my gaze lights upon when I look up is the tiny image, thin and pale and sharp, of his profile reflected in the window of the stairwell on the opposite house. He seems infinitely further away than he would have, had I not had such an unexpected glimpse but only heard him. Though I pay no attention to his words, the distant doubling of his face and hand, flicking up to catch the light, reminds me of how alone we are, how irremediably cut off from the others that surround us, from family, friends, lovers—sealed forever off from even those with whom we find ourselves as intimately close as we can ever know.

The other thought ousts this in a second: *I must reach you—I must get to you. Don't move! Please stay. Don't look away, I'm coming…* I try to move. I note that you are fabulously beautiful. Not grasping that fact, nor its cruelty, you make no response when I mouth in desperation to let me approach, let me shrug off what is keeping me immobile. I am aware it is possible you will smile recognition, emitting involuntary and unmistakable signs that your path across the room to me will be as reflex, inevitable and ecstatic as mine would be towards you, and that we shall soon be together. I also know that it will not happen. I don't know why it won't; most certainly it should. It would be fitting. But despite or because of that, I know it won't. And it doesn't. Your face is gentle, smooth, expressionless, calmly divine in its tranquil hub. Now it grows to fill the glass, a metre wide, pinning me down as the room revolves. The voices round me squirm, boiling up to a crescendo of growling and screeching. The walls and bodies sway beyond control. Helpless, I am floundering in the ocean of a single eye of yours, which has grown to fill the mirror. It is as if I am now the grain in the cylinder, while soft and wide above me through the spy-hole the monstrous wet eyeball of my owner drinks my image as it twiddles the kaleidoscope. It stares through and past me, without communication. A whisper booms, from deep within the earth: "BLINK!… BLINK!…" I try to obey, but cannot. I try to scream "*Stay! Stay! Stay!*" but am frozen. If I don't speak now, I know you'll go. The entire mirror's width is now your iris—now the event horizon of your pupil—now a black hole. My vision pulses light and dark in time with my heart, as it does before my eyes cry. My eyes must cry, must—try to, cannot.

The floor comes up to hit me. I observe there is no mirror, nearly smile with relief. But then a realisation dawns—a straightforward fact, but a thunderbolt—so simple in itself, yet in complexity of horrid implication so dwarfing any nightmare as to cause my mind to reel…

Oh, my Angel.

Oh avenger of betrayal! Ever-watching, devastating, motionlessly powerful black Angel… No ceiling mirror here, no, maybe not. But where, *where* do I remember seeing one? I know the answer, though I'll ask it once again to buy a few seconds more before the axe falls. Where was it, now? A large convex model that I failed to take account of when I juggled with your life?

Above a point beside your bench.

Can I recall my reasoning?… "I am still near the doorway, removed from your sight-line, so you won't have seen my agonised reaction to your tear. My turning back to look and then my horrified discovery of it were silent; the last thing you heard was my audible relief when you failed to blink. Were I to leave now in emotional haste, any glance I might have shot at you from here might plausibly have failed to catch the telltale streak upon your face—especially if my own eyes were also wet. You cannot know if I saw your tear, with all it implies—or if I've yet seen it. *You needn't know…*"

No, so you needn't—if only you or I had closed your eyes. But neither did…

So you watched my sudden agonising, through the ceiling mirror.

So you knew I'd seen your tear, and all it meant.

And I left you.

—Resickened and smiling and soon to come, I think!

*

No music now.

A stereo thud as the stylus slips into the inmost groove and spins, withheld in ticking orbit from the centre pin.

…Did you deduce what wish of yours it was I dreaded? Did you know what wish of mine my cowardice betrayed? Whose death my flight averted? Worse—did you think I was *pretending* to forget the glass I really knew was showing you an acted pain I hoped you would believe? Or did you know that I forgot but would remember it in subsequent reflection, as I have—then, as I do, wonder whether you have known this? Any of these are possible…

The stylus lifts, hovers, floats across the disc and halts, sinks and comes to rest, with a muffled thud in stereo.

No music now.

*

I rise, leave the party and the block, and travel fast to the city's edge. Foiling guards, walls and spikes with the thoroughness, ingenuity and persistence of unqualified obsession, I climb into a garden, stalk unseen across a lawn, seek a means of entry to the building I'm intent upon, and find one.

A small frosted sash, unlocked. Gingerly I raise it, wriggle through into a washroom and close it behind me. With the caution to be expected, I emerge from the room, locate myself, pursue constricted corridors and find yours. I creep to your door and turn the handle. Locked.

Footsteps approaching round a corner. I dive for the handle of the door next to yours—turn it softly, poke my head in, slip inside, close it after me and freeze behind the door. Dim light shows me another little cell like your own, but unoccupied. The footsteps grow louder, pass and recede.

I breathe again and peer around. A bed, a chair, a basin. Where's the light from? Looking up, I see it then. One internal window, near the ceiling. And through it?

Through it is a ceiling. Painted bloodless orange, in a liver-blotched light…

I sit on the empty bed and wait, in case of further footsteps. None. No sound; just the click through the wall, every minute, from your clock.

The more I concentrate, however, the more there is to hear. I freeze again, cock my head and listen hard, as if by hearing what you've heard so long I'll know the vegetations of your mind.

A light buzzes blandly in the yellow rubber corridor, cutting through a sad-voiced duct in a wall. A distant cough, through many walls. Then some tiny shred of sound unidentified and odd, like a twist of cellophane across a valley… And underneath it all (to my excitement and discomfiture and growing fascination) the micro-scopic pipe-line of my bloodsong through the darkness of my head!

Both of us are silent.
Are you ready?

*

OK… I bound off the bed, push the chair against your wall, step up on to it, look up, plan the movement to be made; flex my legs (eyes wide, lips tight) and launch myself upward. My fingertips attain the sill, grip it fit to snap and take my weight, edging forward as I dangle. Feet against the paint-work, working gently. Inching further, sill regripped—too narrow, finger-nails hit glass—now elbows splay as biceps creak, and upward slowly slide… Right forearm onto sill; right side of head (flatter than front) against the glass, to bring my centre of gravity forward as far as I can. Stabilise, breathe. Now my left hand is free, to smash the pane I lean against.

One thing I had not foreseen: being unable to face forward without toppling back, I shall have no chance, until I have shattered the glass, to make out any more than an empty corner of your room—from the rest of which I know I must be all too visible, framed here as if on television.

My right arm is trembling.

I raise my left fist carefully behind me and launch it forward as hard as possible. The pane explodes; glinting shards hit the sink with a clatter that is deafening and somehow unreal. I grip the sill on your side, to steady myself … and look.

I jolt, for there's a shock: you are alone and still on your bench, but have been turned around to face me. Discoloured pin-pricks of light from your eyes transfix me, accusatory. I look away but feel them on me still. I narrow my eyes and frown at the nauseating orange all around me. The *light* in here is worse than ever, like a bad dream: grainy, clotted, teeming, sick, and seeming now to worsen by the minute. If you are in there, it must have turned you mad. On the ceiling, out above a point beside the bench, towards the door—a convex disc.

No sound, but the dripping of a tap.

But there wasn't any dripping tap before, it occurs to me. And there's something wrong with the sound. The drips are oddly magnified. They quicken with my heartbeat, painfully loud in the silence.

The heat is oppressive; I am sweating. I crane my head forward and glance down. The grey metal sink is spotted red. Blood is oozing from my hand, running off my fingers and landing underneath the taps.

I must be quick. I snap what shards remain within the frame and push them out. Another vicious clatter as they hit the sink.

I slide my left leg up through the window and down on the other side; survey the room, astride the ledge. I pull the other leg through, drop to the sink and to the floor. I stride to your bench.

I position myself above you, careful not to look into your eyes. I kiss your forehead, and gently close your eyelids with my fingers.

I whisper three words in your ear. Wrap my hands around your throat. Close my eyes—and clench.

I look. You twitch. Your brown eyes reopen—bulge—glare—glaze, are still. I close them again, dart across to the sink and rinse my hands.

I must get out of this feverish light or I'll vomit. The paintwork is sweating. I am leered at by the wall above the sink—leprous chicken colour, spattered like a blood-flecked cough.

The window beckons, like a finger.

—Redoubled the horror, but just begun.

*

I travel fast, return to the block and to the party. Bottles and bodies strew the floor like cigarette butts soaked in blood and wine. It's nearly over now.

The warm dark room is empty. I recognise the voice on the stereo, one that's been with me for years. That voice—dramatic, naked, intense, a violent silence just before a storm.

Lightly I swing across the floor to the window. The curtain looks strangely solid, almost sculpted. I grasp it, make to lug its heavy-looking folds along the rail; they slide aside at the lightest touch. I step out on a white-lit concrete balcony, contained in tinted sheets of glass a metre high and topped in polished steel. From here, high up in the Midlevels, rearing up to blot out half the sky, the dark cathedral of the Peak squats close. Against my will, my eyes are drawn to a recent crop of tower blocks perched on a site where, in ages past, a stage was set…

Snaking through the curtains behind me from the room seep strains of the music, which dance in my mind till the night is instinct with the ullage of their poison. Reaching for the steadying steel of the rail, I look at what connects me to it—four three-dot ellipses of separate finger bones, wodged in a pink-grey jelly that in some way ensures they do not fall apart either side of the glass. How astounding—how precarious. I try to claim identity with that extraordinary distant pumping inside me; I finger the pulse in my neck, to remind myself this sac of bones and fluid is really mine. What disturbing breakability...

The balcony surrounds the tower block. I float around its circle to the unlit north side and lean on the rail overlooking Hong Kong. Twisting out to mingle with the city's breath, a suppurating scent of musky blue is overpowering the tang from the apartment, from a box of outsize flowers on the parapet—the undulating petals pudgy, succulent, obscene in the stillness, the grubby buds as fat as paws of cabbage... The blooms seem random, redundant. The arbitrariness of their being in just this configuration out of the infinite number possible transmits itself as a buzz, a hum, a very high-frequency *sing*. They are clearer, brighter, harder, cleaner than I ever would have forecast; even the earth they grow in is clean. It is as if I knew they would happen, though not what "they" would be. Bizarre and odd within themselves, yet how pointless, how irrelevant they are to anything outside them. They matter not at all, and they carry on. This is how it is.

I lean on the rail, the entire shining city sprawled below me, charged to flash-point. I look towards the sleepless district, cut by teeming alleys in the thick hot heat, where the people stream as ichor in the veins of a giant, where the red-lit air is tingling alive on the skin, where the broken basement windows sweat the sultry beat of music and the unmarked stairs bleed neon. Then I take a long shot up and out, where the Bank Building soars up in shrieking verticality from Central, where perspectives slice and plunge in spired glass and diamond parallax—refinery of moonstone glistening with night-fire. And underneath it all? Fear and hatred, I sense, like the surge of a pool writhing ugly and grey below a wafer-thin crusting of ice.

There's a movement above. I glance up, but see nothing. I scan the horizon as far as the lightless zones to right and left, in search of a forked pin of lightning. A storm must be drawing near, inaudible but imminent, barbing the air with a prickling of positive ions. My eyes wander over the heavens. On the surface they are matt; but underneath, a fluid chocolate-purple, aglow from within. All is still… There again, no denying it, the same huge movements— monumental shiftings and grindings, always noiseless, as of cosmic bulks of furniture being hefted up some grand stair from one world to another. The sounds come not through eye or ear, but chest and bowels, limbs and diaphragm. I tilt my head further back, and further still and further, till my swimming gaze is whisked from the sky-depths to bob upon the end of the aerial that shoots from the tower roof behind me. I lower my head again—halt transfixed by what I see. Far in the distance of purply-brown air, beyond Hong Kong, beyond the beacons of Kowloon, above the Mainland, the belly of the sky flickers almost imperceptibly. More noises—softer now in timbre, more organic. The sky bulges taut as if pregnant with something that is kicking to escape. The heavens are coming alive… The skin of the night stirs and ripples, like a muscle in the sea. And again and redoubled, that strange translucence.

Now, across a hundred degrees of my circle of sight, a remarkable vision unfolds. Dim shapes appear: features are assuming moist laborious shape. I watch them thrash and struggle to penetrate their walls of grained elastic—pushing out soundless yells to no effect. I can almost see their bodies now, their sluggish senseless deadweight, their feet that claw in vain against the gristle that contains them. Necks slide in writhing desperation, frustrated mouths agape to screech autistic howls of ecstasy… A sickening tension and urgency build up inside me for release, longed-for release. The sky breathes faster, wheezing like a ruptured lung. The outlines thicken, clarify: the outlines of futility, of loss, of stale delusion in your absence. There is now no longer room for the shapes to dance and flip; they must expand, sway, shudder in compression as the walls contract convulsively and each mouth groans below the force that strains to crush it. The pressure mounts, the bodies' oscillation so constricted I can barely see a movement—all their features squeezed within three cells, like bars of soap embedded in a swill of gluey mud. (A moment's inactivity. Kai Tak airport is bathed in a pale green light; the planes have finished flying.) Then, silent and calm, a giant pink cloud hatches out from a fissure in the middle cell, as if from a tear in a spotlit back-cloth. Fussy and deliberate, it trembles and unfolds—inflates, becomes more fungal, more intricately fleshy. Pink light nestles in a thousand flushing wrinkles; minute movements flutter in its branches, which paw and shiver like floating boneless fingers. Storm-clouds brood around it, slate-grey and tubular, staining with a livid arc the western sky inland towards the Pearl River. The cloud blushes prettily to puce, then erupts in a soundless explosion, spurting filaments that gush in ragged skeletons of fire until the sky is streaming blood. These tissues then transmute in weird eclosion in the debris, into myriads of teeming motes and animalcules. Twitching their vanes, the midget creatures mew and signal with tics and dinky squeals, unearthly in the hush. As the cloud in ghastly splendour decays to a worm cast, the creatures gulp the bile that bubbles round it, fatten into mumpish yolks and sprout in profusion like an orgiastic circus. Tougher than the hide of a dried-out puffball, the worm cast is itching ... then it fades out of view. The foetal circus of homunculi, maggoty and sickly, is at last fading too as it continues to proliferate—and sinks, among the coloured hills, beyond the plains of Canton.

The vision done, I bow my head in horror. In the street far below me, a tiny figure scuttles from a door where an orange light streams in a path into dark. There are voices far away through the windows of the party, then some music starts: a new song, now that the old one's done.

I am older than the oldest song, numb, drained and dead. But what are you, my Angel, and where?

I love you still, you know. I want you to be with me—you beautiful, beautiful, beautiful boy. I want your love to fill the void...

But you're not here.

My stomach churns and shifts, sinks—weighs me down, like dead things. I raise one foot to the height of the rail, then I lift up the other and my body with an effort; now both feet are planted on the rail's curve. I steady my balance, stand a moment. Raise my arms and golden eyes up high above me, touching nothing. Lean towards the void.

As I start to fall, I push my body outward from the tower block—outward in slow motion into black glinting stillness, as I lift my head to space and laugh aloud into the sky—

Lights weave and lash, the airs caress...

The ferry creeps slower than a mite across the harbour. The

harbour water coruscates topaz and gold. Hong Kong purrs like a power house.

—Inside us the horror, so silent we shriek…

*

A hand shakes my arm while a figure looms and asks would we like tea or coffee. Swimmily, I realise I am no longer on the balcony or at a party or anywhere near Hong Kong, still less a smudge upon a road in the Midlevels. A dream … and with a rush of indescribable relief, I feel the sleeping warmth of Angel's head upon my shoulder.

"Yes please," I tell the steward, who puts two cups down and sets about filling them. I lean down to peer at his watch, which tells me it is only half an hour since take-off. Is that all? Now Angel raises his head, yawns, and stretches. So vivid was my dream, I almost feel it must have spilled right out of my head into his as we slept. Its details are slipping away even now, though the flavour remains; already I must struggle to recall it… Hazy as my recollection is, however, I have a powerful sense that I would prefer him not to have been tuning in. I shiver. "Sweet dreams?" I ask.

He turns, looks hard at me. "Oh yes," he murmurs, smiling. His hands move to my neck. "Oh yes!…" Then with a sudden whisper *"Was it good for you!?"* he squeezes his hands, so I almost choke.

I start in horror—didn't I just dream…?

He drinks my confusion for a moment, then he titters, kisses me on the mouth again and holds my hand in his, leaning back and closing his eyes.

I shake my head and frown. I'll ask him later.

Focusing beyond him, through the oval plastic porthole, I see that we are high above the cloud-belt, floating free in liquid crystal blue. I smile, sink my head back, close my eyes and look ahead. How beautiful it is to have no plans or schemes or schedules to pursue in New York City, but just to be returning to my home with my love, to be with him…

What I've wanted to do for years!

THE END

If you've enjoyed these tales, then my warm appreciation for leaving a quick rating or just a handful of words of feedback on them, at the online retailer they came from. If you are able to do so, then this really would help me enormously, so very many thanks!

Rohan

Also by Rohan Quine, the following novel is available at most online retailers, as a print book or an ebook or an audiobook, published by EC1 Digital.

THE BEASTS OF ELECTRA DRIVE
a novel

From Hollywood Hills mansions and Century City towers, to South Central motels and the oceanside refinery, *The Beasts of Electra Drive* spans a mythic L.A., following seven spectacular characters (or Beasts) from games designer Jaymi's game-worlds. The intensity of those Beasts' creation cycles leads to their release into real life in seemingly human forms, and to their combative protection of him from destructive rivals at mainstream company Bang Dead Games. Grand spaces of beauty interlock with narrow rooms of terror, both in the real world and in the incorporeal world of cyberspace. A prequel to Quine's other five tales (and a Finalist in the IAN Book of the Year Awards 2018), *The Beasts of Electra Drive* is a unique explosion of glamour and beauty, horror and enchantment, exploring the mechanisms and magic of creativity itself.

www.rohanquine.com/the-beasts-of-electra-drive

REVIEWS OF ROHAN QUINE'S
THE BEASTS OF ELECTRA DRIVE

See www.rohanquine.com/press-media/the-beasts-of-electra-drive-reviews-media for all links to the following.

"Technologically intelligent, socially clever, and supernaturally chilling—a trippy sci-fi tale. […]

There is a strong artistic element woven into this act of creation, allowing us to see how and why Jaymi creates each of his Beasts, giving them purpose and personality as well as form. […] This is a book that would have been entirely serviceable with just the hacking and virtual reality interfaces, but what makes it really compelling is the ability for Jaymi's Beasts to step out into meat-space (*I love that term*) and take on corporeal form. These characters grow, learn, and even challenge their programming—they are somewhat childish in their willful independence, to the point of being sociopaths, although they demonstrate real emotion. There is some wonderful genderfluidity to some of the Beasts, with Shigem never feeling '*quite like a boy, being half a gender to the left*' and Scorpio whose '*nature flowers with so transgender a beauty,*' as well as a gay love affair between two Beasts who were created for one another. Lest you forget that this is a revenge fantasy, however, Amber is modeled after Rutger Hauer's character in *The Hitcher*, while Scorpio's defining moment is the fantasy of dominating an entire prison as the most dangerous boy in a skirt. […]

What really impressed me, however, is the flair for language, with some really beautiful—and beautifully chilling—passages that had me dog-earing pages along the way."
—**Sally Bend** in *Bending the Bookshelf*

"Quine describes [the Beasts'] release like a beautiful dance instead of a strategic infiltration. […]

The novel is a creative mashing together of Hollywood novel, science fiction, eroticism, and dystopia, with a premise that seems at once foreboding and prescient. While the book takes obvious science fictional liberties with technology, there is a real-world parable about superficiality versus authenticity. As the world becomes more digitally mechanized—and we are as much a product of our digital personae as our real-life personae—the book has an important message to tell about what it is to be truly human. […]

Quine obviously has a lot of affection for his Beasts, which has the same effect on the reader. He also injects humor throughout into what is at times a fairly dark storyline, replete with violence and seamy sexuality.

In all, Quine has created a wholly unique look that will appeal to gamers and non-gamers alike. Most readers will empathize with the main character and his suboptimal working situation, and the steps he takes to get out from underneath a tyrannical and uninspiring boss. On a science fictional level, the novel works exceptionally well for its creative use of tech, mixed in with a group of highly imaginative characters.

A prequel to five other works, *The Beasts of Electra Drive* will have readers seeking out Rohan Quine's other books in the series."
—SPR

"This novel is essentially near-future cyberpunk subtly blended with elements of LA noir and dystopic fiction to create a darkly stylish and, at times, visionary glimpse into humankind's future. […] Richly described, the beasts are androgynous characters with full backstories, personalities, and idiosyncrasies. Unleashed upon the world, they allow Jaymi to achieve vengeance in ingenious ways.

This is an intriguing premise, but the story's true power comes from its underlying theme: Humans can choose to live in the superficial, and underlying falseness, of tabloid reality (as gamers do when engaging in the novel's online game), or embrace the 'complexity, unconventionality, beauty and subtlety of truth' of the world around them. Ultimately Jaymi's journey of self-discovery mirrors our own: We all seek happiness in the short time that we inhabit the 'meat space' of this world."
—BlueInk Review

"*The Beasts of Electra Drive*, an unctuously dark piece of magical realism interwoven with biting satire on mass culture." "This book is a marvel." "I had the joy of editing this extraordinary novel that's

part magic realism, part horror, part satire of the media industry, part meditative hymn."
—**Dan Holloway**, novelist, poet and *Guardian* blogger

"Quine's narrative challenges the arbitrariness of commercial gate-keepers and the randomness of success—and has a lot of fun in the process. It's an odd mixture of dark—verging on horror—with more than a bit of kitsch. […] It's a very visual novel too. Quine gives his narrative voice (and sometimes his characters), the eye of a camera mounted on a drone, able to fly across a valley and zoom in on details miles in the distance—like a tiny reflection in the pupil of someone's eye. […]

Reading this book is a little like watching a particularly unsettling art house movie. You will be, in turn, disoriented, enchanted and repelled.

For all the technology involved, this is more magic realism than science fiction. It deliberately pushes the boundaries of the outrageous and challenges you to go along for the ride."
—**Catriona Troth** in *Bookmuse*

"Quine's novel centers more on an interesting cast than fascinating sci-fi traits. Some characters are computer code in bodily form but still have depth. For example, Jaymi created Kim, in part, to be Shigem's lover. (A nice touch: both Beasts are male.) There's likewise a rather sublime religious theme. Though one Beast kneels in prayer in front of 'his creator,' Jaymi, there's an understated notion of free will. Jaymi assigns missions to Beasts (e.g., wreak havoc on Bang Dead) but often leaves them 'to [their] own devices.' The author's lyrical prose is profound and sometimes surreal, especially in character descriptions. 'Inside Kim,' Quine writes, 'there is a lonely savage from the caves, bent on pure first-degree survival, blown by chance and the primal drives of instinct and emotion, alone and uncertain on a dart from birth to death.' […]

Unhurried but engrossing novel in which characters are more enticing than otherworldly technology."
—***Kirkus Reviews***

"[Protagonist Jaymi] discovers that he can bring his incarnations of excessive freedom, sexuality, intellectual seriousness, cool ambiguity, and dark vulnerability to life, unleashing them on 'meat space.' They become his beasts, extensions of his own personality, and through them, he interacts with the executives behind *Ain't They Freaky!* As various elements of Bang Dead's software are released, Jaymi works to help his former coworkers recognize the shallow depravity of their game through unnerving visits to their homes. [...]

This is a powerful book that advocates letting people be themselves, despite how far outside the bell curve of 'normal' they are. Pulsing with sexuality, the story will appeal to readers who enjoy artistic works rich in vocabulary, symbolism, and graphic imagery."
—*The Book Review Directory*

"Part cyberpunk meditation and part erotic thriller, BEASTS is a stylish narrative romp around a fictional Los Angeles landscape that appeals to the heart first and the head second. [...]

THE BEASTS OF ELECTRA DRIVE sounds like a cyberpunk thriller, and it sort of is. It also has an erotic undertone that grows throughout the narrative as the Beasts themselves crawl out of Jaymi's computer screen and gain independence. It's also a postmodern-ish meditation on creativity. Part of Jaymi goes into the creation of each of his Beasts—perhaps something author Rohan Quine can relate to—and as a whole the group is as a kind of kaleidoscope view of its creator. Additionally, part of Jaymi's mission in siccing the Beasts on Bang Dead Games is a retaliation against *Ain't They Freaky!*, an in-universe alternate reality game that embodies empty mass appeal over genuine artistry. [...] the writing grows increasingly smoother, culminating in a hauntingly pretty passage about man's inhumanity to man and ending up with intense backstories for the Beasts.

THE BEASTS OF ELECTRA DRIVE is, as its cover suggests, perhaps more about style than substance. Readers are told not to judge books by their covers—but this is the future. Maybe that's the point."
—*IndieReader*

"A sensual ballet of rich characterisation, alluring subtlety and originality. *The Beasts of Electra* Drive is a novel that I didn't want to put down while I was reading it [...]. I was transported into a domain peopled by characters who felt as if they were beckoning to me. It was as if they were inviting me into a kind of gliding embrace of harmony, within the pages of their author's imagination.

I found myself underlining things on the page, throughout it, because of the allure of Quine's language. I was fascinated with the marriage of his vocabulary and his punctuation. On the few times when I wasn't familiar with a word he uses, I resisted looking up its meaning—so as not to disturb the flow of the prose, but also because the spell of the sentences made the mystery of those words' meanings into an actual part of Quine's sheer creativity.

I felt drawn into his characters, which are complex. In the case of at least a couple of them, I had a strange feeling that they were somehow stroking me, while I was being led around their inner worlds. I was unable to dislike any of them, even those who clearly weren't very nice.

I also loved being reminded of when I lived in the Hollywood Hills. [...] Quine has captured the feel of those hills and canyons, in a way that will be recognised as authentic by anyone who's lived there.

This book creates a luscious and sensuous effect, which you can expand into. I have the sense that it was written by a very unusual and special person."
—**Suzi Rapport**

"An extraordinary genre-defining and fascinating novel. So timely as cynical, talentless and opioid-pushing mass-media owners try and downgrade all popular culture—Rupert Murdoch/tv producers and ilk, I'm looking at you. Like a lyrical poem from ancient times. But more violent and with more gay sex."
—**Hermione Ireland** on Goodreads

"Jaymi's pursuits are a revenge fantasy taken to the next level, with moral and ethical quandaries wound in.

Magical realism meets old school noir in Rohan Quine's technological thriller *The Beasts of Electra Drive*, which poses philosophical questions around reality, humanity, and where to draw the line with tech-infusion. [...]

Distinct writing is filled with lyrical prose and vivid sensory descriptions […] At times, [Jaymi] appears to have moral quandaries about his drastic actions against a rival company. His cyber-creations also lead him to question the nature of existence and his role as a creator—can he ethically order his creations to do his bidding in the real world? […]

The characters that Jaymi creates are refreshing in their diversity of race, gender, and sexuality. The two distinctly male beasts conform to the spectrum of masculinity, with one, Amber, being excessively violent, athletic, and handsome, and the other, Kim, being introverted but boundlessly intelligent and philosophical. These two men are in relationships with Shigem and Scorpio, who are more fluid in their gender and sexual identities. Shigem and Scorpio, along with Evelyn, are of varying nonwhite ethnicities. The scope of variety among the beasts is a nice change of pace.

The Beasts of Electra Drive is a techno-thriller that focuses more on its beautiful prose than on nurturing its thrills. Although sometimes repetitive in format, the vitality of the characters is pleasant and engaging."
—*Foreword* Clarion Reviews

"A crazy, psychedelic and experimental book. A fascinating and genre-defying story of a genius computer games designer waging war on the cynical and cretinous mass-market media and entertainment peddlers that threaten to cheapen and destroy our world. Perfect for adventurous readers."
—**Dartmouth dogwalker** on Amazon

"A fully-wrought origin story like no other."
—*The Bookbag*

Also by Rohan Quine, the following novel is available at most online retailers, either as an ebook (including films and video-book and audiobook) published by EC1 Digital and the Firsty Group, or as a print book published by EC1 Digital.

THE IMAGINATION THIEF

a novel

The Imagination Thief is about a web of secrets, triggered by the stealing and copying of people's imaginations and memories. It's about the magic that can be conjured up by images of people, in imagination or on film; the split between beauty and happiness in the world; and the allure of various kinds of power. It celebrates some of the most extreme possibilities of human imagination, personality and language, exploring the darkest and brightest flavours of beauty living in our minds.

www.rohanquine.com/the-imagination-thief

REVIEWS OF ROHAN QUINE'S
THE IMAGINATION THIEF

See www.rohanquine.com/press-media/the-imagination-thief-reviews-media for all links to the following.

"Rohan Quine is one of the most brilliant and original writers around. His *The Imagination Thief* blended written and spoken word and visuals to create one of the most haunting and complex explorations of the dark corners of the soul you will ever read. Never one to do something simple when something more complex can build up the layers more beautifully [...] suffice to say he is the consummate master of sentencecraft. His prose is a warming sea on which to float and luxuriate. But that is only half of the picture. He has a remarkable insight into the human psyche, and he demonstrates it by lacquering layer on layer of subtle observation and nuance. Allow yourself to slip from the slick surface of the water and you will soon find yourself tangled in a very deep and disturbing world, but the dangers that lurk beneath the surface are so enticing, so intoxicating it is impossible to resist their call."

"*The Imagination Thief* is one of those books that has originality stamped across it with a pair of size 12 DMs. An incredibly dark yet full and balanced with shafts of light picaresque through the recesses of the human psyche, it is an uncomfortable, troubling immersive experience that mixes text, audio and video taking us into places we would rather not go. It could be described as a cubist novel, taking each aspect of the torn mind and laying them out on separate planes through the different media."

"Rohan is one of the most original voices in the literary world today—and one of the most brilliant."
—**Dan Holloway**, novelist, poet and *Guardian* blogger; and see his *Guardian* review at http://bit.ly/13rR45R

"Never read anything like it! Magical realism in NY. Extraordinary."

"An intriguing book that addresses many big issues (love, sex, death, power, the nature and reliability of human memory, history, culture, human potential, the constraints of 21st century society, and more) [...].

[...] described with a larger-than-life intensity that put me strangely in mind of Coleridge's *Kubla Khan*—and occasionally its drug-induced origins too!

It's not an easy or comfortable read, particularly when closely examining mental and physical cruelty and violence between some of the characters. I read with a constant sense of foreboding. However even the most shocking passages are underpinned by the compassion, pity and tenderness of the narrator for all but the most brutal characters. There's also some very welcome, very British understated humour to offset some of the horror. The brevity of the 'mini-chapters' was well-judged—I felt I needed to come up for air after some of the short episodes, and to assimilate the latest action before moving on.

The immediacy of the story is more keenly felt because it is written in the present tense—always more demanding on the reader, I find, and even more so in this case because although most is in the first person, there are also many second-person narratives, where Jaymi is reading the minds of other characters and addressing them: 'You move closer...' That the author is able to keep the reader not only engaged but tantalised by this difficult mode of storytelling indicates the power of his prose.

Though it's very much a modern book, with the constraints of modern life as one of its themes, there are touches of the classic about it too, reminding this reader of Johnson's *Rasselas* [...].

As I turned the pages, I found myself puzzling how on earth this intense tale would end. Without spoiling the plot, I can say I found the conclusion surprising, redemptive and satisfying.

[...] So, here we have not so much an imagination thief, but, to the reader, an imagination expander. Great stuff."
—**Debbie Young**, author and Amazon UK Top 1,200 Reviewer

"It feels like something that will win major awards... I look forward to gritting my teeth and applauding loudly at next year's Booker."
—**Meg Davis**, literary agent, Ki Agency

"Another difficult to classify book, but that's precisely why it works so well. Part literary fiction, part fantasy, it is a surreal experience which makes the most of its equally offbeat location. With a cast of unforgettable characters and a central premise both intriguing and epic, this is what indie fiction does so very well—breaks boundaries and takes risks. In this case, it pays off."
—**JJ Marsh**, novelist

"Rohan Quine not only has several books out. He also has a career in alternative modeling and film to look back on. Naturally, he has gone on to make a series of silent short films to go with an audio track of the author reading from his work. It's flooded with city lights, drugs and darkness. One foot in the New York Nineties, and one foot in today's London, it's both hypnotic and gut-churning."
—**Polly Trope**, novelist and literary editor of *indieBerlin*

"To love some of these characters would be to doom yourself, you are simply asked to observe them; to see them as deeply, as thoroughly as you see yourself, such is the all-encompassing clarity of Quine's descriptive abilities.

[...] Rather than a violation, Jaymi's reading of this motley crew of players is performed with a tenderness and an unending respect for the spectacle of another's soul in its entirety laid bare to us. There is magic in the twisted minds as well as in the sublime.

[...] the decadently rich language of this novel makes it pure chocolate, wine and sex—you will need a cigarette as you turn the last page. This book reads like a musical. The words are liquid and melodic: always entrancing and encaptivating and rising to chorus-line lung-busting crescendos every time Jaymi unleashes his powers and the imaginations of his superbly diverse cast shine out of the page in an explosion of Sound and Vision. Given that he accomplishes this purveyance of the innermost soul with black words on a white page, what is indeed impressive is the sheer level of colour, smell, texture and heat that can be felt during these moments when we are invited to couple our minds with theirs.

As I have stated, this is a piece where the English language is flexed and stretched until it's sweating on the floor in its yoga pants, and yet there are plenty of examples throughout to demonstrate Quine's skill in summing up the state of a character in a few simple words.

[…] there are other characters too, such as Evelyn and Rik, who are able to find light and love in their lives in the same way that Shigem and Kim have, and the warmth and tenderness of these characters serves to further illustrate that in contrast Angel is unable to escape the darkness […].

[…] Despite Jaymi's authority as our narrator, the English language is the true star of this trans-corporeal, trans-reality, trans-possibility, trans-mindf*$k, all-transcending diva of a debut."
—**Jen McFaul**, author

"Rohan is a dazzling writer […] 21st century Beat Generation dreamweaver!"
—**Peter Godwin**, musician

"I finished *The Imagination Thief* late last night, and found it … many things, I suppose, but I know they add up to 'deeply overwhelming'. It took my own imagination prisoner for a long while, and I cannot think of a better accolade for a true novel. I can't recall the details of any earlier version (which is why I've been able to read this as from zero), nor can I find an earlier copy anywhere, but I don't remember that the older version ended the same as this—has it changed? Because now, I read the last few pages—the van trip back to NY—as completely new to me, and I thought you have wonderfully created a quite unforgettably convincingly-constructed exit for the reader from this (again, overwhelming) experience."
—**Dr Michael Halls**, Intercom Trust

"quite brilliantly written. I have now read it twice and think it is full of amazing descriptions—especially those detailing the backgrounds of the various characters as divined by Jaymi in his magic insights. I am not on the whole a fan of magic realism, if one is to call it that, but your prose is so lyrical and beautiful that I felt quite seduced by it. The same applies to your dialogue which is richly colloquial. I am sure that the writing alone will arouse the admiration of the discriminating reading public."
—**Jeremy Trafford**, novelist

"fiery work. How rollickingly it proceeds down to its last bloodily beautiful drop."
—**Willie Coakley**, poet

The four novellas in this volume are also available as four separate ebooks and audiobooks published by EC1 Digital, available at most online retailers, with the following covers.

THE PLATINUM RAVEN

A triple convulsion whereby our heroine Raven escalates herself into the Chocolate Raven and then the Platinum Raven, from London to Dubai to the tower in the hills in the desert—then back down again, forever changed

www.rohanquine.com/the-platinum-raven

THE HOST IN THE ATTIC

A hologram of Oscar Wilde's *The Picture of Dorian Gray*, digitised and reframed in cinematic style, set in London's Docklands in a few years' time

www.rohanquine.com/the-host-in-the-attic

APRICOT EYES

A cat-and-mouse pursuit through the New York City night
involves a preacher, a psychic and a dominatrix, broadcast
live on air—until a horror is unearthed, bringing two of them
together and the third to a sticky end

www.rohanquine.com/apricot-eyes

HALLUCINATION IN HONG KONG

Sliding from joy to nightmare and back, a plane flight frames
a journey into Jaymi's and Angel's polarised identities and
perceptions, where past and present merge in an obsessive fantasy
of love, death, horror and apocalyptic beauty

www.rohanquine.com/hallucination-in-hong-kong

ABOUT ROHAN QUINE

Rohan Quine is an author of literary fiction with a touch of magical realism and a dusting of horror. He grew up in South London, spent a couple of years in L.A. and then a decade in New York, where he ran around excitably, saying a few well-chosen words in various feature films and TV shows, such as *Zoolander, Election, Oz, Third Watch, 100 Centre Street, The Last Days of Disco, The Basketball Diaries, Spin City* and *Law & Order: Special Victims Unit* (see www.

rohanquine.com/those-new-york-nineties/film-tv). He's now living back in East London, as an Imagination Thief, with his boyfriend and two rabbits—a caramel-coloured one with upward ears, and a white one with downward ears.

His novel *The Beasts of Electra Drive* (a Finalist in the IAN Book of the Year Awards 2018) is a prequel to his other five tales, and a good place to start. See www.rohanquine.com/press-media/the-beasts-of-electra-drive-reviews-media for reviews by *Kirkus*, *Bookmuse*, *Bending the Bookshelf* and others. From Hollywood mansions to South Central motels, havoc and love are wrought across a mythic L.A., through the creations of games designer Jaymi, in a unique explosion of glamour and beauty, horror and enchantment, celebrating the magic of creativity itself.

In addition to its paperback format, his novel *The Imagination Thief* is available as an ebook that contains links to film and audio and photographic content in conjunction with the text. See www.rohanquine.com/press-media/the-imagination-thief-reviews-media for some nice reviews in *The Guardian*, *Bookmuse*, *indieBerlin* and elsewhere. It's about a web of secrets triggered by the stealing and copying of people's imaginations and memories, the magic that can be conjured by images of people, the split between beauty and happiness, and the allure of power.

Four novellas—*The Platinum Raven*, *The Host in the Attic*, *Apricot Eyes* and *Hallucination in Hong Kong*—are published as separate ebooks, and also as a single paperback *The Platinum Raven and other novellas*. See www.rohanquine.com/press-media/the-novellas-reviews-media for reviews of these novellas, including by Iris Murdoch, James Purdy, *Lambda Book Report* and *New York Press*. Hunting as a pack, all four delve deep into the beauty, darkness and mirth of this predicament called life, where we seem to have been dropped without sufficient consultation ahead of time.

The six titles are in the process of being released in audiobook and video-book formats too, performed by the author.

CONNECT WITH ROHAN QUINE

If you'd like to be notified of future print and ebook publications, you're most welcome to sign up for my not-too-frequent newsletter at www.rohanquine.com/sign-up. Rest assured, such emails will be at supremely tasteful intervals and your details will be shared with no one else.

And if you wish, thanks for connecting on:
www.twitter.com/rohanquine
www.facebook.com/rohanquinetheimaginationthief
www.goodreads.com/author/show/1089889.rohan_quine
http://theimaginationthief.tumblr.com
www.wattpad.com/user/rohanquine